ANTIGRAVITY

ANTIGRAVITY

Book One

of
The Egress of Humanity series

By
Archie Kregear

AntiGravity

This is a work of fiction. All characters, incidents and dialogue are drawn from the author's imagination and are not to be construed as real.

Copyright © 2022 All rights reserved.

By Archie Kregear

This book, or any portion thereof may not be reproduced or used in any manner without the express written permission of the author, except for the use of brief quotations in critical circles and reviews.

Amazon Print Edition ISBN: 9798401865120

Acknowledgements

During the writing of AntiGravity many people supported me and this work. First and formost, I thank my wife Bonnie who encouraged me throughout the writing process.

Over the years of writing this book I have been blessed with the support of the Kitsap Writers Critique Group who offered suggestions on the early drafts and beta read the manuscript. I am in debt to these fellow writers for their willingness to share their expertise.

Table of Contents

Chapter 1 – Monday	1
Chapter 2 – Busted	4
Chapter 3 – Tuesday and Wednesday	8
Chapter 4 – Thursday–Tuesday	13
Chapter 5 – Weeks 2–6	17
Chapter 6 – May Conference	23
Chapter 7 – Offers	29
Chapter 8 – First Trip	34
Chapter 9 – Memorial Day Plus One	44
Chapter 10 – The Next Week	52
Chapter 11 – Third Monday in June to March	59
Chapter 12 – April to August the Following Year	68
Chapter 13 – Mid-September	75
Chapter 14 – October–Mid-November	80
Chapter 15 – Thanksgiving	101
Chapter 16 – January	113
Chapter 17 – February–March	115
Chapter 18 – March–April	120
Chapter 19 – May	126
Chapter 20 – June	133
Chapter 21 – Late June–July	140
Chapter 22 – July	150
Chapter 23 – Late July	156
Chapter 24 – August	160
Chapter 25 – Mid August	166
Chapter 26 – Late August	169
Chapter 27 – September	173
Chapter 28 – Early October	176

Chapter 29 – AGD-II	180
Chapter 30 – Mid October	181
Chapter 31 – November	184
Chapter 32 – Mid-November	189
Chapter 33 – November	196
Chapter 34 – November	202
Chapter 35 – December–January	208
Chapter 36 – February	213
Chapter 37 – Early March	219
Chapter 38 – Mid-March	228
Chapter 39 – April	231
Chapter 40 – Late April–May	236
Chapter 41 – June	242
Chapter 42 – July	244
Chapter 43 – August and following	249
Epilogue – Years Later	251
Further reading in the Egress of Humanity series	253

AntiGravity

Chapter 1 – Monday

Isaac Thomas and his lab mates entered the physics classroom through the back door just after the bell announcing the start of lunch. "Hi, Mr. Collins. We're here to pick up the rocket launch equipment. We'll set it up on the old handball court."

The middle-aged man stopped erasing the whiteboard and peered over the glasses perched at the end of his nose. "That's right. Today you're scheduled to test and present your project."

"We'll set it up and be ready to go when you get there."

Isaac picked up the half-meter-long rocket and wires from the back lab bench where he had put it that morning. Mohammad took the battery. Hector lifted the launcher, accidentally poking a model of the solar system hanging from the ceiling, causing the planets to swing.

"I'll stop at the restroom and be right out. Don't connect anything until I get there. Remember, safety first." Mr. Collins lifted his coat and hat off the hook by the front door.

Isaac adjusted the lock. "I locked this door. We'll wait for you," Isaac said.

"I've planned for your team to present the launch in class this afternoon."

"I'll have the video ready. We added some red dye to the ejection charge to make it easier to measure the height." Hector said.

"A bright idea," Mr. Collins said.

The three boys maneuvered through the noisy crowded hallway, dodging other students to get to the back door of the school.

It was a clear, cold January day in the Midwest. Students were milling about or going between buildings. The lab team's destination was the cement pad of the handball court that no one used. Isaac and Mohammad began setting up while Hector stood at the edge of the cement and held up his phone to video the launch.

Isaac put the starter into the rocket, while a few feet away Mohammad attached the wires to the battery.

"Dude, what's that?" A boy named Randy peered over Isaac's shoulder then shrugged toward his friends.

Isaac cringed, gripping the rocket tightly with both hands. "My physics project. Don't touch it."

"Oh?" Randy smirked. He seized the rocket in one hand and pried Isaac's hand off with the other. Being a full head taller and a hundred pounds heavier had its advantages. "Hold the runt!"

Archie Kregear

Hands grabbed both of Isaac's arms from behind and hauled him a step from the launcher. Isaac tried to pull away, but the grip tightened. He winced and stopped struggling.

"How does this rocket work?" Randy asked, examining the rocket. "I guess we slide it on the stand."

Mohammad opened his mouth to say something, but all he managed was "Ow."

Isaac noticed a muscular arm go around his lab mate's shoulder. It could have been seen as a friendly hug but was actually a firm pinch on the side of Mohammad's neck.

A couple of other boys walked up. One, carrying a football, said, "Attach the roach clips."

Randy started to attach the wires.

Isaac said, "Don't connect those."

"Quiet, geek," the boy holding Isaac said while twisting his arm behind his back.

Another boy moved in front of Hector, blocking the video.

"I got this," Randy said as he attached the second clip and moved back like he expected the rocket to fire.

"You got nothing," one of the boys said.

Randy moved to the battery. "I get it. If I flip this switch, will it fire?" He held his hand over the switch.

"Stop," Isaac said over the pain in his arm.

The boy with the football chucked it at Randy's head. "Get this."

Randy reacted and batted the football, which clipped the rocket stand, knocking it over. His other hand landed on the battery and flipped the switch.

The rocket fired and took off on a trajectory parallel with the ground. It ricocheted off the side of the gym and toward the school. The smoke trail highlighted its flight toward the building, where it crashed on the right shoulder blade of Mrs. Leigh, Isaac's English teacher. She let out a blood-curdling scream while falling to the ground. The red dye splattered across the back of her beige coat certainly looked like a severe wound.

"Mrs. Leigh's been shot," someone yelled. Other students screamed and shouted, "Shooter! Gun! Run!"

The boy holding Isaac shoved him onto the cement. Randy and his friends sprinted into the crowd of students fleeing in panic.

"Holy shit," Isaac muttered as he crawled to the graffiti-covered handball wall. He sat with his back against it and watched the pandemonium. Hector and Mohammad joined him.

It took a few minutes and a lot of screaming and yelling before everyone realized a model rocket had hit Mrs. Leigh, not a bullet.

AntiGravity

Isaac watched in silence while fellow students crowded around to take photos of the rocket and Mrs. Leigh.

Mohammad had his arms wrapped around his bent knees. "We should get out of here."

"We didn't do anything wrong. So why run?" Hector said.

"I want to keep an eye on the launcher. You two take off if you want," Isaac said.

Mr. Chávez, the principal, ran up. The cold made his heavy breath turn to steam around his head. "You three boys stay right there. Don't move. And don't touch anything." Then he sprinted to attend to Mrs. Leigh.

Mr. Collins walked over with his hands in his pockets. "I told you boys to wait for me."

"We didn't launch it," Isaac said.

"Some jocks did," Mohammad said.

Chapter 2 – Busted

Mr. Chávez escorted Hector, Mohammad, and Isaac to separate rooms in the school office.

Isaac ended up with Mr. Mandy, one of the advisors who handled discipline issues and counseling. While telling his side of the story, Isaac avoided eye contact and let his eyes wander around the room. Pictures of the last twenty valedictorians hung on the wall to his left, while photos of star athletes, including Randy in his football uniform, decorated the right wall. Family photos sat in an arc on the credenza.

After hearing Isaac's side of the story and taking a page of notes, Mr. Mandy leaned forward and folded his hands on the desk. "I realize you're a passenger in this incident. How do you feel about what happened?"

"I don't know," replied Isaac, who had slumped back in the metal chair and folded his arms.

"I sense that you're upset and angry about what happened."

"I guess so. Bullies like Randy tend to turn good things into shit."

"Isaac, one of the truths in life is we can't control the actions of others. What we can control is our reactions to others. Do you understand the difference?"

"Yeah." Isaac picked at his fingernails. "I'll get over it. I've had a lot of practice getting over bullying."

Mr. Mandy sighed. "The other advisors and I will get together later today to review everyone's account of the incident. Your record is clean, so I am not anticipating any disciplinary action." He sat back. "We have a few minutes. Do you have any career goals?"

Here comes the small talk. Isaac thought, then said, "Study science and math."

Mr. Mandy's bushy eyebrows went up like the wings on a ladybug. "What do you want to do with science?"

Isaac cracked a smile. "I don't know. Learn more."

Mr. Mandy flipped the page on the legal pad. "Everyone needs a career. What type of occupation do you see yourself doing in twenty years?"

"Half of today's science careers didn't exist twenty years ago. I want to do something nobody is doing today."

Mr. Mandy wrote on his pad. "That shows me you have a good understanding of the progression of discovery. Why do you like science?"

"Science is easy. It's straightforward. No hidden meanings like in literature." Isaac sat up, leaned forward, and looked at his feet.

"Have you been accepted to a college?"

"I'm going to Wichita State University."

AntiGravity

Sitting back in his high back vinyl chair, Mr. Mandy reached back to a pile of identical books on his credenza and slipped one off the top. He placed it on the desk in front of Isaac. "I'd like you to do something for me. Here is a book on mindfulness. I want you to read it. It will help you become more aware of your inner-self and your feelings."

Mr. Chávez opened the door. "Are you done, Mr. Mandy?"

"I think I understand Isaac's view of the incident."

The principal moved to the side of the desk. "Isaac, I'm afraid I'm going to have to suspend you until we get to the bottom of this incident. The no-tolerance rules are strict in this regard, and I have no other option. Get your things."

Isaac sat forward and stared past Mr. Chávez to Randy's photo on the wall. Then he glared at Mr. Mandy as he shoved the thin paperback book into his backpack.

Mr. Chávez escorted him to the school's front door. "I've notified your mother. She said to have you walk home. Remember, Isaac, school district regulations require that you not come on or close to campus while suspended. I'll contact your parents when I know the results of the investigation."

Isaac trudged home, kicking every rock in his path.

#

Isaac played video games until dinner time. He slogged down the stairs to the kitchen, where his father sat watching the news as his mother was holding an empty frozen pizza box and setting the timer on the oven. He sat down in his usual chair with his hands in his pockets and feet out straight.

Still dressed in his post office uniform, Hermon took a deep breath and said halfway through the exhale, "What do you have to say for yourself?"

"I didn't do anything wrong."

Hermon aimed the remote to turn off the small flatscreen TV attached to the wall by the refrigerator. Isaac realized that, for once, he was more important than the news. He wished he weren't.

"They said the rocket you purchased last week for a physics experiment hit a teacher," his mother said.

"I didn't fire the rocket." Isaac also didn't want his mother to worry about him. When she started to worry, she asked lots of questions about things he'd rather not talk about.

"Then who did?" his father asked, sitting forward.

"Randy and his friends," he said without moving.

"Randy did not take a missile to school."

Isaac looked up at his father and raised his eyebrows. "A rocket." Isaac pushed his collar-length dark hair back over his head and ended with his hands clasped like he was surrendering. He realized that he had just corrected his father, which made him defensive.

"You bought the thing, and it went off. That makes it your responsibility."

Isaac released his hands and held them out. "Right, I'm responsible."

His father leaned forward, pointing an index finger at him. "This is serious. A teacher was injured and the principal suspended you, not Randy. The police are going to investigate. There may be felony assault charges."

"The only thing I'm guilty of is taking my physics experiment to the graffiti wall behind the school," Isaac explained, staring down at his worn sneakers.

His mother stopped chopping lettuce. "What is the graffiti wall?"

"The old handball courts by the football field where students graphically express themselves."

Judy shook the knife in her hand. "What are we going to do, Hermon? Do we need a lawyer?"

Isaac's father glared at his only child and gave a big sigh. Then he sat back and ran his tongue over his lips. "You're grounded during your suspension. Put your phone, games, computer, and all electronics outside your room. And no TV during the day."

"I'm eighteen, Dad. At least let me have my computer."

"No. I think you need to be cut off, especially from games and social media. You got to learn to deal with the real world where the games being played have consequences, and liking friends is not about clicking an icon."

Isaac wanted to argue, but he could see that his parents didn't know how to deal with the situation. In fact, neither did he.

His mom reached out and put her hand on Hermon's hairy arm.

He looked up at her. "I've been easy on him for his whole life. Life isn't easy. He needs to learn that."

"My room is better than the halls of high school anyway." Isaac stood and plodded up the stairs.

After placing his electronic devices outside his room, he pulled the book the guidance counselor gave him from his backpack, read the title, *Meditation, Mindfulness, and Inner Peace,* and sighed. He sat cross-legged on the bed and opened to the first page. *What does this philosophy have to say? Will it cure the world of bullies?*

He was on page nine when his mother came into the room with three pizza slices on a paper plate and a can of soda.

"Here's dinner. I'm sorry if we seem so harsh. All this is so upsetting. You've never been in trouble."

Isaac took the plate and can. "I learn from other's mistakes."

"Would you like to come out and watch TV with us? *Quest for Talent* is on. I'm always amazed by the people on that show."

"No. I'll stay here."

Judy slipped out of the room and closed the door.

AntiGravity

He took a bite of pizza and returned to the book. *Vegetating, mindlessness, and eating pizza, such an exciting life.*

It was late when he finished the book about awareness of thoughts and feelings. He turned off the light. *Is anyone mindful? Who do I know who has reached inner peace?*

Archie Kregear

Chapter 3 – Tuesday and Wednesday

The following morning, Hermon stuck his head into Isaac's room. "Stay in the house while we're at work. Your phone, computer, and game console are in my trunk, so you won't be tempted to look for them."

Isaac nodded at his father. After the door closed, he sat cross-legged on the bed and began to apply the meditation techniques he'd read about the night before.

The world isn't configured for geeks like me. Why do some people need power and others are ruled by feelings? Why isn't science and logic enough? I wish school didn't require history, English, and social studies. If I'd inherited Dad's height, or if Mom were taller, I wouldn't be so short and an easy target for the likes of Randy. As the book says, accept who you are. Control the emotions and focus the mind on what you can be. Easy, except for assholes. Ideas of how to retaliate ran through his mind. Fears arose, making him quiver. *Bullies are competitive. They always find a way to win.*

He reclined against the headboard and let his mind wander. His thoughts turned to what he had been learning in his advanced placement physics class. He caught a vision of Einstein riding alongside a beam of light, figuring out the theory of relativity. The Milky Way poster on his wall took his mind to the heavens. He contemplated the origin of a star, its long-burning life, and its violent death by going nova.

Isaac recalled Mr. Collins' lecture on the creation of heavy elements, bonding, and chemical attraction. Thoughts raced on the physics of how matter interacted, reacted, and formed molecules. He contemplated the principle of gravity that attracted atoms to coalesce into clumps of matter, becoming asteroids, comets, planets, and suns. *Is there a unifying principle? What is it? How does gravity fit into the theory of relativity? How does the planet I'm on keep me from flying away?*

He moved his leg. "Ow!" A cramp. He grimaced and rolled off the bed. He limped around the room to work it off. Hunger made him venture to the refrigerator, where he found the lunch his mother had prepared for him. He sat at the table, enjoyed a sandwich, an apple, and an oatmeal cream pie.

With nothing to do, he put on his coat and hat, went into the backyard, and lay on a lounge chair to soak up the afternoon sun. He daydreamed of flying through the air, wondering what would happen if a person could turn off gravity? The cold and wind soon forced him to go in and return to his room.

After dinner, he sat cross-legged on the Megatron bedspread his parents gave him twelve Christmases ago. His mind soon wandered to gravity and how masses have an attraction to each other.

AntiGravity

Lightning flashed through the window. The immediate thunder rattled the glass, informing him that it was a close strike. He closed his eyes, returning to focus on how gravity worked.

A moment later, he felt a slight bump on his head, and then, pressure, pushing his head against his shoulder. "What the …" Isaac opened his eyes. The ceiling was an inch from his nose. He quickly took in a short breath before the bed absorbed his fall with a boom. Isaac lay sprawled on his bed, wondering what had just happened.

The door swept open. His father's broad torso filled the doorway, and his eyes glared at Isaac. "Are you okay? The thunder scared your mother half out of her wits, then we hear a boom up here. What were you doing? Jumping?"

In the back of his mind, he heard the lecture about not jumping on the bed when he was younger. "I wasn't jumping. I … I think I fell." His thoughts returned to the introspection of how he got to the ceiling.

"Falling, jumping, plopping, whatever! From downstairs, it sounded like a bomb went off up here."

His mind racing, Isaac said, "I'm not sure what happened."

"Well, get sure. You're old enough. Start being sure of what you're doing!" He slammed the door, sending a shudder along the wall.

Mom and Dad are on edge tonight. Isaac picked up the mindfulness book. *Should I give this to my parents? Not now.* He tossed the book on his desk.

Isaac got up and walked in a circle. *Gravity. I was meditating on gravity. My head hit the ceiling. I fell into bed. Let's try this again, only I need a check, so I don't go to the ceiling.*

Using the bedspread, he made a little tent between his chair and desk. He sat down on the floor, made sure his head was clear of the blanket, closed his eyes, and resumed meditating only on gravity.

The blanket is touching my arm. Has the tent fallen?

He opened his eyes. The desk was inches from his nose, and his knee was almost as high as his shoulder. He tried to turn to face down but floundered! He panicked and fell, caught himself with both hands and one foot, hopeful that he didn't make too much noise. He held his breath and his position. The door didn't open. He released a long sigh.

If I use the meditation techniques from the mindfulness book to focus on gravity, I become weightless. Isaac grabbed his physics book, climbed into bed, and reread the chapter on gravity. Then he reviewed Newton's three laws, inertia, force, and action/reaction, to try to understand how to move while weightless. *How did I get to the ceiling the first time? I was meditating while the force of gravity was pulling me into the bed. The first law states that an object at rest will remain at rest unless an external force acts upon it. The bedsprings were applying a force on me, equal to gravity. When I became weightless, the mattress springs pushed me up, causing acceleration. I rose to the ceiling. The forces are different on the floor where there are no springs. Some slight impulse must have caused me to twist in the air.* He lay back, and, with thoughts of the laws of motion acting on a weightless object running through his confused mind, fell asleep.

The next morning, his mother's voice called, "Time for breakfast, dear."

Isaac sat at the table and cleared his throat to get his father's attention from the news. "Dad, I'd like to do some gravity research today."

"Is that what you were doing last night? Gravity research?" Hermon asked.

"Yeah, sort of. May I use the trampoline in the backyard? And may I have my laptop to look things up?"

Judy sat. "When you were eight, we bought you the trampoline, and you've never liked it. If your cousins didn't enjoy it so much when they visit, I would've had your father sell it long ago. Now, you want to jump around?"

"I'm experimenting with the laws of motion, not jumping."

His parents glanced at each other.

Isaac turned his attention to his father.

Hermon sighed. "You can have your laptop and your phone. Your phone is only to call us if you injure yourself on the trampoline. You're doing research and experiments. No social media. Is that clear?"

"Yes, Dad."

"Wear a coat, even if it is supposed to be a warm day for January," his mother ordered.

"I will."

The newsman on the TV caught Isaac's attention, "A bolide, which is an exploding meteor, flew over Wichita last evening. Authorities say it exploded before hitting the ground and put on quite a light show. Not only was there a streak in the sky and an explosion, but it also caused a lightning strike that ripped a tree out of the ground in Maple Park."

"That's just over the river," Judy said.

#

Isaac watched the few videos of the meteor that were online. For a couple of hours, he read on the Internet what he could about gravity. Most things he understood, some he did not. All of this was to work up the courage to try to go weightless on the trampoline. The first thing he decided he needed to do was figure out a way to keep himself from flying off into the sky.

He bundled up against the cold, got a tarp and bungee cords from the garage, and made a covering over the trampoline. With the trampoline's side nets holding up the tarp on top, he had a contained space. He climbed in with a notebook to write down his observations.

As a child, Isaac could never get the hang of jumping straight up and down. After a bounce or two, he always fell awkwardly and, sometimes, painfully.

AntiGravity

Overcoming the fears formed years ago was his first task. He walked around on the trampoline. The old supports creaked with each step. He attempted to control his heartbeat with the meditation techniques he had worked on the night before. Then he bounced lightly for a few moments, sat in the middle, measured his breathing, cleared his mind, and began to meditate on gravity.

The trampoline springs pushed him up as soon as he began to float. Hitting the tarp caused him to lose his concentration and fall in a heap onto the trampoline, where he bounced clumsily.

Grabbing the notebook, he wrote: *I excluded all thoughts and focused on overcoming gravity. I lost focus when I touched the tarp and fell.* Then he did it again and wrote down his observations.

For the next couple of hours, he repeated the experiments over and over until he knew what to do in his mind to turn off gravity. The words of his chemistry teacher from the previous year came to mind: "Science is mostly trial and error." Those words faded to be replaced by a phrase from the mindfulness book, "Meditation is a practice, so it's never perfect."

No, this is more like a video game. Play the game over and over until you've got it down, then record yourself. *That's it.*

Isaac attached his phone to the netting on the side of the trampoline, hit the record button, and meditated on weightlessness. The result was a seven-minute video. After studying the footage and observing himself going into a trance in the last few seconds when the trampoline forced him up and into the tarp, he wrote down his observations.

Six videos later, he was getting faster at achieving a state of weightlessness.

Over lunch, he reviewed the videos and noticed he didn't seem conscious while floating up to the tarp. *I need to be able to remain weightless longer.*

He attached his phone to the trampoline leg, lay in the dirt underneath, and concentrated. He felt a touch on his head, attempted to stay weightless, but fell to the ground. The video showed that he had floated under the trampoline for over a minute before falling. *I need to get to the point where I can be conscious and weightless*, he wrote in his notebook.

Twenty-two videos later, he noticed that the time it took him to go weightless was two minutes. He realized that when he tried to think about floating, he fell. He attempted to write down the mental state he went in to achieve weightlessness, but he didn't know how to explain what was going on in his mind. *Meditate on "no gravity," and it turns off,* he wrote in his journal. Followed by *more trials needed.*

He was frustrated about not controlling his state of mind when gravity was turned off but excited by his progress. *Just like a video game; fail and try again.*

He again set his phone up on the trampoline net, determined to ignore what he touched. After several tries, he recorded himself bouncing around the trampoline for two-and-a-half minutes of a three-minute video. He recorded his observations in his notebook.

"Isaac, time for dinner," his mom called from the back door.

He took a deep breath and let it out quickly. "Wow, this is so amazing," he whispered. He gathered his things and went into the house.

His parents were sitting at the table, filling their plates, when his mother asked, "How did your experiments go today?"

"Incredible," Isaac said as he stabbed a slice of ham with his fork.

"Tell me what was so incredible," she said.

"If an object sitting at rest on a trampoline becomes weightless, the springs will apply a force upward and put the object into motion. I attached bungee cords to a tarp and covered the trampoline to keep the weightless object from floating into space. The tarp then applies a force downward to any object bouncing off the trampoline. The weightless object will continue between the two barriers, losing energy with each bounce until it becomes motionless."

"I think I understand," his father said. "How did you get a weightless object?"

"By thinking I was weightless."

"You spent the day thinking you were weightless?" Hermon's eyebrows fell as he glared at Isaac.

"Yes."

"Very, um … imaginative." Hermon scowled. "I want to see your laptop to check your search history."

"Sure, Dad; it's in my room on the charger."

Hermon immediately stood and went upstairs. Coming back down with the laptop, he placed it on the table. "What's your password?"

"E equal sign MC2. All caps."

Hermon focused on the laptop while Isaac and his mother ate. "Hmmm, six windows open to physics sites. No porn sites."

"Hermon!"

"He's a teenage boy," his father replied.

Isaac continued to eat. *Do I show them the videos stored on my phone? No, not yet. I need to learn to control myself first.*

Chapter 4 – Thursday–Tuesday

The next day, Isaac resumed his experiments on the trampoline, focusing on maintaining a weightless state while his stream of thought was interrupted by touch. It was mid-afternoon when he was able to be fully conscious of his surroundings while he was weightless. He floated between the trampoline and tarp, touching each just enough to stop his momentum until he hovered, in contact with nothing. "I did it. I've overcome gravity," he said out loud, though no one was close enough to hear.

He pumped his fist into the air, pumped his feet, and screamed for joy at a barely audible level. Then he stopped, stilled himself, mentally released the antigravity mindset, and fell bouncing on the trampoline until he was motionless. His heart raced. He had mastered the mental state required to turn gravity on and off while remaining conscious of his surroundings.

#

On Friday, Isaac took two bricks from the garden path and began experimenting on how to control himself when weightless. He held the bricks tightly and set his mind to turn off gravity. The bricks floated with him. He wrote in his notebook, *Objects in my hand become weightless when I do.*

Next, he began experiments with Newton's third law. When an object exerts a force on another object, there is an equal and opposite force on the first object. Isaac changed his momentum by tossing a brick. As soon as he released the brick upward, it returned to the influence of the earth's gravity and fell to the trampoline while he rotated and descended. When he caught a brick, the brick's downward momentum combined with his momentum and pushed him down. The tricky part was throwing and catching a brick in a manner that didn't apply an angular force, causing him to twist and turn. The fun part was throwing a brick down on the trampoline, where it bounced back to him. Both the throw and return added upward momentum.

He threw a brick upward hard into the tarp on one attempt, and his body rotated with the effort. The brick ricocheted off the tarp and hit him in the head. He lost weightlessness immediately and fell to the trampoline. When he took his hand off his forehead, it was bloody. He cleaned up the gash and put on an adhesive bandage that covered half his forehead.

After a few more bruises, he wrote in his notebook, *Bricks should not be used to control momentum by persons with a low level of coordination.*

At dinner, his mom spotted the bandage. "Good gracious!" she exclaimed, leaning to get a closer look. "What happened to your head?"

"I used a brick as a counterforce and applied more than sufficient momentum to it, causing me to twist. It rebounded erratically while I was in an awkward position to catch it, and it impacted on my head."

"I don't understand," his mother said.

His father turned his attention from the TV toward him. "You did what with a brick?"

"In simple terms, I threw a brick upward to change my momentum. It hit the tarp and came down in a manner I was not able to control or avoid, and it hit my head."

"Only you would say that is simple," his mother said.

"I'm fine; just a small cut."

"No more bricks on the trampoline," she commanded.

"I think I have things figured out to the point where I don't need bricks."

"And by the way, Mr. Chávez called and wants to meet with us Monday morning." Hermon picked up his plate. "We can eat in the living room. The guys at work were telling me about a new series on Netflix. Join us, son."

Three episodes later, everyone retired for the night.

#

Hermon put Isaac to work around the house on Saturday first by helping his mother. Vacuum the whole house, clean the bathrooms, and other chores. Then he had to scrub the patio chairs with caustic chemicals for hours to get all the grime and mold off. When he removed the rubber gloves, Isaac's hands ached and were red from the cold.

He's only trying to teach me about responsibility. Go with the flow.

"The glass shop wants a fortune to replace the glass top I broke last year," Hermon said as he surveyed the round patio table frame. "Learn this lesson, son. The manufacturers don't want you to repair their products. It's outrageous what they want to fix things. Put the frame out by the trash."

Isaac slipped underneath the rim into the center where he could lift the table and carry it while imagining he was Saturn, and the table was the rings.

In the afternoon, Hermon watched over Isaac while he changed the oil in the car.

This is easy, except for loosening the bolt.

After dinner, Isaac lasted ten minutes into an episode on Netflix before he fell asleep on the couch.

#

The family attended church on Sunday. The sermon was on the rapture. All Isaac could think about was going into a weightless mode and being a stowaway among the saints on their way to heaven.

After Hermon took them out to eat, he made Isaac join him to watch a basketball game on TV. Isaac imagined he could go weightless and jump over all the taller players to dunk the ball. Otherwise, he found watching a game he was absolutely lousy at a boring waste of time.

#

AntiGravity

When Monday morning arrived, Isaac felt he was a different person than the one suspended the week before. He had a new ability that no one else had. He walked into the school's conference room behind his parents, realizing nobody there knew how he had changed. The room was long and wide enough to contain a table and twelve chairs, five on each side and one on each end. The walls were adorned with student artwork.

Mr. Chávez sat at the end of the long table. He introduced a police detective and Mrs. Leigh, who both sat on his right. Isaac and his parents took a seat to his left. "Thank you all for coming this morning. I'm sorry it took longer than expected to complete the investigation," he said. "I spoke to Mr. Collins. It seems that the rocket was part of an assignment on thrust and gravity. Students may also make other items demonstrating these principles. The rocket is the most dangerous option, and a teacher is required to supervise. The problem before us is that the rocket was fired before Mr. Collins arrived, and Mrs. Leigh was injured. Detective, your findings?"

The detective uncrossed his legs and sat forward. "I questioned several students who were in the area at the time of the incident and concluded that a few boys who were not in the lab team were present. There is no evidence that the rocket was intentionally fired. Isaac, Hector, and Mohammad were not at fault. Unfortunately, the rocket hit Mrs. Leigh." He nodded in her direction. "A ballistics expert diagramed the flight of the rocket. Once it ricocheted off the gym, the resulting impact was terrible luck for Mrs. Leigh. Having the device on campus in a place where others can play with—"

"I didn't let anyone play with it!" Isaac blurted. "Randy connected the wires and flipped the switch while others held me."

"Let me agree," the detective said. "There was no cooperation on Isaac's part when the rocket was launched. The trajectory was altered accidentally by a football. I found no criminal intent in the actions of the other boys. There will be no charges filed."

Hermon sighed in relief.

Mr. Chávez asked, "Do you have anything to say, Mrs. Leigh?"

"I'm appalled by the presence of such a destructive device on campus. The bruise on my upper back is quite painful. I've filed a grievance with the union for compensation and asked for a reprimand of Mr. Collins. Assigning projects to launch weapons is irresponsible. As for you, Isaac, if you put forth even a smidgeon of the effort you give to science in my English class, you would be a commendable student."

The principal gestured toward Isaac's parents. "Mr. Thomas, Mrs. Thomas, do you have any questions?"

Hermon pointed at the principal. "Will you punish the boys who took and fired my son's project?"

"There was no intent to harm anyone. So, no."

"They harmed my son," Judy said.

"There was not enough evidence to accuse anyone," the principal replied.

Judy opened her mouth, but Hermon spoke first. "I should have taught him to fight back in situations like these."

Isaac's gaze dropped to the floor as his father put the blame on himself and conveyed to everyone that he raised a wimp. He'd always felt that he was a disappointment to his father but never had his dad admitted it in public. Now the stupid mindfulness book insisted he accept himself. *What does this new ability make me?*

After a moment of awkward silence, Mr. Chávez leaned forward. "Mrs. Leigh, I will be meeting with the union representatives and Mr. Collins later today. I will inform you of the outcome." He turned toward Isaac. "Since the rocket was a school assignment and technically not a lethal device, there is no further punishment. We expect you back in class tomorrow. Thank you all for your time."

"What about my lab mates?" Isaac asked.

"They returned to school last Wednesday," Mr. Chávez said.

#

The next day, Isaac dropped by the physics classroom at lunch. "Mr. Collins, I'm sorry for letting the boys fire the rocket and make a mess of things."

Mr. Collins stepped around his desk. "Isaac, I don't hold you responsible for what happened. If you ever get the rocket back, I'd like to see a video of a launch. When I was in high school, my chemistry teacher had an assignment to bring in things that smelled. My father had a little vial of skunk scent that he kept in a sealed jar. Well, I brought it to school. My teacher said it was too potent and wouldn't let me take it out. Some of the guys in the class decided that they wanted the jar, so they knocked me down and took it. They opened it and threw it into the girl's bathroom. I learned to be less trusting and grew a little wiser that day."

"What did the school do to punish you?" Isaac asked with wide eyes.

"I was told to tell a teacher if anything like that happened again. However, my father gave me a whipping when I got home for taking his skunk scent without permission." Mr. Collins smiled.

"I'll never bring anything to school again that bullies can use or destroy."

"Good thinking. How was your week off?"

"It was an excellent week. I learned a lot," he said, shuffling his feet and looking at the poster of the International Space Station on the wall behind his teacher. "Someday, I'll have to tell you about it."

"You know, I'm always here at lunch."

Chapter 5 – Weeks 2–6

Every day when the weather cooperated, Isaac practiced and experimented with his new talent in the backyard. In his notebook, he wrote, *My primary concern is getting too high and not being able to come down softly.* Then he thought, *the same problem some of my classmates are having.* He chuckled.

He practiced standing still and going weightless, careful not to push away from the ground. One day it started to rain. He noticed that the drops on his hands and head did not run off. The rainwater collected on his skin and clothes until he looked like a puddle in mid-air. He let gravity take over and landed with a splash as most of the water washed off. In his notebook, he wrote, *Weightless effect is transferred to water when it is in contact with me.*

On a windless day, he lit a ring of incense sticks on the ground under the trampoline, sat in the middle, and turned off gravity. The smoke that came close to his body shot up then slowed. He made notes, *The air I touch is affected but quickly regains the effects of gravity.*

He experimented on objects to see which ones he could make weightless. He gripped a barrel planter and went weightless. When he pulled, the barrel rose as he went down. He noted this was an equal but opposite reaction to the mass of his body and the planter's mass. Letting gravity take over again meant that the planter and he fell. *Lifting heavy objects is possible, but the return to gravity results in a fall. My ability is like a switch. It's either on or off. I wonder if I can learn how to go partially weightless?*

To alter his momentum and control movement while weightless, he needed something to throw and catch that wouldn't hurt him. After getting his father's permission, he used a hacksaw to cut the legs off the junked patio table frame, leaving a round metal hoop that weighed about ten pounds. He began using this to stay in an upright position while floating.

When the weather was stormy, Isaac focused on schoolwork in his nonscience classes. It was too late to make a difference for college, but he wanted to show his teachers that he cared.

He wrote an extra-credit book report on *The Baroque Cycle* by Neal Stephenson for Mrs. Leigh's class. She gave him a C on the paper, stating that the report was too long.

Each day the weather permitted, Isaac practiced with the hoop. Soon, he could twist or rotate it to adjust himself and remain upright. Next was learning to do some modest acrobatics. The first time he attempted to flip, he became disoriented, lost concentration, and fell hard on the ground. He worked tirelessly on making small movements. Gravity punished every mistake he made, and he accumulated the bruises to prove it. By early March, he was able to use the hoop and perform backward and forward flips.

He wanted to show what he could do but feared that he couldn't concentrate in the presence of his parents or classmates. He was afraid he would look awkward when he was weightless. The only person he thought he might be able to trust was Mr. Collins.

One day after physics class, Isaac approached his teacher, who was dressed like always in a button-down shirt with the sleeves rolled halfway to his elbow; his short hair, parted on the right, revealed a receding hairline. "Mr. Collins, I've been working on a physics experiment that I'd like to demonstrate to you," Isaac said, looking over his shoulder to see if anyone was watching.

"Sure, Isaac. What's it about?" Mr. Collins asked while collecting the papers in his in-box.

"It's an experiment with gravity."

"Sounds interesting. Are you ready now? Or would you like to come back after school?"

"Can we do it tomorrow after school? I need something from home. And can we use the small gym?" Isaac asked, hoping his teacher would agree.

"How long will it take? The wrestling team practices in the small gym."

"Only five or ten minutes." Isaac wiped his sweaty hands on his pants.

"I'm sure the coaches can give us a few minutes or a corner of the gym," Mr. Collins said with a reassuring smile.

"I ... I don't want anyone else to be there. I need it empty and quiet."

"Okay, bring what you need, and we can keep it in the classroom during the day. I'll get the gym scheduled," he said as he brought up the school schedule on his computer. "Ten minutes, immediately after school tomorrow. The request is in."

The following day, Isaac walked into Mr. Collins's classroom carrying his metal ring, "Here's the equipment I need."

"We're approved for the gym." His teacher glanced up from his laptop. "A metal hoop. Is that all you need?"

"Yes, sir. And myself."

"Great, see you later. I'm looking forward to your experiment." Mr. Collins smiled.

The day seemed to drag on forever. He barely heard anything his teachers said and couldn't concentrate enough to read. Isaac's preoccupation with showing Mr. Collins his experiment put him further in a hole with Ms. Leigh, who called on him three times before a student next to him punched him. To make matters worse, he did not know the answer to Ms. Leigh's question, and his classmates laughed at him.

In business class, his palms sweated, sticking to the paper he was writing on, and left damp marks on his desk. He reviewed over and over in his mind what he would say and do in front of Mr. Collins. The final bell rang and Isaac went to the physics room to get his hoop before walking to the gym.

The gym smelled like sweat and disinfectant, both of which made Isaac want to pinch his nose. Mats for wrestling practice covered the floor. Isaac walked to the middle and said, "This is an experiment in nullifying gravity. I've never done this in front of anyone. It requires a lot of concentration. Can I ask you to remain still and quiet? We can discuss things afterward."

"I'm here only as an observer," Mr. Collins said, taking a couple of steps back.

Isaac sat on the mat holding his hoop vertical in his lap. He closed his eyes and went weightless. He lightly pushed the mat, giving himself some momentum upward. Then he maneuvered to steady himself. A few feet up, he tossed the ring a little in the air and caught it to stop his upward momentum. Then he flipped the hoop around his body and started a backward somersault.

The wrestling coach's booming voice broke the gym's silence. "What the hailstones?"

Isaac dropped like a rock onto his back.

"Acrobatics without a harness is against the safety rules," the coach bellowed.

"Are you hurt, Isaac?" Mr. Collins rushed onto the mat.

"I'm fine." Isaac took a self-inventory. "Just lost my concentration."

"What the gobstoppers were you doing?" the wrestling coach barked.

"He was floating," Mr. Collins softly replied with raised eyebrows and his mouth hung open.

"Floating? How in flubbergast can a person float?" The coach blurted out, raised his arms and shrugged his shoulders.

"Just a physics experiment, Coach. Mind over matter." Mr. Collins helped Isaac from the mat and steadied him until he gained his balance.

Isaac picked up his hoop and started for the door. His neck hurt, but he was not going to let anyone know.

"No blood, no foul. Isn't that what they say in sports, Coach? My apologies for not following safety rules," Mr. Collins said.

Rolling his hoop, Isaac walked away from the gym.

His teacher caught up with him breathless. "Isaac, were you weightless?"

"Yes, sir."

"Can you explain how?" Mr. Collins asked, wide-eyed.

"I put my mind in a meditative state and think about turning off the influence of gravity on my body. Things I'm holding also become weightless." He held up the metal hoop.

Archie Kregear

Mr. Collins held out his hands for emphasis. "What I hear you saying is you can become an exception to the law of gravity."

"That's what I was demonstrating before I got distracted." Isaac glanced back at the gym door.

"Holy cow!" Mr. Collins said toward the sky as he bent back at the waist. "You'll shake up the physics world and make everyone rewrite the textbooks." He leaned forward. "You'll be famous."

"Maybe then my parents would be proud of me," Isaac muttered. He took a deep breath. "But I'm not sure I want to be famous."

The next day after physics class, Mr. Collins said, "Isaac, the wrestling team has an away match Friday. The gym is available. Would you like to try again to show me what you can do?"

"Yeah. I guess so," Isaac said, moving his head around to test his sore neck.

The gym was empty and silent. Isaac lifted off like he did before and made a backward summersault, then one forward, moving the ring around his body to alter direction. Then, with a few throws and catches, he added downward momentum and landed on the mat. He gave a big sigh and looked toward his physics teacher.

"Amazing. Incredible! This is a monumental moment in the history of science," exclaimed Mr. Collins.

Isaac clenched his shaking hands.

"Now tell me in your own words, what did I just witness?" Mr. Collins leaned in to listen.

"By putting my mind in a state, I can't explain, I turn off the effects of gravity. The effect extends to any matter touching my skin."

"So, you're creating an antigravity field around yourself."

"To be technical, it's not antigravity; it's null gravity. I can't give myself a force against gravity."

"Excellent observation, Isaac. You've worked on this and thought out what you're doing. I observed you using the hoop to control the vectors of momentum. Managing the hoop is a superb demonstration of the laws of motion. Have you documented anything?"

"Yes, sir. I can give you my notes and share the videos I uploaded to my private channel on YouTube."

"I definitely want to see them. Wow, I'm amazed by what you just did. This is the most exciting thing I've seen in a long time, maybe my whole life."

Isaac opened his backpack and handed a notebook to Mr. Collins. "Here are my notes. I'll send an email with a link to the videos to you tonight."

AntiGravity

Isaac walked into school on Monday, and Mr. Collins came running up to him. "I filed paperwork this morning for an independent study day for you and requested a substitute for me," Mr. Collins said. "We're going to work on your paper and a plan to make this public. Let's go." He directed Isaac to the library, which was used mainly as a computer lab. A few tables were along one side against the shelves of books, gathering dust. "You've documented the process very well, Isaac," he said. "I'm impressed at the detail in your notes. If you approve, I'll help you write this up, not that I want credit or anything like that. You get all the credit. Do you have a plan for how you're going to reveal this to the world?"

"You and the other science teachers deserve credit. Everyone stressed the scientific method and documenting experiments," Isaac replied. Then his head began to spin. *I have a unique ability. How will the world react?*

They spent the day in the library, interpreting the data and writing a paper. Isaac's notebook was in order with references to his videos. What they needed was the math supporting the laws of motion experiments. Together, they were quickly able to show how Isaac could alter his momentum using the ring's mass.

Mr. Collins asked, "Do your parents know about your ability?"

"They know I've been doing experiments with gravity. But I don't think they know that I can defy gravity."

"Do you think you should tell them?" Mr. Collins asked with raised eyebrows.

"I did tell them, but they didn't understand what I was doing." Isaac shrugged. "I don't know how to explain what I do."

"How could we introduce your parents to what you can do? How would you like to let this null-gravity cat out of the bag?"

Isaac considered the question while taking in a deep breath and letting it out slowly. He looked up. "I don't know. Open the bag and let the cat out?"

Mr. Collins grabbed his computer and browsed away. "There's a gravity conference in Los Angeles the end of April. I can set this up as a physics-related field trip and pay for it myself. Since it requires travel, I'll need your parent's approval. Do you think you can get it?"

"I think so."

"Great, I'll get us tickets, and until then, we practice. We'll add all sorts of distractions to increase your immunity to sounds and sights. Also, we need to find a better hoop."

They submitted the paper documenting Isaac's abilities to the conference organizers, requesting ten minutes when Isaac could demonstrate his null-gravity ability.

Isaac ordered a one-meter stainless steel hoop and retired the table-top rim. Mr. Collins scheduled the gym every day it was free and played music, blasted bullhorns, and flashed lights. Many times, an external stimulation caused Isaac to lose concentration, and he fell onto the mats. They captured each trial on video, reviewed the failures, and tried again. After two weeks, Isaac was not perfect, but he was less likely to fall.

Chapter 6 – May Conference

On the flight to Los Angles, Isaac's nerves made him sick. *Why do I have to tell the world? I could keep this to myself. Does it matter if I can turn off gravity?* He was miserable during the entire plane ride and tossed and turned in the hotel.

The following morning, they arrived at the conference. Mr. Collins studied the schedule. Lectures all day—no mention of Isaac. He asked the person at the check-in table why Isaac was not on the agenda, and he directed them to a man by the main door.

"Excuse me. I'm Lance Collins. Isaac Thomas and I submitted a paper about null gravity and requested a few minutes to demonstrate the ability during the conference. I don't see Isaac on the schedule."

"You're the people who submitted the paper on turning off gravity?" the bald man asked in a loud voice.

"Yes, that's us," Mr. Collins said.

The man chuckled. "We got a good laugh at the preposterous proposal, and it didn't warrant a response." He cocked his head slightly and fluttered his fingers. "This is a serious conference. Not a place for ridiculous demonstrations."

Isaac had the urge to go weightless just to show this man what he could do. Instead, he slunk inside the open auditorium door to listen, while eavesdropping on his teacher.

"Isaac can turn off gravity. We came to reveal our findings."

"Go inside and try to learn something. You'll realize gravity can't be turned off."

Mr. Collins entered the auditorium and joined Isaac.

Isaac said, "I'm unbelievable."

He put his hand on Isaac's shoulder. "Most discoveries are not accepted initially. We'll have to find another way to convince them."

After the morning presentations, Mr. Collins said, "I hope you got something out of this. The mathematics on quantum gravity is beyond me."

"Me too. I picked up a little on the concepts. The speaker on gravity waves got me thinking. Do I modify waves or nullify them?"

"You seem to turn gravity on or off and thus nullify them to go completely weightless. If you modified gravity waves like a potentiometer, then there would be a state where you weighed less but were not completely weightless."

"I thought about that when I lifted a barrel. We need to design a test to determine if I can modify gravity, not just nullify it."

To Isaac, the afternoon lectures were like the stars on a clear night—way over his head. He wondered, *how am I doing what I'm doing?*

Archie Kregear

The schedule listed a few options for evening entertainment in or near the conference center. One caught Isaac's eye. *Acts that Defy Gravity: The Los Angeles School District Acrobatic Exhibition.* Isaac pointed to it. "This one is nearby. Can we check it out?"

They ate a quick dinner and arrived at the show early, which allowed them to get third-row seats.

First up was an acrobatic act with people flying through the air. The performers were remarkable to Isaac. He wondered if he should try to get into a show like this. He could float and entertain people.

Isaac spotted the conference organizer, leaned over, and pointed. "Isn't that the man we spoke to this morning?"

"It sure is. I see quite a few others from the conference here."

There were a couple more acts of gravity-defying people, flying through the air but always subject to the earth's pull.

Stagehands set up the next act by hanging a streamer from the ceiling. Music began to play. A petite young woman in a blue leotard with long blonde hair danced onto the stage. Her flowing movements seemed to be effortless as she wound her way up the red ribbon. Her acrobatic twists and turns mesmerized Isaac. He was trying to catch his breath and calm his racing heart when he heard a snap, followed by the acrobat's piercing scream. His eyes fixated on the girl hanging awkwardly, her oddly bent foot tangled in the streamer, fifteen feet over the floor.

Isaac stood with everyone else in the audience and joined the collective gasp. People rushed onto the stage, looking up and holding out their hands to the girl who was far out of reach. The stage became a chaotic scene with people yelling and looking for ways to help. Isaac stepped up on his chair, took a deep breath, turned off gravity, aimed his body, and launched himself toward the hanging girl. He glided over the people, reached out, and took the girl's hand, making her weightless.

"Help me," the girl wailed as she grabbed him around the neck in a panic.

He held her with one hand and carefully unwrapped her injured ankle from the ribbon with his free hand. They ascended into the overhead rigging, on which Isaac pushed lightly, giving them some momentum toward the stage.

She held him tightly around the neck. "How are you doing this?"

Isaac couldn't think of what to say as he realized this was the closest he had ever been to a girl his age. The smell of whatever perfume she had on filled his nostrils, drowned out the shouts from below, and dulled his brain. He couldn't believe how soft she was in his arms. Her face radiated the pain she was in, but he saw only loveliness.

The girl looked over her shoulder. "You're flying."

"Actually, we're weightless," he said into her hair that waved in front of his face.

She turned to stare into his eyes.

AntiGravity

Isaac smiled as they floated into an abundance of hands, reaching up to catch them. He timed his release of the acrobat, liberating her into the crowd. Hands grabbed him, and he let gravity take over. Mr. Collins helped him stand upright.

"I think you found a way to show off what you can do," Mr. Collins said. "Maybe someone noticed."

The conference organizer approached them as they headed back to their seats. "That was quite a rescue, Isaac." His eyebrows raised. "I think we need to revisit the paper you submitted. I'll see if I can fit in a demonstration at the end of the day tomorrow if you're still interested."

"Yes, sir." Isaac nodded; his hands shook. "I'm interested."

Isaac couldn't sleep. Between visions of flowing blonde hair around a lovely face, his mind went through the routine he had practiced for the conference. As quietly as he could, he slipped out onto the seventh-floor balcony where there were a couple of chairs and a small table. The city lights lay sprawled out before him, creating a glow in the sky and masking the stars. He sat in a chair and tried to collect his thoughts.

Mr. Collins opened the sliding glass door. "May I join you?"

"Yeah. Sure."

His teacher sat down. "You were heroic tonight."

"I'm not a superhero."

In a mentoring voice, Mr. Collins said, "There are no superheroes in real life. Only people who do good to the best of their ability."

"How can I use my ability for good?"

"If there is one thing I know for certain, you don't have a bad bone in your body."

Isaac studied the lights of the city for a while. He replied, "Is not doing bad good?"

"Excellent question," Mr. Colling mused as he moved the little table so he could put his feet up. "If you do what you think is right, then by your nature, it will be good."

Isaac rubbed his sweaty palms along the metal armchair and enjoyed the warm spring night air and absence of mosquitoes for another hour before returning to bed.

The next morning, Isaac didn't want to wake his teacher, which caused them to arrive after the first lecture was underway. The person checking the badges handed them the one-page abstract of Isaac's paper and said, "You're scheduled for a demonstration at four-thirty."

They took a seat at the back and tried to understand what the man said about space-time breaking down due to the extreme gravity at the event horizon of black holes.

The afternoon presentation covered gravitational distortions picked up by LIGO, the Laser Interferometer Gravitational-Wave Observatory. The speaker focused on an event that led astronomers to the collision of two black holes. Isaac enjoyed the simulations of the crash projected on the giant screen. *If I were near a black hole could I turn off the gravity and not be drawn in? Not an experiment I want to try.*

The presenter said, "There was close gravitational distortion picked up by LIGO last January. The event was associated with a bolide over Wichita, Kansas. The evaluation of the data is ongoing, and currently, there are no working explanations. Those of you who wish to examine the data can find the references on our webpage. We are interested in any hypotheses as to how a bolide could cause a gravitational fluctuation."

Isaac squirmed in his seat. *He's referring to the night I turned off gravity for the first time.*

They returned to their hotel room an hour before Isaac's presentation to get the hoop.

"Are you ready?" Mr. Collins asked.

"No. But I have to take this step." Isaac rubbed his hands on his pants. "Let's go."

They stood in the back of the auditorium to wait for Isaac's turn.

The organizer took the stage. "For the final item on our agenda, we have a demonstration by Isaac Thomas. Initially, we discounted the paper submitted by a person who made the preposterous assertion that he can nullify gravity. Last night, he demonstrated his ability with the rescue of Sally Sykes at the L.A. School District acrobatic exhibition."

"Sally. That's her name," Isaac whispered to Mr. Collins.

"Based on what I saw, I decided to allow Isaac Thomas a few minutes to show us what he can do. Hopefully, all of you received a copy of the abstract this morning. Isaac, come on up. The stage is yours."

Isaac took a deep breath and walked toward down the aisle.

"Stay focused. You can do this," Mr. Collins said.

Isaac walked on stage and sat down with his metal hoop. He went through the routine he had practiced, rose a little off the stage, performed two summersaults, one backward and one forward. Finally, he threw the hoop up and caught it to bring himself back to the floor.

A smattering of applause led by Mr. Collins coursed through the auditorium and died out to the sound of murmuring.

The organizer approached. "I'm standing here on stage and see no external apparatus to assist Isaac in his demonstration. Isaac, can you tell us what you just did?" He held a microphone into Isaac's face.

AntiGravity

The presence of the microphone sent a chill down his spine. "In my mind, I turn off the effect of gravity on my body. Then I used the hoop to control my momentum."

"How was the hoop weightless?" the organizer asked.

"The effect is transferred to materials I'm in direct contact with, like this metal hoop. There are limits, but I have not studied them extensively."

"Thank you, young man. You pose an interesting mystery to end this conference. With that, ladies, and gentlemen, I hope everyone has a safe trip home. Thank you for coming to this year's gravity conference."

A man with a coarse beard and unruly hair came up to the edge of the stage. "Isaac, I would like to invite you to come to my lab where we can evaluate your talent more thoroughly," he said in a heavy German accent.

"You can study with our team at Berkeley instead of going overseas," yelled out a man behind him.

A middle-aged man in a black business suit and red tie strode down the aisle toward the stage. "I'll hire you right now, and you'll be paid well for your services."

A jumble of shouts offering places to go came from the floor. Isaac looked at the men and women, dumbfounded. He didn't have a clue how to respond.

The man in the business suit reached the stage and held out his business card. He bellowed over the commotion, "I'm Doug Cooper, CEO of Stellar Z. Nobody else here can pay you as well as we will for your services."

Mr. Collins bounded up on stage, collected the man's card, and addressed the group. "Ladies and gentlemen. Isaac has another few weeks of high school to complete. The abstract of his ability and experiments includes an email address. Please send us your offers. Isaac and his family will give them equal consideration. Thank you."

The crowd began to disperse. A few people fired questions from the floor next to the stage. Isaac shuffled his feet, confused by the commotion.

Mr. Collins turned to the organizer. "Thank you for allowing Isaac to show what he can do. He wanted to let the world know he could nullify gravity, and now it seems everyone wants to know how. I'm not sure where to go from here."

"There are many great scientists here who can offer Isaac an opportunity to learn about his ability. My suggestion would be to contact NASA," the organizer said.

"Yes. That would be a good place for Isaac. Thanks again." He hurried to Isaac. "Let's get back to the hotel and get ready to leave." He ushered his student to the steps that would return them to the main floor.

Isaac froze. His eyes locked onto the blonde girl in a floral sundress standing next to a middle-aged man in a polo shirt.

The girl held a crutch under each arm. She looked directly at Isaac. "Hi, I'm Sally."

Isaac perched at the edge of the stage with his gaze locked on Sally. He rubbed a sweaty palm on his pants and felt the clamminess of the hoop in his other palm. "I … I know."

Out of the corner of his eye, he saw his teacher descend the three steps and hold out his hand. "Hi, I'm Lance Collins, Isaac's physics teacher."

"I'm Victor Sykes. Sally's father."

Sally hobbled a step forward. "Isaac, I want to thank you for rescuing me last night."

Her voice was sweet to him. Isaac took the steps in slow motion as if he were walking into a swimming pool. "I'd like to thank you for breaking your ankle. They would have never allowed me to demonstrate my ability without you." He blushed and ran a hand through the hair over his ear. "I mean, I'm not glad—"

"You have a unique ability, and I'm glad you were there." Sally showed off a dimpled smile.

"Me too," Isaac said with a gesture that swung the hoop into the back of Mr. Collins.

"Let me hold that for you." His teacher took hold of the hoop.

Sally leaned on her crutches and held out an envelope. "This is for you."

Isaac let go of the hoop and received the card with both hands. "Thank you." His heart was thumping like a dog scratching fleas.

"That was a very unfortunate accident. How's your ankle?" Mr. Collins asked.

"A broken bone and a severe sprain." Sally sighed. "The doctors say I'll be fine by the end of summer."

"If you don't have any other plans, we'd like to invite you to dinner," Victor said.

"I'm afraid we have a flight to catch. We need to be back at school tomorrow. Can Isaac get a raincheck?"

"Definitely. Any time," Victor said.

"It's …" Isaac swallowed and licked his lips. "It's been a pleasure to meet you, Sally."

"The pleasure is all mine," Sally said with a hop. She leaned up and planted a kiss on Isaac's cheek.

Isaac felt the blood rush from his head.

Mr. Collins and Mr. Sykes exchanged smiles.

"Come, Sally, we should let these men get to the airport," Victor said.

"Thanks for coming to meet us," Mr. Collins said to Victor. "I think Isaac's overwhelmed with the conference, his demonstration, and the reaction of the physicists."

"That's enough to stagger anyone." Victor smiled.

"I'll see you later," Isaac said to Sally. He turned and walked up the aisle ahead of Mr. Collins.

Chapter 7 – Offers

Isaac stared at the lights below the plane as it climbed into the night sky. "I can't believe I made such a fool of myself."

"Everyone was thrilled with your performance."

"I mean with Sally," he said to the window.

"Your head was spinning from the questioning after your performance. I'm surprised you didn't fly away."

"I wanted to."

"What did the card say?"

Isaac reached around, pulled the folded card out of his back pocket, and opened it. He read it and handed it to his teacher.

Hi.

Thank you for coming to my rescue. My dad said you flew up from the audience to release my ankle. Amazing. I can't believe that my rescuer is a real-life superhero. I feel honored and grateful. Please get in touch.

Best Regards,
Sally

Mr. Collins quickly scanned the note. "She wrote down her social media links. That's good. There is also a link to her videos and an email address. I would say she wants you to contact her." Mr. Collins gave him a thumbs up.

"I don't know."

"Do you have some paper in your backpack?"

"Yeah."

"Good. We'll work on a reply you can send to Sally."

For the rest of the flight, they worked on the wording of a response.

\#

The following morning, there was a knock on his door. "I know you didn't get much sleep. Come down to breakfast, we want to hear about the conference."

"I'll be down in a few minutes, Mom," Isaac replied. *How much do I tell them? Will they believe that I flew up and rescued a girl hanging from the ceiling?*

Isaac entered the kitchen and slumped in his chair.

Hermon sat forward. "You must have made an impression at the conference. I got a call from Doug Cooper, the CEO of Stellar Z, last night. He wanted to offer you a job."

"Yeah, I know."

"You don't seem very excited," his mother said.

"Everyone wants to study me."

"Study you?" his dad exclaimed. "I thought you were studying gravity."

"They want to study me because I can turn gravity off," Isaac sighed.

Hermon got a puzzled look on his face. "What do you mean?"

"Like this." Isaac went weightless and pushed himself toward the ceiling. "I can float."

Hermon quickly stood knocking his chair over.

"Oh, my!" His mother's eyes grew wide, and her hands came together over her chin like she was praying. "So, this is what you learned to do on the trampoline."

"I used the trampoline to learn how to control myself." He pushed off the ceiling and returned to his chair. "Cooper wants to learn how I do that. So do a lot of other people. I should be getting more offers this week."

"That's fantastic," Judy said, beaming.

With his back up against the china cabinet, Hermon had his hand on his chin; a finger stroked his lips. "Now, let me get this straight. You can turn off gravity, and companies want to pay you to study your ability."

Isaac sat up straight. "Here's the scoop, Dad. I have an ability that nobody else has ever had. I defy the present laws of physics, and if anyone can figure out how, it will change the world."

"So, you're like an X-Man?" Judy said.

Isaac closed his eyes and dropped his head. "Nothing like that. I need to get to school."

"Here's your lunch." Judy held out a paper bag.

He took the bag. "Thanks, Mom." And rushed out the door.

#

Isaac went through the motions in his classes. The bell rang, signaling the end of Mrs. Leigh's third-period class and the beginning of the break. As he stepped into the hallway, he saw Randy leaning against the lockers on the other side.

"I heard you snitched on me." He pushed himself away from the lockers.

Isaac stopped. "Did I tell a lie?"

"You said more than you should have. They wanted to pin me for the injury." Randy grabbed Isaac's arm.

Isaac took hold of Randy's hand with his free arm, turned gravity off, and lightly pushed off the floor.

"Don't make me hurt you." Randy pulled Isaac to him.

"Never again," Isaac said.

Randy flopped his legs and wiggled in mid-air. "Let me go!"

"Gladly." Isaac pushed Randy up and away while he released his grasp. Randy fell in a heap against the lockers with a loud bang. Isaac bumped the lockers across the hall, pushed off the ceiling, and slid down the wall to his feet.

"You're going to get it now." Randy scrambled to get to his feet.

"Randy Torrington!" Mrs. Leigh yelled from her doorway. "Are you picking on students half your size?"

"Everything is cool, Mrs. Leigh. Isaac and I are good." Randy backed down the hall.

Isaac adjusted his shirt. *I acted badly, and it feels good.*

Mrs. Leigh folded her hands and let them hang at her waist. "Isaac, Mr. Collins mentioned to me that you're … uniquely talented. He wants me to allow you some accommodation. I hope you use your ability for good and don't become like Macbeth."

Isaac's mind raced. "Um … He's a Shakespeare play. Right?"

"Maybe a better reference for you is Anakin Skywalker."

Isaac's eyes lit up. He shook his head. "Okay. I understand, Mrs. Leigh. Never. Not me." A shy smile formed on his face. She smiled back.

He started for the library. *Shit. I have to be careful.* He proceeded to the library, where he emailed Sally the response Mr. Collins had helped him write on the plane the night before. *I hope Sally doesn't think I'm totally cringy.*

#

After school, Isaac entered his room, dropped his backpack by his desk, and opened his laptop to check emails. There were dozens of offers, but the email he wanted to find was not there. After printing out the proposals, he put them in preferred order, overseas on the bottom and the ones he liked on the top. Many came from prestigious universities like Berkeley, Stanford, Princeton, MIT, and Cal-Tech. He decided to do something he had never done—ask his father for advice.

Isaac entered the kitchen and placed the pile of offers next to his father's chair. "Hi, Mom. How was your day?"

Judy talked while she prepared dinner. "The same as always, reviewing claims. It's a never-ending job."

"I received more offers today. I printed them out so you and Dad can review them. I'd like to know what you think."

"Your father was excited about the call he got last night from that space company. You must have made quite an impression at the conference."

"I showed the scientists what I can do. Now they want to know how." He patted the pile of paper.

She stopped and turned around. "Why? Why do each one of these companies and schools want you? That is what I would look for. Now, why would you want to go to one of them over the other? What is your motive?"

Isaac leaned on the back of a chair. "I guess letting the world understand me is the right thing."

Hermon came in, gave his wife a kiss on the cheek, and turned on the television.

"Isaac's printed out the offers for us to go through." She pointed to the pile of paper.

His father picked up the pile of offers. "Are any of these offering full scholarships?"

"A few mentioned that they would cover expenses," Isaac replied.

"Does that include tuition?"

"Some include grants. They're in order of what I think is best."

"I'll look them over after dinner. You should at least go for an interview at that something Z company. He offered to pay you."

"His email is in the pile."

"Good. We'll read through them after dinner."

Isaac ate a few bites and went to his room to look for a response from Sally. He followed her on social media. Then he watched her videos.

What is it about Sally that makes me look for a message from her every ten minutes? The mindfulness techniques didn't work, and he couldn't concentrate on anything. He lay on his bed, staring at the ceiling, hoping Sally would get back to him. He worried that he made such an awful impression on Sunday that he had turned her off. It was after midnight when he rechecked his phone.

Sally sent a text. *Thanks for your email. I'm short on time tonight, sorry. I'll message later.*

Isaac felt himself relax and soon fell asleep.

In the morning, the pile of offers was on Isaac's chair in the kitchen. He scanned the notes and questions his father had scribbled on many of them, then shoved them in his backpack.

After English class, he went to the library where it was usually quiet. He checked his email on his phone, Sally had sent him a response.

Hi, Isaac. I'm glad you got in touch with me. I hope I didn't impose on the moment and catch you by surprise after your presentation. I know I've felt awkward at times when someone rushes up to me after a performance. I'm in total awe at your ability to defy gravity and that it's not a trick or an act. A friend showed me a video of you flying up to rescue me. Amazing. I shudder to think how long I would have hung there without you. I can't thank you enough. You're my hero!

I'm graduating in a few weeks too. It will be so great to be over with HS. I'm going to community college in the fall since I don't know what I want to major in.

I'm in English Lit where we have a sub again. Everyone is talking or playing on their phones, like me.

So where do you live? Do you have any brothers or sisters? Write back and tell me about yourself.

He read the message over and over until the bell rang. This day had become the best day of high school—ever.

After physics class, Isaac discussed the offers to study his talent with Mr. Collins. Since there wasn't an offer from NASA, his teacher committed to contacting them.

AntiGravity

When he got home, he sent acknowledgments to all the organizations who made offers to study him. Then he spent the rest of the evening carefully crafting a response to Sally's email.

Thursday, during dinner, his father clicked off the TV. "From all of the offers you received, there are two places we should visit. Stellar Z since Mr. Cooper offered you a higher salary than your mother and I make together, and the University of Miami."

"Why should we visit Miami?" Isaac asked.

"I spoke with a representative from the school today, and he wants the three of us to fly out for a weekend at their expense."

"That sounds like so much fun," Judy said.

"Don't you want me to take the job at Stellar Z, which is in California?"

"All we have to do to get a free vacation is let them show us around the research facility and act interested."

"That doesn't seem honest," Isaac retorted.

"The university made the offer. I didn't ask for it. If they get mad when we turn them down, I'll offer to pay for the trip if you'll loan me the money from your first paycheck."

Judy stood to clear the table. "Every vacation we take is to visit relatives. We haven't gone anywhere with just the three of us since you were little."

"Okay," Isaac said and pursed his lips. He went upstairs and sent emails to Deron in Miami and Doug Cooper at Stellar Z.

A couple minutes later his father came into the room holding his phone. "Mr. Cooper will get you tickets for tomorrow, and you can interview on Saturday. Are you okay with that?"

"Yeah, I guess." He messaged Sally: *I'm interviewing at Stellar Z Saturday and flying in tomorrow night.*

Chapter 8 – First Trip

Isaac arrived in Los Angeles, found his ride to Sally's, got in, and checked his email. A message from Tanya Nash, a Stellar Z astronaut, confirmed that she would pick him up at eight on Saturday morning and be his host for a tour of the facilities and activities planned for him. He felt a sense of importance with the assigning of an astronaut as a guide. He went through some of the mindfulness book exercises to calm his emotions and focus on communication skills. He didn't want to come across as a fool with Tanya, and more importantly, Sally and her parents.

The driver stopped in front of a house in a residential neighborhood. A sidewalk separated the front yard and led straight to the front door. Centered on each side was a round garden area containing a fruit tree with flowers around the base. Golf-ball-sized white stones covered the ground. He walked up the sidewalk, dried his sweaty palms off on his pants, and knocked. An older version of Sally opened the door. "You must be Isaac."

"I'm Isaac. You must be Mrs. Sykes." His voice squeaked.

"Come in, young man. Call me Mary. I've been excited to meet the person who flew and rescued my daughter."

"I-i-it was my pleasure," Isaac stuttered, then blushed.

"Isaac!" shrieked Sally.

She hobbled on crutches toward him. Her golden hair contrasted with her red blouse, and a big smile graced her face. Isaac thought she looked like an angel. She dropped her crutches, took a hop on her good foot, and put an arm around Isaac's neck to steady herself. "I'm glad you agreed to join us for dinner."

Isaac held her lightly, catching a pleasant waft of her perfume. "I'm happy you're doing well."

"Come into the backyard. We can talk there. Mom made some lemonade and her famous lemon-drop cookies."

Sally bent over to pick up one crutch, and Isaac grabbed the other and held it for her.

A kidney-shaped pool occupied the middle of the backyard. Long poles held up a ribbon over a three-foot-thick mat on the right side. Isaac now knew where Sally practiced. Lemon trees framed the yard on the left.

Sally chatted as they sipped lemonade and munched on cookies.

Isaac did not know what to say as he had never been alone with a girl he liked before. He nodded now and then, asked questions about her acrobatics, and listened.

When Victor arrived from work, he took them all out for dinner.

While they waited for their meal, Isaac described how he first learned about his ability to turn off gravity and his experiments to understand and control it.

AntiGravity

Sally rotated her water glass. "You're a lot like me. I needed to practice day and night to learn about ribbon acrobatics, and I tried so many moves to determine what I could do. The only reason I can think of for getting my foot caught the way I did was being too nervous."

Isaac nodded. "I suppose you're right. You looked so graceful before that."

Mary said, "To perfect any ability to the point it can be performed or is useful requires discipline. It sounds like you're very self-disciplined, Isaac. I'm impressed you perfected your ability without a coach. Sometimes we need to encourage Sally to practice."

Sally narrowed her eyebrows and glared at her mother.

Victor changed the subject. "Sally tells us that you're interviewing with Stellar Z tomorrow. Do you think you'll take the offer?"

"It looks like the best option thus far. We will be checking out the University of Miami next weekend. They were offered my parents an all-expenses paid weekend. That reminds me, Stellar Z offered to pay for my meals, so I'll have them reimburse you."

"Nonsense," Victor replied with a wave of the hand.

"Then, when I move out here, if I take the job with Stellar Z, I'll treat everyone to dinner."

"I would be thrilled to have you nearby," Mary said. "I haven't heard of any boys in the area who are as talented as you, Isaac."

"Mother," Sally said. "There are many boys at school who have talent."

"The boys I met from your school have a lot of growing up to do," Victor said.

"I think I have a lot of growing up to do as well," Isaac said. "Working for Stellar Z or going to a university will force me to change."

"You've shown some wisdom by including your parents and physics teacher in your decision. If you have a question about anything, please feel free to ask," Victor said.

On the way home, Sally took Isaac's hand and held it. He could only think about how soft her hand was in his clammy grasp while the rest of him melted into the seat.

After returning home, Sally took him to the backyard, where they chatted into the evening. The longer Isaac was around her, the more comfortable he found it to talk. By the time Victor drove him to the hotel, it was late. Isaac went straight to bed.

Isaac grabbed his ringing phone and saw that it was from his mother. "Hi, Mom."

"Good morning, Isaac. I wanted to make sure you arrived okay."

"Mom, it's six. Couldn't you have waited another hour?" Isaac interrupted.

"It's just after eight here."

"I told you it's a two-hour time difference," his father said in the background.

Judy continued. "I wanted to wish you luck during your interview and let you know it's your choice. Don't accept the offer at Stellar Z if you don't love it."

Half-listening and half-asleep, Isaac said, "When I get home we can talk."

"How's Sally?"

"Her parents are nice, and we got along fine last night."

"That's wonderful. I hope we get to meet her someday. You didn't tell us much about her, but your mood changed after your trip to California."

"If there is an opportunity, I'll introduce you to her."

"I watched the video of her acrobatic act a few times. It didn't show her face clearly. Take a selfie of both of you and send it."

"I'll send it tonight, Mom." Isaac disconnected the call and remained in bed with his eyes closed, but his mind raced with the possibilities of the day. *What will the Stellar Z be like? I've never been to an interview before. And an astronaut will show me the facility. Wow.* He tried to meditate to calm his nerves but couldn't focus, so he got up and showered.

A couple of minutes before eight, he walked out to the front of the hotel. He didn't wait long before a white Acura SUV rolled up with the passenger window down.

The driver leaned toward the open window. "Are you Isaac Thomas?"

"That's me." Isaac stepped up to the vehicle.

"I'm Tanya. Climb in."

Isaac situated himself as Tanya made her way onto the freeway where the Saturday morning traffic rushed. "I'm thrilled to be escorted by an astronaut," he said.

"Mr. Cooper thinks you're special. He volunteered me to be your hostess." Tanya glanced at Isaac and showed off an appealing smile.

"You don't fit the normal picture I have of an astronaut."

"Three African American women flew on the space shuttle, and three others are scheduled to fly on missions. When Stellar Z is ready to send a crewed craft into space, I hope to fly on one of them. That's a year or two away."

"What I meant is that I was thinking you're not in a spacesuit." Isaac rubbed his palms on his jeans. He looked at her navy-blue blouse and matching calf-length pants.

Tanya chuckled. "No spacesuit today. Well, the pictures I've seen of men who can fly all have capes, like Superman."

"I can't fly. I nullify gravity and float. Do you think a cape would help?"

"Probably not." Tanya laughed and continued to ask questions about his life. Isaac explained his ability in the best way he could during the hour and a half drive to Stellar Z's headquarters.

AntiGravity

After a brief stop at the main gate to get Isaac a security badge, they started on a tour of the facilities. The first stop was in a building where they assembled the Osprey space capsule. One was almost complete, and two were under construction.

"Do you think I'll be able to fly in one of those someday?" Isaac asked.

"You can if you apply yourself to the years of training that it takes to become an astronaut."

Should I commit to being an astronaut?

Next was the design lab, busy with lots of people working.

"Why are so many people here on a Saturday? Don't they get weekends off?"

"Each project has a deadline. From what I hear, most of the projects are behind schedule."

Isaac nodded and was unable to think of a response.

They proceeded into another building. "In here is the materials research lab. One of my friends works here. I'll introduce you to her."

He walked through the lab, noticing racks full of boards, metals, and ceramics like what he'd seen at a Home Depot.

"Isaac, this is my friend Monica Shultz," Tanya said, nodding toward a woman wearing a white cotton lab coat and matching pants approaching them. "She is an expert with materials and can tell you about the properties of metals, plastics, ceramics, and composites. When an engineer designs a component to an engine or spacecraft, they come to Monica to get the material to use."

"It's a pleasure to meet you," Isaac said.

Her honey-blond hair was pulled back in a bun while a few stray hairs fluttered out from her temples. "Hello, Isaac. Tanya told me she had a date today with a man who can defy the laws of gravity."

"That's my claim to fame and the reason I'm here."

"I heard that you could transfer the effect to objects in your hands. Is that correct?"

"Anything touching my skin also becomes weightless."

Monica rubbed her hands together. "If you join us, you and I are going to spend some time together evaluating the transfer of your ability to a wide range of materials."

"There is one question I have not tried to answer. I don't know how much mass I can make weightless. Would you help me with that?"

"Definitely. And we'll find out if the amount varies depending on the material. Kind of like heat transfer or how fast sound waves travel through various substances. Every material has different properties. I hypothesize that every material reacts differently when you make it weightless."

"That will be a lot of work." He looked back at the shelves.

"It is, but we'll be doing novel research, which is always exciting." Monica smiled. "We'll be publishing a lot of papers on our findings."

"I have to get Isaac to lunch," Tanya said. "We'll talk later."
"I'm looking forward to working with you, Isaac," Monica said.

Over lunch, Tanya introduced Isaac to some of the employees. So many, he couldn't remember any of their names.

"The first thing on the schedule for the afternoon is a meeting with the company president, Mr. Cooper."

Tanya took Isaac to the top floor of the tallest building, where Isabelle, Mr. Cooper's assistant, met them. "Go right in, Isaac. Mr. Cooper is expecting you."

Isaac stepped through the tall wooden door into an office with windows on one side and pictures of rockets and spacecraft on the other. Doug Cooper sat behind a mahogany desk ten paces from the door.

"Isaac! Welcome to Stellar Z," Doug said with enthusiasm. "I hope you're enjoying your tour of our state-of-the-art space facility. Are you ready to become part of the team?"

Isaac stopped, and a shiver ran down his spine. "I'm not ready to commit today."

"We have the best people, new facilities, and we are well funded. Tell me about a better place than Stellar Z to work and discover the abundance of your talent."

Isaac steadied his hands on the chair across from the massive mahogany desk Mr. Cooper sat behind. "I have not evaluated all of the offers that I've received."

"I'll spare no expense to make you comfortable here at Stellar Z. All our scientists reviewed your paper and videos. They're impressed by how well you experimented and documented your ability to turn off gravity. You're a scientist and should be with scientists who are working to make the world a better place, not some university or research facility that's trying to make a name for themselves."

How do I get away from this? He shuffled his feet and looked out the window for a moment. "I promised my parents I would make them a part of my decision."

"Your father and I had a few pleasant conversations. He came in a lot lower on what I thought your starting salary should be. I'll triple what he said if you'll agree to join Stellar Z today. I'm sure he'll agree."

Isaac shuffled his feet. *The last time I felt like this, Randy was launching my rocket.* "I'm not ready for commitment. This is happening so fast." Isaac's stomach turned like he was about to upchuck lunch.

Mr. Cooper put his hands on the desk and pushed his chair back, then stood. "Alright, Isaac. Tanya will take you to the astronaut training facility and introduce you to the equipment. We'll talk after you've had a chance to discuss Stellar Z with your parents. Let me know if you have any questions or if there is anything you need. I only ask one thing. Promise me that you'll let me make a counteroffer before you decide to go somewhere else."

Isaac swallowed hard. "Okay." He turned and walked quickly out of Mr. Cooper's office. A bead of sweat trickled down his brow.

AntiGravity

"Are you okay?" Tanya asked as she met him. "You look a little flush."

"Some fresh air would be good."

Tanya grabbed a couple of water bottles from a glass case in the lobby before they walked outside into the heat of the midday sun.

Isaac stopped and took a few deep breaths and a big gulp of water.

"Are you feeling alright?"

"I'll be fine." He focused on relaxing his muscles. "I'm overwhelmed right now."

"Did Mr. Cooper pressure you to join Stellar Z?"

"Yes," he answered, but didn't want to dwell on the issue.

Tanya leaned in slightly. "He is excellent at convincing people to accept what he wants."

"I can't sign on to work here right now." Isaac looked down at the sidewalk.

Tanya took a step forward. "Let's go to the training facility. I think you'll enjoy some of the equipment. It's a place where we can have some space, and you can relax."

Isaac caught up with her and they walked on.

"Listen, I don't want to pressure you to be here if you don't want to," Tanya said.

The training facility was about a hundred meters away. By the time they got back into an air-conditioned building, Isaac had gotten his wits back.

Tanya showed Isaac the different ways she trained as an astronaut. The physical training in the gym, the classroom, and a swimming pool. Tanya led Isaac through a wide archway. "In here are the extravehicular suits. We wear these and walk around the pool to simulate being weightless. Would you like to try one on?"

"Yeah. Can we go into the pool?

"When we enter the pool, there needs to be a safety team present to haul a person out if there is a problem. But you can put on a training suit and walk around."

Tanya pulled a frame from the wall with the suit hanging on it. Then she moved a three-step ladder to the back. "Climb up and hold onto the frame and slide into the suit."

He followed Tanya's instructions. Once his feet were out of the legs, she had him sit back as she put on and secured the boots. "Stand up and put your hands down the arms of the suit."

Isaac felt the excitement of doing something he had dreamed of as a kid.

"Good," Tanya said. "Now, make sure you're steady. The suit is about thirty pounds, which is a lot less than the spacesuit used by the first men on the moon. Those weighed about two hundred pounds." She released the supports holding the spacesuit. "Take a step forward, and I'll fasten up the back."

"This suit doesn't seem that heavy."

"We'll get the gloves and helmet on and see how well you can move with the extra weight."

"Isn't there an oxygen pack that I need to put on?"

"I'll attach a pack that simulates the size and mass of the real thing. But we won't close the visor on the helmet and thus, won't need to engage life support." Tanya attached a forty-pound backpack to the suit.

Isaac took steps like he was tired and walking up a hill.

Two men walked in dressed in sweaty T-shirts and shorts. One said, "Hey, Tanya. I didn't know we had a new astronaut on the team."

"This is Isaac. He's interviewing with us today. Isaac, this is Blake and Trevor, two members of the astronaut team."

Isaac took two awkward steps forward and held his hand out. "I'm pleased to meet you."

"Welcome, Isaac. Aren't you a little young for an astronaut?" Blake asked.

"I'm eighteen."

"Not to say you won't be part of this team in a few years, but you'll need to gain some muscle to handle that suit," Trevor said.

Isaac turned off gravity, and his feet came off the ground. "I don't need muscle when I'm weightless."

"What the ... How are you doing that?" Blake gasped, stepping back a few feet. "Tanya, what's going on?"

"Isaac has the unique ability to nullify gravity. Mr. Cooper has offered him a position with the company with the hope he can teach us how he does this."

Isaac had floated up to the ceiling, where he gave himself a push downward. His feet weren't underneath him when he let normal gravity take over, and he fell on his face.

"And I hope to learn how to control myself better when I'm weightless," Isaac said from a prone position.

"The first thing to learn about flying is that before you go up, you need to know how to land," Trevor said, smiling.

Isaac struggled to push himself up, but the extra weight was too much for him.

Trevor, Tanya, and Blake all reached to help him as he turned off gravity. For the next few seconds, the four were weightless and flailed their arms and legs. The three astronauts let go of Isaac like he was a hot pan. Tanya landed on her feet while Blake and Trevor stumbled before regaining their balance.

Isaac was put into a slow spin by the handling of the others. "Don't grab me. Touch me lightly to stop the rotation and straighten me out." After a few pokes and prods, Isaac allowed gravity to take over, and he landed on his feet.

"You know, this will make the training for spacewalks a whole lot easier," Trevor said.

AntiGravity

"And a lot less wet," Tanya said with a smile. "Now, let's get you out of the suit."

"Good to meet you, Isaac," Trevor said. "See you later, Tanya."

Feeling embarrassed, Isaac exited the spacesuit as fast as he could.

"Our next stop is the flight simulator," Tanya said.

Together they went on a simulated mission to Mars, or at least the takeoff and landing portions.

"Now that we are on Mars, can we walk around on the planet?" Isaac asked.

"It's after four. I should get you back to where you're staying."

On the drive back to the hotel, Isaac's phone rang. "Hi, Mom," he answered.

"Hi, Isaac. How was your interview?"

"I've learned a lot and met some great people. The facilities are amazing!"

"You'll have to tell me all about them when you get home. I wanted to tell you we confirmed our trip to Miami for next weekend. Deron is making all the arrangements."

"That's great, Mom. I'm on the way back to the hotel. Can I call later?"

"Hopefully I didn't interrupt anything important."

"Not at all. Bye."

Isaac looked at Tanya, who glanced in his direction.

Isaac put his phone into his pocket. "My parents want me to check out Florida because it's so nice there."

"I'm sure you have a lot of options. Where to go now is a difficult decision to make, one which will direct the rest of your life. If you can transfer your ability to others or if you can reveal the secret to gravity, then you're extremely valuable."

"I don't know what to expect. It was all so easy when I was experimenting on myself. Now I need to decide who will experiment on me."

"Stellar Z is a good company with good people. The pace is demanding since Mr. Cooper wants to be the number one company in space exploration. We work long hours and weekends to meet his goals. Being a part of the team is exciting. There's also a lot of stress, which not everyone can handle."

"I like everything about the company, except Mr. Cooper makes me feel bullied."

"Is that what you felt when you came out of his office?"

"Yes," Isaac said in a quiet voice. He looked out the window at the passing hills.

"Mr. Cooper wants to be the best or the first. He pushes people to do and be more than they would without him. I feel I'm a better astronaut because I work for Stellar Z. The downside to this is that I'm achieving his goals and not mine."

"I don't have any goals. I mean, I've always wanted to study physics, but I don't have any goals related to gravity."

"I read a quote by Lewis Carroll that said, 'If you don't know where you're going, any road will get you there.' Figure out what you want to be, then study the roads."

"Good advice." Isaac stared out the car window.

A few moments later, Tanya stopped in front of the hotel.

Isaac opened the door. "I enjoyed spending the day with you. Thanks for showing me around."

"You're welcome, Isaac. It was my pleasure."

Isaac felt a bit melancholy when Tanya drove away. *Making decisions is hard, especially when I don't know where I'm going.*

He headed inside the hotel. While in the elevator, he sent a message to Sally. *I'm at the hotel.*

Before he could get to his room, Sally responded, *Dad's going to grill some chicken. Can we pick you up in 30 minutes?*

I'll be out front, he typed before searching his pockets for the room key card. His heart fluttered.

Over dinner, Isaac told them about his Stellar Z tour and how the CEO pressured him to join the company.

Mary was thoroughly impressed with everything, kept asking questions, and listened intently to Isaac's answers. Sally added many, "Oh my, that's so cool, wow," and other exclamations to Isaac's narration of his day.

When Sally's parents took the plates into the kitchen, she said, "You know Stellar Z wants you. All you have to do is decide you want them. The best thing is that you'll be close so we can see each other."

For the first time in his life, Isaac realized that a girl liked him. A shiver rose up his spine as he looked at the prettiest girl he had ever seen. Tanya's words blasted in his mind. He hadn't given any thought to what he wanted in a girlfriend or how life would be with Sally. The images flew by as if he were standing on the freeway with the cars racing past. And there was no way he could get a vision of what a relationship with Sally would mean for his life. His head spun as he considered the roads to take.

"I like being with you," Isaac said. He could sense himself falling out of control, which would probably cause him to say something stupid. So, he stopped talking.

Sally leaned forward. "What I like about you is that you're not trying to impress me. You're genuine all the time."

"I like that you like me."

"Do you like all the girls who like you?"

"I'm not aware of any other girls who like me."

"You don't think that any other girls have liked you?"

"If anyone in high school liked me, the fear of ridicule for liking a nerd would make them keep quiet."

AntiGravity

Sally leaned back in her chair. "You're right. The girls at school can be brutal about the guys. I told them that an attractive man rescued me when I broke my ankle."

"And they believed you?" Isaac said.

"You *did* rescue me."

"I'm referring to the attractive man part."

"I showed them the video, and no one said you weren't handsome."

"There's a video?"

"They were recording all of the acts. Here, it's on my phone." She held it out for Isaac to watch.

Isaac was mesmerized at how he left his seat and glided to Sally. He recalled how she felt in his arms and how exciting it was. The video ended when Sally was carried off the stage. He took in a deep breath. "Pretty unbelievable." He felt a butterfly form in his stomach. "The video doesn't show my face."

"And thus, my friends have to take my word that you're attractive."

Mary sat a lemon méringue pie on the patio table. "Eat up. You have a busy day ahead of you tomorrow."

Isaac dug into dessert, keeping an eye on Sally, and wondering what life would be like with her as a girlfriend.

Archie Kregear

Chapter 9 – Memorial Day Plus One

The following week went by slow for Isaac. School was boring, responding to emails and calls from researchers was tedious, and he constantly checked his phone for texts from Sally. *Am I obsessed? The girls at school don't pay any attention to me, and I don't pay much attention to them either. I'm just fooling myself, thinking I could attract a girl like her.*

By Friday, Isaac convinced himself that he wouldn't allow his initial infatuation with Sally to rule his actions. He just wished his gut would follow his mind. The Thomas family went to the airport and parted for their afternoon flight to Miami.

#

They arrived in Miami and approached a man who held out a sign with their names on it.

"Hi, I'm Mr. Thomas."

"Welcome Mr. and Mrs. Thomas. Hello Isaac. I'm Deron," said the man in a white polo shirt and tan khakis. "I hope the three of you had a pleasant flight. Let me take your bags." He took Judy and Hermon's bags and started out of the terminal. "Just a short wait for our ride." He sets the bags down on the curb. "I'm excited to tell you that a wealthy alumnus to the university has offered his vacation home to us for the weekend. The best way to get there is by boat. Maybe not the fastest way or the easiest way but it's the most scenic. But first, we have to get a ride to the marina."

The ride as promised was short. Deron showed them to a bright red boat.

"This is incredible," Judy said, grinning from ear to ear. "We get to ride on a luxury yacht."

"This isn't at the luxury level, but it is a nice cruiser." Deron helped them step aboard. "Our program is backed by private capital, which allows us a few indulgences for special guests. The owner of this yacht is another one of our generous donors." He handed their bags to a man in an off-white short-sleeve shirt and shorts. "Please have a seat inside or outside while we get under way."

Isaac followed his mother into the galley. "This is almost as big as our kitchen," she said.

A rectangle table with bench seats was on one side and a counter with a sink on the other. Seat and steering wheel were in the front right corner with gauges and controls.

"Pretty fancy." Hermon ran his hand along the wooden cabinets.

A moment later, Deron joined them. "My specialty is mojitos, but I also have beer, wine, and a few other options for mixed drinks."

"Mojitos please." Hermon gave an affirming nod to his wife who smiled.

"Isaac, can I interest you in a can of soda? Or do you call it pop in Kansas?"

"Pop. I'll take a Coke if you have one?"

AntiGravity

Deron served mojitos with cheese and crackers. "Consider this an appetizer. Dinner will be served later. The lavatory is down the steps to the left. When you're down there check out the lovely stateroom. This is the galley. The boat can be piloted from here or up on the fly bridge. The power comes from dual diesel engines. All the latest navigational gear is onboard, including GPS, autopilot, and course computer system. But that's all boring stuff; I'm sure you want to see the city, and the best view is from above." He ushered them up the stairs.

Isaac followed his mother and father to the bridge. *Nice. But he's trying to impress my parents?*

The boat idled down the Miami River. The lights of the tall buildings at night were spectacular as they passed through the heart of the city. Once into the Atlantic Ocean, they turned south and increased speed. The waves were light and the ship cut through them without a lot of jostling.

The wind blew Isaac's hair, so he kept his face in the direction they were travelling. Behind him his mother laughed at something Deron said. *She's having a good time.*

It took about fifteen minutes before the pilot tied the boat up to a dock. Isaac looked up at the manicured yard and immense house.

After a grilled tuna dinner with wine, Isaac's sensed his parents were a bit tipsy. He slipped off to his assigned room to give Sally a call and told her all about his trip so far.

Isaac sat and looked out at the sunrise over the ocean. He checked the time on the clock on the nightstand, six-thirty. *Just get through the next twelve hours, and we'll fly home.* He dressed in jeans and a white polo shirt and headed downstairs.

The living and dining area was empty, but sounds could be heard coming from the kitchen. He wandered out to the deck by the pool.

Deron came out. "Can I offer you something to drink? Coffee, tea, juice, or other?"

"A coffee with cream and sugar."

"Coming right up."

A moment later Deron walked out with two mugs. "Do you like this place?"

"It's very nice. Is this how the university recruits football players?"

"There are rules preventing this level of treatment for athletics these days. You are not covered by the same rules."

"Are you a professor at the University of Miami?"

"No. My role is to bring you to the professors today."

"So, you will not be involved in the experiments to reveal how I can nullify gravity?"

"Not directly." Deron was at least half a foot taller than Isaac, and his muscular arms and shoulders filled the black button-down shirt he had on. "Today we'll start the journey that I expect will reveal the secret of gravity. Many others will participate. Have a seat at the table and I'll check on breakfast."

Who are these others? I hope I'll get to meet them. It doesn't matter. Play along and let Mom and Dad enjoy themselves.

"Good morning, son," Hermon said. "Wonderful day."

"It is nice, but I don't think that I'd be staying in this house if I agreed to come here."

"Probably not." He strode over to the pool. "It's great to experience how the wealthy live for a couple of nights."

A woman pushed a cart loaded with breakfast options up to the table. "What would you two like? We have eggs, bacon, sausage, waffles, croissants, grits, and pastries."

"Good morning, Isaac." His mother strode in wearing a peach sun dress and a big smile.

"You look splendid this morning," Hermon said.

Isaac wondered what to say about his mother's looks without sounding too cheesy. "That dress looks good on you, Mom."

"Thank you, boys." She joined them at the table.

Isaac ate more than usual, as did his father. His mother confessed to having too much to drink and she wasn't hungry.

Deron walked up. "Is everyone ready to take a tour?"

"I'm very curious about what a research facility looks like," Judy said.

"Me too." Isaac stood.

Hermon downed the last of his coffee.

"Meet me at the dock when you're ready. It's just a short boat ride from here."

Judy put her hands on her stomach. "I don't know if my stomach can handle another boat ride."

His parents and Deron took seats in the cabin while Isaac went up to the bridge.

The pilot cast off the lines, climbed to the bridge, and powered away.

Isaac enjoyed the morning air even though the humidity was making him feel sticky. Seeing the land and sea from the bridge gave him a feeling of freedom. He was soaking it in when he realized they were heading away from land into the open ocean.

"Where are we going?" Isaac yelled over the sound of the wind and motors.

The pilot looked over at him from his seat in the captain's chair but did not answer.

The land was far in the distance. Isaac stepped next to the pilot. "Why are we heading out to sea?"

The man shrugged his shoulders then stomped a foot.

AntiGravity

Deron came up to the bridge and made eye contact with the pilot who nodded towards Isaac.

Isaac looked at Deron. "Where are we going?"

"Why don't you come down to the cabin where we can talk?" Deron reached out to take Isaac's arm.

He yanked his arm away and moved to the corner of the bridge.

Hermon appeared, stepping up the ladder. "Aren't we a long way from shore?"

"Mr. Thomas, return to the cabin. We'll be right behind you." Deron said over his shoulder.

"NO!" Isaac yelled. "You'll explain now."

"If I don't where will you go?" Deron smiled and held at his hands towards the expanse of water.

Hermon reached the top step. "Listen, my wife is getting seasick. Probably from too much to drink. Take us back to the house or directly to this facility."

Deron turned to face his father offering a polite smile. "I have just the thing for her. Shall we go down to the cabin?"

"Answer Isaac's question first." Hermon stood firm looking his host in the eye.

Deron turned his head and pointed away from the pilot, "Oh look, there's dolphins."

As soon as Hermon looked where Deron pointed, the man scooted behind the captain's chair. The pilot pointed a gun at Hermon.

Everyone froze in place for a moment. Then Deron took the gun from the pilot.

"This is where we expected you to realize you are my guests for the weekend. Mr. Thomas, please back down the stairs and enter the cabin."

Isaac nodded at his father, held his hands by his ears, and took a step towards Deron.

Hermon took a step down. Then another.

Isaac moved to the center of the open bridge and faced Deron. "You're kidnapping me?"

"Such a harsh way to explain the situation. I'm making sure we have the opportunity to learn about you." Deron kept the gun pointed at Hermon while reaching across with his left hand to grab Isaac.

Isaac let Deron take hold of his right hand, then lunged to grab the pilot with his left. Then he turned gravity off and lifted the pilot from his chair.

Deron yanked Isaac toward himself which pulled the trio upward and back, off the bridge. As they floated over the railing, Isaac caught it with his foot enough to stop their ascent then pushed to get them away from the boat. This also sent them in a backward head over heal slow spin.

"GET AWAY," Isaac yelled as he passed over his dad's outstretched arms.

"ISAAC!" Judy screamed, rushing from the cabin to the back of the boat.

47

The pilot pried Isaac's hand off his arm and fell into the water. The boat motored away from him.

Deron wrestled Isaac around and held him around the throat with a gun to his head. The two continued to travel near the same rate as the boat.

"My orders are to not harm you." Deron said into Isaac's ear and turned the gun towards the boat. His parents scrambled into the cabin.

Isaac kicked his legs as the gun fired, hoping to spoil the aim. The recoil changed their angular rotation adding more spin.

Deron waited until he could get shots off at the boat, each time the recoil wildly changed their movement.

Still, Isaac saw and heard bullets hit the wood and fiberglass. Isaac went limp when the gun clicked. His ears rang, and he had a sweet gunpowder taste in his mouth.

"You will not get away," Deron growled in his ear.

They continued to flail about in the air.

"Where are you going to take me now?" Isaac asked.

"How long can you float in the air?"

"Long enough for my parents to get away and for those boats to get here." Isaac tried to point, but the flips they were doing had him pointing in all directions.

The two floundered about. The closest boat, driven by a man and woman, picked up the pilot and sped toward them with a second boat close behind.

"Next time, I will not be so nice." Deron released his grasp and fell the ten meters into the ocean. The closest boat stopped, and the pilot hauled Deron aboard. Then Deron and the pilot threw the couple in the water.

As Deron started to race away, the second boat arrived. They picked up the two people in the water.

Isaac let gravity take over, and he fell awkwardly into the water with a smack. He surfaced, gasped a breath, and flailed about in the choppy water. The side of his face stung, his left shoulder had a sharp pain, and the rest of his body ached. A life ring landed behind him, and he reached with his right hand to grab it.

"Who are you?" a voice yelled.

"I'm Isaac Thomas," he said, trying to regain his senses.

"What are you doing out here?"

"They were trying to kidnap me." He let himself float in the water. Isaac felt a tug on the ring. They pulled him into the boat, where he fell to his hands and knees.

"Are you hurt?" a woman asked.

"Nothing major."

Isaac heard a man talking to the Coast Guard, giving a description of the boat.

"The leader is named Deron." Isaac sat back on his feet and finger-combed his wet hair back.

"What direction?" the man asked.

AntiGravity

"I don't know. Look for a red yacht. My parents are on the boat."

The man relayed the information and a minute later said, "We're to take the three of you to the Coast Guard station in Miami."

Isaac took a seat in the back. *That was close. I hope my parents are safe.*

The trip to shore was slower and the seas rougher than Isaac expected. He thanked the boat owners for picking him up and apologized to the couple who lost their boat to Deron. Mostly he sat and thought about his parents and what he was going to tell Sally.

A uniformed man ushered him into a room at the Coast Guard station with a small metal table and four chairs. "Someone will be here to speak with you in a few minutes." He left a bottle of water.

Isaac looked at the photos of boats and ships on the walls while sipping. He learned that there was a class of cutters referred to as Famous.

The door opened, and a uniformed woman entered. "I'm Ensign Guilford. Please tell me your name."

"Isaac Thomas."

"Date of birth and city of residence."

"December 15 and Wichita, Kansas."

"What are the names of your parents?"

"Hermon and Judy. Have you found them?"

"What was your mother wearing when you last saw her?"

"A peach-colored sundress."

"Where were your parents when you last saw them?"

"They were on a red yacht cruising east."

"Were your parents experienced boaters?"

"No. I don't remember them being on a boat before this weekend."

The Ensign pursed her lips then turned her tablet towards Isaac. "Is this what your mother's dress looked like?"

Isaac looked at a photo of a hand-sized section of cloth. "Yes." His chest tightened.

She swiped to the next photo. "Does this look like the boat they were in?"

Isaac recognized the yacht. "Yes. Where are my parents?"

The woman took a deep breath and let it out slowly. "Your parents called in a mayday from the boat. We were able to guide them through the procedure of turning on the autopilot with coordinates for this station. When we were able to get on board—"

"Were they hit by the bullets?" Isaac looked directly at the ensign.

"No. We suspect a bullet damaged the exhaust. The cabin filled with carbon monoxide."

The woman took a deep breath. "I'm going to ask you to verify that the next two photos are your parents." She showed him one.

"My father," he said quietly.

Then the other.

"My mother." His response was barely audible.

"I'm terribly sorry for your loss, Isaac," she said, then sat in silence.

The rest of the day was a blur. Isaac answered questions from the Coast Guard and police, filled out forms, ate what was given to him, and responded to a grief counselor who said many times, "You did the right thing."

It was dark when he was ushered into a nearby motel room with the clothes on his back and the counselor's card in his hand. His phone didn't work, and he had never memorized Sally's number. He had never felt so alone and helpless.

The following morning, he met again with Ensign Guilford. "Isaac, here is what we know. You and your parents arrived Friday night and met Deron, who put you up in a house south of downtown Miami. We are looking for the location. The boat was leased by a company with no recorded history of owners."

"Deron said he was with the University of Miami."

She shuffled a couple of papers. "The FBI checked that out. There is no person with that name associated with the university. Students with that name do not fit your description."

"We tracked the hijacked boat toward international waters where all electronics were disabled. There was a two-hundred-foot yacht in that direction. We made an inquiry but have not received anything back. These things take time.

"The bottom line is whoever wanted to kidnap you to learn about your ability is smart and well funded."

"Wow," Isaac uttered.

The ensign's phone chimed. She glanced at it. "Stay here. We can release your belongings that were recovered from the cruiser. I'll have them brought in."

A few minutes later, Ensign Guilford returned with two plastic bags containing the belongings his parents had on them. "Sign these documents which say that I am giving these items back to you. The last form is a release to allow the FBI to access your phone records and those of your parents."

Isaac signed the forms. "Thank you," Isaac choked out, looking at the ensign with blurry eyes. "I guess we were pretty naive."

"Most people are unaware of the levels the scum of the earth go to to get what they want. You set your parents free and saved yourself. I'm sorry for your loss." She walked out of the room.

Isaac sat silently wondering what to do next.

A few minutes passed and Ensign Guilford returned. "Do you have any friends or relatives in Miami?"

"No."

"Is there anyone you can call?"

"My phone doesn't work, and I don't know anyone's number."

"Give me a minute to gather some paperwork and we'll get you on a plane home." After meeting with TSA to confirm Isaac's identity, she bought Isaac a one-way ticket home.

"Thanks. I have your number and address." He held up a piece of paper. "I'll repay you when I figure out how."

"Let me know you arrived home safely."

"I will."

He bought a charger with money from his dad's wallet. He composed an email to Sally. *My phone got wet so using my dad's email. Deron tried to kidnap me. We got away. I'm about to board the plane home. I'll call tomorrow.*

Chapter 10 – The Next Week

Isaac was thankful to have his dad's keys so he could drive himself home from the airport. He entered his home and turned on the lights, feeling the emptiness, the quiet, the stillness of the air. Stepping forward, he noticed for the first time a creak in the hardwood floor of the entryway. Climbing the steps, he studied each photo on the wall, noting the people and time they were taken. There was the wedding photo of his parents; they looked so happy. Now his new talent had ended their lives. *Damn, I wish this gravity thing hadn't fallen on me. Why?* His legs buckled, and he lay on the wood stairs with tears dripping from his chin. *What am I going to do?*

After a few moments, his dad's phone chimed with a message from Sally. He ignored it and went to bed to lie in the dark, wondering what to do next.

Monday morning, the doorbell rang. Isaac looked out to see a man in a black suit holding up an FBI badge. He opened the door. "Hi."

"Good morning. Are you Isaac Thomas?" the agent asked.

"Yes, that's me. Are there more questions I need to answer?"

"Not that I am aware of. I'm here to inform you that the FBI will be watching to make sure you stay safe. We will set up a few cameras around the house, and you may notice our presence in the area." The agent took a black plastic item from his pocket about the size of a remote car key but thinner. "If you are in any trouble, press the button. It will send us an alert with your location. Otherwise, we'll stay out of your way."

"Thanks," Isaac said. The agent stepped off the porch and walked down the street. Isaac put the remote in his pocket.

Around noon Morgan, his dad's brother, and his wife arrived. They took over dealing with the funeral plans and informing other family members and friends.

He called Sally when he knew she would be out of school. He told her the whole story and talked about it for a few hours.

On Thursday, he attended the next-to-last day of high school, more to get out of the house than to be with his classmates. He noticed the agent follow him as he walked to school. The agent met another, and both remained in a car across the street.

Throughout the day, he felt like he didn't have anything in common with the other students. They were signing yearbooks, reminiscing, and having fun. Isaac didn't order a yearbook, and in physics class Mohammad and Hector asked him to write in theirs. In both, Isaac drew a ticket and wrote in it, "Good for one free passage to space."

Mr. Collins called him up after class. "How was your trip to Miami?"

AntiGravity

Isaac took a deep breath. "It couldn't have been worse. Deron wasn't with the University of Miami. He tried to kidnap me. I got away but my parents died after escaping."

"Oh no. I'm so sorry, Isaac."

"I'll fill you in on the details another day."

"I wanted to tell you that I got a reply from NASA. They will contact you by email."

"I'll check when I get home."

Later in the evening, he found NASA's reply.

Dear Isaac Thomas,

We are interested in having you come to the Johnson Space Center in Houston to conduct gravity research. I'll call Wednesday at four in the afternoon.

Best regards,

Director Anderson

Isaac replied with his dad's phone number, then sat on the edge of his bed. *Why do I want to let scientists study me? Scientists studying the X-men or anyone with special abilities always ends up bad.* He laid face down and beat his fists against the pillow. *I've already killed my parents. I don't want problems!*

After a mental debate about staying home on Wednesday or going to school, Isaac decided that the day would go faster if he went to school. Most of the day, he played games on his phone. At lunch, he was eating alone when a half dozen students ran over to him.

One girl said, "Isaac, we're from the Student Council and have selected you to be the fourth most likely to succeed. Congratulations." She held out a certificate.

An ironic smile grew on Isaac. "Thank you," he said. "What do you think I'll succeed at?"

Jerome, the student body president, said, "You're the smartest guy in math and physics. We know you'll do something great."

Isaac held the certificate in both hands. "Fourth most likely to succeed. Who are the first three?"

The girl who spoke first blurted out, "Jerome is first. We all know he will be President someday. Melody was voted second most likely to succeed because of her voice, and Randy will be a football star."

Isaac rubbed the certificate between his thumb and index finger and looked over the group of popular students standing before him. "When I get to space, I hope you'll look up to me and wave."

"That would be so cool." One girl giggled and waved at the ceiling.

Isaac said. "Good luck on becoming President, Jerome. I wish you all the greatest success in life."

"Group photo," another girl said, and they gathered around him to take a picture.

After they left, Isaac got up and walked to the physics classroom. "Hi, Mr. Collins. The director of NASA is calling this afternoon. I'm too nervous to think, so I'm going home."

He stopped what he was doing. "How are you holding up?"

"I'm okay."

"Good. I'm always available, even after school is out. Let me know what happens with NASA."

"Will do. If they accept me, I'm sure they will be able to figure me out. They can have this ability."

"They're the best scientists in the world. You'll give them something they'll cherish forever." The bell rang, signaling the end of lunch. "I'll send a quick note to your other teacher, letting her know that you're helping me out for the rest of the day."

As he walked home, he felt relieved to be done with the bullies and status games of high school. Yet he wished that Randy would bully him now with the FBI watching.

When the phone call came, Isaac rubbed his sweaty palms on his pants and answered. "Hello, this is Isaac."

"Good afternoon, Isaac. This is Director Anderson, and I have Don Greenwell here with me. Don is an electrical engineer here at NASA. Should you come down, he'll be assigned to work with you. First, on behalf of NASA, I want to extend my condolences on the loss of your parents. I understand there are many things that you need to take care of, including your graduation. Do you have an idea of when you think you'll be able to come to Houston?"

Isaac thought for a moment. "I think I can be there in two weeks." For the first time, he wondered what needed to be done to take care of all his parent's stuff. "Maybe three."

"Great. Come down a week after Memorial Day. I'll email the contract and Don's contact information. He'll work with you on the details."

Isaac replied. "I guess that will work."

"You sound a little hesitant, Isaac. Is there anything we need to discuss?"

"No. I just want to get rid of this ability or at least get the knowledge out so that I'm not the only one."

"From what I've seen, you have a unique ability. If you wish to share your knowledge with the world, we can make that happen. The most important thing in our research will be your safety and security."

"That's why I'd like to come to NASA. I know you're more interested in my well-being than knowing how to turn off gravity."

"Absolutely. From this time on, all of NASA's resources are at your disposal."

"Thanks. I'll be in touch after everything comes together." Isaac ended the call and thought about being in Houston. *That's too far away from Sally.*

AntiGravity

Isaac wanted to tell Sally directly about going to NASA, so he waited until he thought Sally would be home from school.

It was eight when he called via video. "Hi, Isaac. We're on our way to the beach. Can I call you tomorrow?"

A voice came from behind Sally. "Is that the guy who can fly? Let me see him."

Isaac saw Sally go wide-eyed before another girl's face was on the screen. "You're cute."

"Let me see," came another voice.

Isaac turned the phone toward the ceiling. "Call me tomorrow." He ended the call and tossed the phone onto the bed. *How can such an attractive, popular, talented girl like me?*

On Saturday, Isaac's aunts and uncles sat down with him to go over the funeral and estate. He told them that he was going to Houston to work for NASA, and it would be best to sell everything. As the family went into the details, Isaac only wanted a phone call from Sally. By dinner, all he wanted was to shoot monsters in video games.

By the time his phone rang, Isaac was engrossed in Call of Duty. He paused the game and answered. "Hi, Sally." He pulled his headphones down around his neck.

"Hi. Sorry to get back to you so late. It's been a busy day. Guess what? I still have a summer job at Universal Studios. They accepted me months ago, but I went in to make sure I could work with a cast on my ankle, only now I'm a cashier in a store. How are you doing?"

Isaac swallowed, but the emotions wrapped up inside him about his parents, his infatuation with Sally, going to NASA, rumbled as he choked out, "I'm going to Houston in a couple of weeks."

"I'm so happy and proud of you."

He forced back a sob. "I won't be coming out to California."

"Hey, I'm coming out next weekend for the memorial service. I like you, and we'll have to figure out how to have a long-distance relationship."

"I don't know how to do relationships and have no idea how to do a long-distance one."

"Do you like me?"

"I do. I think about you more than I do my parents." He stood and began to pace. "But I'm wondering if I'm just clinging on to you as I have nothing else." His headphones, having reached the end of the cord, jerked off his neck.

"I'll accept being the person you cling to because I like you. You're honest, transparent, talented, and intelligent. You've bottled up your feelings and sealed them tight. We're going to work on that."

"But we'll be so far apart."

"That will force us to take things slow and grow together. Too many couples take it too fast."

That Thursday, Isaac graduated. They spent another hour on the phone and talked each day the following week.

Friday, after Sally graduated, she and her mother took a late flight to be at Isaac's parents' funeral.

#

After the afternoon service, there was a reception at Isaac's house.

The place was packed with five uncles and aunts and fifteen cousins—three married and two with infants. Isaac snuck out to the front porch with Sally. They sat in the chairs his parents might have been in on a warm summer evening like today—Isaac closest to the door and Sally to his right.

Isaac stared through the fresh leaves of the maple trees in the front yard to the houses on the other side of the street, catching the last of the sun's rays. He made a note of the SUV with the FBI agents. *Watching me must be the world's most boring job.*

Sally slipped her fingers through Isaac's and held his hand lightly. "This is a nice home. Our yard is all rock, cement, and lemon trees. I like the green lawn and big trees,"

"This has been a good place to grow up. I don't think I'll miss the house now that my parents are gone. The place doesn't feel the same."

Isaac adjusted himself in the chair. The screen door creaked as it opened. "There you are," Morgan said, stepping onto the porch. "So, how long have you two been dating?"

"About a month," Sally said. "Isaac rescued me when I broke my ankle. I kind of fell for this guy."

"Pun intended?" Isaac looked over at her.

"Of course," she said, showing off her dimples.

"With that smile, I can see why Isaac has fallen for you. Did you go to school with Isaac?"

"We met when I was in California," Isaac said, hoping to give short answers to avoid a lot of questions.

"So, Isaac's your hero?"

"He is, but I've found him to be an intelligent and nice guy." Sally gave Isaac's hand a slight squeeze.

"I've been around here for most of the last two weeks, Isaac. You should have told me more about Sally."

"He hates to talk about himself," Sally said.

"Yes, that has always been true," Morgan said. "Just so you're aware, Isaac, as I passed the women in the kitchen, they were telling Sally's mother all about you."

"A dull conversation if I'm the main subject." Isaac swatted at a mosquito.

AntiGravity

"Sally, let me say one thing that my younger brother said more than once about his son. This young man is the smartest person he had ever known."

Isaac looked up at his uncle. "I always felt I disappointed him. He wanted me to be athletic, like your sons."

"That's true. I can also say he was frustrated about how to challenge you. You never needed him to help with homework. When he tried, you would always say, 'I know how to do it.' And by golly, you always did."

"I don't know enough about people. If I did, I wouldn't have let my parents go to Miami."

"You said that was their choice," Morgan said.

"It was. But if I could have perceived Deron's motivation, then they would still be alive."

Sally gripped Isaac's hand tighter, her eyes focused on Isaac.

"Do you think your parents' death wasn't an accident?" Morgan asked.

"Yes and no. Deron was taking us somewhere, and we needed to get away. I took the kidnappers off the boat and left them to drive away."

"Hold it. You have not mentioned kidnappers."

Isaac leaned forward. "Technically, it wasn't a kidnapping because I thwarted the plan."

"How did you get this Deron guy off the boat? And why would anyone want to kidnap you and your parents?"

"A trick with gravity. That's why Deron wanted me and why I'm going to NASA next week. My parents were being held to get to me and what I know."

Morgan shook his head. "Wow, that puts a whole new twist on things."

"I don't want to talk about this now." Isaac clenched Sally's hand like a life preserver.

Morgan took a couple of deep breaths. "You'll have to fill me in next week." He brushed the sweat off his forehead. "One last thing, Sally, seeing the two of you together like this warms my heart. I'm super pleased you're here." He went into the house.

"It's been a pleasure to meet you, Morgan," Sally said as he vanished. She turned toward Isaac. "You have a nice family. I'm worried that you haven't told them everything about your parents and your talent."

"It's like you said." Isaac stared across the street. "I don't like to talk about myself."

Sally released Isaac's hand and lightly wiped her hand on her dress.

The family started to leave—each person sharing their condolences to Isaac as they passed them on the porch. Isaac appreciated the comforting presence of Sally next to him as he suffered through the attention and the mosquitoes.

They sat in silence for a few minutes after the last of the family left. Sally sat forward. "You made it through the day. All week you were worried about the services and holding up around the family."

"I spent hours on the phone this week with my therapist. You made this possible."

"And I'll be at the other end of the phone as you go to Houston."

"I wish you were going with me," Isaac said with a loving stare.

Sally moved to sit on Isaac's lap and gave him a long kiss.

The screen door creaked. Sally's mother peeked out the door. "I'm going to use the restroom, and then we can leave." She went back in.

Looking into Sally's blue eyes, Isaac choked out, "I'm sorry I'm not coming to California."

"We've been over that. That is the best road for you to go down. We'll figure out how to meet in the distance. Until then ..." Sally planted her lips onto Isaac's lips.

Chapter 11 – Third Monday in June to March

"Good morning, Isaac," Director Anderson said as he got up from behind his desk.

"Good morning, sir." Isaac shook the director's firm hand, which seemed twice as large as his.

"I'm sure Don has gotten you situated."

Isaac looked over at the man who had picked him at the airport the previous day, helped him check into a hotel, and got him his badge. "Yes, sir."

"I want you to know that I'm always available to help with anything. I have total confidence in Don, but feel free to call or drop by if he's unavailable. The finance department agreed to a three-year contract paying ten thousand a month. Don, what's on Isaac's schedule today?"

"Human resources to get paperwork signed and a visit to medical."

"My apologies, Isaac. We have to make sure that we don't design a test that will fail because of a health issue. Don't let the medics overdo things, Don."

"I'll keep him away from the aliens and their probes," Don said as he turned to leave.

"So, there are aliens with probes," Isaac said as they walked across the campus, where the trees waved in the warm, humid breeze.

Don was quite a bit taller than Isaac and a lot heavier. No one would call him obese, but he carried a little extra weight. His upper body stretched out the polo shirt he wore and showed the muscle he acquired as a wrestler in high school. "Not really. But when the doctors are all masked up, who really knows?"

"I think I'll tell my girlfriend that there are aliens on the medical staff here who probed me."

"Good idea. What's your girlfriend's name?"

"Sally."

That evening, Sally got a good chuckle out of the alien story during their conversation. Isaac continued to be amazed at how easy it was to talk to her.

The next day, Don gave Isaac a tour of the Johnson Space Center. Isaac took it all in and realized there was more history at NASA than with Stellar Z. The facilities were much more extensive than what Tanya had shown him in California. Don did not try to impress him as they walked around. When Isaac asked to try on suits or take simulated missions to Mars, Don said he would schedule it for another time.

By the end of the day, Isaac was more confident that this was the road he needed to be on, even if it led him away from Sally.

On Wednesday, Don showed Isaac the test facility. It was a three-story square room, seven meters on each side. Thick pads covered the floor, and four large fans covered by a wire mesh were in the ceiling. On one side was a door and one-way window to the control/observation room. Along another wall was a long bar with an angle support that could be swung out for help when walking on the mat.

Don explained how there were video cameras in each corner, side, and one in the ceiling. The fans could create an upward or downward air current.

Thursday, the experiments began. Don gave Isaac the instructions. "All we want for today is proof. Stand in the middle of the mats and do what you need to do to nullify gravity. I'll keep you from getting too high with the ceiling fans. At any time, you can stop the experiment and fall into the mat."

He stood in the middle of the mats and realized he had not gone weightless since the death of his parents. It took him a few minutes to concentrate and go weightless. The buoyancy in the mats pushed him up into the room. He felt the breeze from above slowing his ascent. The first couple of times, the wind pushed Isaac down to the mats. "Less fan Don, and I can stay up longer," Isaac said to the smoky window.

Isaac wished he had his hoop to control his position while in the air. If he found himself rotating too much, he would let himself fall to the mat and start again. If he got too close to a wall, the fans would push him to the mat. Isaac lost track of how many times he went weightless and came down.

They took a break at lunchtime, where Don said, "A couple more hours of testing, and I'll send the videos off to be studied."

"Who is studying me?"

"The core group is a research team of six scientists. Then anyone with clearance can look at the data."

"Aren't you the person studying me?"

"I'm the technician. I'm responsible for performing the experiments and collecting the data. I know how all the equipment works and get to play with the toys. More fun this way."

Isaac went back to eating.

Friday, Don presented Isaac with a couple of pages of questions. "The team has a few questions. Write out your answers to the best of your ability."

By the time he was getting tired of writing, he had finished. "Don, here are the answers. What's next?"

"No more testing until Monday. We do need to get you moved into an apartment."

NASA security met with Isaac on Saturday. They had approved of only one single-bedroom place for Isaac to live at the edge of the Space Center. Isaac liked it as it was close to restaurants he enjoyed and the stores he might need. Security did not want him to get a car, but they did help him get furniture and the items he needed to furnish his apartment.

AntiGravity

The following few weeks, experiments on Isaac got into full swing. There were tests with weights. How much mass could he make weightless? They stopped at ninety kilograms for safety. How long could he keep the mass floating? The experiments ended at one hour. Did the type of material affect how much he could make weightless? Each test of material took more time to swap items than it did for Isaac to test.

There were a few times in the schedule when Isaac met with a counselor who ensured that he dealt with his parents' death. He requested a meeting the day after receiving a report from Miami police. He let the counselor read the information. "What do you think?" Isaac asked.

"Deron put your family in a precarious situation. You did your best to resolve the conflict in a nonviolent way. The real issue is how do you feel about what happened?"

Isaac slumped in his chair and folded his arms. "I'll get over it."

"Talking about them is the best way to process emotions."

"I talk with my girlfriend about things every day. I just wanted a second opinion that my actions on the boat were not wrong."

"Your parents did get away safely."

Thoughts of what he could have done differently continued to plague him. Other than allowing Deron to take him away, he had taken the best option.

The subsequent tests performed in late July were ones that Don expected to reveal Isaac's ability. He began to set up electromagnetic sensors around the room.

Isaac asked, "Can I help?"

"Yes. Let me show you how and explain what we are doing. This is an excellent opportunity to teach you about the equipment."

The more Isaac knew about the purpose of each experiment, the better he was able to reveal his talent to the instruments. There were multiple tests to measure electromagnetism. Unfortunately, each picked up zero change. One test that Don thought was sure to work involved a tight-fitting skull cap filled with sensors. The test showed zero change in electromagnetism while Isaac was weightless. This surprised Don.

Every day Isaac would call Sally, tell her about the experiments, and listen to what was going on in her life. Other than Don, she was the only person he spoke to regularly. He became more isolated as the summer progressed.

Isaac was able to enroll for the fall semester in a nearby college and started classes in September. Most of the courses he took were online, which gave him time to continue testing.

The psychological tests also started in the fall. One person or sometimes a group came to interview him. Some attached sensors to monitor brainwaves, heartbeat, sweat, and other physiological conditions. To each one, he explained the thoughts that allowed him to nullify gravity. He repeated the night of his first experience with each person and told them about the meteor and how LIDO detected it. The men and women would end by thanking him, but he sensed they weren't thrilled with the results.

Sally invited him for Thanksgiving. But after security told him that they would send three people with him, he felt he couldn't deny their time with family to be with his girlfriend.

One rainy day in January, Drs. Oborsky and Boyes, both doctors in physics, came in to participate in an experiment. They wanted Isaac to hold their hands and make them weightless so they could document the experience.

Isaac led them to the middle of the room, took their hands, got them to stand still, and turned off gravity. He knew the null gravity would transfer to them. The air pressure in the pads gave them a slight upward momentum. The doctors initially were wide-eyed and smiling. Dr. Boyes even chuckled as her hair floated out from her head then began to flutter in the breeze from the fans that Don had turned on to slow their upward drift.

Dr. Oborsky took a stress ball from his hip pocket, held it out, and dropped it. "It falls normally."

"So, this is what the astronauts experience in space. I've always wanted to be weightless without the ups and downs of the Vomit Comet." Dr. Boyes smiled from ear to ear.

Isaac focused on being still to avoid adding in any additional motion. But Dr. Oborsky pulled Isaac closer, then twisted and reached out to push Dr. Boyes in the shoulder. Both began a slow rotation backward with their feet coming up between them. They started to thrash out to remain upright. Isaac did his best to still their movements, but when Dr. Boyles' feet got higher than her head, the airflow pushed her skirt over her waist. She panicked.

I'm sorry, Dr. Boyles," Isaac said as he let the scientist fall. He tried the same with Dr. Oborsky, but the man wouldn't let go. Isaac made sure they weren't over Dr. Boyes and let gravity take over. As they landed on the air-filled pad, they launched Dr. Boyes into a bottom-exposing flip.

Don rushed out of the control room and swung the support bar out to Dr. Boyes. She reached the platform by the door to the control room and started laughing. "I'm going to get you for this Oborsky."

"I'm just getting even," he said with a wide smile.

"I think I embarrassed these boys," she said.

Isaac's face was red. "I'm terribly sorry, Dr. Boyes. Once I saw that things were going south, I had to let you go."

Dr. Boyes laughed. "Young man, you have a way with words."

"I erased the videos of today's experiment," Don said. "All testing in the future will require flight suits."

"Come along, dear," Dr. Boyes said.

AntiGravity

Dr. Oborsky looked at Isaac. "She's my wife."

Isaac and Don went into the control room.

Isaac plopped in a chair. "Did you know they were married?"

"No. I do feel like we were set up today. They weren't experimenting; they wanted an experience." Don sat in another chair.

Isaac breathed heavily. "I don't want to be a fucking sideshow act." He stomped out and walked around for an hour, vaguely aware of the security agent who followed him.

That night, Isaac stayed up until Sally got home. They talked about Boyes and Oborsky and how it made Isaac feel like entertainment for other people. Performing was one thing; being used was another.

The next set of experiments were to test the extent of the transfer of null gravity. The Boyes/Oborsky test, as it became known, proved that Isaac could transfer null gravity to at least two adults. Further experiments were performed on the amount of mass Isaac could make weightless and the distance the gravity field would extend. The safety limit for the new mats was two thousand pounds. The tests ended when Isaac floated up with that amount of weight.

By March, Isaac was bored with experimenting in a cube, bored with school, with video games, and even a little bored talking with Sally. "Don, isn't there something we can test outside?"

"There might be. How would you like to take a ride on the Vomit Comet?"

"Is that the zero-gravity plane? That might be fun. I wonder how the flight would be if I were at null gravity?"

"That experiment is in the planning stage and might occur as early as next week," Don said with a smile.

A week later, Don and Isaac strapped themselves into the Boeing 727-200F with the other passengers. The interior of the plane had pads around the open fuselage. Once the aircraft was at 24,000 feet, passengers moved to the open area and lay down. The plane ascended, applying a force of one point eight times gravity. Isaac was waiting until the aircraft began to descend and put the passengers into a zero-g environment. He turned off gravity in himself and found that he was at a negative one-g relative to everyone else. He walked on the ceiling of the plane.

Don yelled over the noise of the engines, "The pilots see no change in the flight with you at null-g."

Isaac pushed himself to the floor and relaxed as the plane leveled out and began to climb.

During the ascent/descent changes, Isaac only went weightless while the plane fell. He experienced a one-g upward force allowing him to sit on the ceiling.

While on an upward climb, Isaac said, "I'm going weightless now. Then I'll flip to the ceiling as the plane levels out and starts to descend."

"Okay," Don replied. He relayed what Isaac was going to do to the co-pilot.

As the plane began to level off and prepared to descend, Isaac flipped from standing on the floor to standing on the ceiling. Over the next two parabolas, Isaac transitioned from floor to ceiling with ease.

Isaac then noticed that Don was talking a lot to the pilot. Don motioned to him to cut off the weightlessness. Isaac settled next to Don as the plane began to ascend again.

"Isaac, this time grab the metal bars on the ceiling. We'll see how your ability is transferred to the plane. The plane leveled off and was ready to descend. Isaac went weightless, pushed himself to the ceiling, and grabbed the bar.

Don yelled at Isaac, "The pilots are going into a dive."

Isaac closed his eyes, held tight to the metal bar, and concentrated on making the plane weightless. It seemed like a long time to Isaac compared to the other descents.

"The pilot says to stop," Don said over the noise of the plane.

Isaac let himself return to normal and held onto the bar as the plane dropped, sending Don and the other passengers to the ceiling. The plane began to level out, and everyone returned to the floor except Isaac, who held on to steady himself. Once he was still, he dropped to the floor.

"That was fun," Isaac said.

"The copilot was a little panicked," Don said, lying beside Isaac. "Time to return to our seats for the landing.

"Do you think I made the whole plane weightless?" Isaac asked Don.

"You had some effect on the plane. I'll be interested in the pilot's report and the flight data."

When Isaac returned to his one-bedroom apartment, he texted Sally. *Call me when you get off work tonight. I had a fun day.*

It was after midnight in Houston when Sally video-called. "Sorry it's so late. I had to close tonight. Was the Vomit Comet fun?"

"It was loads of fun," Isaac began, and then he told Sally all about the flight.

The following day, Isaac received a text from Don, *Take the day off. We are going over the data from the flight yesterday.* He was relieved and rolled over to go back to sleep, where he dreamed about flying in a Zero-G aircraft.

Don was bent over what Isaac first thought was an old gaming computer tower. "What's with the computer?"

"This is an instrument that measures the stress in materials. We'll load it onto the Vomit Comet and take a reading when you're creating a null-gravity field and compare it to normal."

"Do I get to fly again?" Isaac said with a bounce.

"You do. But first, I need to make sure this instrument is working properly and get it installed onto the plane this afternoon."

Isaac watched Don for a while and realized how he was a lot like him. Intelligent, focused on tasks, and not very personable. He decided to get Don talking. "Where did you go to college?"

"Purdue University."

"What did you study?"

"Electrical engineering."

"So, do you have a doctorate like everyone else around here?"

"No, I stopped at a masters. Getting a doctorate was not practical. I like getting my hands on the equipment, and having another degree wouldn't add to my skills."

"My high school physics class didn't teach me much about electronics. A little about electricity but not how devices work."

"In high school, I knew more about electronics than my teachers. It's a fun skill to have but can be annoying when everyone wants me to fix their broken toy or tool."

"I know how that feels. Other students always wanted me to help them with their math or science homework. How did you get assigned to me?"

Don stood up straight and addressed Isaac directly. "Everyone thought your ability would be related to electromagnetism. I've worked on several experiments with EM, I'm single, I enjoy experimenting instead of theory work, and I thought you would be interesting."

"Am I interesting?"

"You're the most interesting puzzle on the planet right now. I also find you to be an interesting person. You have a gift, if I may put it that way. And you don't want to keep it or show it off. In that respect, you're teaching me a lot."

"How am I teaching you?"

"For the first time, I'm working with a person. My whole life, I've stuck my face in devices like this one," he gestured.

"Aren't you working with people all the time?"

"Yeah, I work with people all the time. This situation is different. I'm just trying to figure things out."

"That's what everyone wants, to figure me out, but I'm pretty unfigurable outable."

Don began to laugh. Isaac realized that what he said was kind of funny and started laughing.

Don said, "I'm going to get you a T-shirt that says 'Unfigurable outable.'"

Isaac continued to chuckle. A couple of minutes passed before he spoke. "Do you think that you and the scientists here will ever be able to understand how I nullify gravity?"

Don stepped back and sat in a chair. "I don't know, Isaac. At this point, I really don't know. Tomorrow we'll try another experiment. I'll keep thinking until we do, if it takes the rest of my life."

Isaac stared into the three-story padded room. "Thanks."

"Take the rest of the day off. Get some rest or play video games all night."

Isaac got something to eat on the way back to his apartment. He noticed the security that followed him. *Will I need protection for the rest of my life?*

Two men strapped Isaac into a fixed seat inside the Vomit Comet. His helmet contained numerous electrodes connected to his scalp, and he wore a suit designed to monitor every biological function the NASA scientists could think to record. Various other instruments were bolted to the fuselage around his seat. Don adjusted a microphone adjusted in front of his mouth. "Speak normally, and everyone will be able to hear you," he said.

"Don, you didn't tell me I was going to be this confined today." Isaac looked up at Don with pleading eyes.

"I didn't know everything the science team wanted to test. They kept adding things."

Isaac watched a Don strap himself into the adjacent seat and access a monitor. Then he said, "Cabin is ready for takeoff. Isaac's vitals are excellent."

"Welcome back aboard, Isaac. This is Captain Archer. I'll be your pilot today. My request is to use your null gravity ability only at my command. If I say stop, please release immediately."

"I understand, Captain Archer."

Don's voice came over Isaac's headphones, "I'm confident we're going to get some great data today."

The plane took off, and Isaac wished Sally were present to see him. He felt like this would be a defining day in his testing. While they climbed he thought about what their relationship would be like if the world understood gravity. *Probably nothing.*

Captain Archer said, "We are at thirty thousand feet. The sky is clear, and we are heading out over the gulf. I'll give a countdown from five. At zero, Isaac can nullify gravity. Anyone not ready?"

"This is a fifty-ton aircraft. I don't know if I can make it weightless," Isaac replied.

"Do what you did the other day," came Don's voice.

In the silence, Isaac could feel his heart beat faster.

Archer counted down, "Five, four, three, two, one."

Isaac gripped the metal handles tightly and turned off gravity.

"Let's get this level." Isaac heard the pilot's voice. "Adjusting to return to thirty thousand."

AntiGravity

Isaac thought, *the lift of the wings must have shot us up when the weight was reduced.*

"Weightless for two minutes," the pilot said. "How are we doing, Isaac."

"I'm fine," Isaac said.

Dr. Oborsky walked into the padded area in front of him and said, "Interesting that we can't float around?"

"The aircraft is in null gravity, but you are not part of the plane," Boyes came in to view. "Hold onto the metal handle, and you're weightless, let go, and gravity takes over."

How did they get on the flight? Isaac wondered.

"Coming up on five minutes," said the pilot.

Boyles and Oborsky hurried past Isaac.

Captain Archer said, "Ending test in five, four, three, two, one. Isaac, stop."

Isaac released. The aircraft resumed normal flight.

A week later, Don said, "The conclusion is that the last Vomit Comet flight revealed nothing."

"Unfigurable outable." Isaac slumped in the chair.

Chapter 12 – April to August the Following Year

Isaac rotated himself while floating in the middle of the test room. "Hey, Don, here's a bit of data for the scientists. Blood doesn't rush to my head when I'm upside down."

Don's voice boomed from a speaker over the window. "Astronauts on the space shuttle have the same experience. And you're not upside down. You're standing in the same direction as the people in Australia."

"So, down is always the direction of gravitational attraction?"

"Not always," Don said. "Sometimes it's goose feathers."

"Good one." Isaac rotated to have his feet down. "You said we are starting a new series of tests today. What are we trying to determine?"

"The question is whether your strength increases with the exercise of turning gravity off."

"The variable they can't control is boredom." Isaac folded his legs and assumed a lotus position. "Play music or let me have my computer so I can do homework or watch movies. A better question to test is how many movies can I watch on the flat-screen television they are going to install?"

"The goal is to make you more powerful so the instruments can pick up what you're doing. Exercise for a month, then repeat all of the tests, looking for how you change your environment."

The exercise period began with a daily routine interspaced with repeated experiments and a few new ones.

Isaac and Don traveled to the Kennedy Space Center, where equipment designed for Isaac tested how much mass he could make weightless. The results showed that the type of material and distance from Isaac were factors in negating gravity. How to have over twenty-thousand kilograms near him became a safety problem. Even with that mass, instruments were unable to detect changes in the electromagnetic spectrum.

The exercise program for Isaac added running, weightlifting, swimming, and yoga. NASA also began to control his diet, weaning him off of fast food and pizza and toward what an astronaut-in-training would eat.

After six months of training, Isaac was worn out. Add in a full schedule of classes that he started in the fall, and he had no spare time. The routine, including nightly calls to Sally, was getting to him.

The staff at the various training facilities were excellent. However, when he started to float in the yoga class, walk across the swimming pool, and run around the walls and ceiling of the indoor track, the staff began to worry. The day he put all the weights in the gym on a barbell, lifted it over his head, and used it like a gymnast on a high bar was when they called the counselor.

"Where am I going?" Isaac refused to sit and paced in the small room.

The counselor adjusted his glasses. "Where do you want to go?"

"I don't know anymore."

"You wanted to become a physicist. What has changed your mind?"

"Seeing what they do to me."

"What are you dissatisfied with?"

"They haven't determined how I nullify gravity."

"Maybe the task is more yours than theirs. You came here a year and a half ago to have NASA understand who you are. I think it's time for you to understand who you are."

Isaac stopped pacing. "You're right." From that day on, he made sure that he understood the experiments and trained to make the tests successful.

At Thanksgiving, Isaac went to Los Angeles and stayed with the Sykes. He had matured in everything except being flustered around romantic things. The relationship strengthened over the weekend. Together, they knew they needed to remain on separate roads while expecting those roads to merge in the future. For Isaac, it reassured him that what he was doing was the right thing and that he needed to figure out his gift.

The following nine months went by slowly for Isaac. He focused on his classes and making the experiments work. He trained hard and grew stronger. One day, as he and Don conducted more tests, he asked, "Can we try to make the Vomit Comet weightless again?"

On a warm, muggy day in August, Isaac boarded the test airplane again. Don was busy checking the various sensors and test equipment he had installed over the previous days. Two men strapped Isaac into a seat in the middle of the fuselage. His helmet contained numerous electrodes connected to his scalp, and his suit was designed to monitor every biological function the NASA scientists could think to record.

One man adjusted the microphone in front of Isaac's mouth. "Speak normally, and everyone will be able to hear you."

"Coming up on five minutes," the pilot said.

"No need to give the time. Just let me know when we have to land because we're out of fuel."

"Available fuel gives us six hours. For everyone's information, the lavatory is unavailable while weightless."

Isaac closed his eyes and focused on the thoughts that allowed him to turn off gravity. He could tell that it took more effort to keep the mass of the aircraft weightless than anything he had nullified before.

Archer said, "The flight plan has us on a NASCAR type course today. We'll be making left turns every few minutes."

Isaac felt the plane lean to the left then straighten out. Over and over.

Don said, "Now at one hour."

The hum of the engines was consistent. Cool air blew lightly across his face.

Keep the lines straight. Isaac thought. *Keep the lines straight.* He felt like a headache was starting.

#

"Oh my god. WAKE UP!"

Isaac felt two hands shake his arm. He opened his eyes to see ceiling tiles an arm's length away. He clenched his fists only to realize he was holding onto bed railings.

"Wake up," a woman's voice yelled. The bed banged into a wall.

"Code violet in four-oh-nine," came over the intercom.

I'm not on the plane. I'm strapped to a bed. He looked directly at the nurse. "Move away. Stand back. I'm awake."

She stepped back, her face looking like she was facing a monster. Another nurse entered the room and bumped into the first.

Isaac let go, and the bed crashed to the floor. The IV stand fell over with a bang. Isaac looked at the frightened nurses. "Why am I in the hospital?"

The nurse took tiny steps forward with her hands held up in a defensive position. "You were brought in two days ago. You've been unconscious the whole time. How do you feel?"

After taking a mental inventory of body parts, Isaac said, "I don't hurt anywhere. I feel like I want to get up and stretch." He flexed his muscles under the restraints.

"Please don't go floating around again," the nurse said between heavy breaths.

"Please be assured I will remain under normal gravity."

Two muscular orderlies barged in and looked prepared for action.

"I'm okay," Isaac exclaimed. "At least I think so."

The orderlies and nurses put the room back in shape. Then one recorded his vitals. "Still normal."

Isaac lay there wondering what happened on the Vomit Comet.

Don burst into the room. "Isaac. Thank God you're awake."

"What happened?"

"At an hour and twenty-three minutes, you passed out. The doctors have run every test known to medicine on you."

"What did they find out?"

"There's nothing wrong with you."
Their eyes met, and they said together, "Unfigurable outable."
"Nurse, can I get out of here?" Isaac asked politely.
"The doctor can release you. I've let her know that you're awake."
"Don, do you know where my phone is? I need to call Sally."
"I left your things in the control room. I'll go get it and your clothes."
"Text Sally and let her know I'm fine, and I'll call her soon. The password on the phone is pi to six places."
"Got it."

#

Don picked up Isaac's phone and typed in 3.14159. It rejected the password. He added a two then texted, *Sally, Isaac is fine. He'll call in a little while.* He grabbed Isaac's clothes and started for the door. Isaac's phone rang, it was Sally. *Should I answer or not?* He accepted the video call and saw a cute blonde girl.

"Where's Isaac? How's he? Who are you?" Sally asked frantically.
"Hold on, slow down. I'm Don Greenwell. I work with Isaac."
"Isaac's told me about you." She looked to the side and said, "I have to take this call. Cover for me." Then she turned back to Don.

I have to explain this simply. "Isaac is awake. The doctors found nothing wrong with him. He's just been asleep for two days."
"Why?"
"I think he was tired."
"Why couldn't the doctors find anything wrong?"
"I don't think there was anything wrong. His mind wanted to sleep."
"I don't understand why he would be so tired?" Sally's exasperation came through over the phone.
"Maybe a better term is exhausted. The working hypothesis is that the experiment we were doing drained him of energy. He passed out and slept for two days."
"Passed out? And I've heard nothing. Why haven't you called earlier?"
"Isaac woke and asked me to let you know he was okay."
"Isn't there a list of who to call in case of emergency?"
"Yes."
"Why wasn't I on it? I've been so worried."
"I'm taking this phone to Isaac. He'll call you."
"How long?"
"I'll have it in his hand in"—*double the time*—"about thirty minutes."
"I expect a call from Isaac or you within half an hour."
"You have my word on it." Don ended the call to prevent Sally from asking more questions. *I knew I shouldn't have answered that call. Never again.*

Twenty minutes later, Don walked into the hospital room where Isaac was served a tray of hospital food. Here's your phone. I promised Sally you would call within the next ten minutes."

"She's probably worried. We haven't talked since Wednesday."

"Level ten frantic if you ask me."

"Yep." Isaac sheepishly smiled.

"Good luck. Call me if you need anything." Don stepped out and closed the door behind him. He stopped at the nurses' station on the floor and asked, "When will Isaac be released?"

"The doctors want to keep him here through a normal sleep cycle. So, tomorrow morning is the earliest."

Don went home. His house was a modest three-bedroom near the NASA facility. The garage and two bedrooms looked more like an electronics repair shop. Stacks of electronic components, parts, and test equipment covered the tables that filled the rooms. Tools were orderly, placed for easy access. The open kitchen, dining, and living room were neat and simply furnished.

#

Isaac said, "Everything is okay. The doctors couldn't find anything wrong with me. My brain was in a deep sleep."

"I was so worried when you didn't call, and I had no other way to get in touch with you. I'm checking flights—I'll be in Houston by six tomorrow morning."

"You don't have to come out."

"Don't you want to see me?"

"I do. There is nothing I want more."

"My boss is signaling that I need to get back to work. I'll call later."

Isaac tapped Don's number. "Hi, Don. Sally is catching a red-eye flight from California tonight. I need to ask a big favor. Can you pick her up at the airport at six tomorrow morning?"

#

Isaac sat on the hospital bed, legs folded under the tray, holding breakfast dishes.

Sally rushed through the halls into Isaac's hospital room. He moved the tray away as she wrapped her arms around his neck. "I got so worried." Tears dribbled down her cheeks.

"Just overexertion. I'm feeling great." He smiled through the hair lying across his face. "It was worth it to have you in my arms again."

"The hell it was," she said in his ear before pushing back to look him in the face. "I haven't slept in three days. I thought you might have died, and I'd never hear anything about it."

"Um, ah, I see how that is bad. I won't do this again."

AntiGravity

Don came in. "I signed you out. Get dressed, and we can leave."

Isaac jumped up, seized his clothes, and headed to the bathroom, his open gown flashing his behind.

A minute later, he was in jeans and a T-shirt.

A nurse entered with a wheelchair. "Mr. Greenwell, I'm passing custody of our patient to you."

"I can walk out," Isaac said, taking Sally's hand.

"Policy states that you ride out."

Isaac sat and pulled Sally onto his lap.

"Let's get out of here," Isaac said over his shoulder.

Don took hold of the handles. "I'll get them out safely."

With her arms around Isaac's neck, Sally glared at the nurse.

The nurse hesitated, grinned, and opened the door.

Don drove them to Isaac's apartment. The main room had a couch, TV, assorted video games, and a table with two chairs. School books were piled on the coffee table. Isaac rarely ate there, so the kitchen counters were clean. The garbage was full and had stunk up the place.

"Whew." Don picked up the trash and took it out.

Isaac opened a couple of windows.

Sally looked around the room. "This looks just like I expected."

"I'm sorry, my apartment is a mess. I hoped to have a clean place for you to see."

"I'm not offended. You have simple needs. The place could use some decorations on the walls."

"Would you like something to drink? I have soda in the fridge."

"Anything else?" She opened the fridge to see six soda cans. "That's it."

"I eat out."

"Most guys would have moldy leftovers." Her dimples formed as her eyes narrowed. She looked at him and swung the fridge door closed. "What's your favorite place for breakfast?"

"There's an IHOP nearby."

"Let's go." She headed for the door.

After Don took them to breakfast with two security agents at the next table, Isaac took Sally on a tour of NASA. But feeling sleepy, she cut it short in the afternoon. When Isaac offered to pay for a room at a local hotel, Sally refused. They grabbed something for dinner and returned to Isaac's place.

Taking things slowly in a long-distance relationship came to a lovely end.

Isaac watched Sally pack. "I don't want you to go back to California."

73

"I don't want to go home." Without folding, she stuffed her clothes into her suitcase. "As soon as I can, I'll come back for good. I love being with you more than anything."

"I love you more than anything." He reached out to hold her. "Don will be here in a few minutes to drive to the airport. Hopefully, they have some data from the Vomit Comet that will release me from this curse."

"It's a gift, Isaac. I feel that you'll do something wonderful with it. There is more to discover, and we'll do it together."

Tears formed in his eyes as he held her close, releasing his worries and fears.

Chapter 13 – Mid-September

It was a rainy day in the first week after Labor Day when Isaac showed up in the control room for the first time since the trip on the Vomit Comet.

Don removed a battery from a fan and checked the charge. "We'll resume your testing today. You can use this fan to maneuver around the room. The experiment is to see how long you can remain weightless in a stress-free situation."

Isaac surveyed the pile of wires and connections. "Do I have to wear all the electrodes?"

"We have to collect brain activity somehow."

Don helped Isaac wrap the wireless communication belt around his waist and attach the sensors to his chest and wrists. Isaac pulled a snug cap containing the brain sensors onto his head while Don plugged it into the belt.

"Here's the fan. There's a thumb switch for low or high speeds. One variable is how long the battery will last. Just use it to stay in the middle of the room."

"We did this a couple of years ago, only with the hoop."

"Yes, we did. A change was noted in the data when you passed out on the Vomit Comet. Some think the transition is significant. Others said it looks like you fell asleep. We're now testing the same thing differently."

"Do I need to fall asleep while floating to show the same conditions?"

"We're not going to let you get that tired again."

Isaac took the fan and flipped the switch to low and then high. He pointed it at his face and said, "Cool."

"No sweat today, Isaac."

Isaac went into the test room and walked out on the mats.

Don's voice boomed over the speaker. "Today's test, endurance with a handheld fan." A light over the door went from red to green.

Isaac turned on the fan, pointed it at his feet, and went weightless. He rose off the floor and began to rotate backward. In a couple of seconds, his feet were over his head. Adjusting the fan applied new angular forces resulting in his tumbling in midair. When the fan pushed air away from Isaac's center of mass at a perpendicular angle, Isaac moved straight. But finding the center and not overcorrecting was a difficult task. *How long will it take to figure out how to control myself with a fan?*

There was nothing to tell Isaac how much time had passed. Don was strict about external variables intruding on an experiment.

Once he was motionless, floating with nothing to do was boring. Isaac began to experiment on how to move in a controlled fashion around the room with the fan. He straightened himself as if he were standing at attention and pointed the fan away from his navel. He flipped the switch on, which pushed him backward. The hard part was turning around and reversing momentum while compensating for the movement induced both by the pushing of air and the counterrotation of the fan blades, which wanted to spin him in the opposite direction.

Going from random tumbling back to a stable position took an unknown amount of time. But the challenge kept Isaac from being bored out of his mind.

Next, Isaac extended his arms over his head and pointed the fan at his face. He flew like Superman. By adjusting the fan right or left, he could change direction. He ended up with too much momentum a few times and banged into the walls in slow motion. He tried going up and down in the building, accelerating up, then reversing the fan to slow himself before accelerating down. Up and down, he went at the speed the fan propelled him.

One time, Isaac left the fan pushing down too long and could not slow himself before impacting the pads. The rebound off the pads gave Isaac some momentum upward and an odd spin. He kept the fan on full as he moved up and attempted to adjust his rotation. The fan sputtered and quit. He couldn't slow his upward momentum as he approached the metal mesh over the fans in the ceiling. He returned to a state of normal gravity and fell from three stories high toward the floor.

It only took Isaac a second to realize what he had done and another second to return to weightlessness, but gravity had accelerated him towards the floor. He panicked and wished he could stop his descent. He did, just above the pads, and accelerated upward. It took him another second to realize he was accelerating up and resumed normal gravity. His momentum still carried him into the ceiling. Then he fell, focused on stopping, only to reverse gravity again. His rate of descent took him into the pads from which he rebounded and accelerated up. This time he returned to normal gravity quicker and did not hit the ceiling as hard.

Up and down, he went fighting to control his ascents and descents. His heart raced as he impulsively made split-second decisions to reverse gravity or allow normal gravity. Falling from the ceiling to the floor took less than three seconds. The same was true for going up as Isaac reversed gravity. With such short reaction times and in his panic, Isaac continued to overreact. His mind was confused by the fact that he was able to reverse gravity and fall up. Plus, he was disoriented, tumbling while going up and down, making quick decisions to stop his fall down or stop his upward momentum. He had no idea how many times he went up and down in the room before being able to control his descent and let himself fall into the pads.

As soon as Isaac was motionless in the pads, Don grabbed him. "Isaac, Isaac, I got you. Relax. Lie still. What the hell were you doing?"

Isaac's breathing was as labored as if he had just finished a mile run. Beads of sweat covered his face. "Reversing gravity."

A couple of men entered the room. "Who is injured?" one asked. "What's the emergency?" asked the other.

Don replied, "Isaac got out of control. No impact injuries, but his vitals are high."

"I'm alright." Isaac sat up on the pad and attempted to balance in the movement of others walking around. "I just need to catch my breath."

Don steadied himself and Isaac. "Take it easy, buddy. You set off the automatic trigger for emergency response. We need to let them check you out."

Isaac ran a shaking hand over his face and across his shirt, leaving a wet handprint. He looked at Don. "What did you see me do?"

"You scared the crap out of me is what you did. We'll have to go back to the video and the data to figure out what happened."

Isaac took a deep breath and let it out slowly. A couple of paramedics entered, carrying black cases with the NASA logo on the side. "I'm fine," Isaac said as he stood.

"We need to check you over," a paramedic replied.

"Isaac's vitals are being recorded. We can take a look at them in the control room," Don said, holding Isaac's arm as the two paramedics stepped carefully through the pads.

"Per the policy we put in place last month, we'll have to transport Isaac to the medical center for a thorough checkup," a paramedic said.

"Oh, crap, another inspection," Isaac said as he stood and walked toward the door while ripping the sensors off his body and head.

Isaac remained in a bad mood because he had to experience more examinations, scans, probes, and questioning. "There's nothing wrong with me," he told every doctor, nurse, technician, and psychologist.

They all replied, "We have to check."

By the end of the exam, the doctors concluded Isaac was in excellent shape.

That evening, Sally asked, "What's wrong? You're answering questions with single words."

"Nothing's wrong," Isaac said. "Everybody is testing me to see if they can find something wrong. I've never felt better."

"Is there anything I can do?"

"Talk about anything but me."

They changed the subject to the classes they were taking, and the assignments Sally needed to work on.

The next day, Isaac and Don met with a team of scientists in a small conference room. Don projected his computer onto a forty-inch monitor on the wall. Isaac had met most of the men and the women during his first year at NASA but couldn't remember all their names.

Don said, "For about three hours, Isaac, in a weightless state, experimented and learned how to control himself with the fan. I'll fast forward through most of that." He paused while he adjusted the video. "Here is where Isaac begins to propel himself in circles around the room."

"Why were you attempting this, Isaac?" a man with dark wavy hair asked.

"I was bored."

They watched the wide-angle view of Isaac change to going up and down in the room.

Don said, "This is the upward movement where the fan quits. Isaac reverses the fan to point up, but the fan is off. He impacts the ceiling and drops, but before he hits the mat, he slows and accelerates upward." He changed the display to a graph. "This shows the subject's rate of acceleration and height in the room. We see the downward acceleration at nine-point-eight meters per second and upward acceleration at the same rate. He didn't just nullify gravity. He reversed it."

"Is there any variation in the subject's brainwaves?" a woman asked.

"We see increases in panic and stress. Nothing else," Don replied.

"Incredible," the wavy-haired man said.

Don pointed to the graph. "Gravity on, gravity reversed. On, reversed. Over and over."

A middle-aged woman in a lab coat said, "We need to design some controlled experiments where the subject can repeat this behavior."

"Why am I being referred to in the third person?" Isaac asked.

"Sorry, Isaac. What can you tell us today that you didn't say yesterday?" a heavy-set man asked.

"It's like thinking between two colors. Red then green then red."

"This is a significant step ahead—the actual reversal of gravity. I wish we understood how you do this, young man." the wavy-haired man said with excitement in his voice.

"Isaac, you are incredible," said one woman.

"I agree. You are shaking up the world of physics and biology. The problem is that I don't know how to continue with the experiments. We need to do some brainstorming," a man said.

Isaac sighed and let his shoulders droop.

#

"Did you have a better day, Isaac?" Sally asked as their nightly call began.

Isaac stared at the screen, collecting his thoughts. "I ... I can do something different. I can reverse gravity."

"What does that mean?"

"I'm able to accelerate up at the opposite speed of gravity. Going up as fast as I fall is scary because there is no way to land without turning my ability off. Like the astronaut at Stellar Z said, 'Don't go up until you know how you're going to land.' I don't know how to come down easy."

"That's frightening. I'm sure Don will figure out how to keep you safe, but now I'll worry about you."

AntiGravity

"I'm wondering how I do it. It's a whole new aspect of my ability. The NASA scientists are excited and perplexed."

They stared at each other over the phone for a few moments.

"What if you tied yourself to the ceiling with silk ribbons like I use?"

"That might work if the negative gravity isn't passed through the ribbon to whatever they are tied. I'll suggest it to Don tomorrow.

"How's school?"

"It's good."

They discussed their classes until late in the evening. Isaac helped her with her math, and she edited an English paper of his.

It took a week to get the long aerial silk strands and another week for NASA to test their strength. As hoped for, the antigravity ability did not transmit more than a meter through the material. Don hypothesized that the silk was porous and thus was a poor conductor of Isaac's nullifying gravity ability.

The experiments involved attaching a silk strand to each of the top four corners of the room to keep Isaac from falling. Isaac hung from them to demonstrate normal gravity. The four silk strands in the bottom corners would keep Isaac from rising when he exercised reversing gravity.

With the silk apparatus, Isaac demonstrated he could reverse gravity as well as nullify it at will. This began the repeating of the experiments with weight, metal bars, and other materials.

With classes at the university, the experiments, and his nightly calls to Sally, Isaac kept busy. It was mid-October, on a call with Sally, that Isaac's world took another turn.

"Brace yourself, Isaac. I need to tell you something."

She's got a new boyfriend. This is over.

Sally's eyes fluttered on the phone. "Isaac, you're going to be a father."

"What?"

"I'm pregnant."

"Huh? What? How'd that happen? No. I know. You're—I'm—We're parents?"

Sally laughed. "Yes, Isaac, we're going to be parents."

"I—I'm speechless. Oh boy." Isaac took a deep breath. "I guess I need to ask, will you marry me?"

"Yes." Sally's smile melted Isaac's heart.

Archie Kregear

Chapter 14 – October–Mid-November

Sally informed Isaac that the best time for the wedding was the first weekend in December. Don helped Isaac find a two-bedroom apartment close to NASA. Isaac was super excited about being with Sally and planned to fly out before Thanksgiving.

During October, Isaac practiced his negative gravity capabilities and was now able to control the magnitude. He could fly up at a controlled rate and, more importantly, descend at whatever percentage of Earth's gravity he wanted. It was a relief to Sally to know that he could regulate his descent and land softly on the ground.

Don and the other scientists were super excited. Until they adequately documented Isaac's new ability and made every attempt, within safety parameters, to understand how Isaac altered gravity, they would not announce it to the public.

They had tested the main theories of gravity and proven that Isaac disproved them. NASA eliminated electro-gravimetric pulses and magnetic effects but held the nucleo-gravitic option utilizing the strong force to neutralize a gravitational field—something they could not test. Both bismuth and moscovium have exhibited anti-gravitational forces extending beyond their nucleus, much more with element 115, moscovium. The hypothesis is that these elements influence the strong force. Of course, any mineral that nullified gravity would be absent on the earth's surface.

As the experiments progressed over the years, the NASA scientists concluded that they would not discover the secret to altered gravity. How Isaac managed to reverse gravity was beyond the abilities of present-day measurement.

"I straighten the waves," Isaac told them.

"We are unable to measure gravity waves at the scale you claim to alter them," was the scientists' response.

Don explained what the equipment measured and how. Isaac did his best to have the sensors pick up something. Since stress testing was currently not an option, by mid-November, the list of experiments grew short.

On November fifteenth, with his wedding in a few weeks, Isaac said, "I'm bored. Can you at least play some music?" He was motionless, floating three stories up in the test chamber after lifting a thousand kilograms of padded lead. Only the ceiling silk connected him to the building in today's test of his ability to nullify gravity.

"I can't play music," said Don. "The test parameters require no distractions. No more talking."

"How long have I been up here?"

"You know you're not supposed to know the time."

AntiGravity

Isaac repelled gravity and lifted himself and the mats toward the ceiling. Fans in the ceiling came on. The closer he got, the fans turned faster, making it harder for Isaac to reach the top of the chamber. If he couldn't give his ability away, he wanted to fly away from all the testing and be with Sally.

"You're going to exceed your limits, and the safety folks will have both of us in meetings. Plus, you're ruining today's data collection just because you're bored. I have to sit here and monitor all the instruments collecting data on you. Now that's boring," Don said.

Isaac returned to the stationary position. The fans whirred to a stop. "So, Don, who else in this world gets paid to float around in a three-story padded cell?"

"Who else has a job to record every aspect of a person floating in a padded cell?"

"What do you do to alleviate the boredom?"

"I figure out sixteen-square sudokus."

A beep came from the control panel. "Isaac, I'm getting a red light here."

"What's wrong?" Isaac asked. He adjusted his body so he could look down from thirty feet above the floor to see the red light over the command window flash off and on.

"I don't know. It's not an equipment failure. It looks like the emergency is campus wide. I'm terminating the experiment."

"I'm coming down." Isaac lowered his load to the floor, then let himself gently on the padding.

Don flipped switches on the control panel, shutting off the equipment that monitored Isaac's physiology and brain waves.

Isaac undid the belts of the harness and shed himself of his burden. He entered the control room, loosened the strap to his helmet, and pealed the sensor cap with the wires from his head. He shook his head to free the mats in his hair.

Both of their phones chimed. *ALL HANDS REPORT TO THE AUDITORIUM* flashed on their screen.

"All caps. Must be important," Isaac said.

"I hope someone brought donuts," Don added.

They exited the test facility and walked across the park between buildings with every other employee at NASA's Houston Space Center. Isaac and Don found seats on the right side near the back. An inquisitive buzz of conversations filled the air.

Isaac was looking around at the crowd when he noticed the talking dying down. He turned forward to see Director Anderson walk across the stage. He leaned toward Don. "I haven't seen him in a long time."

"Me either. He's a busy man."

"Ladies and gentlemen," began the director. "There has been an incident with the International Space Station. At 10:13 our time, we received an emergency broadcast from the ISS. The cause and extent of the emergency are under investigation. What we know at this time is that five crew members are safe in the US orbital segment. The status of the Russian section is unknown. The status of the European spacecraft that was scheduled to arrive at the ISS this morning is also unknown. Everyone's focus today is on bringing the five astronauts safely back to Earth. Every idea, no matter how farfetched, is to be forwarded to my office.

"The emergency teams may need technical assistance. Watch your notifications and jump into roles as they're posted. If you have nothing else to do, pray. Thank you." He walked swiftly off the stage.

Isaac noticed Don scrolling NASA's internal internet portal. "What are you looking for?"

Don kept searching. "I'm looking for messages that request electronic assistance."

Isaac pulled out his phone and started to look. "Who needs an eighteen-year-old whose only ability is to alter gravity?"

"Yeah. You might as well head home. Experimenting will be a low priority until the astronauts are on the ground."

"Maybe I could just jump up and rescue them?"

"They need an electronics specialist in building twelve. See you later." Don stood up and left Isaac sitting alone in the auditorium.

Isaac started to walk back to the test facility, engrossed in the real-time updates on the ISS.

Five alive. One unconscious. Others with minor injuries.
Stellar Z's Osprey is ready, but the first-stage booster will take five days.
LMB's Starship will be ready for launch in six days.
The orbital segment will run out of oxygen in twenty-six hours.
ISS has broken up. The US segment is tumbling out of control.
Russians announce that the Soyuz Crew Return Vehicle status is unknown.
The European Space Program says they have lost contact with the capsule, which was to dock with the ISS today.

Isaac slowly made his way through the park in the middle of the Johnson Space Center complex. His mind was racing with how he could help. He queried the internet to get the size and weight of the Stellar Z *Osprey* spacecraft. Twelve and a half thousand kilograms. *Only twelve times more than I easily lifted earlier. A lot lighter than the Vomit Comet. What would Cooper say? If I could make the Osprey weightless, would there be a way to give it enough thrust to match the space station's speed and meet it in orbit?*

He took a deep breath and typed into the NASA web page: *Need the assistance of an expert in acceleration and trajectory.*

AntiGravity

Fifteen seconds later, he received a response from MillerS: *I'm available. Where are you?*

Isaac typed: *I'm in the park. I'll come to you. Building 4S basement.*

Taking the stairs two at a time, Isaac reached the basement hallway and started to type.

"Are you looking for trajectory assistance?" asked a woman wearing dark blue pants and a light blue blouse standing halfway down the hall. Her long brown hair slipped behind her ears and down her back.

"Yes. Are you Miller S?"

"Susan Miller. And you are Thomas I. What does the 'I' stand for?"

"Isaac."

"Are you the Isaac who can turn off gravity?"

"That's me, the floating lab rat. I had a crazy idea and wanted some help to see if it would work. If you're not doing anything else and can run some numbers, I'm wondering if it would be possible to float up to the space station?"

"What do you plan to use for a vehicle?"

"The *Osprey* with a second-stage booster. If I can make it weightless, how much thrust would be needed to get it to the space station?"

Susan began to think out loud. "Getting a weightless object that high is easy. Having it match the orbit of the ISS will take some doing. Let's see ..." Susan searched the web for the specifications. "We take the mass of the *Osprey* and booster, bring it to a speed of 27,600 kph. This program doesn't like a value of zero for gravity."

"Enter in a negative one-tenth-G."

"Are you going negative gravity now?"

"I have, but I haven't tried anything that large."

"Gravity is a constant in this equation. If it's negative, then the software thinks we are accelerating down."

"I'm unsure how long I can maintain a negative gravity."

"Okay. Let me make sure I'm getting this. You can exert a negative gravity over a mass and provide lift?" Susan worked away on the computer.

"That is correct."

"Using the second stage and *Osprey* with maximum fuel, you won't achieve the ISS orbit. It will get you over twenty thousand kilometers per hour, but that's about it. Add in your weight, and it falls well short. You can't achieve orbit without the stage-one booster."

"What if we put in a negative fifty-percent G? Or how much would I need to provide?"

"Hold on. Let me rewrite the equation to find the optimum negative gravity and allow for sufficient fuel for reentry with added passengers. Can you get me a Dr. Pepper from the end of the hall?"

"Yeah, sure." Isaac started down the hall, his stomach churning with the idea that he would have to go negative with more mass and for more time than he had attempted in tests. He got Susan a Dr. Pepper and a Sprite for himself. *If Susan can make the figures work, then I'll have to take the Osprey into space. Am I up for this?* As he walked back into her office, he hoped that she couldn't make the numbers work.

"Thank you, Isaac. This is the most interesting problem I've worked on in my fifteen years at NASA. At fifty percent negative gravity, you can get there. If you can go over fifty percent, then making orbit with the ISS is a sure thing. Oh my god, you're shaking. Are you alright?"

"As I walked down the hall, I was hoping you'd fail. Since your calculations tell you this crazy idea can work, now I have to try."

"If you definitely can achieve negative gravity with the mass of the *Osprey*, then it might be worth the investigation. The ship is designed to land from space. There is no risk to the occupants of the *Osprey* unless they run out of fuel. Listen, since we have orders to send all ideas to the command team, I'm going to review the numbers and forward the data." Susan focused on the screen before her and typed away.

Isaac looked over her shoulder, trying to make sense of the information on the computer. The numbers and graphs changed too rapidly for him to keep up.

"This will work if there is a second-stage booster available to provide horizontal thrust. Okay, let's get a quick message to the director and his team." Susan typed frantically for a minute before hitting send. "Okay, I told them that you could maintain a negative point five gravity for fifteen minutes. If you fail, then the *Osprey* can bring you back down. I copied Stellar Z to confirm this possibility." She looked at Isaac. "My god, you're white as a sheet. Let's get something to eat. I have a feeling this afternoon will be busy."

They briskly walked to the employee cafeteria where Isaac selected a ham sandwich. Their phones chimed as he took a bite.

"Eat while I respond."

"What does the message say?" Isaac asked and took another bite.

"They want to know where you are. I'll let them know we're in the cafeteria."

Isaac finished half of his sandwich when Director Anderson barged into the cafeteria. "Isaac and Susan. Your idea and calculations have had a quick review. They look possible. Stellar Z responded, insisting that we try. They're confirming the calculations, and my staff is double-checking as well. Since time is critical, we need to get Isaac on the way to the *Osprey* while it's being prepared for flight. Let's go." Director Anderson yelled at a person behind the buffet line, "Get me some pastries to go." He walked to the buffet and received a pressed cardboard container.

Isaac stood and looked anxiously at Susan.

Susan looked directly at Isaac. "I'm going to go revise the equations to allow for variability in your reversal of gravity. I'll make sure they work. Good luck."

"Isaac, we need to go," the director said.

They hopped into a golf cart and sped away, leaving Susan on the sidewalk with her hands on her hips.

"Isaac, I've been reviewing the reports documenting your ability to go negative. There was no mention of how far negative. How far can you go?" Director Anderson wove his way between buildings.

"I can hold a negative one G. But I don't know how much mass I can take negative. The test room is too limiting."

"I guess we're letting this secret out of the box. I don't know if this will work. But if we don't try, we'll forever regret it. Once you're at Stellar Z, you'll be under their command. I'll monitor everything they do from here. They're all too eager to perform the rescue, and I'm sure they will take all the credit. I don't want your effort to be a publicity stunt for Stellar Z, but that won't matter if we save the astronauts up there. And understand Isaac, if this rescue attempt doesn't succeed, don't feel bad. Without you, there would be no rescue attempt at all."

They approached the old Huey helicopter used for campus security. Its blades were already spinning.

"Do what you can," Director Anderson said, putting a hand on Isaac's shoulder.

Isaac's stomach corkscrewed. He instinctively bent halfway over and jogged to the helicopter. Two men helped him on board, strapped him in, put a helmet on his head, and adjusted a microphone in front of his mouth.

"Package secure," a voice said over his headphones.

One man jumped out while the other strapped himself into a seat behind the pilot.

"I need to test something," Isaac said. "How much does this chopper weigh?"

"Stay in your seat," one voice said.

"About five tons," said another.

"With your permission, I'm going to provide some lift to get us in the air."

"You're the kid who can turn off gravity, right?" the pilot said.

"I can also go negative and transfer that to solid matter. Can I see if I can lift five tons?"

"Don't start until I say go," the pilot commanded.

Isaac felt the blades speed up. He balanced the box on his lap and grasped the seat tightly with his hands.

"If you think you can lift this chopper, give it a go now."

The helicopter leaped straight up into the air.

"That works!" the pilot yelled. "Now ease off and let me get control."

"I'm easing off slowly," Isaac said, trying to return to normal gravity at a slow, steady rate so the pilot would have time to adjust.

"We're over a thousand feet already," the pilot said. "Falling up is a new sensation."

"If I'm going into space, I needed some confidence with this much weight."

"What are you lifting into space?"

"I'm going to provide lift to Stellar Z's *Osprey* to help it get up to the space station."

"Best of luck to you, kid. That's a hell of a lot more lift than you did here."

"Yeah. I need to lift a lot harder for a lot longer." Isaac opened the container—a couple of pastries and a donut. He took the donut and offered the pastries to the man sitting opposite him.

"Thanks," the man said, taking one and putting the box next to the pilot.

"I love it when the passengers bring food and entertainment," the pilot said.

I can move a helicopter. Can I lift the Osprey *into space? I have to. I better let Sally know I won't be calling her tonight.* Isaac pulled out his phone and typed: *I won't be able to call tonight. I'll text later. Lov U.*

Is this about the space station? Sally texted back.

Yes. Full emergency at NASA. Everyone's working on the rescue.

Are you helping?

Isaac furrowed his brow. *How do I respond without making Sally worry?* He sighed and typed: *Of course. So far, I've delivered a Dr. Pepper and pastries.*

They flew a few miles northwest to Ellington Field. Men grabbed and ushered Isaac to a T-38, where the pilot was in the cockpit, ready to fly. They picked him up and shoved him into a pressurized flight suit, crammed a helmet on his head, and shoved him up a ladder to the rear seat of the astronaut training plane.

"Flight T-75. Cleared for takeoff," a voice reported in Isaac's ear.

The engines roared.

"I'm taking us to three-G thrust. Hold on."

Isaac relaxed as the pilot accelerated. He felt himself sink back into the seat. His arms and legs felt like they were glued to the chair.

"You must be special. Command gave me clearance to Mach one point two. Relax, the flight time to California is about eighty minutes."

Isaac's stomach felt like he was about to lose his pastry and grabbed a barf bag before closing his eyes, trying to think of something else besides going into space.

"Flight T-75, you're clear to land," a voice said in his helmet, awakening Isaac from his short nap.

AntiGravity

He was at an airbase surrounded by military planes. Uniformed men ushered him into a Humvee, which raced down the runway to where the *Osprey* waited.

As he got out, he saw Tanya standing in a sky-blue flight suit. She said, "Hi, Isaac. It's good to see you again. I'm the commander of this mission."

"I'm glad that it's you," he said, looking over her shoulder at the spacecraft a few meters away.

Monica, her long blond hair flowing in the wind, approached. "The equipment is stowed."

Tanya turned her attention and said, "Thanks. Remember Isaac?"

"I sure do. Good luck on the mission, Isaac."

"Come, Isaac. These men will get you into a different flight suit."

Three men helped Isaac change. The suit fit loosely, even after they cinched the waist up as tight as they could. They helped him climb inside the *Osprey* and into a seat.

"The handles next to the seat are connected to the structure of the ship. We were told to strap your hands to the handles to ensure a good connection," Tanya said.

The men assisted Isaac, putting on a helmet, then exited the craft.

Tanya put her helmet on, pushing stray hair into the sides. "Can you hear me?"

"Loud and clear," he replied.

"How much negative gravity do we need? And for how long?" asked Isaac.

"I got some equations from Susan Miller that allow for variations in your ability. At twenty percent negative G, we'll need about an hour. If you can do more and get the craft out of the atmosphere quicker, we reduce friction. A full negative G will give us the altitude we need in less than twenty minutes. There are six mini solid-fuel boosters I can use for initial vertical momentum or save for later. The calculations show that if we can use all of that thrust to give us lateral momentum, the second stage can easily match the space station speed. Computers will be monitoring our speed and altitude, and I can adjust thrust accordingly.

"They said you haven't lifted something this big for so long. If we don't get there, I'll bring us back nice and gentle."

"You sound like you don't think this will work," Isaac said.

"Do I think you'll replace a two-hundred and fifty-ton rocket? Not really. But there are five people up there who are hoping with all their hearts that we succeed. Doug Cooper is holding a press conference right now, asking everyone to pray. Maybe we'll get an angel or two to help us. Cooper boasted, 'The important thing is we try.' A fellow astronaut called this a fool's errand when in reality it's great for public relations."

"Director Anderson said something similar—'We'll regret not trying forever.'"

"That sounds like NASA doesn't expect us to succeed either." Tanya watched the final system checks and tapping her screen.

What was I thinking when I said I could lift the Osprey? His nervousness shook his whole body except for his hands, which were securely bound to the handles.

"Ten seconds and you can reverse gravity," Tanya said.

Isaac took deep breaths and counted down in his head.

"Lift!" she commanded.

Isaac closed his eyes and gritted his teeth. He felt himself get light.

A soft voice said, "You're doing great, Isaac. Amazingly wonderful. Keep it up."

Rigid with effort, his hands grasping the handles as tight as he could, Isaac pushed himself.

"Negative point three Gs, up to point four. Keep going, up to point five. You're holding steady. Now give me everything you have for five seconds."

Isaac strained, imagining himself on a race to the moon.

"That's enough. Back off some," Tanya said.

Time didn't matter to Isaac. He forced himself to relax a little while keeping focused.

"Breathe, Isaac. Take steady deep breaths. I don't want you passing out from lack of oxygen."

Isaac did as instructed while easing back on the lift.

"I'm rolling us over and igniting the six solid boosters to increase our horizontal momentum. I'll ease us to two G acceleration. How are you doing, Isaac?"

"Good. How much more do we need?"

"Ten more minutes at negative point four G. You're awesome."

Isaac felt a renewed confidence. He looked out at the stars, more points of light than he ever imagined, and he was flying to them.

"Keep us steady, Cowboy. You're increasing lift again."

"I don't have experience with controlling the strength of going negative. I'm learning."

"Maintain your focus. I'll let you know when to stop. The more I talk, the more you fluctuate."

"Okay."

Isaac closed his eyes again and focused on staying steady.

#

Tanya watched the reverse G scale slowly decrease. Fifteen minutes later, Isaac's effect on gravity was at zero.

She ejected the spent solid-fuel rocket boosters.

Isaac's heart rate and breathing registered normal levels on her monitor. He was asleep or unconscious, so she turned off his headphones.

She checked on the flight. The computer showed them speeding into an identical orbit with the US segment of the ISS.

"Come in, Mission Control."

AntiGravity

"We're here, Commander."

"Isaac is out cold."

"Copy that. The medical staff is monitoring his vitals. No emergency at this time. We'll keep you advised. Congratulations, you've commanded your first space mission. Switching to a private channel." She waited. "Tanya, you're doing a great job."

"I haven't done anything. Isaac got us up here. Do I abort as planned or proceed to the ISS?"

"The trajectory looks good. You're on track to rendezvous with the ISS. I say get there, and I'll split the hundred bucks I bet the boss that you could do this. They'll have about two hours of oxygen by the time you arrive."

"So, Cooper bet against me. I knew he only wanted the data on Isaac," Tanya said. "He didn't want to lose the *Osprey*."

"The rescue will be worth millions in sales."

"Our attempt thus far is worth millions in publicity. Now we're going to do this for the stranded astronauts," Tanya added.

"Sit back and relax. Let Isaac rest. Approximately six hours until you reach the ISS."

"Copy, Mission Control."

Tanya sat back. She noted the orbit lines for the *Osprey* and the ISS on the command screen crawl around the earth. The spacecraft would be near critical on fuel for the descent, but the computer said they could still make it.

She gazed through the windows at the stars above and the earth revolving below, amazed at the incredible beauty of the planet containing all of humanity. She felt fantastic to have come from inner-city Cleveland to see the entire world through one portal. And to do it working for a public company. She savored the moment. The sight of Earth was far grander than anything she had ever experienced. Her monitor showed that Isaac's heart and breathing rate had increased. She turned the sound on in his helmet. "Are you waking up, Isaac?"

"I'm awake."

"We are on an intercept course, and it will be a few more hours. I heard you'll be married soon."

"Yes. Sally is expecting our first child in May."

"Aren't you expecting, too?"

"I guess I am."

"Do you know if you're having a boy or a girl?"

"We want it to be a surprise."

"You set a record today as the youngest person ever to go into space."

"Oh, great. Another thing I'll be famous for. How old are you?"

"I'm thirty-two. After today, I'll be the youngest ever to command a space mission. Last year, I rode into space on a test mission. But going to the space station today is not what I expected when I got out of bed this morning."

"I didn't plan on this either. Thanks for being the commander."

"I think it's good that NASA asked us to help with this rescue mission. Someone there was thinking outside the box when they put this together."

"It was my crazy idea." Isaac gave Tanya a big grin. "I hope we can do what I set us up for."

"NASA has kept you and your abilities top secret. Nobody at Stellar Z knew you could go to negative gravity and transfer the negative to so much mass."

"It's been a couple of months since I figured out how to go negative. Tests inside a building are so limiting."

"Can I ask if NASA has figured out how you change gravity?"

"You can ask. By contract, I can't answer."

"No problem. Do you want anything to eat or drink? We have about three more hours before we get to the ISS.

"Yes, please."

Tanya released Isaac's hands and showed him how to take off the helmet. They ate, drank, and engaged in some small talk. Tanya encouraged Isaac to get some more rest.

She watched him as he dozed off. *A good kid who stepped up and is risking his life to rescue others. And Cooper only wanted data on him. I have to make it a success.*

With the computer controlling the approach of the *Osprey* to the ISS, Tanya stared out the window and viewed the wreckage. *Tumbling* was the term NASA used to describe the motion of the US segment, but her heart jumped into her throat when she saw the solar arms flailing about randomly through space. "Mission Control, are you seeing this?"

"Visual is clear. Let's hope Guds nät will work as designed," Mission Control replied.

Isaac shook as he startled awake. "Are we there yet?"

"We're close," Tanya replied. "Sit tight while we pick up passengers." She turned her attention back to the space station. "Control, I'm opening the nose. When we get within thirty meters, I'll deploy Guds nät." Tanya switched to Isaac's headphones. "You can get up and watch this if you want."

The *Osprey* glided toward the ISS as the orbital maneuvering system lined them up with the US segment.

"Deploying Guds nät now." Tanya stared out the portal.

"What's Guds nät?" Isaac asked.

"It's a square cable net with sixteen small thrusters recently designed by a Russian space engineer to capture old satellites. He named it from the Swedish term for God's Net. When deployed, the corner thrusters carry the net and wrap around an object in space. Magnets attached to the thrusters hold the net in place while an onboard computer analyzes the movement and coordinates their firing. If it works, the captured object, in this instance, the US segment of the ISS, will be stabilized. It's never been used before, but this situation is what it's designed for."

"The module is gyrating in all directions," Isaac said as he looked over Tanya's shoulder.

Tanya hit her hand next to the portal. "Shit! The net caught on a solar panel. The panels are moving faster than the net's thrusters can react."

The net swung like a fisherman twirling a net over his head.

Tanya grabbed a computer pad and began to manipulate the thrusters manually. She attempted to gain some slack and free up the corner tangled on the solar panel with the three thrusters attached to the main section.

After a few attempts, she muttered, "Fuck it." She hit the engage button. An algorithm evaluated the movement of each thruster in relation to the control unit in Tanya's hands. The program turned the thrusters and initiated short bursts to change the rotational vectors on the module. After several attempts by the AI, it stopped and flashed "ERROR" on the screen. She hit the "Stop" button.

"Commander Nash," said a voice from Mission Control. "We suggest that you disengage Guds nät and redeploy."

Tanya pressed the disengage button and watched the net get more tangled on the spinning ISS segment. "ERROR" flashed on the screen again. "Damn it."

Isaac had watched what Tanya was doing. "Let me try. I've had a lot of experience tumbling weightless. Maybe I can think this through." He held out his hand to Tanya, who handed him the computer pad.

He studied the controls for a moment and then the tumbling ISS. He tapped on a thruster, gave it a direction, and a little boost. Then another and another. After numerous thrusts, he freed the tangle over the solar panel and wrapped that end over the ISS. He looked at Tanya and smiled. "Sometimes, during a test, I would get to tumbling. I only had a fan in my hand to get us steady. Now let's see how the program works." He pressed the engage button.

There was a pause for what seemed like an eternity. Then Guds nät went to work as advertised. The thrust counter steadily rose to twenty, forty, a hundred and thirty. A couple shorter bursts and the hatches were aligned.

"Guds nät is incredible," Isaac said.

Over the headphones, Mission Control said, "Good job, team. The next challenge is to cut the net away from the docking port. Suit up commander; the tools you'll need are in locker three. Readings show the astronauts have about one hour of oxygen left."

"Isaac, we need to get you hooked up to life support," Tanya said, opening a panel on the interior of the *Osprey* near the hatch.

Archie Kregear

"I'm fine. Why do I need life support?" asked Isaac.

"You need a supply of air while this craft is depressurized." She pulled out a hose and attached it to the connectors on his thigh. Tanya retrieved an extravehicular support backpack from a locker, put it on, and attached a tether. Then she secured and checked Isaac's helmet and gloves.

She placed some cutting tools in a pouch on her belt, depressurized the cabin, and opened the hatch.

The two ships were about ten meters apart, flying at over 27,000 kilometers per hour when Tanya pushed out into space.

Mission Control said, "Tanya. The engineers here have evaluated the cables. Are you getting the image on your helmet?"

"Affirmative."

"The engineers are determining the order of cuts. They want the higher tension cables cut first. The rest will absorb the stress. There is a double wrap here, so this may be tricky. Cut the highlighted one first where circled. Attach your second tether to the cable circled in green to keep you in place."

"Copy, Mission Control."

She took a twenty-five-centimeter-long cable cutter in both hands and snapped the first cable. A circle appeared at a second location on her helmet screen. She cut where indicated, then made four additional cuts.

"The next cable seems to have absorbed most of the tension after the last couple of cuts. Be careful," Mission Control said.

Tanya worked to get the cutter in place. "There is another cable next to this one. I can't get the tool around the cable." She put her hand around the cable and put a foot on the ISS to give herself leverage and pulled. The cable moved as she intended, but it slipped and smashed her left hand against the ISS. "Ow!" She lost her footing and turned toward the *Osprey*.

"Commander Nash. Advise," came the voice of Mission Control.

"My hand is caught." Her voice reflected her pain.

"Can you turn and get a camera on your hand?"

"Give me a second." She moved around to look at her hand, firmly caught against the ISS by a cable.

"Hold still, Commander. Isaac, can you hear me?"

"Yes, sir."

"We need you to put on an extravehicular pack. Look for a panel labeled EVP-2."

"I see it."

"Open it up. Slide into the arm straps."

"Okay."

"Secure the clips across your chest and pull the straps tight."

Isaac worked to make sure the pack was tight. "Done."

AntiGravity

"Let your arms hang. Slip them back, and you'll feel a knob with each hand."

"Got it."

"Pull them up to release the pack."

"This pack has a lot of mass."

"It's about forty kilos. Now here's the tricky part. I know we have never done this before—"

"What's that?" Isaac said, thinking that moving around weightless was easy.

In a stern voice, Mission Control said, "Reach around behind you with your right hand. Grab the round hose from the bottom of the EV pack."

Isaac reached back and felt for a hose. After searching around, he said, "I think I have it." He pulled the hose out in front of him.

"Now, listen carefully. We need to replace the life support hose attached to your thigh with the one in your hand. Swapping is usually done in a pressurized environment. So, what I'm saying is that life support has never been disconnected in a vacuum before. Once you disconnect, if you can't connect the EV hose, you'll need to disconnect Commander Nash's tether, close the hatch, and pressurize the *Osprey* before you pass out."

"Um, are you telling me that if I don't get the EV hose connected, then everyone will die?"

"Basically. By the time it will take you to close, pressurize, hook up, reopen, cut the cables, reenter the ship, close it up, pressurize, dock with the ISS, and open the hatches, it will be too late. You'll be able to help Commander Nash, but not the astronauts."

Isaac grabbed the life support hose, shoved it in place. It popped out like a cork out of a champagne bottle. He felt the reduction in air pressure within his suit as he repositioned the EV hose on his thigh. He pressed, but it did not connect. He hammered his fist down on the connection. It seated, but the pressure inside his suit immediately pushed the hose out. He felt another reduction in air pressure.

"Isaac, we need you to release Commander Nash's tether."

He hammered the connection again, trying to apply the twist needed to make the connection. The hose popped off.

"Isaac, this isn't working. Pressurize the craft!" Tanya yelled.

I need to reduce the pressure inside the suit enough that I can force in the hose. He hammered over and over, each time releasing a little air pressure.

"Isaac. If you pass out, everyone dies," Tanya said.

He felt himself getting dizzy. He pressed down with all his might and twisted the hose into place. Fresh air rushed in and inflated the suit. Isaac took a couple of deep breaths and tried to still his heart, but the adrenalin rush prepared him to conquer anything.

"That was too close," Mission Control said. "Get tethered up."

Isaac located where the tether connected Commander Nash to the *Osprey* and found another clip. He attached it to his spacesuit and pushed himself into space.

In a moment, Isaac was next to Tanya. He brought his helmet face to face with hers. "You're going to be fine."

"Isaac, move along the cable holding Commander Nash's hand. We need to find the best place to cut," said Mission Control. "The astronauts inside don't have a lot of time."

He followed the cable to one side and then the other.

"Good, Isaac. The engineers have circled a point they feel is the best place to cut. Take the cutters and snip it."

"Um, I um ..."

"Is there a problem, Isaac?"

"I'm worried that cutting the cable at the point you specify will release the cable, and it will whip around and hit Commander Nash. I suggest cutting the cable on the other side in three places to relieve the tension, then releasing the thruster holding the tension on the other side. Let me show you." Isaac moved and indicated the place of three cuts on one side and then the thruster. "If I release the thruster first, the cable will move across her hand, causing more damage."

"Your suggestion is acceptable. Proceed."

Isaac snipped the cables on one side in quick succession and then released a thruster on the other.

"I'm free," Tanya said.

"Commander Nash, return to the *Osprey*. Isaac, you'll have to finish."

Isaac took hold of Tanya's right arm. "Let me help Commander Nash in."

"Get those cables cut!" Tanya yelled.

Isaac let her go and went to work on the remaining cables covering the dock on the ISS. He secured the wire ends to make sure they did not float in and interfere with the docking. Then he slipped back inside the *Osprey*.

"Ready to dock." Tanya hit the icon on her screen. "Closing hatch."

"Put the *Osprey* on automatic and dock," Mission Control ordered.

"On automatic," Commander Nash said. A few seconds later, she added, "Docking engaged."

Once the coupling of the *Osprey* and ISS was completed, the cabin of the *Osprey* pressurized and Engineer Ted Wright's voice came from the section of the ISS. "Our hatch is open. Oxygen is nearly gone."

Commander Nash went to the hatch and pressed the buttons to initiate opening. A red light came on. She pushed herself to the command chair, flipped open her helmet, and studied her screen. "The pressure is unequal, mission control. The hatch won't open unless the pressure is equal." She yelled at the hatch as if talking through a door. "Ted, what's the pressure over there?"

"The pressure is point eight nine atmospheric units."

AntiGravity

"Mission Control, how do we reduce pressure by eleven percent?"

"Standby. I'm waking up every engineer employed by Stellar Z with your question."

"Shit. There has to be a way to get the hatch open," Commander Nash said to herself loud enough for everyone else to hear. "There has to be a manual override." She pounded away on the command screen. "There, it's on manual." She leaped to the hatch, grabbed it with one hand, and pulled with a blaring grunt.

Mission Control said, "Commander, the hatch was designed to be unopenable at this pressure difference. Unfortunately, environmental control is programmed to maintain one atmosphere in the *Osprey*."

"How can I change the program?" Nash demanded.

"That's the question I posed to the engineers. One says he can get a software fix by the end of the day."

"Tell him we need it within twenty minutes," Ted Wright said from the segment of the ISS.

Isaac, still inside his spacesuit, said, "The pressure is affected by temperature. Can we lower the temperature?"

"The environmental control unit will maintain the pressure no matter what the temperature is," replied Mission Control.

"That gives me an idea." Tanya punched at the command screen for a moment, then went to a panel behind the seats.

"Commander, are you disabling the air pressure maintenance system?"

"Affirmative, Mission Control, and bringing the temperature down."

"I hope we can get the cooling system to drop us far enough," Isaac said.

"A quick calculation and I figure the temperature needs to be about negative ten degrees Celsius," Mission Control said.

"It doesn't have to get all the way there, just enough to equalize the pressure, and I can pull the hatch open," Tanya said.

Isaac heard the woosh of air inside of the capsule. He felt warm inside his spacesuit while floating in the middle. "What can we do?" asked Isaac.

"While we're waiting, we should get out of these EV packs."

Over the next few minutes, Isaac was busy following the commander's instructions to stow away the EV packs and tools.

Tanya grimaced every time something touched her left hand that she held close to her chest.

"Not to rush anyone, but we are reading that we have ten minutes of oxygen left," Ted said.

Tanya replied, "I'm reading eight degrees Centigrade. I'll try the hatch again in a few degrees."

Archie Kregear

The seconds ticked by slowly. Isaac watched the temperature dial, thinking it was the same as watching a pot come to a boil. An annoying BONG, BONG pierced the air.

Commander Nash swerved over to her chair. "The alarm for low pressure and temperature has gone off. Time to get that hatch open." She swung to the hatch, placed a foot on either side, and grabbed the handle with one hand. She bent her knees, straightened her back, and grunted.

Isaac joined her, putting his feet by the hatch and lifting on the hatch. The whoosh of air told them the pressure was equalizing. The hatch gave way. Tanya drifted away from the hatch towards the back of the capsule. Isaac let out a big sigh.

"The hatch is open!" she yelled.

Ted floated into the capsule, "Permission to come aboard, Commander?"

"Permission granted," Commander Nash said in an emphatic tone.

The survivors from the ISS floated in. They carefully moved the one unconscious man through and into a seat. Isaac helped secure him for the trip home. The rest entered, and the capsule interior soon looked like a game of three-dimensional musical chairs as they maneuvered for seats.

Isaac closed the hatch while Tanya reset the environmental controls to normal.

Ted Wright introduced the other astronauts and ensured they were strapped in. Then Ted started opening and closing panels.

"Is there something you need?" asked Commander Nash.

"Water?" Ted asked.

"The storage cabinet on the right side, halfway up," Tanya replied with a tone of indignation in her voice. "Please take a seat while we begin to descend." She entered commands to undock from the ISS, leaving it to float amongst the rest of the station debris.

A wave of accomplishment washed over Isaac. He looked at the men and women he had helped rescue with the realization that their lives would continue after today. *They still have a future. What's my destiny?*

"Congratulations. The difficult part is over," Mission Control said over Isaac's headphones. "Commander Nash, you're free to bring your passengers home."

"Initiating reentry preparation." She turned to the passengers. "Please secure everything and buckle up."

Ted said, "With that hand, are you able to—"

"Just a couple of buttons to push, and I could do that with my nose. No problem," Tanya said.

"She's got this, guys," Isaac said.

An astronaut named Anders passed Isaac some water.

"Mission Control, passengers secure. We're ready for reentry," Tanya said.

"Initiate."

"On our way." She pushed a button, and nothing happened.

AntiGravity

"Aren't the retro rockets supposed to fire?" Isaac asked.

"The computer says we have eighteen minutes before we reach the position to begin our descent." Tanya took a deep breath and let it out.

A man at Mission Control said, "Isaac, we have a few minutes. Open up the medical cabinet. Get a couple of ice packs and wrap them onto Tanya's hand. Leave the glove on."

One of the astronauts assisted Isaac. In a few minutes, they had her hand wrapped and arm secured to her chest.

Isaac buckled Tanya in and heard her ask Mission Control, "What's your take on the fuel?"

"Critical."

Isaac focused on Tanya's reaction.

She turned to him. "I'll need your assistance with the landing."

"Tell me how much and when," Isaac said.

Tanya typed away on the command screen with one finger. The deorbiting thrusters fired for eleven minutes, initiating their descent.

"Is everything OK?" Ted asked.

"We're overweight," Tanya said.

"Shit!" Ed exclaimed. "You should have left me up there."

"No one gets left behind," Tanya said.

"We got this." Isaac calmly adjusted his grip on the handles by his seat.

"God, I hope so," one of the women said.

"The retros fired too long," Ted exclaimed.

"Because of our mass, we need to slow down," Tanya replied.

"We'll go in too steep," Ted said.

The windows glowed bright red as the spacecraft streaked into the atmosphere. The deceleration pushed Isaac back into his seat.

"Isaac, we have a narrow window. Reduce gravity too much, and we skip; too little, we burn up," Tanya said. "Reduce gravity by twenty percent now."

Isaac's eyes closed and he took the *Osprey* to a negative one gravity.

"Way too much. STOP."

"The amount is hard to control." Isaac adjusted in his seat.

"Try again. Now."

Isaac focused on making the spacecraft lighter.

"Let off just a little," Tanya said. "Good. Hold that.

Isaac focused on maintaining the present change in gravity.

A little smoke floated through the cabin.

"Add more lift," Ted said. "We're too hot."

"Still in danger of skipping. Hold steady, Isaac." Tanya calmy said.

"Are we in a safe flight path or not?" Ted demanded.

"Communication blackout phase for the next few minutes," Tanya said.

Isaac wanted to wipe his wet hands. He could feel them slip on the handles.

Smoke now filled the cabin, stinging Isaac's eyes. Time passed ever so slowly as he focused on maintaining a steady reduction in gravity.

"Comms back. We're a little high."

Ted said, "I can see the flashing red on your monitor through the smoke. What's up?"

"We don't have enough fuel to land. Isaac, you'll have to help me put this down softly."

Mission Control came on the comms. "Commander Nash, you're coming in too fast. Get some lift."

"Isaac," Tanya said with a raised voice.

He increased his lift on the craft.

Mission Control said, "You'll have to get to negative g forces until slow enough to deploy the chutes."

Isaac strained, forcing all the lift he could muster into the craft.

"More Isaac. We need to gain altitude."

He thought about being the rocket he would launch for Mr. Collins.

Tanya said in a hushed voice, "Great, Isaac. You're doing what we need."

Mission Control said, "Deploying chutes. Isaac, resume a twenty percent reduction."

Isaac didn't move.

"There, that's it. Steady. Good. Keep it there. Fifty meters to touchdown. Twenty ... ten ... and we're on the ground! Relax, Isaac."

Isaac let out a deep breath. His hands slipped off the handles.

#

Don and everyone around him looked to the west, trying to see any sign of the *Osprey*. He had flown from Houston to Los Angles, rented a car, and drove to Stellar Z's facility before sunrise. He received updates on the mission by text from Houston. The folks at Stellar Z ignored his questions and him. He hadn't come prepared for the cool desert morning, and he wished he had stopped for breakfast. Almost at once, the people around him began to run to vehicles. "What's happening?" He shouted and got no response. He typed, *what's happening? Everybody here is running.*

The Osprey has overshot the landing zone. Follow them.

The convoy of emergency vehicles, cars, trucks, and vans sped east down Interstate 40, and he was in the rear.

For Don, this was the longest hour of his life. He didn't relax until he received the text that everyone on the return craft was safe.

He made his way through the randomly parked vehicles at a farm outside of Barstow. Still in his spacesuit, Isaac lay unmoving on a stretcher as the medics checked his vital signs.

"Anything wrong besides being unconscious?" Don asked frantically.

AntiGravity

"He is in deep sleep or coma," one of the medics said. "We're going to get him to the hospital where they can check him thoroughly."

Commander Nash came over. "He was fine until just before landing. His vitals after we landed read like he was sleeping."

"Did he receive any blows to the head during the mission?" a medic asked.

"No. He used his ability to help slow the descent, then passed out as we landed."

"This has occurred before when he overexerted himself. Give him fluids, and let him sleep," Don said. "Where will you take him?"

"To a medevac helicopter at the airbase. You're coming with us, Commander Nash?" the medic asked.

"Yes."

The medics put Isaac into an ambulance.

"Which hospital?" Don asked.

"Excuse me, who are you?" Tanya demanded.

"I'm Don Greenwell with NASA. I work with Isaac." He held out his badge. "I'm here to bring Isaac back to Houston."

"It's good to meet you." Tanya pointed with her good hand. "Give the woman by the *Osprey* your number. I'll call you when I know the hospital where they take Isaac and me. Also, ask her for Isaac's things."

"Okay. Thanks." Don walked over to the woman who was unloading equipment from the spacecraft. "Hi, I'm Don. Tanya told me to give you my number and get Isaac's things."

"Hi. I'm Monica Schultz." She set a metal box about the size of a banana crate into the back of a van and stood straight, arching her back from the heavy load. "Isaac's things are on the passenger seat." She walked around the van while taking out her phone. "What's your number?" She typed as Don recited the number.

"I noticed the electronics you unloaded from the *Osprey*. What was being measured?"

Monica's head turned quickly to look at Don, her eyes wide. "I can't talk about that."

"Since I work with Isaac, I'm interested to see the data collected during the flight."

Monica quickly walked to a canvas bag, picked it up, and held it out. "I just move the boxes. I don't know what they do."

Don took the bag and gave Monica the complete look over, from her white walking shoes and matching scrunchie to the jumpsuit with "Dr. Schultz" stitched on front. *She's lying to me about the electronics.*

He pulled out Isaac's phone to call Sally, but the battery was dead. He plugged it in and drove back down the long desert highway, slower and in the opposite direction. The sun was bright behind him in the high desert. With the car window halfway down, Don enjoyed the fresh night air and found a working station on the radio.

A reporter interrupted the music. "We have breaking news about the accident at the space station. We take you to the CEO of Stellar Z, who is live."

"Yes, America. We did it," boomed the ever-enthusiastic Doug Cooper. "The five astronauts stranded in space are now back on solid ground due to Stellar Z and our new space capsule, the *Osprey*. We launched yesterday from our test site at the Mojave spaceport and returned a few minutes ago. The attempt was not announced, as even I was skeptical of getting a test spacecraft to the space station with a boost package that had never been used before. Hell, nobody had even thought of boosting a rocket into space the way we did. The need to rescue these astronauts sparked some incredible innovation.

"Stellar Z is proud to be able to do what NASA, Boeing, and Russia were unable to do. We got the *Osprey* up two-hundred and fifty-five miles above the earth and met the International Space Station. The commander and crew performed the first-ever deployment of Guds nät to stop the tumbling of the segment of the space station where the astronauts were trapped. I hope to get the incredible video of the taming of a tumbling container holding five astronauts released within the hour. This mission by Stellar Z has to be the most heroic rescue in the history of humanity."

Cooper always sounds like he's selling something.

"The five astronauts, the mission commander, and one crewman are being taken to a hospital. A medical checkup is standard procedure after every flight. I'll have a press conference later this afternoon with all the details, but I wanted to get the incredible news out. Thank you for your prayers and have a stellar day."

Isaac's phone rang. Don knew it was Sally and that he needed to let her know what was happening. He slowed and pulled to the side of the road. He texted Sally. *This is Don. Isaac is fine. He's on his way to the hospital with everyone else on the mission. He was a big part of saving the astronauts from the space station. Get some rest. I'll have him call you when I catch up to him.*

I knew he was involved in this. I've been worried all day. You're supposed to take care of him. Why did you let him go?

Long story. I've got his phone. I'll get back to you in three hours.

Don knew he had a long drive. Hopefully, he would have a few minutes to find out how Isaac was before contacting Sally again.

An hour later, Don received a text from Tanya with the hospital's address and the message *Isaac is still unconscious.*

Chapter 15 – Thanksgiving

A doctor who looked younger than Don had come out to provide him an update. "So far, everything is normal. We are doing a complete medical check."

"Last time Isaac overexerted himself, he slept for three days. The doctors found nothing wrong with him. Who authorized the tests?"

"The doctor in charge."

"Isaac is with NASA, and his medical data must not be shared with anyone."

"For that, I need you to talk to the folks in admissions."

Don sent a text to Sally. *Isaac is asleep like he was last summer. The doctor says all tests are normal.*

Where's Isaac? Sally responded.

Don shared his location.

I'm coming.

Don went to admissions. After a few minutes of waiting, he spoke to an admissions clerk and demanded that Isaac's test results be confidential.

The admissions clerk said, "The hospital doesn't have authority over Isaac Thomas' medical records."

Don shook his head. "I don't understand."

"Stellar Z employs the doctor in charge of treating and evaluating the returning astronauts."

He turned away from the counter. *Crap. These guys are intent on gathering all the data they can on Isaac.*

Don heard over his shoulder, "What room is Isaac Thomas in?"

The admissions person said, "Mr. Thomas is in radiology. Please take a seat. I'll let you know when he is available for visitors."

Don looked at the woman dressed in a pink blouse and matching calf-length pants. "Are you Sally?"

"You must be Don. Can you take me to Isaac?"

"No, we're both stuck here until they tell us."

"Why did you let him do this?"

"He was on a plane to California before anyone told me about the rescue mission. Last time, everything turned out fine. I'm sure this time will be the same."

"He better be."

"I haven't eaten all day. Would you like to join me?"

Five hours later, the same young doctor approached Don and Sally. "Isaac is resting. We found no injuries."

"Can we see him?" Sally asked.

"Only family can visit."

"I'm his fiancé. Our wedding is less than three weeks away."
"Isaac has no family. I work with him at NASA. Do you work for Stellar Z?"
"I'm interning at this hospital and helping the doctors in charge."
"All medical data belongs to Isaac and NASA. Please pass that on," Don said.
"Are children considered family?" Sally said.
"Yes, they must—"
Sally stepped forward and pointed to her belly. "This is Isaac's child. What room is he in?"
He looked at the five-foot-tall woman in front of him and took a deep breath. "I'm not authorized to tell you that Isaac is in room three-twelve. Now, if you'll excuse me, I need to get to the ER."
"Let's go." Sally took off for the elevator.
They watched Isaac breathe for a while, then a nurse ordered them to leave for the night.
The third morning, Don and Sally entered Isaac's hospital room. She kissed her fiancé on the cheek. "If you don't wake up and shave, I'm going to have to shave you."
Isaac's hand sluggishly moved to his face. "Is this a three-day beard or four?"
"Four," Don said from the end of the bed.
Sally leaped across Isaac's chest and held him. "Don't you ever do this to me again."
"Every time I do, you come to see me." He wrapped his arms around her.
Don texted the folks at NASA. *Isaac's awake and is doing fine.*

#

Isaac and Sally were relaxing in the Sykeses' backyard pool on the day after Thanksgiving. He had stayed in California until the wedding, now only eight days away. His phone, lying on the patio table, rang for the third time.

Mary picked it up and looked toward the pool. "I'll just tell them to stop calling."

"Let it go to voicemail." Isaac knew it was probably just another reporter wanting an interview.

"Hello, Mr. Prescott. I'm sorry, Isaac is unable to talk right now."

Sally began to swim toward the side of the pool. Isaac decided to ignore his soon-to-be mother-in-law.

"I'm Mary. Isaac will soon be married to my daughter, Sally." She lowered herself into a chair. "Oh, I love your show, Mr. Prescott. I watch it whenever I can," Mary said excitedly.

Sally had gotten out of the pool and left a wet trail of footprints as she walked toward her mother. "Give me Isaac's phone," she whispered and held out her hand.

Mary stepped toward the sliding glass door. "That's wonderful." She opened the door and turned to Sally, whispering, "It's Mr. Prescott from the Sunday Morning

Show." Stepping into the house, she said, "I agree. He should tell the world how he saved the astronauts on the space station. No, I didn't know he went to space until the day after." She closed the sliding glass door behind her in Sally's angry face.

"I'm sorry, Isaac," Sally said in an exasperated tone. "She loves Prescott's morning show."

Isaac folded his arms on the side of the pool. "It's okay. It's fine if she talks to Prescott. She seemed so excited. Come back in the pool."

Isaac admired her as she walked toward him in a turquoise two-piece swimsuit. "She's overly excited about having a hero as a son-in-law."

"Not as excited as I am about having her as a mother-in-law." Isaac grinned.

"Why are you so excited?" Sally reached the edge of the pool and looked down at Isaac.

"Because that means I'm married to her daughter."

Sally jumped in close enough to Isaac to drench him with the splash.

Isaac splashed back, and the play ended with passionate kissing.

Mary exited the house and laid Isaac's phone back on the table. "Sorry to interrupt you two. Allen Prescott wants a live interview."

"I don't want to be interviewed."

"You rescued those astronauts and should be recognized for it."

"No, Commander Nash was in charge."

Mary's eyebrows went up, and she nodded. "She couldn't have done it without you."

"I wouldn't have been there without her."

Mr. Sykes strode through the open sliding glass door. "Why are you two talking so loud?"

"Your son-in-law is a hero and is afraid to tell the world."

"They always want me to demonstrate by floating."

"A little publicity might help in landing employment in the future," Mary said.

"I'm *not* a sideshow act."

"No, you're NASA's *lab rat*. Those are *your* words, not mine," Sally chimed in.

"Mary," Mr. Sykes took his wife's arm.

Isaac's eyes narrowed, and his lips tightened together. He felt Sally's arms around his neck, pulling him close.

Mr. Sykes ushered his wife toward the house.

"It's okay, Isaac. We'll figure it out," Sally said.

Isaac took a couple of deep breaths through his nose. "She's right, you know. What's a lab rat going to do when there's no more cheese?" He turned to look into Sally's eyes, his arm around her back. "I need a way to make some money for us. Let's call Prescott back and get a little publicity."

After changing, Sally and Isaac sat at the patio table and put the phone on speaker. "Hello, this is Isaac Thomas. I understand you called and wanted me to come on your show."

"Yes, Isaac. I would love to have you come on and tell the world about how you rescued those stranded astronauts," Prescott said.

"I didn't rescue anyone. Commander Tanya Nash was in charge of the mission."

"My sources say you made the mission possible."

"I wouldn't have left the ground without Commander Nash, and I won't come on your show without her."

Sally shook her head and smiled.

"I'll get in touch with Commander Nash. The first open date is the second Sunday in December. Will that work?"

"It will."

"I'll see if I can get the producer to agree with that. Anything else?"

"Yeah, one more thing. My future mother-in-law, who you spoke to earlier, wants to meet you and get your autograph."

Sally's eyes got wide, and she shook her head rapidly and mouthed, "No."

"Congratulations. When's the wedding?"

"A week from tomorrow."

"Super. I'll agree to a photo with Mrs. Sykes as long as I get to meet Sally and get a photograph with both of you."

Always wanting something in return. Isaac thought, then gestured to Sally, who leaned toward the phone.

"I'll be there, and I'm excited to meet you."

"Thank you, Sally. Thank you, Isaac. I'm looking forward to meeting you in person. Someone will be in touch next week to make all the arrangements."

"Thank you, Mr. Prescott."

Isaac sat back in the chair and rubbed his hands on his shorts. "I'm already nervous."

#

Isaac met Don, who had stayed in L.A. to take a vacation for lunch on Monday at a local burger place. The smell of the burgers and fries during the wait in line ahead of Agent Johnson, there to provide security, made his mouth water.

A few minutes later, Isaac finished his hamburger and asked, "What am I going to do after you finish testing me?"

"You're smart. What do you want to do?"

"I have no clue."

"I'm not the best person to ask. I'm as good as anyone with electronic test equipment. When your contract is over, I'm on to the next boring experiment."

"So, I'm a boring experiment now?"

"No, you're not. It's the propeller heads who design the tests and the safety folks who have made it boring."

"It's only when I do something outside of the tests that becomes interesting, like falling up and down." Isaac rolled a french fry in ketchup.

"We know you have limits. The tests to find them have been dangerous. The flight data we got from monitoring the *Osprey* shows that the landing was a miracle. I wish I had the data from the instruments Monica was unloading."

"Do you think there's some good information there?"

"I've analyzed the flight. At one point, you must have taken the *Osprey* to at least negative one-point-two Gs. It was short, less than a minute. The instruments they had on board should have caught the extreme change in whatever stuff in the universe you can alter."

"What if the data isn't there?"

"Then we're not going to find it. NASA is not going to take the risk of outdoor experiments." Don pushed his partially eaten burger aside.

Isaac wiped his face with a napkin. "Don, Stellar Z jumped at the opportunity to put me in the *Osprey*. Why? Because figuring out how I turn off gravity is worth a thousand times more than the publicity from rescuing the space station crew. The rescue was secondary to them."

"That makes sense. There were at least fifty kilos of measuring equipment on the *Osprey*, probably more. It was the equipment that made the craft too heavy to land. Without you, they would have crashed."

"I should ask Commander Nash for the information they recorded," Isaac said.

"Remember, NASA employees can't talk to Stellar Z employees."

"They have my data."

"That's it!" Don said, raising his index finger. "They gathered your personal data without your consent. Since it was your data and medical information, *you* can ask for it. It may be data on how you affect gravity, but it's still *yours*. I wonder if there was a contract between NASA and Stellar Z. Did you sign anything?"

"No, I didn't sign anything. By the way, you have to come with me when I do the interview."

Don's head shot up straight. "What interview?"

#

Isaac enjoyed seeing his aunts and uncles, who flew out for the wedding. His ability was now the topic of discussion with his family, and he finally found the courage to tell them the whole story of how his parents died. Being able to talk about their deaths was another bottle of emotion he was able to uncork.

Isaac was sick to his stomach the morning of the wedding. *A flight suit is more comfortable than this tuxedo*, he thought as Don adjusted his tie. For the last couple of nights, he had stayed in the same hotel as Don, who was the best man at the wedding.

Sally's cousins filled out the groomsmen, and her friends were bridesmaids.

He rubbed his sweaty palms against his trousers as Sally started down the aisle. *What in the stars did I do to deserve a girl as gorgeous and radiant as her?* His mouth went to cotton, and he felt faint. He almost went weightless to keep himself from falling, but Don's hand under his arm held him up.

"Steady, Isaac. Breathe," Don whispered behind him.

"She's taken my breath away," he whispered back.

"You're the luckiest man in the universe right now."

Isaac took Sally's hand, stumbled through his lines, and kissed his new bride. He walked on air down the aisle with Sally while everyone applauded.

The newlyweds took a couple of days in San Diego with FBI agents always close when they went out. They visited the zoo and Mission Beach, and had a nice dinner for Isaac's twenty-first birthday.

A week later, they were ready to go on Allan Prescott's Sunday Morning Show.

Victor, Mary, Don, Sally, and Isaac arrived at the studio a couple of hours early.

After introductions, Allen Prescott posed with Mary for a picture, then he invited the newlyweds over for a photo. "The two of you are a stunning couple. Give the photographer a big smile. And if you'll excuse me, I see our other guest."

The photographer took several photos, posing them in many ways.

Isaac began to hate the process, but Sally enjoyed the attention.

When the photographer finished, the couple joined Don and Sally's parents. Isaac pointed to Allen. "He's talking to Tanya and Monica. Tanya has the cast on her hand, and I met Monica during my Stellar Z interview. She's a materials scientist."

Don leaned over to Isaac. "I need to talk to Monica again."

On stage, Prescott sat behind a large wooden desk. Stagehands ushered Tanya into an upholstered chair next to him, and Isaac sat next to her.

The live show started with Isaac and Tanya recounting the rescue of the five astronauts from the International Space Station. Tanya gave Isaac credit for making the mission possible. Isaac praised Tanya's leadership and gave all the credit for the successful rescue of five astronauts to her.

"We have some dramatic video of the rescue supplied by Stellar Z.," Allen said. "Tanya, would you narrate?"

"This video starts with an image of the space station tumbling. Here we deploy Guds nät, which translates to 'God's net.' And here's when the thrusters counter the movement and align the station with the *Osprey*."

"So, tell me how you broke your hand."

AntiGravity

Tanya explained how the cables across the hatch needed to be cut, and while she was doing that, a cable smashed her hand against the station module.

Mr. Prescott gave a concerned look. "Now, let me get this straight. You're on a spacewalk at over seventeen thousand miles an hour, attempting to cut the cables holding the space station hatch closed, behind which are the astronauts needing rescue, and your hand gets smashed under a cable. If you don't get your hand free, you die, and the rescue doesn't happen."

Tanya gave a nervous smile. "That's right."

"What happened next?" Mr. Prescott waved his hands like he wanted more dramatic moments.

"Isaac came out, finished cutting the cables, freeing my hand, and—"

Allen interrupted, "Isaac, have you trained to do a spacewalk?"

"Not directly. But I've floated weightlessly more than anyone. I felt comfortable going outside the spacecraft. The scenery was spectacular."

\#

Don was off stage, and he noticed Monica watching the interview. He walked over to stand beside her. In a whisper, he asked, "Did you find anything interesting in the data you collected?"

Her head jerked toward Don.

"Sorry to startle you, Monica."

"No data that concerns you."

"It does concern us," Don replied, looking onto the stage. "The only use for that equipment would be to monitor brain waves and material distortions."

"There's nothing there."

"I can believe that. I've got lots of data and nothing of significance."

Monica turned to face him. "So, NASA hasn't figured out how Isaac affects gravity?"

"My conclusion is that Isaac is unfigurable outable. I was hoping that stressing his ability might show something."

"Everyone is hoping, and I have no answers." Monica pressed her lips together and walked away.

\#

Allen's voice grew louder. "Now, ladies and gentlemen, for the first time since their rescue, four astronauts get to meet their rescuers." The host waved to the side stage behind Isaac. He turned around as four people in flight suits walked onto the stage. With knees wobbling, he stood, and each astronaut hugged him and thanked him.

Allen had each astronaut give a statement about the event.

Isaac felt uncomfortable as each one confessed they wouldn't be alive if it weren't for him and Tanya. Then the astronauts, Tanya, and Isaac posed for a group photo.

Tanya elbowed him and said, "Smile, kid."

Isaac smiled.

"We have a few seconds left," Allen said. "This show wouldn't be complete if Isaac didn't demonstrate how he can turn off gravity. Isaac, take my hand and make me weightless. We all know I need to lose forty pounds. Here goes Isaac nullifying two hundred and forty pounds." Prescott reached out and grabbed Isaac's hand. Prescott looked him in the eye with the message, Do it.

Isaac took a deep breath and hesitated. *Gravity to zero, no negative. Be careful.*

Isaac looked at Prescott and went to zero-g. Their feet lifted off the floor. Mr. Prescott began to lean backward. Isaac saw the panic in his eyes, and before he could let go of the show host, the man jerked his arm to keep from falling back. Isaac freed his hand as he flew over Mr. Prescott's shoulder. Prescott stumbled forward and righted himself. Isaac remained weightless as he flew leisurely over the desk and into the curtain backdrop, where he let himself fall and rolled under the curtain. A couple of stagehands helped him to his feet, and Tanya pulled the curtain up. Isaac stood to the applause of the crowd.

"Isaac, are you hurt?" Mr. Prescott yelled from across the stage.

He held a thumb up and smiled as Tanya helped him under the curtain.

Mr. Prescott smoothed his hair back with one hand. "That's our show for today. One that I will never forget. A big thank you to Tanya and Isaac, a couple of real American heroes."

The stage lights dimmed, and the show's theme music played while Allen shook everyone's hand.

Isaac took a few steps and sat in the chair behind the desk. "I'm glad that's over."

Sally put her arm around him. "You were great, Isaac. You always are."

"I'm sure that flying across the stage looked spectacular."

Tanya came over to Isaac and Sally. "Congratulations on your marriage and expected child. Thank you for everything. If there is anything I can do for you, let me know."

"I want all the data collected on the flight," Isaac said.

Tanya's head twisted a bit and shook. "The company won't let me give that to you."

"Tanya, I have the utmost respect for you. Stellar Z collected my personal data, respiration, brainwaves, and so on without my consent."

She apologetically said, "I don't have the authority to give you the data."

Isaac stood. "Listen, I don't want to be the only person who can turn off gravity. It makes me a sideshow freak or a lifter of talk show hosts. I want the world to know how I alter gravity. I'd like to see if that data will help."

She took a deep breath. "Monica says there is nothing significant in the data. She's under a lot of pressure to find your secret."

AntiGravity

"NASA will publish their findings when we figure me out," Isaac said. "Then everyone can have the secret to gravity."

#

Monica waited for Tanya to get her seatbelt fastened, then pulled out of the parking garage and headed for the freeway. "Don came up to me and asked for the data."

"Isaac asked me for it as well."

"We can't give it to them, or we'll be fired or charged with breaking our contracts."

"For Isaac's sake, I wish there was information in the data that helped him understand his gift."

"Just between you and me, Tanya, there may be information there that I don't understand."

#

Mary talked about how excited she was about her famous son-in-law. She took out the 8x10 autographed photos and showed everyone. "I'm going to hang these in the hallway with the other family photos. Can we stop and pick up some frames?"

"We can do that after we drop Sally and Isaac at the airport," Victor replied.

Isaac reached over to take Sally's hand. She moved her hand away. "Is everything okay?" Isaac asked.

He got the glare from Sally that something was wrong a second before he heard what it was. "When were you going to tell me that you went spacewalking?"

"I ... I didn't know how to tell you that Tanya needed me."

"I know that you don't know how to communicate things, especially things that are important to me but don't seem to be important to you. Over our conversations last summer, you got a lot better at sharing about yourself. That has dropped off since we became engaged and married. Especially things like flying into space."

"I'm sorry," Isaac said more as a defense to the attack than a soulful apology.

Mary had turned in her seat. "You know, dear, men in general don't talk about themselves, and we have to coax things out of them. Isn't that right, honey."

"Yeah. It's not a topic I want to discuss while driving," Victor said while checking his rearview mirror and changing lanes.

"Is there anything else that went on up there that I should know about?" Sally asked.

"I had a hard time putting on the EV suit."

"What's an EV suit?" Mary asked.

"The extravehicular suit." Isaac proceeded to explain how he had a problem connecting the EV suit while Tanya was trapped and the astronauts were running out of air.

Sally crossed her arms. "Another time where you almost died and left your child fatherless."

They stopped at the airport. "I hope you kids have a nice trip home," Victor said.

"Hold on. Isaac," Mary said, "how did Tanya fly the *Osprey* with one hand?"

"I'll have to tell you later," Isaac said as he got out. They retrieved their luggage and started for the terminal.

Sally said, "You'll tell me on the plane."

#

The following day as Tanya arrived at the Stellar Z facility, she got a text message from Monica. *Cooper wants to see me at nine. I think I'm in trouble.*

Another text message arrived from Isabelle. *Good morning, Ms. Nash. Mr. Cooper would like you in his office at nine this morning.*

Tanya parked in her regular spot then texted Monica. *I've also been summoned to Cooper's office at nine. See you then.*

Doug Cooper closed the laptop on his desk. "Come in, Ms. Shultz, Ms. Nash. Have a seat. There are a couple of things I want to talk about."

The women sat in the leather swivel chairs in front of the massive desk.

"One is the talk show yesterday morning. You were there to promote Stellar Z, not yourself or that kid Isaac. Do you know how much that mission cost? And in front of the cameras, you tell the world that Isaac made the rescue possible, not Stellar Z. Your mission was to gather data on Isaac, not risk a quarter-billion-dollar spacecraft. Yeah, you succeeded. What you need to be saying is Stellar Z succeeded! Here's the press release sent out this morning." He picked up a couple of pieces of paper and slapped them down facing Tanya. "What does that headline say? Read it to me."

Tanya looked at the paper and then into Cooper's eyes. "Astronauts praise Stellar Z for their rescue on Sunday morning talk show."

Mr. Cooper grabbed a newspaper and slapped it down over the press release. "What does the L.A. *Times* headline say?"

Tanya shivered and read, "Astronauts praise Isaac Thomas and Commander Tanya Nash."

"Stellar Z is not mentioned until the end of the article, and I'm not mentioned at all!" He stood, turned around, and looked out the window. "You have no clue what it takes to run this business."

"I'm sorry, sir," Tanya choked out.

"Now for you, Ms. Shultz." He turned to face Monica. "You were responsible for figuring out how Isaac changes gravity. Do you have anything new to tell me?"

"Only that NASA doesn't understand Isaac."

"And when were you talking to NASA?"

Tanya came to Monica's defense. "We spoke to them briefly yesterday."

"And did you share with them what the data says?"

AntiGravity

"I haven't found anything abnormal in the data," Monica said.

Cooper planted both fists on the desk and leaned toward Monica. "Exactly, YOU have not found anything. You had one simple task: get the instruments on the *Osprey* that will record what Isaac does. Either you didn't put the right instruments in the craft, or you can't read the data." He stood up straight and circled behind his high-backed leather desk. "One thing is clear. The lock preventing easy access to space is gravity. The *key* to unlocking gravity is Isaac Thomas. Get to work. Get me some answers!"

With clenched teeth, Tanya followed Monica out of Cooper's office with her hands over her face. Once out, Tanya put one arm around Monica and accepted a pack of tissues from Isabelle. She handed the tissues to Monica.

"Do you want to meet for dinner tonight?" Tanya asked.

"I'm going to my office." Monica sniffed. "I'll let you know."

"I'll be in the gym punching some bags if you need anything."

#

Isaac met with Don in the control room on Tuesday morning.

Don brought up a calendar. "There are no more experiments scheduled until January. I'm going to go home to my parents' for the holidays, so that leaves this week free."

"Great, we have nothing to do." Isaac stated.

"I will be completing the documentation of our experiments so the writers can turn them into articles. Documenting the rescue. What do you think about letting the director know that Stellar Z has additional data on the flight?"

"We need to get what they collected on the flight and at the hospital."

"I'll write up what we know and get it to Director Anderson. Anything you want to do this week?

"I should see if my teachers will allow me to get an extension on my classes."

"I'm sure they'll give you more time."

"I also want to practice going slightly negative and letting myself down slowly."

"We can set that up for later in the week."

On Wednesday, Isaac explained, "It's like thinking of food and my mouth waters. I think of going weightless, and I float. Flip the switch to negative, and gravity is reversed."

"You've said that a thousand times. What does gravity look like to you?" Don said with some exasperation in his voice.

"Gravity waves are like straight lines that are curved by large masses."

"And what do you do to the gravity waves?" Don was hoping for something new.

"I guess I reverse the curve in a small area."

"We can't publish that you 'guess that you reverse the curve.' We have to know. You and I have been working at this for thirty months now. I'm leaving on Saturday for the holidays. We'll retackle our quest in the new year."

"I'm sorry that I've been hard to work with."

"No need to apologize."

"I'm sorry not just to you but to me, to Sally, to the world, and my parents," Isaac said with remorse. "You're the best, and next year, we'll figure this out."

"Yep, next year will be the best. I'll let the director know we are shutting down Friday for the holidays."

Chapter 16 – January

Monica paced across the living room floor of her apartment, phone to her ear. "I gave two weeks' notice New Year's Eve, but they want me to stay for another month to try to bring my replacement up to speed. As dense as this guy is, it would take me a year. Can you believe they had hired someone before Christmas? It's like they knew I was quitting."

"How long will you stay?" Tanya asked over the phone.

"Two weeks, and I don't know if I can hold myself together that long."

"I'm always here for you."

"I know, but the advice I got was not to take down my friends as I leave. That's why I've avoided you. You're still my best friend, but in this company, I'm radioactive."

"You don't need to be. The schedule for space flights for the last half of this year was released today. Guess who's not on it again."

"Oh my god. I'm so sorry, Tanya. What are you going to do?"

"Wait three months until my stock options are vested, then join you and the other job hunters."

"Listen, I'm serious about this. I don't want to drag you down as I leave, so I'm not going to talk to you until you have completely cut ties with Stellar Z. Guys like Cooper look for disloyalty."

"I know. I'll call you when I'm free. Let me know where you end up."

The next day Monica called in sick and left to visit her parents in Northern California.

#

With the hood of his raincoat over his head, Isaac walked across the Space Center in the rain. He entered the hallway of NASA headquarters where Don met him. "Did you enjoy the time off, Don?"

"Yeah, seeing my family was great. But Ohio is too cold this time of year. How's married life?"

"It's great to have Sally here. We're making adjustments." Isaac studied the photographs of former astronauts that hung on the high walls. "How many of these astronauts have you met?"

"Quite a few in the ten years I've been here. I haven't kept count."

Director Anderson quickly came down the hall. "I'm sorry to keep the two of you waiting. A meeting went on longer than planned." They followed the director to a conference room where the table had ten chairs on each side. Don and Isaac took seats. The director remained standing. "Isaac, on behalf of NASA and the whole country, I want to thank you for your part in the rescue mission. I've reviewed all the reports and video a few times and am totally amazed by your heroism. The families of the rescued astronauts have been asking me for a chance to meet you and thank you in person. The public relations director has a tentative schedule for the first Saturday in February."

Isaac brushed his hair back and stared up at the ceiling. "I don't know."

"You can do this," Don said. "All you have to do is shake a few hands and say, 'You're welcome.'"

"The other thing I have caught up on is the experiments results of the testing from last fall. The concern everyone has is there are no results providing an understanding of how you control gravity."

"I'm not sure we have the technology capable of detecting what Isaac does."

"Everyone agrees with that conclusion. All of NASA's scientists, engineers, and the best technician I know can't figure out why Isaac doesn't hit the ground when he falls off a wall."

Isaac slumped in his seat and folded his arms.

"Isaac, what I want you to do is catch up on school. I saw that you took an incomplete in all your classes last semester. And you now have a wife, and I expect you to spend time with her. All experiments are suspended until further notice. We'll reevaluate your contract at the end of the semester."

"Yes, sir."

"Don, in the meantime, there is a project at White Sands that needs our best man. I'd like you to consider going to New Mexico for a few months."

"Yeah, forward the details and I'll consider it. One other thing that needs looking into …" Don leaned forward. "Stellar Z collected data on Isaac during the ISS rescue mission."

"Do you think the respiration data will show us anything we don't already know?"

"There is a lot more data on Isaac and the spacecraft that might be useful," Don said with a hint of hesitation.

Isaac sat forward. "They put a cap on me full of electrodes and had electrical equipment secured to the floor. I asked Tanya about the data after my interview, and she admitted there was information, but they didn't know if it meant anything."

"I'll put in a request for the data. I doubt Stellar Z will cooperate. I appreciate the excellent work you've done over the past two and a half years. We'll meet again in June." He left the room.

"Study hard, Isaac. Keep in touch and call me when the baby is born." Don patted Isaac on the shoulder. "I'll see you in June, and we'll figure this out."

Chapter 17 – February–March

Sally and Isaac studied the video on how to tie a tie.

"The video is the opposite of what I see in the mirror," Isaac said.

"Let me see if I can help."

They got the tie to look right, and Sally slipped into high heels. She was stunning in the black formal dress she had bought for the occasion.

They came out of their apartment where Don stood by a limousine.

"You're picking us up in that?" Sally said in amazement.

"Yeah, get in," Don said.

"Overkill," Isaac said.

"For you, maybe," Don said. "For Sally, not enough."

"How's New Mexico?" Sally asked.

"A lot drier and a lot less people." Don said.

Isaac rubbed his hands along his thigh. "I would appreciate both right now."

Sally grabbed his arm. "Relax and let the evening happen. Don't worry about anything."

Isaac took a big sigh and leaned his head back in the cushy seat.

Once seated at the front-center table, Isaac didn't want to look behind at all the people who were there to honor him. Sally and Don sat on one side and Director Anderson and his wife sat on the other.

After dinner, Director Anderson addressed the audience. "Last November, the International Space Station encountered a disaster."

Isaac felt his stomach turn as the director went on with his speech. His ears stopped hearing, and his eyes focused on the napkin crumpled before him.

"Come on Isaac. I'll go with you." Sally pulled on his elbow.

He kept his eyes focused down while she led him to the center of the stage. He saw the director's hand, shook it, then received the microphone, and his ears opened up to hear the applause.

He took a deep breath and held the microphone up. "I ... I wish there was an *Osprey* here." He pointed to the stage beside him. "I'd get in and go to space, so I wouldn't speak ... wouldn't have to speak." He heard a few laughs. "But I won't because my wife would disown me." He glanced at Sally. "I wasn't this scared jumping out of the *Osprey* and into space." His stomach gurgled loud enough to be picked up by the microphone. "Gotta go." He shoved the microphone into Sally's hands and sprinted off stage.

"He gets nervous." Sally looked to where Isaac ran, then faced the audience. "I first met Isaac when I was hanging twenty feet over a stage with a broken ankle. He became my hero when he floated up and rescued me. The next day, I went to thank him. His response was, 'I'd like to thank you for breaking your ankle.'" She smiled and took a couple of steps until the laughter died down. "Today, almost three years later, I'm also glad I broke my ankle and met that amazing man. I'm proud of Isaac for stepping up, and as he would say, being a part of the rescue team. Thank you all for coming out tonight to honor Isaac."

Sally exited to a standing ovation and met Isaac off stage. He was wiping his face with a towel.

He took her hand. "Whoever said opposites attract probably didn't have stage fright and stage presence in mind."

#

"Hey, Don, how's the testing coming along?" Oskar, the balding man who six weeks ago had become his boss, asked.

Don looked up from his workbench cluttered with electronic parts and testing equipment. "The components work. I'd have used more modern technology for some. Isn't there anything more important to do than test outdated electronics?"

"It's proven to work in previous satellites. Maybe you can get on the team for the next satellite. I do have something more exciting for you. There's an interview this afternoon, and I need a fourth person for the team. Be in the conference room at one."

"I'm lousy at doing interviews. You'd be better off with someone else."

"Nobody likes interviews. Everyone gets their turn, and we share the pain." Oskar smiled and walked away.

Don purposely arrived at the conference room ten minutes after one. "Sorry I'm late," he said, and his mouth dropped upon seeing the interviewee.

"Dr. Shultz, meet our electronic test specialist, Don Greenwell. Don, this is Monica Shultz." Oskar slid a copy of Monica's resume and application to Don.

"We've met." Don took a seat without taking his eyes off Monica. He matched her nod with one of his own. "Professionally, a couple of times," he added.

Oskar continued. "Dr. Shultz was about to tell us why she left her position at Stellar Z."

Monica took on the face of a confessor. "Last fall, I was assigned a task that was outside my expertise. The results weren't what management expected, and I was personally reprimanded. I resigned to take my expertise somewhere where I will be appreciated."

Ms. Maynard, the human resources head sitting at the other end of the table from Don, asked, "To what do you attribute the failure of finding the expected results?"

"The data did not reveal anything significant." Monica's voice cracked.

"Unfigurable outable," Don said under his breath.

AntiGravity

"Do you have something to say, Mr. Greenwell?" Oskar asked.

Don half smiled. "I had a similar task that I worked on for two and a half years, and I'm here because I too did not find the expected results. The task Monica was assigned does not have a solution. If you refuse to hire her based on why she left, you have to fire me."

Monica gave Don a "you're not helping" look. "I'm sorry. I didn't know you were in New Mexico."

Ms. Maynard said, "Gentlemen, give us ten minutes."

Oskar and the other man, who Don had seen around but had never been introduced to, headed for the door. Don hesitated, then followed. Outside the conference room, Don told Oskar, "She's the best person for the job." Then he went back to work, hoping that they would never invite him to an interview again.

An hour later, Monica sent him a text. *Thank you for your help during the interview. Can we meet for a drink later?*

Don didn't want to seem too anxious or too negative. *I'm available. I'll need to eat. How about Pueblo Cafe. Easy to find. I'll meet you at six.*

Perfect

#

They entered the sandstone adobe building and placed their orders. Don noticed Monica twisting her napkin around her fingers. He realized he was tapping his heel.

She looked at him and said, "Thanks again for supporting me in the interview."

"What I said is the truth. I couldn't determine how Isaac manipulates gravity. You shouldn't have been punished." Don nervously tapped his finger on the table. "But I don't think that's why you invited me to meet with you."

Monica placed her hands on the table in front of her and clicked her fingernails. "I know how much you want to figure out what Isaac does. I didn't expect to find you here. But this whole mess has stressed me out, and maybe I can get some relief by telling you." She took a deep breath. "There are some anomalies in the data on the rescue flight that neither I nor anybody else at Stellar Z understood. The anomalies probably don't reveal anything, and if they did, there's no way to replicate the test. For Isaac's sake, I wanted to let you know."

"Thanks for the information. We can't replicate the experiments with Isaac exercising his full power. It's too dangerous. I think we were lucky Tanya landed the *Osprey* without killing everyone." Don watched Monica continue to click her fingernails. "There's more. Am I right?"

"I have a copy of the data on my laptop."

Don sat up in his chair. "You have a copy of the data?" he whispered.

"I do." Monica shook her head in small movements.

Don looked around the room to make sure nobody was close enough to hear. "Are you trying to get me fired? NASA sued Stellar Z to get the data on Isaac."

"And NASA will never get it."

"I know I'll never see your anomalies while I'm working for NASA."

"Is Isaac also here at White Sands?"

"No. Isaac is still in Houston. They have run out of safe experiments. I was reassigned to test outdated electronics. What are you going to do if NASA doesn't hire you?"

"Keep looking, and I'm thinking about doing some consulting."

"Becoming a consultant has also crossed my mind. It's the uncertainty that keeps me from taking the leap."

"There is security in working for a large organization. It's management that makes my life miserable."

"I read your resume. The research you have done and the forty patents Stellar Z has applied for with your name on them are impressive."

"Thank you. I imagine you have your name on many patents as well."

"Only two. I do have a few journal articles published and another half-dozen on Isaac that have been submitted." He played down that his expertise had been used on many other projects.

Their meals arrived, and they both focused on eating.

Don was almost finished when he looked up and said, "Would you be interested in consulting together?"

Monica swallowed and took a drink of her tea. "I was just thinking the same thing. I think we're both scared of working alone and would benefit from consulting as a team."

#

When Don arrived at work the next morning, he received a message from Ms. Maynard. She wanted to see him as soon as possible. He reviewed the resignation letter he had composed the night before, printed it, and headed to HR.

"Mr. Greenwell, come in," she said from behind a large metal desk. "Please have a seat."

Don remained standing beside the cushioned office chair. "You wanted to see me?"

"I needed to discuss what happened yesterday. To get right to the issue, your behavior during the interview with Doctor Shultz was unprofessional and has put us at risk of a lawsuit should we not hire her."

"Then offer her the position. I've worked with many materials scientists at NASA, and she's as good, if not better, than any of them. I doubt the work here at White Sands will challenge her and utilize her abilities to the fullest. Like myself."

"Are you dissatisfied with your current responsibilities?"

"I'm testing equipment that's older than I am."

"The testing is important to the project. And you're an essential person required to complete the mission." She leaned forward and folded her hands on the desk.

"I feel my abilities could be better utilized."

AntiGravity

"There are many times in every person's career where they feel they hit a plateau. Usually, they're at the top of a step that leads to another step. You're a professional with an exemplary record at NASA. I sympathize with you having to move from Houston to New Mexico. The adjustment can take a while, and HR sponsors a group that meets weekly to assist with the transition." She turned to the computer on her desk. "Let me send you the information on the group."

"There's no need. I've decided to resign. Here's my two weeks' notice." He placed a paper on the middle of her desk. "I'll make every effort to complete the testing within two weeks or stay a few days longer if necessary."

"After what I saw yesterday and your demeanor here today, I'm considering accepting your resignation effective immediately."

Don started to walk out of the office. "Your call, Ms. Maynard. I have some testing to complete." On the way back to the lab, he listed out what he needed to do. *Message Monica to let her know I'm free in two weeks. Let Isaac know. Complete the testing without error as fast as I can. Figure out how to become a consultant.*

Chapter 18 – March–April

In late March, Don and Monica formed a company and started to market their services to companies in Albuquerque. They picked up a few small contract jobs and felt that they would succeed as a business.

They rented five hundred square feet of space in an industrial park near the airport. Inside, it smelled of a mixture of solvent and ninety-weight oil. The transmission rebuilding company, which had been in the shop, left metal shelves that extended halfway down one wall; the rest of the space was empty. They purchased a couple of chairs and two wooden office desks that had seen better days from a secondhand store and got them set up in their new office.

Don sat back and put his feet on the desk. "Tomorrow, I'll bring in my tools and test equipment."

"I finished the contract I was working on."

"I thought you quoted a week?"

"It was an easy problem once I understood what they were looking for."

Don took a deep breath and said what he had wanted to say for a while. "Are you ever going to let me look at the data?" The words echoed in the large room.

"Bring your chair over, and we'll go through it."

Don spent the afternoon and evening going through the data collected on Isaac during the rescue mission. After synchronizing the information collected by the various instruments, he could see that changes in Isaac's heart rate, breathing rate, temperature, skin moisture, brain waves, facial expressions, eye movement, and electromagnetic aura coincided with the changes in gravity, acceleration, altitude, speed, and a dozen other measurements taken on the *Osprey* and the materials of which it was made.

It was late when they picked up a pizza on their way back to the building where they had each rented one-bedroom apartments. The place wasn't fancy, but it was close to their office space and they could commute together. Don and Monica sat at the table in his apartment and resumed reviewing the data.

"Did you put the brainwave sensors in Isaac's helmet?" Don asked.

"Yes. We have a cap that snaps inside with all the sensors."

"Did you account for Isaac's small head size?"

"No. We didn't have time to fit him."

"That may account for these weak, long-wave readings. I think they're echoes from the sensors being out of alignment."

"There are some wave changes like that in the data for the ship's hull."

"Faint, but the changes in both wavelengths are in line with changes in gravity."

"Is the data within the margin of error?"

"Yes," Don said.

AntiGravity

"So, this *isn't* evidence of Isaac changing gravity." Monica sat back in the wooden chair and looked at Don.

Don stood and stretched his five-foot, ten-inch frame. "Nope. Nothing new to me here. Okay, what do we know? Gravity is the attraction of particles with mass to each other. It's a very weak force, but when the mass is great, the force increases and becomes the largest influence on the physical universe. Most theories ascribe this force to a particle called the graviton. None of the theories to explain gravitons work out mathematically, but we do know there is an attraction between masses and variations in the attraction can be measured, which this data supports."

"So, where does that leave us?"

Don ignored her question. "What Isaac can do is turn off the mutual attraction his body has with the earth, and if he's in contact with another physical object, the effect is transferred to that object. The data shows a minuscule change in particles in the extremely low-frequency range."

"Okay, so we are still in the measurable energy range," Monica added.

"Right. The equipment can measure wavelengths in the range of a million kilometers. Hypothetically, gravitons have a natural wavelength about a million times longer, one point six light-years.

"This indicates we may be able to measure only the edge of the wavelengths Isaac is affecting. But it also indicates Isaac's meditation might be countering the graviton's wavelength amplitude, which nullifies gravity. Plus, since Isaac has demonstrated that he can go negative, he's reversing the graviton wave or its effect on him and what he is in contact with."

Monica nodded and stood. "One of the tests I performed on materials at Stanford was a vibration test. Many metals carry vibrations extremely well, and some don't."

"Vibrations? Like sound waves?"

"Right. Some substances are poor conductors of vibrations. What we need to do is find a substance, or substances, which can affect extremely low-frequency wavelengths. If a substance has a mass-to-weight ratio that's not equal to one, then it would be a poor conductor or super conductor of these gravity waves."

"Any substance with a ratio approaching infinity nullifies gravity and would have left Earth long ago."

"Not necessarily. Isaac alters gravity waves, but under normal conditions, he responds to gravity like everything else." Monica typed furiously on her computer while talking. "A material substance might alter gravity waves under the right conditions. Kind of like a super-conductor that works when in extreme cold or high pressure. We just need to find the research I remember faintly by someone, somewhere, who claimed a substance changed weight under pressure."

"That sounds promising."

"The research couldn't be replicated," she said. "I'm going need to find the article. Give me some time."

"How much time do you need?"

"If I'm really lucky, maybe an hour or two. Maybe a few days if I'm just lucky." Monica picked up her laptop and headed to her apartment.

#

The next day, Don poured himself into his computer to find more evidence of Isaac's ability in the data but came up empty.

Monica's eyes stayed glued to her laptop, searching publications for materials that varied in weight under stress.

Two revolutions of the earth later, after a total of ten hours of sleep, six meals brought in by Don, washed down by liters of coffee and Mountain Dew, Monica announced, "I think I found it."

Don scooted his chair over. "Tell me anything but the turtle holding up a disc-shaped Earth kneeling at Isaac's telepathic command."

Monica chuckled. "That might be better than what I've come up with." She paused, deep in thought. "Do turtles kneel?"

"I don't know. Tell me what you found."

"The material reported to lose weight under pressure has a phonon of zero."

"Help me with phonon."

"The transmission of compression waves in a material is measured in phonons. There is a thulium-based ceramic that does not conduct waves and is not compressible. The debunked study showed evidence that by applying perpendicular pressure on the center of a meter rod of the material, it changes weight."

"You said debunked."

"Yep. Both of the experiments attempting to replicate the results broke the sample. Since the sample is made with a rare-earth element in an expensive process, there were no further attempts."

"Now, that sounds promising. Who makes this ceramic?"

"Only one place. The Colorado School of Mines."

#

The laboratory of Dr. Emmil Trask was in the basement of a sixty-year-old building on the Colorado School of Mines campus. At the bottom of the stairs, Don and Monica met Michelle, a grad student who handled all correspondence for Dr. Trask. Michelle had them sign a standard nondisclosure agreement before she would let them see him.

Michelle put their papers into a file. "Let me show you to Dr. Trask's lab, where he spends all his time." She led them down a concrete-floored hallway whose sea-green walls needed a new coat of paint. The hanging fluorescent lights plugged into light bulb sockets revealed an attempt to update under a budget. Wooden doors with painted-over windows suggested the people doing research here did not want anyone spying on them.

She stopped at a door with a glass window painted the color of the walls and a warning sign: Materials Lab. Authorized personnel only. "Here we are. Dr. Trask is autistic. He won't look at you when he's talking and tends to ramble on about what he wants to say instead of staying on topic. I updated him about your meeting today." Michelle took a deep breath and opened the door. "Dr. Trask, Don Greenwell and Monica Shultz are here for your meeting."

A middle-aged man in a short-sleeved lab coat straightened from where he had been hunched over a long table. "Are you the two who wanted to examine the thulium ceramic?" He slowly turned his head. Thick prescription safety glasses, held on by an elastic band, made his eyes look larger than normal.

"Thank you for meeting with us today," Don said. "We'd like to see the ceramic and how you tested it to alter the weight."

Dr. Trask walked toward the end of the lab while talking. "I do a load test by hanging a rod of the material by the ends on a scale and then adding weight to the middle. Lasers measure ductility. The thulium ceramic is not unique in having a zero ductility and a phonon of zero. Under stress, it will fracture easier than glass." He stopped at a metal arm holding a scale with a hook hanging below. A plexiglass door could be pulled down in front of the scale.

"Can you show me how you performed the experiment that revealed that ceramic affects gravity?" Monica asked. "I've never seen a ductility test performed on a hanging scale."

"I use this large scale so I can enclose brittle substances. Fewer flying fragments and the cleanup is easier. Here's a meter-length rod of the ceramic, two centimeters square. First, we tare the scale to zero it out," he said, examining the digital readout. "Now, we clamp the lasers to the end and middle of the rod and attach the ends of the rod to the scale using thin strands of silk ribbon. I also use a silk basket to add weight. See how light it is?" He offered the basket to Monica and Don to hold.

"It weighs almost nothing," Monica said, holding the basket in her hand.

Dr. Trask took the basket and tied it to the middle of the ceramic rod. "Next, we line up this device to drop beads, each with a mass one-tenth of a gram, into the basket."

The device looked like a toy conveyer belt that carried a bead at a time up and plopped it into the silk basket.

He closed the plexiglass doors around the scale, which also prevented air currents from affecting the tests, and pressed a button to begin.

"How much weight do you need to show the effect?" Don asked.

"Between thirty and thirty-five grams. The ceramic breaks at around forty grams, so I'm setting the maximum weight to thirty-seven grams. It will take about ten minutes before we get enough weight to see the effect." Dr. Trask walked toward the other end of the lab and gave his attention to some instruments on the bench.

"Dr. Trask, what did the labs attempting to replicate your experiment do differently?" Monica asked.

"They didn't use silk ribbon."

"That's it," Don said. "I know from testing Isaac that silk ribbon doesn't conduct the reverse gravity, where a direct connection to the chains would."

Dr. Trask spun around and looked directly at Don. "If you're involved in testing the antigravity boy, Isaac, then you must be with NASA. You said you're only researchers and not with any company."

"I *was* an employee of NASA."

Monica added, "And I was an employee of Stellar Z. We got together to do consulting and see if we can understand how to replicate what Isaac does. We won't share your information with anyone without your permission."

"I—I need to have Michelle talk to you." Dr. Trask moved his gaze to the wall.

"We will honor the nondisclosure agreement Michelle asked us to sign," Don said.

"NASA didn't. There are many of my materials in spacecraft that I did not give them permission to use. Stellar Z then stole the patents from NASA."

"We will honor any patents should this ceramic do what I think it can. Payment will come if we can perfect the technology."

"No communication with NASA or Stellar Z," Dr. Trask said, clearly agitated. "Unless the college is paid in advance."

"Agreed," Don and Monica both said at the same time.

Ding!

"The test is finished," Trask said, pushing Don aside as he strode to the scale and opened the plexiglass hood. He untied the silk bag and disconnected the thulium ceramic.

Monica stepped up. "May I help?"

Dr. Trask slid in front of her cutting her off from the equipment. "No," he said and poured the beads used into a container that fed the conveyor belt. "We can look at the data across the hall."

Don looked at Monica with raised eyebrows.

She shrugged her shoulders in return. Then they raced to catch up with their host.

A moment later, graphs of the experiment were on a TV screen hanging on the wall. Dr. Trask pointed at a definitive, downward spike in the line showing the weight of the rod and equipment coinciding with the increased mass of beads at 32.4 grams. "This is the weight change I reported in the paper I published."

"The weight of the rod and what is attached to it is increased more than the beads, but it's not decreased. Why more, not less?" Don asked.

AntiGravity

Monica said, "The silk bag pulls down on the ceramic, increasing the gravity curve. When the pull on the ceramic exceeds the wavelength of gravity, the amplitude is no longer the sum of the two, and gravity takes over."

Dr. Trask rubbed his thumb into the palm of his other hand. "You two understand how this is affecting gravity better than I do. I'm always happy to help those who can use the materials I come up with. My price, or I should say the School of Mines' price, is one hundred thousand upfront, plus ten percent of the profit. And that's not negotiable."

"Doctor Trask, can we run the experiment again with the silk pulling up?"

"I have two rods of this thulium ceramic. That will be one for each of you at a thousand dollars apiece. Pay Michelle, and I'll pack them up. You can test them any way you wish. Remember, they're brittle." He shut off the computer and projector and walked out of the room.

"There goes another two grand," Don muttered.

"Well worth it if this works."

Archie Kregear

Chapter 19 – May

Isaac sat on a bench next to a seldom-used sidewalk and pulled out his phone. The message Don left that morning was to call when he could talk privately. Lunchtime on campus was as private as Isaac's life got. He nodded at the NASA security person and dialed Don.

"Isaac. I need to talk to you about what we found and the company we're forming."

"Have you figured something out?" Isaac took a bite of pizza.

"We have. There's a promising material that will allow us to mimic what you do with gravity. We need to do a lot of testing."

"Incredible!"

"Monica and I formed a company. Do you still want in?"

"Yeah, sure. Why wouldn't I be in?"

"Equal investment into the company by the founders. Monica and I are each putting in fifty-thousand dollars."

"Why so much?"

"The license to use the patent on the ceramic is a hundred grand, and we need some equipment for the lab. After proof of concept, we can get outside investors."

"Okay, I'm in. The estate of my parents is just sitting in savings. Let me know how to get you the money."

"Monica and I will complete the paperwork to add you as a partner. Look for the details in the mail."

"Can you make Sally part of my partnership? or does she need to be separate? And remember I need to stay with NASA until the end of June, and we have a baby coming."

"No rush to join us. We have a lot to figure out."

That evening Isaac presented to Sally the option to join Don and Monica in Albuquerque. They agreed that this was the best option to take after the contract with NASA ended in June.

#

Monica had her legs stretched out on the couch when her phone rang. "Good evening, Tanya. How are you holding up?"

"Stellar Z is worse than ever," Tanya complained. "Cooper has me training new astronaut recruits while everyone else goes into space."

"Yikes, that sucks. What are you going to do?"

"I'm documenting things, and when I have enough evidence of their discrimination, I'll sue."

"I'm always a phone call away when you need someone to talk to."

"Thanks. I know folks sense that I'm on the bosses shit-list, so they're steering clear of me."

"Maybe I have a way out. Don and I started a company. Why don't you join us?"

"What will I be? A sympathy add-on, an employee, or will you bring me in as a partner?"

"I'd love for you to be an equal partner. Don, Isaac, and I are each putting up fifty grand to start. If you can match that, I'll talk to the guys about adding you."

"As soon as my options are vested, no problem. Do you believe in the technology you're developing?"

"We have something worth devoting ourselves to. If it works, we'll be rich and famous. If not, maybe we can sell Isaac as a sideshow act."

"Let me know what Isaac and Don say."

When Monica brought up Tanya to Don, he said, "Sounds great. I approve."

"Should I call Isaac about Tanya, or would you like to call him?"

"I think you need to get to know Isaac better, so give him a call."

When Monica called Isaac, he enthusiastically agreed that Tanya should be part of the company.

#

Tanya struggled with the realization that her goal to be an astronaut had come to an end. She had done everything right, from being accepted to college until training at Stellar Z certified her as an astronaut. She may not have been the best at anything, but she was better than average at everything. All academic scores placed her in the top ten percent, and her physical skills were better than most. Her peers accepted her as one of them, but the male executives treated her differently.

She sat on her sofa, recalling the meeting with her guidance counselor at the end of her high school freshman year. She had earned straight As for the first time in her academic career. The counselor presented her with the basic schedule for sophomores. Six classes. Tanya wanted to take one additional course, Advanced Placement English Language and Composition, to give her a boost and free up her schedule to take more AP classes during her junior and senior years. The counselor discouraged the idea. She had pleaded with the counselor, "Teachers have always told me that I could do and be anything I wanted."

The counselor calmly replied, "You *can* do or be anything. But you *can't* do and be *everything*. Choose what you want, and we'll focus on getting you there."

Tanya felt now as she had felt then. She didn't know what she wanted to do or be. Her future was an empty void. She had replied to the counselor, "What I'm determined to do is live up to my potential. I just haven't figured out what my potential is."

The counselor's words set her on the path to this point in her life. "The sky's the limit." Then the counselor signed off on the extra class.

Now, she had gone as far as she could in Stellar Z. Maybe it was a glass ceiling, the color of her skin, the limitation of being an astronaut instead of an executive, or just reaching her goal and having nothing new to challenge her. The door was closing. Monica was inviting her to follow into a new room. A few more weeks, and she would make the move.

#

"Isaac," Sally called from the bedroom.

He had lost track of time while studying for his English final and was happy for the interruption. "I'm coming."

"It's time."

He found her sitting on the edge of the bed and helped her to stand. He began to work down the checklist they had rehearsed many times. Late the next morning, Sally gave birth to their daughter, Emily. Isaac held his new daughter and trembled with joy and admiration for his wife for what she went through to bring Emily into the world. He wondered what his parents would have thought and felt about having a granddaughter and felt sad that they wouldn't know her.

The following day, Isaac picked up his mother-in-law at the airport and brought Sally and his daughter home later that afternoon. He had never imagined what it meant to be a father.

The following two weeks were a blur. The lack of sleep, semester finals, and being ordered around by his mother-in-law brought him to the point of exhaustion. Yet, he felt the happiest he had ever felt in his life.

#

When he wasn't asleep, Don worked with the thulium ceramic to exploit the weightless property. Replicating Dr. Trask's experiment with upward pressure was not difficult. Refining the force applied by adding micrograms of weight eventually produced the desired result. The ceramic and attached metal became weightless.

After a couple of weeks, a working antigravity device sat in their office. A metal pipe contained the meter-long ceramic. A micro screw accessed the ceramic via a hole in the center of the tube. Specific pressure could be applied to the ceramic rod in increments of micrograms, providing the change in gravity waves. He installed limits to the screw to prevent too much pressure and possibly damage the rod.

With the battery and wireless control mechanism, the device weighed about twenty-two kilograms, the maximum weight for checked baggage.

To celebrate, Don left Monica a note. "It works." Then he went to his apartment and slept for a full day.

#

One afternoon in a new father daze, Isaac took Emily to rock her to sleep.

"Isaac, what are you doing!" Sally shouted.

AntiGravity

"I'm rocking Emily."

"You're floating around the room with Emily in your arms. Get down!"

Isaac realized where he was and lowered himself like a feather, landing on the edge of the bed. "She's safe," he said in his defense.

"She wiggles a lot. I've nearly dropped her several times. Having her that high in the air makes me nervous," Sally said, taking Emily from Isaac's arms.

"I would never let her fall."

"I know. Having her in the air makes me nervous."

Isaac shuffled into the living room, sat at the desk. *How can I turn my ability into a money-making business without being a sideshow? I can replace a crane. I can provide lift for a plane. I can take cargo to space. But I can't get Dr. Seuss out of my head. I'm twenty-one, married to the girl of my dreams, and have a daughter. What am I going to do after the NASA contract ends? I hope Don finds a way to make antigravity work.*

His phone rang. NASA wanted him in to meet with another psychologist. To him, it seemed like every shrink in the country wanted to determine his thought patterns when he turned gravity off. The ability was now natural to him, and he played with gravity like a dimmer switch on the wall. He just couldn't explain how his head worked.

#

The next day Isaac entered the three-story padded building at NASA and was introduced to Dr. Grayson, a hypnotherapist. Isaac reached out his hand. "I'm pleased to meet you, Doctor Grayson. What can I do for you today?"

"It is my pleasure to meet you, Isaac. I sense you're more than willing to let me search for your riddle. Shall we sit?" Dr. Grayson asked.

Two chairs were in the middle of the room, facing each other. They each took a seat.

"That's my job. I'm being paid to let NASA figure out why I can do what I can do. If that makes sense." Isaac blushed a bit at how his words came out.

"I find that the human mind is a mystery. Even after studying it for the last fifty years, I have more unanswered questions than I had when I started. You're unique, as are many others, such as math or music savants. I've attempted to probe many minds using hypnosis and have found each to be an original masterpiece full of surprises. Like the secrets of the savants, I predict the enigma of your ability will remain hidden, but we may find a few clues that others may find useful."

"Where would you like to start?"

"I started two weeks ago by reviewing the research about you that has been documented during the last three years. Did you know your mind is one of the most studied in the history of humankind? There is a plethora of information available. I must admit that the questions I have are repetitive, but I will ask them after I place you into a hypnotic state. To start with, do you have any questions or concerns?"

"No." Isaac shook his head.

"You have an unusual calmness about being questioned. Can you explain why you're so accepting about being probed?"

Isaac sighed and thought for a moment. "I don't like being the only person who can manipulate gravity. If others could do it, then I wouldn't be an object to be studied. I could be ... me."

Dr. Grayson cocked his head slightly. "Aha hmm. I see. Well, let's get started. I'm going to place you into a hypnotic state. Stay relaxed, and this will be over before you know it." A few minutes later, Dr. Grayson said, "Isaac, in a moment, I would like you to turn off gravity. As you do, tell me everything you're thinking and doing. Feel free to verbalize everything, no matter how minor. Are you ready?"

"Yes."

"Please proceed to turn off gravity."

"I sense gravity waves, and I'm straightening them out. Gravity is turned off." Isaac floated from his chair slightly. "I bend them a little perpendicular and invert the pull." Isaac rose in the room.

The doctor crossed one leg over the other. "What do gravity waves look like?"

"Long lines with a slight curve. I sense the mass of the earth bending them."

"And you're able to straighten them out?"

"I guess that's what I'm doing."

"Can you extend the lines beyond your body?"

"Only to the things I touch. I've answered these questions before."

"Yes, I know. As I said before, I expect nothing new. Is there anything, any bit of information you know about, that NASA has not asked about?"

"Only the data from the instruments in the *Osprey* when I went to the space station."

"What was found there?"

"The data showed that I straighten the lines of gravity in objects I'm in contact with."

"Which is something documented in previous experiments, if I recall."

"In studies, this phenomenon had been measured in Bismuth and Muscovium, but the gravity effects were minor."

"Yes, I read that in previous reports. How is the data from the *Osprey* relevant? Tell me more."

"Don told me that Monica had measured the effect I had on the structure of the *Osprey*. NASA has not put me in a craft that I can exert my ability like I did that day," Isaac said. "Why am I telling you this? Monica and Tanya will get in trouble if anyone knows." Isaac returned to the floor and stood, glaring at Dr. Grayson.

"Hypnotism may allow you to tell more than you wish. Secrets may slip out."

AntiGravity

Isaac shook his head.

"One last question if I may?" Dr. Grayson said. "How much do you need to bend the gravity waves to turn off gravity?"

"Hardly at all. It's like making a straight line straighter."

"Interesting."

The door burst open, and Director Anderson strode in. "Isaac. What instruments did Stellar Z have aboard the *Osprey*?"

"I don't know, sir."

"Is this why Don left? Has he found something in the data to exploit?"

"The data did not reveal anything we don't already know."

"Then why did he leave, and what is he doing now?"

Isaac shuddered. "I ... I can't say."

"Can't or won't? If Don left because of what they found out on the *Osprey*, that data is our property." Director Anderson stomped out of the room.

Dr. Grayson turned to Isaac. "Many see your ability as having tremendous value. I can understand why you want to reveal this talent to the world. There is incredible stress knowing that you have something of value and can't let it go."

"I think I've made things worse," Isaac muttered.

#

About that time in Albuquerque, Don said to Tanya, "There it is. Zero weight on a total mass of thirty kilograms."

"How does this work?" Tanya asked. She had arrived in Albuquerque a few days previously, and this was her first day in the office.

"Pressure is applied to the ceramic, and it counters gravity."

Tanya examined the apparatus Don had set up in their office. "Can you make it go negative like Isaac can do?

"No. I have no clue how Isaac can invert a gravitational pull. By slight variations in the pressure, I can go from zero-g to any fraction of gravity, but never negative. I'm now working on calibrating the instruments so I can remotely control the gravitational change."

"What can I do to help?"

"You can come with me to pick up some weights," Monica said from across the room. "I found someone selling their gym equipment on Craigslist. I didn't know dumbbells were so expensive." She picked up her coat.

"I'm hoping for at least a couple hundred kilos," Don said.

"That's why I'm taking Tanya along."

"We can set up a gym if this fails," Tanya said.

#

That night after Sally went to bed, Isaac called Don. "Listen, I was under hypnosis today, and they got out of me that Monica has data on the flight that NASA did not know about."

"That's OK. They can have it. We—"

"No! Don't tell me anything about what you found out. They will be questioning me further, and the less I know, the less I can tell them."

"You sound frazzled. Settle down. The data isn't important."

"Are you sure?"

"Definitely. And per your instructions, I won't tell you why. Continue with NASA until your contract is up."

"That's next week."

"By that time, I hope to have something we can show off to some venture capitalists."

"That soon? Wow."

"Take care, Isaac. Give Sally and Emily my love."

"Thanks, Don. Say hi to Monica for me."

"Tanya has joined us. I'll pass on your message to both."

"Super. Later Don."

#

Don hung up from his conversation with Isaac at the same time as Monica's voice called out, "Don, can you help us with the weights?"

"Sure thing." He went outside, into the cold winter air, and grabbed a couple of the larger dumbbells from her car. "Isaac called while you were gone. He wanted me to tell you both hi."

"How's he doing?" Tanya asked over her shoulder as she carried some weights inside.

"Isaac's good. NASA hypnotized him today and found out about the data from the flight."

"They're going to be coming after us," Tanya said.

"Let them have the data. We need to protect the ceramic," Don said.

"Let's get these weights in, then make a plan," Monica said.

A few minutes later, they were sitting around a desk. "What do we need to do to protect our information?" Monica asked.

"Secure servers and a way to keep papers and equipment safe," Don replied.

After a few minutes of discussion, they planned to find an IT specialist for the computers, keep essential papers with them, and leave all equipment dismantled at night. If someone were to break in, they would only find pieces of equipment lying around.

They set out to make their new enterprise secure.

Chapter 20 – June

On the first Monday in June, Don encountered a well-dressed man outside his apartment.

"Are you Don Greenwell?" the man asked.

"I am," Don said, realizing this was the encounter he'd expected and dreaded.

"I'm here to deliver some legal papers. Please sign this." The man held out a clipboard.

Don sighed, read the acknowledgment of receipt, and signed it.

The man handed him a half-inch thick envelope and left.

He sat down at the two-person table in his apartment and reviewed the documents. NASA was demanding he provide all information and data related to Isaac and his ability to alter gravity. Everything he knew was published in journals, but Monica did have data NASA had sued to get from Stellar Z.

The next day Monica and Tanya received similar documents from their former employer.

They sat down in Monica's apartment. Tanya said, "Now let me see if I understand what's going on. We recorded data on Isaac during our flight to the space station. Stellar Z and Monica both have a copy. NASA sued Stellar Z to get the data because Isaac is an employee. Both companies sued us to get our copy."

"They don't know I have a copy," Monica corrected.

"They only *suspect* that we have the data," Tanya corrected herself.

Don added, "NASA is suing us because Stellar Z denies having the data. Stellar Z is suing us to keep us from giving it to NASA."

Tanya stood and began to pace. "What did you find that led you to what you're researching now?"

Don and Monica looked at each other.

"Don was explaining gravitons and gravity waves to me, and something I read while at Stanford popped into my head. After a few days of research, I rediscovered the article on the thulium ceramic."

"What I said about gravity was published by others. Others made the ceramic. We just collaborated."

Tanya stopped pacing and leaned on the table. "If you two actually have something, we need to document it and keep it secure."

The next day, Don went in search of someone who could provide security for their computers. The first computer company he talked to referred him to a one-person company specializing in cybersecurity.

Archie Kregear

On Route 66, through the old part of Albuquerque, sat a small storefront sandwiched between two larger buildings. *WE B Security* was painted above the door. Don entered and took the half step to the glass counter.

"What can I help you with?" came a loud voice from the backroom.

Don took a deep breath and tried to speak at an equal decibel level. "A couple of friends and I left our jobs to form a new company. We need help to keep our information secure."

"Is the total number of people in the company three?" A man in a Steely Dan T-shirt and jeans came through a doorway.

"One more will join us in a month or so."

"Keeping your information safe from others and any form of potential destruction is what I do." He gave a fake smile.

"That's what we need. How much?"

"Ten thousand. If you're worthy clients."

"Um... There are only three of us. Why so much?"

"The hardware, software, and time are the same for a company of one hundred, one thousand, or four. How much experience do you have with computers?"

"I have a degree in electrical engineering and—"

"And your partners?"

"One has a doctorate in materials science, and the other is an astronaut," Don said with pride.

"Good, you're tech-savvy. I don't do basic user support."

"I hope we are proficient computer users. Can we get an introductory level package?"

"The threat is the same no matter how large of a company you are. I also monitor every network I install for attacks."

"Can I get a little background on you? Your education, experience? If I'm going to agree to a large contract ..."

"Yep, here's what you need to know. I'm Chris Pathan. I was a teenage hacker who got caught. The NSA got me released into their custody, which meant I did my time working for the government in cybersecurity. I hated DC, so when my time was up, I headed west and stopped here. After five years here, you walked in my door."

Don felt he had to pry. "The guy who referred me said you're the best—"

"I know the subjects where I'm *not* the best," Chris said. "And for those areas, I know who *is* the best. Take a card and contact me when you're ready."

"I'm ready."

Chris sketched out a plan to keep the data on computers safe. Then he told Don to make sure the building was secure.

Over the next week, Chris installed a network firewall in their building and encryption software on their computers. He implemented a backup plan and security on the entrances to their office. As he finished reviewing what he had done, the subpoenas for Don, Tanya, and Monica came as expected.

"Now we need a lawyer," Monica said.

"No, we don't. If we found nothing useful on the data, give it to whoever the judge decides," Tanya said.

"I agree. Give it back, as there is nothing there to indicate how Isaac alters gravity," Don said.

#

Isaac kissed his wife, who was only half awake. "I'm going to my exit interview. Get some rest."

"I'll try. Every time I get to sleep, Emily wants to be fed."

"What do you want for lunch? I'll pick it up on the way home."

"Anything and everything."

"I'll be back soon." Isaac trotted across the Johnson Space Center in the humid air. *I'm going to miss this place. But time to move on.*

Isaac entered the conference room. Director Anderson and a man and woman, both formally dressed, sat at the long table.

"Good morning, Isaac. Take a seat. Joining us today is the lawyer who is working on getting access to your data and the writer who is finalizing the articles on your gravity-altering abilities."

Isaac nodded at the others and felt intimidated as he was dressed only in a polo shirt and khakis.

Director Anderson took a deep breath and folded his hands on the table. "Tomorrow, we'll be meeting with Don, Tanya, and Monica. We know that you plan to join them after your contract here is up. We have reason to believe that Don is using information from his time at NASA to work on an antigravity device. I think that the data acquired on your flight to the International Space Station is key to what they're developing.

"Over the years, the United States government has spent billions of dollars researching gravity in the hope of finding a way to put it under humanity's control. Such a device should be in the hands of NASA rather than a corporation like Stellar Z. Let me ask this directly, does Don have an antigravity device?"

Isaac's hands began to sweat, and his mind began to race. "I'm not aware of such a device."

"Do you know what they're working on?"

"No, sir. To avoid any conflict of interest before my contract expires, we agreed to cease all communication." Isaac felt himself go flush.

"When did you agree to this?"

"The day I was under hypnosis and told you about the data from the flight."

"Do you know if there is anything significant in that data?"

"No."

"Why did Don start a company with Monica Shultz from Stellar Z?"

"Don and Monica are both competent people in their fields. They wanted to do something that exercised their full abilities."

The director raised his voice. "Was there anything in the data that was significant?"

Isaac wiped his hands on his pants under the table. "They have not told me anything."

"Why would they form a company if there were nothing significant?" the director pressed. "If NASA has the information, we can release it to the world. If Stellar Z controls antigravity, the world is under their control."

Isaac shook at the implications of the director's words and stared at the oak conference table.

"Well, Isaac. Tell us what you know," the attorney ordered.

Isaac looked up at the lawyer and then addressed the director. "I like NASA. Everyone here has been great. I don't know anything right now. If I find out that Don and Monica developed a device that alters gravity, I'll contact you immediately, but only if you promise not to try to control or take it from them. But honestly, I think I will be the only antigravity device in existence forever."

"What do you think you'll be doing when you join them?"

Isaac dropped his eyes back to the table. "I'll help take things into space or provide rides to paying customers who want to experience zero-g."

"If you find a completely safe way for you to do that, I'm sure NASA would consider working with you." The director paused. "The position of NASA at this time is that you shouldn't lift people or extreme loads. The risk of overexertion prevents me from approving you working in that manner."

"Yes, sir," Isaac said, feeling like his future just got swept out from under him.

"Anything else for Isaac?" the director asked.

The attorney said, "We'll draw up a simple document stating that you agree to inform NASA of any form of antigravity technology should you acquire knowledge of such a device."

"The articles we are releasing explain that your ability is beyond understanding. That should be enough to deter folks like Deron from forcing the information from you."

"I wish you and Sally the best for the future."

Isaac shook Director Anderson's hand. "Thank you, sir."

Isaac left, hoping that his agreement would keep Don and Monica out of trouble and wondering what he would for a career.

#

At the hearing, Stellar Z argued that the data was theirs since their employees collected it with their equipment. NASA asserted they had not permitted anyone to collect data on Isaac, their employee.

Monica said, "There is nothing in the data that Don or I did not already know. The data is available to whomever the court decides." She handed the thumb drive to the judge. "We have erased the data from my personal computer."

"Is this your only copy of the data?"

"Yes, Your Honor."

"Your Honor," the lawyer for Stellar Z said, "we would like to have a restraining order placed on Don Greenwell, Commander Tanya Nash, and Doctor Monica Shultz from using the data stolen from Stellar Z."

The NASA lawyer added, "To take this a step further, Your Honor, NASA requests full disclosure on what these three are working on. Only by full disclosure could we ensure that they're not using proprietary information."

"There is nothing there to use," Don replied.

"Let me review the case, and I will respond in one week."

#

The next morning, Don was woken by a call from Chris Pathan, the cybersecurity expert. "Meet me at the Pancake House at six."

"What?" Don said as he dragged his mind to alert.

"I'll talk to you then." Chris hung up.

Don looked at his phone. It was a few minutes after five. *What does Chris want this early?* He checked the messages and e-mail on his phone. As usual, there was nothing significant. He showered, dressed, and drove to meet Chris. He arrived fifteen minutes early to get some coffee and clear his head. Chris was already there, clicking away on his laptop.

"Good morning, Chris," Don said as he slid into the booth.

"Hey, Don." Chris waved at the waitress. "Get your order in so we can talk uninterrupted."

Don ordered his usual eggs, bacon, and lots of coffee.

Chris closed his laptop, leaned into the table, and said, "Last night, there was a high-level attack on your computers. They started with the usual things which would hack most laptops. The firewall I put in probably surprised them. Whoever it was then began one of the most sophisticated attacks I've seen since I left the NSA. I monitored the attack from my office and alerted some of my buddies. They're working to trace where the attack is coming from."

"Did they get anything?"

"If you left a laptop at work turned on, they may have. But the hackers would have only gotten encrypted files, which will keep them busy for weeks unless they get lucky."

"We take our computers home. Mine is right here."

"Good, keep it off."

"Are we going to be able to work today?"

"I was hoping to know who's behind the attacks before you arrived here. I need to make some changes to your network. Then maybe."

Their food arrived.

Chris began shoveling in blueberry banana pancakes. Between bites, he said, "Listen, I don't know what you guys are working on, and I don't want to know. If you hadn't come to me when you did, everything you had would now be in someone else's hands. And your computers would probably be useless."

"The invention is hardware," Don said. "I think we can reduce the information on the computers, so if someone did get in, they wouldn't have enough to replicate what we're doing."

"Great. I'll set up a decoy computer and then a minuscule path to it. We'll give them some false stuff that they can play with. Maybe a mole while we're at it. Are you up to going on the offense?"

"We don't want to piss anyone off more than we already have." Don sighed.

"Who have you pissed off?" Chris asked with a smile.

"Our former employers, NASA and Stellar Z."

"Some big boys, and it's probably the latter or someone you don't know. Always good to know who the potential opponents are. I'll meet you at the office later this morning. Nobody can turn on their computers until I say you can." Chris grabbed his laptop and headed for the door.

Don picked up the tab and sent a message to Monica and Tanya. *Don't turn on your computers.*

Chris arrived at the office a little after nine. "Good, you're all here. The probing of your firewall is continuing. With your permission, I will set up a computer and let them have everything on it. The data will have simple encryption that they will break in a day or less. A mole program will then propagate on their network and send their location out onto the net where I'll find it. We'll know where these folks are in a few days. Are you in?"

"Are you sure this is how we should handle this?" Don asked.

"Someone out there is committing a federal crime against you. I'm doing what the NSA would do if you were a large corporation. The difference is we don't have to keep your computers working. I'm assuming you have something to do without your laptops today."

"I can continue," Don said.

"I don't have anything to do anyway," Tanya confessed.

"Not to be critical," Monica said, "but we hardly know you. How do we know you're not the one stealing our data?"

"Good," Chris replied. "You must be skeptical of everyone, including me. To be honest, there isn't enough gold or bitcoin in the world to make me hack again. Whoever is trying to hack you has devoted more resources to the attempt than you have. Personally, I enjoy a cat and mouse game. Hackers see themselves as defenders of the mouse until they figure out it's usually other mice who get hurt. Hack a bank, take some money from accounts, does the bank suffer? No. It's the account holders who must fight to get their money back. I set up a firewall to stop random hackers from messing with you. You were the target of a lion. All you need to do to stop a lion is to expose them, like a bird in a tree alerting the antelope."

"Do we have another option?" Don asked.

"Are the two of you sure there is nothing in the data you used to come up with the antigravity device?" Tanya asked in a frustrated tone.

"I only used information that's in published articles," Don said. "Monica came up with the materials that allowed us to design the device. Also published information."

"You guys are now talking above my need to know," Chris injected.

"Forget what we say, Chris." Don stood and ran his fingers through his hair as he began to walk around the room.

"Sorry. I didn't mean to let it slip," Tanya said.

"No worries," Monica said. "Maybe we should write up the device, apply for a patent, and publish the technology."

"Whoa," Chris said. "I can't unhear a global game changer. If this gets out there, you'll be swallowed up in a black budget military project faster than you can sneeze."

"We need a plausible reason to be a company that we can present to the world. Something we can publicize to cover what we're really doing," Tanya said.

Don sighed and scratched his head. "Okay, Chris, you go find the lion, and we'll figure out how to camouflage ourselves."

"On it," said Chris. "The first thing is to remove the batteries from your computers. Nobody can access something without power." He proceeded to work on their laptops.

"I'll make a coffee run," Don said and grabbed his jacket from the back of his chair.

Tanya moved her chair next to Monica. "What have we got ourselves into?"

Chapter 21 – Late June–July

Isaac carried their sofa to the truck by himself to show off to Sally and the movers.

Sally stood in the empty living room when he came back for another load. "You don't want to be a sideshow act, but you'll use it to try to impress me."

"Does it work?"

"It has, but not as much as it would if you could get me into an air-conditioned place."

"Go sit in the car."

"We're going to be in the car for the next three days."

"Albuquerque is not as humid as it is here."

"Then we need to get going soon."

"I'll hurry."

Isaac double-timed it while moving boxes from the apartment to the moving truck and the items they needed for their trip into the back of their used Prius. To avoid the heat of the day, they drove at night. With lots of stops, it took them two nights to make the trip.

#

Don added an angular piece of metal to the meter-long tube containing the ceramic sample and a hook in the elbow. It now looked like a giant coat hanger. To keep it upright, he attached reaction wheels. To operate from the ground, he added the electronics for remote control, and tested it by raising it to the ceiling. He left it raised to answer the buzzer at the door. "Isaac, you made it. I have to show you this." Pulling Isaac into the office, he pointed to the ceiling. "Look up there."

"Is that what I think it is?" Isaac pushed himself off the floor toward the device.

Don rushed for the remote control to bring it down. It dropped off the ceiling as Isaac reached for it.

Isaac was able to grab it midair. The combined momentum stilled him and the device with only a few wobbles before the reaction wheels steadied him. Isaac floated them to the floor. "It works."

"I was testing the remote when you got here. I want to add fans for movement." Don helped place the device on a hook on the wall.

"Hi, Isaac." Monica walked from the back of the room.

Tanya, a step behind, said, "Welcome to Albuquerque."

"It's good to see both of you again. I guess we'll be partners now."

"And we all get to work together after all," Tanya said.

"What name did you come up with for our company?"

"Adynamia. We liked the way it sounds."

Isaac nodded. "I like it. Nice choice."

"Where's Sally and Emily?" Monica asked.

AntiGravity

"At the apartment."

"Has your furniture arrived already?"

"No."

"You left your wife and daughter in an empty apartment? Here are my keys. I know Sally must be tired, so use my bed," Monica said.

"I came over to ask Don for his keys. He already said we could crash at his place."

"Nope. My apartment. I'm leaving to meet with MoonBeam Exxcursions." Tanya dangled her keys before Isaac and nodded toward Monica. "Besides, you need to drive me to the airport."

"The logic says Tanya's place." Isaac took her keys.

Monica picked up her purse. "After I drop Tanya off at the airport, I'm going to get some dinner. Do you want to join us?"

"I think we're too tired to go out tonight."

"Thanks, but I want to get this drone connection finished so that when we test the device, we'll be able to capture video from the air," Don replied.

"We need a better name than 'the device,'" Tanya said.

"AGD?" Isaac said.

"What?"

"The antigravity device. I just acronymed it."

"That means we're a real tech company with our own acronyms." Monica smiled.

Don chuckled. "Have a good time at MoonBeam Excursions."

"Hopefully, I can create some working arrangement." Tanya went out the door. Monica and Isaac followed.

Don went back to work, making sure the camera feed from the drone was displayed correctly on the remote-control monitor.

The buzzer to the door chimed. He glanced at the monitor by the door and checked the outside video security camera to see a man wearing a DHL hat standing outside, holding a large box. Don opened the door.

"Delivery for Monica Shultz at a company called Adynamia. Is that you?"

"Yes, I'll take it."

"It's heavy. I'll bring it in and set it down," the delivery man said, looking around the side of the box.

"Just set it down near the door." Don stepped back out of the way.

The man set the box down, then punched Don hard in the stomach as he stood up.

"Urgh!" Don doubled over. Then a gloved fist smashed into the side of his head. He went down in a heap. Lying on the floor, Don blinked the blurriness out of his eyes.

The man stood over him. "Where is Isaac?"

"He's not here." Don raised his arms in a defensive position.
"His car's still outside."
"He must have gone with Monica."
"My boss thinks you have something. He sent me to get Isaac or it. This place is so bare except for that thing on the wall." The man, dressed in a black skin-tight T-shirt and pants, moved towards the AGD.

Don rolled to his hands and knees and watched the blood drip from his head. He caught his breath as the man went out the door with the antigravity device over his shoulder.

He felt the side of his head then looked at the blood covering his fingers. *Get the drone to follow him.* He crawled to retrieve the remote control and picked it up. He stood, grabbed the drone, and went to the door. As soon as he had it open, he held the drone up in his left hand and swiped the remote control against his side to turn it on. Then, he let go.

Leaning against the building, he looked at the monitor on the remote control. "Shit." He saw that he had also activated the AGD.

On the monitor, he could see the drone catching up to the AGD. The man was hanging on, feet off the ground. The device was moving at the same speed the man had been running. He estimated the man was now about ten meters or so in the air and rising. Don put his hand on the switch to deactivate the antigravity device, then halted. *If I turn it off, the guy will likely be injured or killed. I can let him down slowly, but he will get away with the device. How long can he hold on?*

Don's eyes locked onto the monitor, watching the man and the device float like a released balloon to the south. A couple of minutes later, the monitor showed the AGD nearing the golf course. The man had hooked his legs over the AGD and was pulling at the parts. "You're not going to destroy it by hand, you asshole," Don said out loud.

Once the man was over the golf course, Don decided to lower the AGD enough that he could let go without dying. The man let go near one of the lakes and disappeared into the trees. In the dark, he could not see the man land or a splash. Don let out a chuckle. He kept the device weightless for about a half-hour before letting it down in a gully south of town. He clambered back into the office and called Chris.

"We've had a robbery. I followed the thief with a drone. The device is in a gully south of town. Can you pick it up?"

"What happened to the robber?"

"He let go over the golf course."

"What?"

"I'll fill you in when you get here. My head is bleeding, or I'd get it. I'll send you the location of the drone."

"Where are the others?"

"Out to dinner."

AntiGravity

Chris arrived about an hour later with the AGD and the drone. Don was holding a bloody towel to his head. His white polo shirt was half red, and his stomach ached.

"Shit, dude. Are you okay?" Chris asked as he sat down his load.

"I don't know." Don pulled the bloody towel away from his head to let Chris look.

"Holy shit," Chris exclaimed. "You're going to need some stitches in that. Let me secure this place and get you to the hospital."

"Take the AGD apart. Start with the screws in the ends. Put everything in a pile in the back," Don instructed while lowering himself into a chair.

A few minutes later, they were on their way to the hospital.

Chris asked, "Now, what's our story?"

"What do you mean?"

"When the police start asking questions, what do we tell them?"

"I'm a lousy liar," Don admitted. "There is no way we can fabricate a story to cover all of the facts. Airport radar had to see the device go across the end of the runway. I'm surprised no one has shown up."

"You said the man let go over the golf course. Maybe we'll see him at the hospital. If I can get a picture, I'll send it off to see if his face is on file anywhere."

"Shouldn't we tell the police instead of hiding?"

"Yeah. If we try to cover this up, we'll only get ourselves in deeper trouble. Let's get you checked in, and I'll let the police know about the assault."

"Black ops, here I come." Don sighed.

"Not you. You won't have the security clearance," Chris said as they pulled up to the emergency room door.

Don started to climb out, then paused and said, "Call the antigravity device an advanced guided drone, AGD for short. We don't need to explain how it works unless they ask."

"Great idea," Chris replied.

#

While Don was checking in, Chris called the police.

An officer met them at the hospital and took their report. He focused on where the robber might have let go over the golf course and then requested a search of the area. The police officer requested a copy of all the video footage, to which Don and Chris agreed. Then the officer left to join the search for the alleged robber.

Just after midnight, Chris dropped Don off at his apartment. "Get a good night's sleep. I'll make a copy of the video for the police. Call me in the morning when you want me to pick you up."

"I can drive myself in."

"Your car is at the office. Are you sure your head's okay?"

"No. It's pounding inside this mummy wrap. I'll let you know when I need a ride."

"Alright, I'll see you in the morning."

#

Don's head throbbed when he woke up around eight. He called Chris, who drove him to the office. They entered the office about nine to find a detective talking to Monica.

"Don! What happened?" she yelled out as she rushed across the room to his side.

"I was assaulted and robbed."

"Who assaulted you, and what did they take?"

"I don't know who, but they took our advanced guided drone," Don said, emphasizing the name, hoping she would catch on to the terminology.

"Did they want anything else?" Monica worriedly asked.

"Detective, aren't you supposed to be asking me questions?" Don said.

A big smile came over the detective's face. "Doctor Shultz is doing a great job. You must be Don Greenwell. I'm Detective Eddleson. Tell me, Don, how are you feeling this morning? I read the report. You took quite a beating."

"My head is throbbing. I'll be fine in a few days. Thank you for asking," Don said and raised his eyebrows in Monica's direction.

"Last night's report answered most of my questions. I wanted to pick up the surveillance and drone videos you said you had. And is this the box that was delivered?" He pointed to the box by the door.

"Yes, that's it."

"I'll get the evidence boys to come and collect it. And this advanced drone you mentioned, is it here?"

"In the back in pieces."

"Okay, so you retrieved what was stolen?"

"Yes, sir." Don shuffled his feet and swallowed.

"Is there anywhere he that might have left a DNA sample? Anything he touched."

"His bare arm was draped over the drone."

"I'll send someone over. Don't touch it, and we'll need a DNA sample from anyone in the company who might have touched it."

"The videos are on this thumb drive." Chris pulled a small plastic bag from his pocket.

"I didn't catch your name," the detective said, taking the bag.

"My name is Chris Pathan. I installed the security system. There are five videos: two cameras outside, two inside, and the drone footage."

"You're the person who filed the report. Always good to put a face to a name."

"Did they find the robber last night?" Don asked.

"No one was on the golf course. I read the report where you said the video shows where the man let go and fell."

AntiGravity

"Yes, sir."

"I'll go investigate after I watch the video. Thank you." The detective nodded and left.

"So, what happened last night?" Monica demanded. "Why didn't you communicate? I arrived this morning. There is blood outside and on the door handle. When I came in, blood was all over. I called the police, and they said they were aware of the situation, and someone would be dropping by. Then Detective Eddleson shows up and starts asking questions. I don't have a clue. He tells me nothing, and I was worried sick."

"Okay, okay," Don said, holding his hands in surrender. "I'm sorry I wasn't thinking straight last night."

"Let me show you the video highlights." Chris opened his computer.

Don narrated while she peppered him with questions. He explained why they called the AGD an advanced guided drone. "The airport radar had to see the drone. Our secret is out of the bag."

Monica asked, "Do you think the military will confiscate our technology?"

"Yep," Chris said. "It's been nice working with you folks. I'll continue to search for who is trying to hack you. Talk to you later."

Chris left.

Silence filled the room.

Monica said quietly, "What if I had been here instead of you? I don't want to be here alone."

"New procedure. We come and go together," Don said. "We get pepper spray for everyone."

"Good idea." Her phone rang. "Tanya. We have a lot to talk about." She walked to the back of the office.

A few minutes later, she said, "Don, Tanya will be back late this afternoon."

Don went home to lie down.

#

The following day, Isaac rode in with Monica and Tanya.

Don greeted them. "Can you fill me in on what you found out at MoonBeam?"

Tanya pulled out a stack of paper. "Here is a proposal. After they ran the numbers on the fuel reduction, even if Isaac provides the lift and the reduction of one paying passenger, there is no profit."

"How much do they charge for a ticket?" Don asked.

"Two hundred and fifty thousand dollars. The real cost to them has been building a spacecraft and airplane to get into the air. They questioned Isaac's ability to provide consistent lift, flight after flight. For safety, they want to be able to complete a flight without his assistance. In a nutshell, Isaac does not increase profit."

"It makes sense that I won't make a difference."

"When we get our device working, we can do it cheaper," Monica added.

"Did everyone get the notice from the judge informing us to meet with a mediator?"

"Yup." Isaac said.

Tanya and Monica shook their heads.

"Definitely. Anything on materials?" Don asked.

Monica took a deep breath. "I've been looking into ceramics and metals that are lighter and potentially more conductive of Isaac's ability. Now that Isaac is here to work with me…" She smiled at him. "We can get a lot done. I'll transfer a working plan to both of you by tomorrow."

"Tanya, do you have an electronic copy of MoonBeam's proposal?" Don asked.

"I do."

"Great. Let's get to work."

#

Isaac went home to help Sally that afternoon.

Don and Monica were reassembling the AGD after double-checking that all the parts were still intact from the previous night's adventure when Chris buzzed at the door.

"Here is your new decoy computer. Any file you want the world to find, just upload to the documents folder using a thumb drive. I added a honeypot. You need to come up with a new name for the file."

"What's a honeypot?"

"This is the program they think they want. When the hackers decrypt the honeypot and try to open it, it will bring up a ton of charts, graphs, and other gibberish that will take mathematicians days to figure out. While it is open, it invades the kernel and begins to send out the location and specifics of the computer."

"Cool!" Tanya said, beaming at Chris.

Monica added some files on materials that she had ordered but left out information on thulium. Don included numerous documents on drones to lead the hackers astray. Tanya put on the MoonBeam proposal with Isaac providing lift and a bogus spreadsheet of their finances. Chris made sure everything looked realistic, renamed the honeypot "Guidance Specifications," and connected to the network.

#

Two days later, Chris called to let them know he was on his way over. He checked on the decoy computer as soon as he arrived. Everyone stared at him in silence. After a couple of minutes, he said, "Someone has hacked the system. Good thing I disabled the audio and video."

"Do they have the honeypot?" Monica asked.

"Definitely. Now we wait and listen."

"What is going on?" Isaac asked.

Chris filled him in and took Isaac's computer.

AntiGravity

Don's phone rang. He answered and mouthed, "It's Detective Eddleson." A moment later he said, "Yes, Sir. Four o'clock. We'll all be there."

After Don hung up the phone, Chris smiled sheepishly and asked, "Does that include me?"

"I'm afraid so."

#

Tanya, Monica, Don, Isaac, and Chris sat at one end of the conference table. They waited for the detective in nervous silence for fifteen minutes. When he finally came in, he plopped a stack of manila folders on the table and stood, staring at them. "The four of you, now five, have created quite a stir over the last few days. The airport recorded your drone and filed a report. Our policy is to offer a stern warning for the first offense. Consider yourselves warned. Any more drone use around the airport or within the city limits will result in the confiscation of your equipment. Is that clear?"

"Yes, sir," Don said while everyone else nodded.

"After reviewing the videos, I looked for any evidence of the person who fell from your drone. There is none. DHL has no record of delivery of a package to your address two days ago. The assailant was unidentifiable from the videos. The box and hat hid his face most of the time. The assailant does fit the body dimensions of Mr. Pathan." He glared at Chris.

"On first pass, this could all be a hoax except for one thing—your injuries, Mr. Greenwell. I investigated the insurance angle and found only minimal insurance on your business. Just to let you know, I wouldn't sign off on an insurance claim should you file one.

"I did a routine background check on all four of you. Everyone is clean except for Mr. Pathan, whose crimes are classified. Your former boss at the NSA told me to say 'Hello.'"

Chris nodded his head. "He's a great guy."

"Your boss also asked me to let him know if you're involved in any questionable behavior. We agreed that this incident didn't qualify. However, the cybersecurity center has been monitoring the attacks on Adynamia. Someone desperately wants what you have.

"That brings me to the lawsuits filed against you by NASA and Stellar Z, alleging that you stole data from your former employers. The judge told me you're cooperating. Am I missing anything?"

"No, sir," Don said. Tanya and Monica shook their heads.

"Um ... one possible thing," Chris said.

"What's that?" Detective Eddleson leaned forward and placed his fists on the table.

"I set up a decoy computer with a honeypot. The hackers grabbed it last night. When they find the decryption key, which I'm sure they're capable of, we'll know where the cyberattack is coming from."

"What do you mean by a honeypot?"

Chris went over the function of the honeypot.

"Are you taking over their computers?"

"This one does no damage to the hacker's system. The only purpose is to expose the computer it activates on."

"Get me the information on this honeypot, and I'll forward it to cybersecurity."

"Gladly, sir."

Detective Eddleson stood up straight and heaved a big sigh. His eyes darted between them. "I don't know what you're up to, making advanced drones or whatever. I don't want it to be my problem. The four of you are the focus of some powerful entities, both corporate and government. Since I swore to protect the citizens of this city, I will. But all I see is trouble." He put his hands on his hips and let his eyes pierce each one of them. "Keep me informed on anything suspicious. I'll increase patrols by your offices and apartments." He gathered his folders and walked out.

As they got into Don's car, Tanya confronted Chris, "You didn't tell us that you're a criminal."

"I confess. I told Don."

"He did tell me," Don said and got a sheepish look on his face.

"I was a teenage hacker. Nothing major. But enough to put me in jail for a while. The NSA broke me out and gave me a job."

"Pretty cool," Isaac said.

"Compared to you, I'm cold." Chris grinned.

While Don drove back to the office, Monica said, "Guys, I didn't expect all this. I want out. I'm going back to L.A."

"Monica, we need you," Don said.

Tanya took her hand. "Hey, I know this is stressful. Part of my training covered how to handle stress. I'll help you get through this."

"I'll go live with my parents until I find something else."

Chris turned around from the front seat. "You're missing something here. Whoever is after this company will see that you have left. Then you're a weak link, and they will target you. Hang in there until I expose the lion."

"The lion is coming to us. I know it!" Monica exclaimed.

"I'm sleeping on your couch from now on," Tanya said. "You're my best friend, and I won't let anything happen to you."

Isaac spoke as they pulled up to the office. "We are going to influence the future, and I want you here. There is nobody in the world who can do what you do."

"Plus, I like having you around," Don said.

AntiGravity

Chris got out and into his thirty-plus-year-old Honda Prelude. "See y'all at the mediation next week. I'll be prepared if it's Stellar Z hacking us."

Don drove them to get fast food, then back to the apartments.

Chapter 22 – July

Tanya looked stunning in a stylish light brown business suit as she entered the conference room first. Don followed her in. He had dusted off his midnight blue suit and found an old paisley tie to wear. With a spruce green pantsuit and blond hair, Monica could've turned heads anywhere.

Isaac wore a polo shirt and khakis.

Mr. Brooks, the lawyer they had recently hired, entered a few seconds later. Dressed in a charcoal suit that fit too snugly, he sat mid-table.

They took seats at the far end of the massive table circled by several chairs.

Detective Eddleson entered and sat opposite from Mr. Brooks. He plunked down a stack of folders topped with his laptop, which he opened and began to click away.

The NASA lawyers followed Director Anderson in, and they took seats near the door. A minute or so later, a four-person legal contingent representing Stellar Z entered and sat across from the NASA lawyers.

Mr. Draper, the court-appointed mediator, walked in at a fast pace and sat near the detective. A stenographer took a chair next to the wall behind him and adjusted her stenotype machine.

After introductions and opening formalities, the mediator stated, "The essence of this dispute is that both Stellar Z and NASA claim the rights to any technology Adynamia has acquired using proprietary information from the respective companies. Adynamia asserts that they have not developed a technology based on proprietary information from either plaintiff. NASA also alleges that Stellar Z recorded information on one Isaac Thomas during a space flight without authorization. They claim a right to the information collected."

Isaac lifted his hand off the table. "That's me."

Mr. Draper continued, "My objective in this arbitration is to see if we can find a simple way to agree without an extended court battle."

Chris strode into the room in his usual jeans and a rock-band T-shirt; today it was *Born Under a Bad Sign* by Cream.

"Is there any additional information relevant to this case to present?"

"I have something, Your Honor," Chris said, holding up a stack of paper.

"I'm Mr. Draper, the arbitrator. And you are?" He cast a disgusted glare.

"I'm Chris Pathan."

"Now, what's your association with this dispute?"

"Mister Pathan is here at my request," Detective Eddleson said. "He is handling security for Adynamia."

Chris handed a half-inch stack of papers to Adynamia's lawyer. He whispered, "A summary is on the first page."

Mr. Brooks scanned his finger down the first page and stood. "I have evidence of the hacking of Adynamia's computers." He held up the stack of paper held together by a gem clip and read from the top page. "What I would like to submit are trace logs demonstrating that an intensive cyberattack was made on Adynamia by Stellar Z."

A middle-aged man with perfectly groomed hair stood and buttoned his jacket. "I'm Roland Abernathy, representing Stellar Z. This is a preposterous claim that has no bearing on this case. The company we represent would never engage in hacking another company."

Detective Eddleson waved his hand slightly to get attention.

Mr. Draper looked at Roland. "Objection noted." He turned his head. "Do you have something to add, Detective Eddleson?"

"I've been working with the national cybersecurity center here in Albuquerque regarding the attacks on Adynamia. They have evidence that may verify Mr. Pathan's allegation."

"We object, Your Honor. We don't see how this is relevant to this case. We move to dismiss the allegation."

"Noted. Can anyone link the cyberattack on Adynamia to this case?"

Tanya stood. "May I address your question?"

"Please do," Mr. Draper said, holding out an open hand, inviting Tanya to speak.

"The cyberattack by Stellar Z broke into a computer in our office. The information on projects we are currently working on was taken. The real issue is, what did they expect to find? Would it not be the same information they wished to acquire from this lawsuit? I'm sure the expenses of these fine lawyers are greater than a hacking attempt. Thus, if it weren't for the expertise of Chris Pathan, I think Stellar Z would be ending this legal action."

"Unsubstantiated allegations," Roland said.

"From this data breach, does Stellar Z now have the business plans of Adynamia?" Tanya demanded.

Draper held up a finger. "Miss Nash, please keep this meeting a civil discussion."

Tanya sat.

Monica leaned over to her. "You're letting your emotions speak for you. Let me speak next time."

"I would like to put the cybersecurity issue aside for a moment," Draper said. "The dispute revolves around what Mr. Greenwell knew about gravity from working at NASA and then consulting with Doctor Shultz to evaluate the data obtained on a flight of the *Osprey*. Is any proprietary information from these two companies being used at Adynamia in research and development, Mr. Greenwell?"

Mr. Brooks said, "My clients are using only published information in their research and development."

"Mr. Greenwell, you examined the data from the flight of the *Osprey*, and you claim that you have not used any of that information. Is that correct?" Roland asked.

"My client found nothing worthwhile in the assessment of the experimental data," Mr. Brooks said. "All developments are based on previously published research. There was nothing new to be found in the data acquired on the rescue mission."

A Stellar Z lawyer wrote on a legal pad and shared it with Roland.

Director Anderson spoke up. "Since there are no spectacular advances in science from the data collected on the *Osprey*, I request that NASA be allowed to review it. There are some health issues regarding Isaac Thomas that require evaluation. NASA accepts Mr. Greenwell's assessment of nothing new in the data."

"If Stellar Z provides access to the data, NASA can't claim or use anything they find except for items related to the health of Isaac Thomas," Roland said.

Director Anderson looked at the NASA lawyers. A couple of them nodded. "We can agree to that. Upon delivery of the data collected on the *Osprey* rescue flight to NASA, we will drop all claims against Stellar Z. And drop all claims against Adynamia immediately."

The team exchanged surprised glances.

The arbitrator said, "Very good. We are getting somewhere today."

"Thank you all," Director Anderson said as he and the NASA lawyers gathered their things and left the room.

"Now we are down to the claims of Stellar Z."

"If I may," Mr. Brooks said. "What technology do you think is being researched at Adynamia that you are claiming?"

"Any technology related to space flight or gravity."

"Does Stellar Z have ongoing research into gravity?"

"I'm unable to confirm or deny what we are or aren't researching currently," said Roland.

"There *was* no research related to gravity," Monica said emphatically. "Doug Cooper told me to put the equipment onto the *Osprey*, hoping to find some revelation into Isaac and his ability. The mission was never intended to succeed. 'Gather the data on Isaac and come down,' was Cooper's command to Tanya and me. The extra weight almost got everyone killed." She sat forward. "Tanya and Isaac heroically rescued those astronauts. I lost my job over this despite doing everything I could to get Cooper the information he wanted."

"Please, Doctor Shultz," Mr. Draper said. He turned to Roland. "Do you have a response?"

"Until Adynamia reveals what they have, we can't release them from the claim that they're not using Stellar Z's proprietary information."

Mr. Brooks said, "In addition to the alleged cyberattack on Adynamia, there was an attempted robbery and assault last week in which Don Greenwell was seriously injured. We believe the only people who could be behind the attempted robbery is Stellar Z."

Roland jumped to his feet. "The false accusations being thrown at our company have exceeded the ridiculous!"

Mr. Draper held out his hand. "Civil discussion, please." He turned to the other end of the table. "Mr. Brooks, do you have any evidence that points to Stellar Z?"

"From my count, there are fewer than twenty people who know these four people are in Albuquerque: half are family." Mr. Brooks sighed. "On the videotape of the robbery, the man who assaulted Mr. Greenwell said, 'He came to pick up something.'" He pointed his finger to the ceiling and shook it slightly. "Someone told that robber what to take. The lawyers in this room represent the only people in the world who think Adynamia has something of enough value to attempt a robbery and know where they are." He looked at Don. "Am I correct in saying that the advanced guided drone had not been out of the office until the robber took it out?"

"That's correct."

Detective Eddleson, who had been sitting quietly with his arms folded until now, turned his head to look sternly at Chris.

"All suspicion leads to Stellar Z," Mr. Brooks said.

"Or Mr. Pathan," Roland said.

"No way. Not me. I don't do that type of thing," Chris exclaimed, waving his hands.

Roland's eyes focused on Chris. The folds of skin between his eyebrows enlarged. "If you, Mr. Pathan, are in any way, shape, or form part of the attacks on Adynamia and deflecting the blame on my client, we will defend our reputation to the fullest extent the law allows."

Chris leaned hard into the back of his chair, which rolled to the wall. "If you think anything I say is false, then bring it on." He folded his arms as he returned the glare.

"I think we have made some progress today," Mr. Draper said. "Let's take a couple of weeks to review our positions and meet again. Is that acceptable to both parties?"

"We are good with two weeks," Mr. Brooks said.

"We'll be in touch," Roland said.

Draper let out a long sigh. "I'll wait to hear from you before scheduling our next meeting."

Mr. Brooks motioned for his clients to stay. He waited for everyone else to leave. "Mr. Pathan, from now on, please let me know about cyberattacks. I don't want to be surprised."

"Oh, yeah. I'll catch you all later," Chris said before hustling out of the room.

"Detective, did you get the information you needed?"

"Yeah. If Stellar Z is behind the attacks, they're sufficiently compartmentalized that these lawyers don't have a clue."

Mr. Brooks turned his chair to face his clients. "This case seems to be changing quite rapidly with Chris attributing the cyberattacks to Stellar Z. Those lawyers were here to scare you into complying with their demands. They knew nothing about the robbery or cyberattack. I see them as a third method to get their hands on whatever you're developing. If it's something new, let's get to work on patents. If not, then letting them know what you're up to is the best way out."

Tanya, Isaac, Monica, and Don exchanged glances.

Monica spoke up. "We'll get to work on patents."

#

The following day, Monica and Tanya fixed breakfast in Monica's one-bedroom apartment. Don came over, and the three sat down to eat at the small table.

"Let's review what we need to accomplish," Tanya said.

Don said, "I have the remote control calibrated to alter gravity in one-percent increments. The brackets to hold the batteries need to be designed and attached to the frame. Then, I'll add in the fan assembly so we can control movement."

Monica put down her coffee mug. "I've been evaluating materials to see which, if any, are better at reacting to the changes in gravity. I would like to find materials other than silk that don't transmit the changes in gravity. We need insulators around the device. I'll order more ceramic in different sizes to test. Plus, I've ordered about a hundred other exotic materials as decoys and to play around with."

"Sounds good," Tanya said. "I'll continue to work on a control unit that will make the device acceptable to the FCC. The GPS, transponder, reaction wheel, and automatic control backup must be integrated and set up in the remote control. I'm leaving out control motion gyros for now. Financially, we have enough cash for the next couple of months. But we need to start looking for sources of capital."

"We know the device works. What applications are there besides taking a payload to space?" Don asked. "What can we work on to make some investor hand over at least a million bucks?"

"Elevators," Monica said.

"Airplanes and a flying car," Tanya said.

"Or an attachment to helicopters so they don't crash. Something fails, and our device automatically lowers it safely to the ground," Monica added.

"My grandmother could have used one of those, then maybe she wouldn't have broken her hip," Tanya said.

AntiGravity

"That's it!" Don exclaimed. "Rig up a small AGD that prevents people from falling hard. For the elderly who have trouble walking. If they fall, the device can let them down slowly and make it easy to get up. I can set up a trigger that reacts in microseconds."

"You know some crazy people will adapt it to jump off buildings and cliffs," Tanya said.

"A one- or two-meter per second acceleration from altitude will still result in a fatal landing. It would be too expensive to add in variable gravity with altitude control," Don responded.

Monica added, "Not to mention the liability issues."

"Add a timer. The antigravity resets in a minute or so," Tanya suggested.

"Good idea," Don replied.

Isaac entered. "Good morning. What's new?"

Chapter 23 – Late July

Don was conducting a test of the remote controls when Tanya came over and handed him a box with a couple of antennas. "The instrumentation package required by the Federal Aviation Administration is ready to go. Data from the flight is displayed on the tablet in real-time."

"Fantastic!" He took the box and secured it under the two thirty-centimeter fans that would provide thrust and above the hook where a payload would hang. The new version of the AGD looked like a giant two-and-a-half-meter inverted coat hanger. A metal tube across the top contained a two-meter thulium ceramic rod and the mechanism to apply the proper pressure to alter gravity. Two equal-length steel rods connected the bottom hook in a triangle to the ends of the metal tube.

"How will weightless loads react to the directional changes?" Tanya asked.

"That's a concern. If the AGD is moving forward, it should remain steady. Turns are the main concern as a load will swing, and the reaction wheel has trouble reacting to the shifting load." He pulled the five-pound weight attached to the bottom hook by a short chain and let go. The weight swung back and forth, transferred the motion to the AGD, and the wheel took a few seconds to steady the whole thing. "I need to get this into the air to see how the AGD responds to changes in direction and the wind. Isaac held loads for hours in a padded room with no problem. We played around a bit with fans for movement, but there were no external forces."

"Speaking of Isaac, have you seen him today?"

"I'm giving Isaac all the paternity leave possible. He's grown up a lot in the last six months."

"We should let him know about tomorrow's test."

#

The following morning, Don drove Monica and Tanya to the desert while Isaac, Sally, and Emily followed.

Isaac unloaded the AGD.

Don noticed Monica shivering. "Are you okay?"

"The mornings are chilly," Monica said through chattering teeth.

"It will be warm enough soon."

Tanya worked on a tablet. "I'm disabling the transponder for the test, so we don't broadcast our position."

Sally held Emily and watched.

As the sun broke over the distant mountains, Don flew a camera drone around a half-mile circle to look for any other people in the area. He saw six grazing deer and a hawk looking for a morning meal.

Tanya performed a final check of the AGD controls while Monica released the follow-drone and confirmed it was recording a video of their invention.

AntiGravity

"The area is clear," Don said, bringing his camera drone to the ground before retrieving the AGD controls from the back of Tanya's SUV. "Everybody ready?"

"Rrready," Monica chattered with her arms hugging her chest.

"Take it up," Tanya said with confidence.

The sunlight gleamed off the metal as the AGD rose in the air. The small fans turned the AGD left or right, and the thirty-centimeter fans propelled it forward or back with perfection. The small center fan gave it lift, and it rose higher.

For an hour, the device floated over the barren landscape, following Don's commands from the remote controls. The drone stayed ten meters above and behind, recording the flight as Don took it through several movements.

They were all smiles when the AGD returned and sat down softly.

"Isn't this great?" Isaac said to Sally. "Monica and Don figured out how to mechanically turn off gravity."

"I'm amazed at what they are doing," Sally said.

Don changed batteries and attached fifty kilos of weight. As he feared, the load began to swing. The AGD's self-correction mechanisms were not able to keep up. The only way to completely halt the weight undulation was to lower the AGD to the ground.

Isaac walked over. "I never wobbled this much in my tests. The cargo has to be secured tightly to the AGD, not hanging."

"I think you're correct."

"What's left to test?"

"The final test is to power off the controls and let the automatic failsafe bring the AGD and the load back to Earth."

When Tanya flipped the power switch off, the device fell like a rock from thirty meters above to the ground.

"Shit!" she yelled.

"Oh my god," Monica said.

"I think we have a failure in the failsafe," Don said in a calm voice.

Tanya and Monica ran to the crash site, about thirty meters away. Isaac leaped in a single bound. Don followed at a trot.

"Some of the fans broke, but the frame looks undamaged," Tanya said.

Isaac removed the weight, and Don lifted the AGD. "Let's get it back to the lab and figure out what went wrong."

"I got the weights," Isaac said.

#

Isaac knew he had a promise to fulfill with Director Anderson. That evening, he sent a text message, *Don and Monica have developed a null-gravity device. It can't go negative as I can. Monica came up with the material after Don explained how gravity works. They have one device working and are developing an anti-fall belt.*

"How's the AGD coming along?" Chris asked as he walked into the office with his mug of coffee.

Don looked up from his workbench. "We had a shorted wire and crashed the AGD during our test flight. It's back together now."

"I came to tell you that there has been another hack of your computers."

"Stellar Z again?" Monica walked up from the back.

"Nope. The Chinese. They made it look like the North Koreans, but the honeypot is transmitting from an industrial complex near Beijing. Maybe the Koreans did the hacking, but the files were decrypted in China."

"The world is after us now." Isaac pushed himself off the ceiling and came down.

"How would the Chinese know we are here and what we're doing?" Tanya asked.

"Hacking attempts can be monitored. All they did was decipher who was attacked and then formulate their attack. They do this all the time. The bad thing is the NSA is now actively monitoring all traffic on your systems. They know about my honeypot and the Chinese. Another lion exposed to the world."

"Crap." Don hit the bench with his fist. "We don't need any more attention."

"Exactly. That brings me to my next suggestion."

"What's that?" Tanya asked with her hands on her hips.

"Move to a more secure location."

"Where is more secure?" Don asked.

"If you relocate near the air force base, I can route all your network traffic through the NSA cyber defense center."

"Wouldn't that expose us to the government?" Tanya asked.

"They're already watching you," Chris said with a know-it-all grin.

#

Monica banged her phone on the desk. "Hey guys, I just got off the phone with the Colorado School of Mines. Professor Trask wants his hundred grand for the rights to the thulium ceramic before he will make us more rods."

"We have that in the budget. But we need to find funding fast. Especially if we move to a more secure location," Don replied.

"Does the hundred grand include instructions on how to make the ceramic?" Tanya asked.

"Yes," Monica said. "We get full rights to the ceramic, including patents. The setup to make the ceramic will be expensive, and we need a lot more space."

"I agree with Tanya. It's time to focus on funding." Don returned his attention to working on the antifall device. He hoped this would be of interest to an investor.

Tanya went back to calling potential investors for the antifall device.

Isaac headed home to give Sally time to finish the business plan.

AntiGravity

Monica returned to materials research.

Chapter 24 – August

It was a little after five on an afternoon when the air conditioner could barely keep up with the heat outside. Don wiped his brow with a rag. "I think I have something that will work. Who wants to try it out?"

Monica waved her hands in front of her. "I don't think I could make myself fall. Isaac or the astronaut should test it."

Tanya walked over with her hand out. "Isaac's playing dad. Give it to me."

Don handed over a nylon belt. Attached to it was what looked like a small cell phone with a cigar tube on top. "Make sure the metal part is in contact with your skin, and the belt is tight."

"We'll have to make these more comfortable," Tanya said as she tightened the belt and pulled her shirt down to cover it. "So, if I hop off a chair, this will let me down slowly?" She dragged a metal chair into an open space.

"You'll fall at twenty to twenty-five percent of gravity," Don said.

Tanya stepped up on the chair.

"Hold on. I want to video this." Monica adjusted her phone. "Okay, go."

Tanya hopped off the chair and landed on the floor.

"Nothing happened," Monica said.

"It worked perfectly. As soon as I started to descend, I felt light. Two meters per second acceleration was still enough to get me to the ground quickly, but I landed light as a feather. And I'm still light," Tanya said and took a giant hop.

"That's so a person can get up easily after a fall. Press the button on the end to reset to normal gravity," Don instructed.

Tanya hit the reset button. "Back to normal. Now to test it again." She climbed up and jumped off. "This is fun. Let me try with a load in my hands." She picked up a dumbbell and hopped off the chair. "The dumbbell is a lot lighter. The effect will transfer, allowing a person to carry more weight. Another application we can sell."

"The effect may not transfer to something like a bag of groceries. We need to be careful how we pitch this," Monica said.

Tanya stepped onto the chair again. "Come and jump off with me, Monica. I'll hold on tight."

"No, I'm afraid of falling."

"That's the whole idea," Don said. "Put the belt on and try it yourself."

"Not interested." Monica picked up her soda cup and slurped up the last of the Diet Coke from lunch, then she dropped the empty container into the trash. "Ew, we have ants again!" The ants chaotically scurried as her cup landed.

Don picked up the trashcan and looked at the ants feasting on their lunch leftovers. "Anything else to add before I take this to the dumpster?"

Tanya added a few things to the trash.

AntiGravity

"Figure out where we're going to dinner while I'm gone," Don said as he stepped out the door with the trashcan.

Tanya continued to hop off the chair, trying different ways to test the new antifall device.

Monica went to the restroom. When she returned, she took her purse out of the desk drawer and placed it over her shoulder. "I'm craving a taco salad. How does that sound to you?"

Tanya leaped off the chair, touched both toes while coming to the floor at twenty percent gravity, and said, "Wonderful."

The door opened, and Don stumbled into the office.

Two men dressed in black, wearing knit masks and holding guns followed him in. One held the back of Don's collar and shoved his face down on a desk. Don grunted loudly as the remote-control unit skipped off the desk and fell to the floor. "Stay there," the assailant commanded.

Monica let out a piercing scream, backed to the wall, covered her head with her arms, and slid down to a sitting position.

Tanya took a step back into the room with her hands in the air. "Take whatever you want and go."

One said something in a foreign language and pointed at the dumbbells attached with chains to the AGD. The other knelt to disconnect the weights.

The first whipped his head and gun back and forth, watching both Tanya and Don.

Monica cowered next to the desk.

The weights clung to the floor, and each intruder took an end of the AGD on his shoulder. As they hustled to leave, Monica reached over and swatted the switch on the remote control like she was swiping at a fly, and the AGD went weightless. The running steps of the men pushed them up toward the ceiling. The one in front, holding the gun, let go. Without his feet under him, he fell to the floor with a thud. The weapon slid away from him into the far corner.

Don pushed himself up and turned around.

Tanya grabbed the mace on her waist and sprayed the man still hanging from the AGD.

The man on the floor leaped into Don's midsection. The two crashed to the floor in front of Monica.

The hanging man dropped to the floor and covered his eyes with one hand to avoid the mace. He jump-kicked at Tanya and managed to knock the canister from her hand. She quickly leaped back as he charged.

Don struggled with the man on top of him, trying to keep the attacker from getting a firm grasp of his neck. With both hands, Monica grabbed an arm of the intruder and pulled.

Tanya's attacker charged and seized her arm. She performed a falling roll onto her back, catching the charging man with her feet. She threw him over her head, realizing the gravity belt transferred through her hand to her attacker. Thus, the man didn't weigh much, and she launched him toward the back of the room as if he weighed forty pounds. Her attacker let go and flew high in the air to land upside down in a pile of boxes. Tanya grabbed a ten-pound dumbbell, which felt like a two-pound weight, and threw it underhand at the man as he struggled to get up. The total mass of the dumbbell hit him in the chest.

The other intruder managed to jerk his arm out of Monica's hands and again went for Don's throat. Monica frantically rifled through her purse for a can of mace. A second later, she sprayed the face of the masked man on top of Don. The attacker flailed with one hand at Monica and tried to get away. Don held him to let Monica spray.

Tanya retrieved her can of mace while her attacker got to his feet. The man pulled out a thin four-inch blade. From a distance, Tanya sprayed the mace with little effect. The man held his left arm over his eyes and charged. Tanya jumped up and swung her right foot back while her left foot moved forward. The man slashed blindly, cutting Tanya across the shin before she kicked with all her might. Her sneaker-clad right foot connected with the man's chin. She winced as she got a blast of pain from her toe and landed on the other foot.

The attacker crumbled to the ground and grabbed his face. Tanya picked up a dumbbell and smashed the hand holding the knife against the floor. The man screamed. Tanya clouted the dumbbell across the man's jaw. He rolled into a fetal position and moaned.

In her frantic panic, Monica emptied her mace can at the intruder's mask. The attacker coughed violently, yanked his right hand away from Don, and grabbed a knife from his belt. As he brought it forward, Monica kicked out, caught the man's hand, and redirected the thrust that would have gone under Don's ribcage across his stomach. The attacker swiped back across at Monica, cutting a gash in her right knee.

Monica shrieked.

Tanya picked up the cordless drill from the workbench and mashed it into Don's attacker's left shoulder, boring a hole to the bone. The attacker wildly swung with his knife at Tanya. She pulled back. Don grabbed the knife hand with his right fist, keeping the attacker twisted. The attacker tried to stand, and Monica kicked him in the side. Tanya shoved the drill at the moving attacker and ended up drilling into the attacker's eye socket, spewing pieces. The attacker screamed, dropped his knife, and scrambled toward the door.

Tanya gagged at the sight of the eyeball remaining on the drill bit and threw up.

Don moaned as he covered his bloody belly with his hands.

Monica took out her phone and pounded on "emergency."

The attacker in the back of the room held his jaw with one hand, and the other mangled hand pressed to his chest as he followed his friend out the door.

From the speaker on Monica's phone came, "Nine, one, one. What—"

"HELP! HELP! Police! Ambulances! Now!" Monica screamed.

Tanya hobbled over and took the phone from Monica's trembling hands. "Hi, my name is Tanya Nash. Two men attacked us at Adynamia. They have exited the building and are injured. Inside, we have one serious injury and two minor injuries. Both attackers wore ski masks and are dressed in black."

Monica rotated to kneel over Don and cried, "Oh, Don, Don, please don't die." Then she fainted, falling over Don's chest and arms.

#

"Can I see my friends?" Tanya asked the nurse who pushed the curtain aside.

"Let me guess which of the other four people here in the ER are your friends."

"There is one in surgery for an abdominal wound."

Tanya gave an anxious look.

"No vital organs were damaged. He'll be fine."

"How about a blond woman with a gash on her knee?" Tanya asked.

"Treated for shock, a few stitches, and we gave her something to calm her nerves. There is one fellow who will be eating through a straw for a while."

"I broke my toe on his jaw." *And smashed his face with a dumbbell.*

"Ouch. Not your friend?" the nurse asked with a slight smile. "Another came in with an eye injury."

"Seeing what I did to him made me sick"

"If you did that, he'll never be your friend."

Tanya chuckled. "Thank you for everything you have done for us tonight." Tanya slid off the bed, gingerly putting weight on her right foot with her big toe three times larger than usual.

"You're welcome. Monica is resting across the hall. Remember to put ice on that toe when you get home. Change the shin bandage daily and let us know if you notice any infection."

Tanya limped across the hall and slipped between the curtains. "Monica."

"Tanya, have you seen Don? How is he? I'm so worried."

She continued to Monica's bedside. "None of Don's vital organs were damaged. He's in surgery now. How are you?"

"I can't believe I got twelve stitches in my knee. I've never had stitches before. My mom always told everyone I was a big baby when it came to blood and pain."

"And she was right," Tanya quipped.

"I know," she said with a sad face.

"Tanya Nash. May I speak with you?"

Tanya turned toward the voice. "Detective Eddleson, good to see you this evening." She turned back to Monica. "I'm going to talk with the detective. I'll be back soon, and we can go home."

"Don't be long," Monica said with urgency.

"I won't."

The detective led Tanya to a consultation room. "Miss Nash, are you willing to talk to me about today's events?"

What should I not say? He knows a lot already. "I'm willing to talk."

He took a recorder out of his jacket pocket and turned it on. "This is Detective Eddleston with Tanya Nash." He set the recorder down on the table. "Tanya, while the incident at Adynamia is fresh in your mind, I'd like you to tell me what happened."

Tanya took a deep breath and began the story of the two men barging into the building behind Don. *Do I tell him about the antifall device I wore through the whole fight? I still have it on. We've always said to be truthful with the detective.* She reached down and unfastened the belt and laid it on the desk between them and looked him in the eye. "I'm going to trust you with this corporate secret"—she pointed to the belt—"but I won't talk about it." She told her view of the fight, blow by blow, and tried to identify the foreign language they spoke. When she got to where she drilled the attacker's eye, she moved to the trash can, gagged, but held on.

Detective Eddleson turned off the recorder. "Does this belt turn you into a superhero?"

"No." *What can I say.* "It doesn't give me any abilities."

He furrowed his eyebrows and gave Tanya a look showing that he wanted more.

"The belt is important, but I won't explain why."

"Just like the advanced guided drone. Things that are causing me a lot of work."

"We're sorry about that, sir. We don't want to cause problems."

"I know." He sighed and stood. "I'll mention in my report that you were wearing a belt. Nothing more. I will expect a copy of the security footage in the morning."

"Yes, sir."

Isaac arrived and picked up Monica and Tanya. "When you left me the message, I immediately downloaded the video and skimmed it. I'm glad everyone came out alive. One thing I noticed in the video is that you were craving taco salads. I picked up a couple on the way over. They're in the back."

"Thank you. That was very thoughtful. But I don't think that I can eat," Tanya said.

"I feel so bad about Don," Monica said from the back seat.

"When are you going to admit to yourself that you like him?" Tanya asked.

"Never."

Isaac adjusted to look at Monica in the rearview mirror. "Don is a great guy. He would be a super catch."

"I've heard that about men before," Monica said sadly.

"Monica has had poor luck with the guys," Tanya said. "So have I, for that matter."

"There are a few reasons why I'm single," Monica said. "All of them are former boyfriends."

There was an awkward silence for a couple of minutes.

Tanya broke the silence. "Could you determine anything about the two men who attacked us from the video?"

"They wore black pants, T-shirts, and ski masks. One has a broken jaw and hand, and the other is missing an eye. Otherwise, no."

Archie Kregear

Chapter 25 – Mid August

"Monica, Don? I'm here with Chris," Tanya called out as she limped into Don's apartment.

"We're in the bedroom," Monica replied.

Don was lying flat in bed. Monica sat in a chair next to him.

"How're you doing, Don?" Chris asked.

"I've been worse. If I lie still and don't breathe deeply, it doesn't hurt."

"How deep was the cut?"

"The doctor said less than an inch deep but over six inches across my stomach. It's a good thing I have a little fat, or he might have caught an organ."

Tanya moved next to Monica at Don's bedside. "Chris and I were at the office. Detective Eddleson wanted to know how to get the AGD off the ceiling. I turned it off, and the failsafe lowered it to the floor. We now know it will stay weightless for two days and not drain the batteries. The investigators took a lot of photographs of it. The place is a mess."

"I asked Eddleson about the attackers," Chris said, leaning against the doorway. "He wouldn't tell me anything."

"At least the police caught them this time. Maybe they can find out who is behind the attacks," Don said.

"I haven't eaten all day. Have you guys had lunch? I can go get us something," Chris said.

"Monica made me a sandwich."

"All he has in the house is peanut butter and jelly." She rolled her eyes.

"I'm going to get pizza," Chris said as he headed for the door.

Tanya's phone rang. "It's Eddleson," she said before answering. "Good afternoon, detective. What else can I do for you?" She shook her head while listening. "Can you text me the address? Thanks, I'll check it out." She ended the call and put the phone into her pocket. "Detective Eddleson is sending me an address to check out. He said it's a larger space in a secure area."

"We need somewhere where we can't be found." Don tried to sit up, grunted, and lay back down.

"Rest for now and let Monica take care of you. And leave me some pizza," she said as she headed out the door.

The map application on Tanya's phone directed her to a large gate where an armed guard in a US Air Force uniform stepped out and approached her vehicle.

"I'm Tanya Nash. I was given this address as a new office space for our company," she said out the car window.

AntiGravity

Another armed guard with a German shepherd circled her car. Tanya glanced at the mirrors to watch as the dog inspected the vehicle. It had taken her a few months of working at Stellar Z to get used to bomb searches at the gates of their facilities. For her, this was a formality that left her positive about the facility she was entering.

"Please pull through the gate and wait for your escort," the guard said and motioned to the guardhouse.

The solid gate rolled open, giving her a view of the other side.

She pulled through and parked next to a sign that read, "Waiting area." The map application on her phone showed her location near Kirtland Air Force Base. *We're being absorbed into the air force. Chris warned us. Damn, there goes our independence.*

"Ms. Nash."

The voice startled her.

"Yes."

"Please follow me," said a tall, handsome uniformed man with short hair. He got into a cart and sped off; she followed.

They stopped next to a long, corrugated metal building.

"I'm Lieutenant Meyers." He held out his hand, which Tanya shook. "I oversee security for our tenants. A memo came earlier this afternoon saying your business, Adynamia—I hope I said that correctly—needed a secure location. This is what's currently available." He unlocked a metal door and stood back.

"Adynamia is correct. I wasn't told anything about this place," Tanya said and hesitated.

"This facility is for contractors and anyone whom I'm commanded to protect. What your business does or what any of the tenants do is outside of my need to know. If this is suitable, I'm authorized to hand over the keys, and you can come and go as you please."

Tanya swallowed hard. "Thank you." The lights turned on automatically as she limped into the building, avoiding putting weight on her right toe.

The room was rectangular, about fifteen meters wide by twenty-five meters long. A windowed office was walled off in one front corner, and a bathroom was in the other. *The two stories will make antigravity testing a lot easier.*

Lt. Meyers pointed to the back. "The bay door in the back can only be opened from the inside. The walls and ceiling are soundproof to a hundred decibels. The fiber network is by cable only and runs through the cybersecurity facility. You will need to set up access with them."

She scanned the room. *This is what we need right now.* She looked at Meyers. "How much is the rent?"

He stood with his hands behind his back. "That's between you and whoever assigned you to be here."

Who is Detective Eddleson working with? "I'll check with my referral."

Archie Kregear

"If this is suitable, I'll need names of the other Adynamia personnel. We'll make you a temporary badge and provide a key to the door," Lt. Meyers said.

"It may be a week or two before the others come to get their badges. One is laid up right now."

"They can pick up badges upon their first visit."

Tanya limped toward the back. *Do I decide without talking with Don and Monica? I need to know who authorized this and how much it will cost.* She reached the back of the room and turned around. *Monica needs this. We can't remain where we are.* "This space will work. Out of curiosity, are there larger rooms available if we outgrow this one?"

"There is one larger available now. There are a couple of hangers large enough to put a C-130 in, but those are currently occupied. Would you like to see the other available space?"

"This building will be fine." *I can return the badge if Tanya and Don don't approve. Plus, I can quiz Eddleson on who directed us here.* She hobbled toward the door.

"Follow me to my office, and I'll get you a temporary badge."

Chapter 26 – Late August

Over the next few days, Tanya left several messages with Detective Eddleson. It was almost a week since the attack when his assistant called back with a time to meet. By this point, she was irritated about not knowing who the attackers were and who had set them up at the air force base.

Tanya strode into the detective's office, where he sat behind his desk.

"Hello, Commander Nash. Can I get you something to drink? Soda, coffee, tea, water?"

"No, thanks. All I want is to know what's going on."

"Your attackers remain in custody. I refer to them as Assailant one and Ass two."

That got a big smile from Tanya.

"Neither one carried any identification, and neither their fingerprints nor DNA are in any database. Clothing, gloves, and masks are all common retail. Their SUV was stolen from a paring lot L.A. two months ago, and the New Mexico license plates were also stolen. The FBI has taken over the investigation into their identity."

"Who set us up with the facilities at the air force base?"

"I did. The base commander and I served together in the Gulf War. Whatever you're doing at Adynamia is getting a lot of attention. I called in a favor to reduce the resources needed by our understaffed police department. Luckily, he had space available. I hope it suits your needs. It's a win-win situation all around."

"Who's paying the rent?"

"You will be. It's cheaper overall for the base to watch over you than hiring security personnel. The staff already in place at the base will be sufficient to prevent any further physical attempts on acquiring your drones," he said the last word with a skeptical inflection of his voice.

Tanya adjusted her stance and glanced around the room. She returned her attention directly to the detective. "May I speak confidentially?"

"Please do."

"We are concerned that we might be ..." She licked her lips. "What can I say? We fear that the military might absorb us. We don't want to become a government project."

Eddleson folded his hands on the desk. "Adynamia is a four-person company with something that everyone seems to want. Confidentially speaking, you *need* to be part of something bigger. The government or a company where you can be buried under layers of security. Put the word out today and become rich tomorrow."

"We want to do this our way."

The detective scratched the stubble on his jaw. "I understand you want to do this your way. Thus far, the attackers seem only to want to take your drones, and the physical assaults have facilitated the theft. I fear that they may escalate to abductions to get what they want. And, despite my opinion, I want to give you every chance to succeed on your terms. I know too much about what you're doing, mostly speculative knowledge, but this invention is too big. I'll do my best to protect you and the"—he flipped his eyebrows up—"drones. But I need to know anytime you venture outside the base or area where you live. I'll stretch the department resources to provide security. I also asked for housing for the five of you on the base. But when your way ends up with your death, or your invention in the hands of one of our nation's enemies, or one of my men is killed, then I will have regrets. And regrets keep me awake at night."

Tanya felt like the detective had just sat on her chest and slapped her over and over. She took a deep breath. "I appreciate everything you're doing. I need to keep Monica, Don, and Isaac and his family safe. I'll communicate your housing offer to them. I came in here needing better communication. You've cleared things up. I need to know I can trust you."

"You can. But I need to trust *you* and the rest of Adynamia. The technology you have is a way to turn off gravity. Am I right?"

Tanya felt like she was betraying Monica and Don. "Yes. Monica and Don figured out a way to turn off gravity. AGD is an acronym for Antigravity Device."

Eddleson sighed. "Which may be the most significant invention since the atomic bomb. And I'm here responsible for its protection." He sat back in his chair. "How is Don? Is he able to get up and around yet?"

"He's starting to. His stomach muscles will take a while to heal. Monica has been taking good care of him."

"I hope Isaac and his family are settled."

"They are adapting to the area and to being new parents."

"The FBI sent me a notice that he had been under a security watch, which is another drain on the department's resources. How's your toe?"

"Sore. I can't wait to start running again."

"So that you know, I have a couple of officers who work out at the gym when you do. They're on the alert. We're also watching the apartment complex and office."

"Thank you."

"By the way, that was one hell of a fight you put up."

"Thank you, sir." A smile formed on her face.

"Does the belt turn off gravity?"

"It reduces gravity for the person wearing it by eighty percent."

He smiled. "I'll leave that out of my report."

She limped out of his office feeling more scared than when she went in.

#

Monica stepped through the hanging plastic strip doorway of her enclosed work area. "Don, Isaac, here are the latest ceramics for the belts. I'm working out the process to make this in quantity. What I need are an industrial kiln and a walled-off clean room. I have one on order, which will allow me to make rods up to two meters or forty-eight belt ceramics."

Isaac picked one up with his free hand while holding Emily in the other. "I am so amazed by this."

Sally said, "This shows what can be accomplished when great minds work together."

There was a knock at the door. "This is Tanya. All clear."

Monica let her in.

Tanya wiped her forehead. "I met with Eddleson, and he is behind the housing offer. I think we need to move on base. There are some one-bedroom houses available on the base we can rent at a reasonable price. I checked them out. They're old and dated, but we would be in a secure area."

Isaac looked over at Sally to see her reaction, knowing she desired to get a house with the money they had saved. "Maybe as a temporary place while we look for a house, or we could have time to build one."

"For the time being," Monica said, "I think we need to take the housing on the base for our security."

"Until we get some investors on board, we need to save money. So, I'm in," Don added.

Sally took a fussing Emily from Isaac. "As long as the housing is temporary. Isaac and I will have time to look around and find the perfect place. It would also give the business some time to get going, and we wouldn't be putting our money in a house only to have to sell if your company fails." She took an uneasy look at Isaac.

"We're not going to fail," Tanya said. "Actually, we have already succeeded. We just need to begin making money."

The next day, the five and Emily went to check out the housing on the base. Lt. Meyers met them and showed them around.

Sally walked through the small one-bedroom house and looked at the backyard. "Look there, Emily. There are some other children you can play with." She turned to Isaac. "Why are we on a military base?"

"We'll find a perfect home that fulfills all your desires, honey." Isaac wrapped an arm around her waist to reassure her.

Sally's face grew white and stern. "This is like Houston, where we weren't free to move about."

"We can go about our lives. The whole world knew who we were in Houston. Only a few people know who we are in Albuquerque," Isaac said to curtail Sally's emotions.

"Tanya and I will be next door if you need help with anything." Monica smiled. "You're part of the team. The business is not about Isaac's ability. We have a device that can do what he does. It's a world changer. We need to work in a secure place so we can develop it into a profitable business."

"No, it's the same." Sally spoke with force. "In Houston, it was all about exploiting how Isaac works. The risky experiments, test flights, and all the secrets. Here, I'll just be stuck with Emily all the time while you're off flying around."

"We'll tell you everything we are doing and give you a key to the work area. I'll make sure you're involved in the business," Tanya said as if she were in charge. She strode to where Lt. Meyers stood. "We'll take the four houses on this street."

The next day, everyone packed up the old office and moved their stuff to the new building. Don used their AGD to haul items from the office onto a rental truck and then into the new space. They moved the limited furniture from the apartments to the houses on base. Don and Monica put their belongings in the same house. Isaac enjoyed showing how he could move heavy objects with ease. He figured that no one would die if he dropped a stack of boxes or a washing machine.

AntiGravity

Chapter 27 – September

Monica came out of the ceramic lab and removed her lab coat. "It's finished."

"The kiln works?" Don asked.

"I fired it up to two-hundred and fifty degrees Celsius, and it worked perfectly. All the equipment is in place."

"Is the seven-meter square space adequate?"

"As long as I don't have to store much in there. Shuffling the carts around may be a challenge. But since I'll be the only person in there most of the time, I'll keep things in order."

"You always have your things in order." Don thought about how she put clean clothes at one end of her closet and took out what she would wear from the other end.

Monica looked at the mess on the workbench where Don sat. "I don't know how you work in such a mess. It looks like nothing has its place."

"Everything is where I put it last, here on the desk or in the toolbox." He smiled. "They say opposites attract."

"Are you about done for the day? Tanya said dinner is at seven."

Don glanced at his desk and stood. "I can leave this for tomorrow."

While everyone was feeding their faces, Sally, showing a slight sunburn, said, "I made a couple of friends today. We had a picnic with two other women who have children close to Emily's age. The people here are friendly, and there are fewer bugs than in Texas."

"That's great, honey. What do their husbands do?" Isaac said.

"They didn't say, and I didn't ask because I don't know what I could say about what we do."

Tanya said, "If they ask, tell them that we are contractors working on a secret project."

"Tell them that if you told them, you'd have to shoot them," Don said.

"That's not nice," Sally said.

"That's an old joke," Tanya added. "We do need to remember to travel as a group. Ask Lieutenant Meyers or Detective Eddleson to provide security if you need to leave the base."

"I'm the only mother around here who needs an escort to go shopping."

#

Don was showing Isaac the details of how the antigravity device worked. Isaac asked, "Do you remember me saying that I go negative by straightening out the horizontal waves?"

"I remember. Do you have any idea how we can make the AGD go negative?"

"What if we change the ceramic to a circle and add pressure in the middle?"

Don scratched his head. "Interesting idea. What do you think that will do?"

Isaac spread out his hands. "With a rod, the AGD works along a line." He made a circle with his arms. "The circle will work on the entire plane of gravity waves. They come from all directions."

"Let's give it a try." He opened the door to the lab. "Monica."

"What do you want, dear?"

"Isaac has an idea I want to try. Can you make a circular piece of ceramic?"

"I can make almost any shape. Would a diameter of ten centimeters be adequate?"

"Perfect! You're wonderful."

Don and Isaac went to work making the mechanism they would need to apply pressure to a ceramic circle.

#

Three days later, the circular AGD was ready to test. The device looked like a metal cowboy hat. Don applied pressure to bring it weightless. Then he adjusted to add enough pressure in the center of the ceramic to repel gravity at a few percent. The device gradually rose to the ceiling. He reduced the pressure and allowed the new AGD to float down, then Isaac proceeded to connect two kilos of dumbbells to the device.

"Take it up," Isaac said.

The new device carried the weight to the ceiling, where Don let it hover.

Monica clapped and cheered as the device rose.

"How much power is required to keep it in the air?" Isaac asked.

"There is a small amount of power required to apply the pressure. Most of that's mechanical. Once applied, it stays until the force is reversed."

"That makes sense," Isaac said, putting a hand on his head. "I have to maintain the force to negate or reverse gravity. Once the force is applied to the ceramic mechanically, it remains. The natural gravitational force is negated with pressure and reversed because we are working in all directions." A smile spread across his face.

Don brought it down, and Isaac secured it. Then he grabbed Isaac and Monica in a big bear hug. "We did it. We did it."

Monica kissed Don on the cheek.

Tanya walked in. "What are you three doing?"

"Celebrating," Isaac said.

"The new device can go negative." Monica bounded over to hug Tanya.

"Fantastic." Tanya skipped over to take a look at the metal hat.

"So, what's next?" Isaac asked.

"Continue working on patents," Monica said. "I've submitted what I think we have that's patentable. Mr. Brooks is completing the paperwork."

"We need to get to work on presentations," Tanya added. "I've made contact with a couple of investors who want a demonstration of the antifall device."

"I'll help Monica with the patents. How many do we have ready to file?" Don asked.

"I've identified sixteen things we are doing that have no patents. I'm trying to separate them so that the final assembly is not defined. We'll patent the pieces now. When we are ready to go public, we'll submit the whole device."

"Isaac, can you help me with the presentation? I think the two of us should go see the potential investors," Tanya said.

"Sally has the business plan ready to go," Isaac said.

"For the most part, we are doing things that only we can do. The rest is administrative, and I don't want to just dump paperwork on Sally," Monica said.

"I agree." Don pointed to a corner. "Can we turn the office over there into a room for Sally and Emily? We can make a list of what we are doing, and Sally can choose what she wants to help with."

"We need to incorporate her more into the team, same with you." Tanya gestured toward Isaac. "That also means we help Sally with some of the things she's doing, so she has time to work with us."

"Like what?" Isaac raised an inquisitive eyebrow.

"Like cooking, cleaning, shopping, laundry, and watching Emily."

"I already do those things."

Don added, "If the rest of us work together on those tasks, we'll have more time overall."

"I like this," Monica said. "Isaac, call Sally and tell her that Don and I are bringing dinner over tonight. We'll discuss what she can do to help and how we can help her."

#

Daily, Monica continued to make ceramic discs and rods in the kiln.

When he got tired of patent paperwork, Don tested the circular ceramics and found the pressure needed to change graviton waves varied with the size. From the small ones, he could determine the maximum weight an AGD could take weightless. By the end of September, he had enough data to chart out the dimensions of a ceramic needed for any amount of weight.

Chapter 28 – Early October

"Isaac, what are you doing?" Tanya hollered.

"This is my Jetson's car." He landed between her and Monica. "Watch. I can fold it up and carry it." He began to disassemble the car and put it into a duffle bag. "Monica had this stuff that is strong and easy to shape." Isaac held out a thin sheet of foggy plastic toward Tanya.

"3M developed it," Monica said. "I liked the properties, so I bought a test sample for a few bucks. I did some research and found out how to make it. We need a license before we take it out of the room."

"So, you made a car, Isaac."

"Yep. All I needed was some flexible tent poles and a folding metal chair."

From halfway down the room, Don yelled, "I'm working on making an AGD for the car with the disc we used for testing. It will have a one-tenth g max ascent or descend limit."

"Super!"

Isaac bought a cheap battery-powered leaf blower and installed it. By the end of the next day, they had a replica of the Jetson's car. He took it for a spin around the warehouse, testing the AGD, smiling and waving like he was riding an amusement park ride. "Tanya, you're next." Isaac landed near her. "Pull the handle toward you to go up, push away to go down. Left and right moves the rudder. Be careful. It turns slow. The foot pedal operates the blower to move it forward."

Tanya circled the hanger and performed a couple of figure eights. She landed and opened the plastic dome. "This is so much fun! I'd love to fly this around town."

"On a windless day, I think it would work. Maybe we can get clearance to use this during the balloon festival in October," Isaac said enthusiastically.

"Is the license to make the plastic expensive?" Don asked.

Monica said, "A couple thousand."

"Get it," Isaac said, beaming.

"It will be very useful," Don added.

#

On the last day of September, Tanya and Isaac had a meeting with their first potential investor, Augsburger Manufacturing, headquartered in Dallas. Isaac brought his flying car to show off, but only if they had a deal on the antifall belt. He found a used golf club travel bag at Goodwill that held the folded-up car.

Since they had requested ample space for the demonstration, Mr. Augsburger and five others met them at the shipping dock of one of his manufacturing facilities. Tanya did all the talking and performed the demonstration of the antifall belt. They asked if Mr. Augsburger or someone from his staff would like to try it out. A young man wanted to try.

After falling a couple of times, the man did a flip without resetting the belt. He jumped higher than he expected and flipped nearly twice before landing awkwardly. "This thing is amazing."

"This is a medical device to be worn only by people who are at risk should they fall. No healthy person should wear an antifall belt. It ..." Tanya paused as she thought of how she overcame her two attackers because of the belt. "It allows people to do things they're not trained to do."

Mr. Augsburger asked a few questions about the two of them. He seemed to be vastly curious how the two heroes of the rescue from the ISS were together starting a company. After about ten minutes of grilling, he asked Isaac, "Are you going golfing later today?"

"No, sir."

"Do you have something else to show me?"

Tanya stepped forward. "What we are asking for is a million-dollar investment for a ten percent stake in a company we're forming to build and market the antifall belt." She clasped her hands together to keep them from shaking. Tanya had never asked for anything to help her get what she wanted.

"I'll be honest. I'm not interested in the belt. I'm interested in the two of you and how this belt works. What other applications might this technology have? Could I put it on and jump off a building?"

"No, sir. The belt slows gravity but does not stop the accumulated acceleration of the fall. It adds safety for those who have their feet on the ground and reduces the potential injuries in a fall downstairs. We designed it for the elderly and others who are at risk of falling."

"I assume it is not good for rock climbers?"

"Definitely not."

He rubbed his chin for a moment. "There's a lot more potential here than you're telling me and letting me in on. I want all in or not at all."

Tanya glanced at Isaac, who shook his head slightly. "Thank you for your time and consideration, Mr. Augsburger."

"One favor to ask if I might, Isaac." Mr. Augsburger scratched the back of his head. "I've always wanted to see you float in person. Would you be willing to demonstrate your ability?

"I was planning on that if we had a deal."

"So ..." Mr. Augsburger stood and rubbed his chin. "To see you float will cost me a million dollars."

"It will require a partnership. I'm always happy to show off for partners."

"Will I get a hint of other applications to this technology?"

"Yes, sir."

"How many partners does Adynamia have?"

"Five are partners at this time: Doctor Monica Shultz, a materials scientist. Don Greenwell is an electronics engineer. Isaac, his wife, and myself."

"So, nobody with experience in manufacturing or in running a business."

"The money we are asking for will allow us to hire people with that expertise."

Mr. Augsburger motioned to the other five people in the room. They walked to the side of the warehouse and huddled.

Isaac wiped his hands on his pants and whispered, "Do we come down on the price if he says no?"

"We offer him the first option at all other products of the AGD."

"Not ones for space travel."

"Agreed."

The huddle broke, and Mr. Augsburger led his team back to Tanya and Isaac. "Alright. I'm in for a million on the belt, but I want twenty-five percent of the company."

"We'll include only the first option to secure the rights to future applications that are not related to space travel," Tanya replied.

"Do you believe that this technology can be used for space travel?"

"The potential is there. We need to get a simple product out to fund further research."

Mr. Augsburger stared at Tanya and Isaac. He rubbed his hands over his mouth, then licked his lips. "I think it's worth the risk. I agree as long as I get the first look at anything and can have an engineering team evaluate possible products. I will also appoint a business manager and a marketing manager to work with you on the belt. This will give me an inside view of the finances."

"Adynamia will retain all patents and control of the technology. We agree with the rest," Tanya said. She opened a folder and took out some papers. "Here is an additional nondisclosure agreement. This one covers everything Adynamia has now, all future technologies, and products we develop."

Mr. Augsburger handed it to an assistant. "Review and sign."

Isaac opened his golf case and assembled his car. "This is my little toy. It assembles quickly, and I can climb in and pull the cover over my head." He checked the controls and lifted a few feet into the air before circling the loading dock. He landed in front of Mr. Augsburger, pulled back the canopy. "My demonstration of antigravity."

Mr. Augsburger let out a loud laugh. "Oh my god, I never thought I would see a working Jetson car. Wonderful."

"Now the real show," Isaac said. "Tanya will drive."

Tanya stepped in and strapped herself to the chair. She pulled the canopy over her head and flew around in a circle, followed by a figure eight.

"Do you have the ability to turn off gravity like Isaac?"

"No, sir. With a little training, anyone can drive this car."

"You have a flying car."

"This is not a safe vehicle outside of a closed space. There are years of development and testing before we have a real flying car."

"Let me know when you need some cash for this."

Tanya looked him directly in the eye. "Your investment is an important step for Adynamia. What's critical is we keep our technology a secret."

"I understand confidential technology."

Tanya and Isaac looked at each other. Isaac shrugged and nodded. "We are pleased to have a partner," she said.

"Wonderful!" Mr. Augsburger said. "Jeremy Goble, my choice for business manager, will be in touch with you within the week." He strode out as Isaac disassembled his car.

Chapter 29 – AGD-II

Two days later, Don was ready to do an outside test with the new version of the device that could go negative. He began calling it AGD-II. Tanya called Detective Eddleson, who suggested an abandoned ranch south of town as a test site. The next morning, before sunrise, they loaded up and headed out.

Detective Eddleson led them to the ranch nestled in the foothills. He would stay at the turnoff and make sure no one ventured their way.

Isaac took his car up and circled the area looking for anyone who might witness the test. Don also thought that anyone around would be watching Isaac and miss their testing. Tanya set up to monitor the video feed from the follow drone.

They set up a canopy for Sally and Emily, who enjoyed seeing the countryside.

For a couple of hours, they took the device up and down. They tested the maneuverability and then repeated everything with two hundred kilos of weights attached. By ten o'clock, Don and Monica were satisfied. Don raised the AGD II into the air and turned off the controls. The device lowered itself to the ground and landed softly. The five cheered and danced in the morning sun, happy that they had perfected an antigravity device that could transport loads safely. They packed up and met Detective Eddleson on the way out.

"Did you get the results you wanted?" he asked.

"Perfect results," Don replied.

AntiGravity

Chapter 30 – Mid October

Tanya got up from her desk. "Hey, folks, I just got off the phone with Spencer Elliot from MoonBeam. I explained we have an alternate lift option. They're willing to set up a test."

"When and where?" Don asked.

"They will fly in a new test plane two days from now, and we can perform a flight test. This has got to work." Tanya crossed her fingers.

"I believe in this guy and the ceramic." Monica rubbed Don's neck.

"Time to double-check everything," Don said as he patted Monica's hand on his shoulder.

The test plane was designed to train pilots for MoonBeam's excursion craft. It had a large rocket engine and two smaller jet engines on the wings. Don hoped there was sufficient space to install the AGD-II. The company was hoping to make it big in the space tourism industry with flights and an orbiting hotel.

After looking over the plane, they determined the best way to connect the AGD-II was to remove three seats along one side. Don would take the other seat in the cabin. The plan was to use only the jet engines and not fuel the rocket. It took over a day for the MoonBeam machinists to extract the seats and modify the connections to install the AGD-II.

The first flight would confirm the device could take the plane weightless. Don had trouble fitting into a flight suit. Tanya and Monica stuffed him in and got him ready.

The pilots took the plane to twenty thousand feet.

"I'm going to reduce gravity in ten percent increments as planned," Don said.

"Copy that," a pilot said.

"At ninety percent gravity," Don said.

"All normal."

"Going to eighty percent."

A couple of minutes later, the pilot said, "We sense the difference. Proceed to seventy."

Every few minutes, Don reduced gravity on the plane. Each time the pilots checked the plane's reaction.

At twenty percent gravity, the plane acted like it was in a lot of turbulence. "The craft is too light. The air variations are knocking us about."

Don, not used to flying, especially in a plane rocking up and down, adjusted quickly to fifty percent. The aircraft went into a short dive.

"What the hell happened?" the pilot exclaimed.

"I adjusted to fifty percent so you could get control."

"Talk to us. Let us know before you make a change. We're going back. Turn that thing off."

The pilots were angry. Don felt bad for ruining the test.

Tanya came to his defense and addressed the pilots. "He's an engineer and not used to flying. Let's try again tomorrow, and I will control the AGD-II."

"Do you think you'll do better?"

"I designed many of the controls for the AGD-II. Having been an astronaut, a little turbulence does not scare me."

The president of MoonBeam walked over. "Report."

The pilot glared at Don before turning toward his boss. "The device works. It makes the plane lighter. At twenty thousand feet, a light plane encounters too much turbulence to control easily. I suggest forty thousand feet or higher. Plus, we'll have a former astronaut on the AGD-II controls instead of an engineer."

Isaac and Tanya walked Don back to the hanger.

Don said, "I'm sorry. I almost blew it."

"Rookie mistake," Isaac said. "The first time I was weightless, I panicked and fell. My dad was pissed at me for jumping on the bed."

The next day, Don remained on the ground. Monica was happy to have him stay with her instead of having him on the test flight.

MoonBeam planned to take the plane up, achieve a speed of two hundred miles per hour and then reduce the gravity to fifty percent. The pilots could get the feel of the lighter aircraft in denser air. They wanted to gauge the fuel savings as they went up to fifty thousand feet.

The pilots ran through a series of tests, checking on the maneuverability of the lighter craft at high altitudes. The next test was to increase speed to seven hundred miles per hour, where the pilots again checked on how the plane handled. A half hour later, the pilot said, "Everything checks out at high altitude. If we can get clearance, I'd like to go higher, faster, and to zero-g."

Tanya, who had sat nervously in the cabin while the pilots worked, now breathed a sigh of relief. "I'm good for tomorrow. What g do you want to descend at?"

"Keep it at fifty percent until I tell you differently. I do want to be at full gravity to land."

"Copy that."

The next day, they did go higher but did not go much faster as they did not have clearance to break the sound barrier. At eighty thousand feet, they took the plane to zero-g. By design, a plane's wings provide lift against gravity. Without the downward force, the pilots fought to keep the aircraft level.

AntiGravity

Tanya felt the pilots struggle to keep the plane level. The computer controls reacted as if the plane was in free fall.

After landing, the pilots said, "There need to be some design changes to be at zero-g in a plane. The best option is to use the AGD-II to get to altitude then accelerate. The device will be best in a capsule similar to that in which Tanya rescued the astronauts. Wings aren't necessary. Or make a craft specifically designed to fly with the AGD-II."

The CEO of MoonBeam briskly left and boarded his private jet.

Don glanced at Tanya, who shrugged.

Archie Kregear

Chapter 31 – November

Tanya put a bowl of scrambled eggs on the table. "Jeremy Goble from Augsburger Manufacturing will be arriving at nine this morning at the old office to take over the belt assembly and packaging. What do we need to do to get him up and running?"

Don poured five mugs of coffee. "The components for the first one-hundred belts should be ready to pick up. I will take Jeremy by the machine shop, the electronics wholesaler, UPS, where the belts are ready to be picked up, and FedEx has the shipment of sensors. Monica is making the ceramic."

"I have forty-three rods ready to go," Monica said.

Isaac jumped into the conversation. "I thought you said you made a hundred."

"I've made a hundred and ten. Forty-three are flawless." Monica buttered her toast. "I'm working on the process to increase the yield. Most of the rest will probably work, but I don't think we want to take a chance with ceramics that are not perfect."

"Sally, how are you coming with the documentation?" Tanya asked.

"I've finished editing the assembly instructions and test procedures. Today I hope to get to the user manual and warranty. I'll send those to Mr. Brooks for his legal review. He committed to having the patents for the belt back to us today for final approval."

"Last night, I came up with four more patents on materials. A layered plastic we can use to weatherproof our devices and three other materials that will divert attention from the rest. Do you guys have anything else to patent as diversions?" Monica added.

"I'm working on drone controls, but the research is bogging me down," Don said.

Tanya added, "Everything we are using for flight controls is patented. I'll keep looking for new ways to do things."

"I'm watching Emily today to free up Sally and studying. Is grilled cheese okay for lunch?" Isaac said.

#

When Don and Tanya arrived at the old Adynamia facility, Jeremy Goble was standing outside dressed in an expensive suit and holding a computer bag over his shoulder.

"Welcome, Jeremy, I'd like you to meet Don. Don, this is Jeremy."

"Hi, Mr. Greenwell, Ms. Nash." He held out his hand. "I'm Mr. Goble."

"It's a pleasure to meet you, Mr. Goble." Don shook his hand.

"I prefer Tanya," she said, accepting the handshake.

Don opened the door and led them into the empty shop. "This is where we can make the antifall belts. I've ordered enough materials to make one hundred belts as

AntiGravity

a start. Everything is ready to be picked up today. I'll let you take over the entire operation."

Jeremy took a few steps into the empty room. "Did my uncle put up the funds for an empty room? Where is the rest of your facility?"

"We have another secure facility where we work. We moved out of here a few weeks ago."

"I was told to come and oversee the operation of the company. There is nothing to oversee."

Don shot a glance at Tanya.

Tanya picked up his clue, "The plan was to hire someone to run the manufacturing, packaging, and approval process. When your uncle told us you were coming, we decided to let you set up everything. Are you here to take charge or to keep an eye on what we do?"

"I expected a functioning business operation."

Don went off. "The product is ready to be assembled. All we need are tables, a person or two to assemble the belts, and a testing area. We were hoping that Augsburger, being manufacturers, could help with packaging. The belts don't require approval from the FDA or any other agency that I'm aware of. We can research medical marketing companies for distribution but were hoping for some help from the promised marketing person. How much of this do you want to do? And what should we hire out?"

"The belt company needs to be separate from our research and development," Tanya added.

"So, you're looking to me to build this from the ground up?"

"Someone has to do it. After we pick up the materials, we can write a job description to run the company and put it up on recruiting sites. Do you want to be involved in hiring that person?"

"Okay, I get it." Jeremy looked around the room. "I was sent here to make sure that the investment is working to make money. What you expect is for me to make the money."

"The success of the belt company can be all yours," Tanya said. "What do you want on your resume? I oversaw a company that made X millions. Or I started and ran a company that made X millions."

"Started. But I don't own any of it." Jeremy slipped his hands into the pockets of his slacks. "A professor I had said, 'You can watch the horse race, you can own a horse in the race, you can operate the racetrack, or you can own the racetrack. You guys own the racetrack, my uncle has a horse, and you want me to operate the track."

"You got it." Don pointed at Jeremy. "Make sure your uncle's horse wins big, then we all win."

Archie Kregear

Tanya spoke in a reconciling voice, "The rest of us at Adynamia need two things. First, time to research other products. Second, cash flow. Prove yourself worthy with the belts, and then there are other possibilities."

"Okay, I needed to be clear about where you're at. Let's go get the parts." Mr. Goble headed for the door.

Don and Jeremy picked up parts all morning. Don handed over the invoices for the materials that were already paid. Jeremy peppered Don with questions about the suppliers and each part's costs and took notes on the answers. By the time Don carried the last of the parts into the new antifall manufacturing facility, as Jeremy did not want to get his suit dirty, he felt they had a new partner who could handle the belt company. He hadn't expected a Harvard MBA grad right out of school, but Jeremy would get the job done. He messaged Chris to see if he could come over and get Jeremy set up on the network. While they waited for Chris, Don and Jeremy went over what they would need for assembly and test.

"Hey Don," Chris said as he came in. "Is this who I need to get secure?"

"This is Mr. Goble. He will be running the belt company."

"Nice to meet you. I see you have a laptop running Windows. I brought a secure PC."

"This is all I require," Jeremy replied, gesturing to his laptop with an expression that read, "Can't you see, dumbass."

Chris looked at Don. "Um, has Don told you about the cyberattacks?"

"My computer has the latest malware and virus protection."

Don held up his hand toward Chris and addressed Mr. Goble. "Adynamia has been the focus of cyberattacks attempting to acquire our technology and trade secrets. We require the highest level of protection available."

"You don't think my laptop is secure enough?"

"Nope," Chris said matter-of-factly.

"You can keep all of your personal information on your laptop. Anything company-related needs to be on a secure computer," Don said. "Chris, have there been any attacks lately?"

He leaned back on the desk. "Someone is probing. They're leaving the honeypot alone, but they look at the files I change. I'm working on a new honeypot."

"I'm keeping my computer. Just give me internet access." Jeremy folded his arms.

"Maybe we can use it as a picnic basket. Can I add a honeypot?"

"What?"

"When all of your information is stolen, I'll be able to track who took it."

"Nobody is getting into my computer!"

"They may already have. How long has your computer been turned on?"

"About an hour," Don said.

AntiGravity

Chris opened his laptop and began working away. A minute later, he said, "You just received an update to your malware. They're in. Shut everything off."

"What?" Jeremy said.

Chris took Jeremy's laptop and turned it off. Then he pulled out a screwdriver and began to take it apart.

Jeremy stood. "What the hell are you doing?"

"Let him work." Don moved between Jeremy and Chris.

A moment later, Chris held up the battery. "They can't access a dead machine. Unless you want the Chinese and Stellar Z to know everything on this computer, and also the NSA who is monitoring all the cyberattacks on Adynamia, you'll let me secure it."

"Why should I trust you?" Mr. Goble yelled over Don.

"Trust *me*," Don said. "Chris knows what he's doing."

"You didn't tell my uncle about the cyberattacks!"

"I've got them under control. I have some new information for you, Don. I didn't want to mention them in front of Mr. Goble. Remind me to fill everyone in on what I've found."

"Why don't we all get together for dinner. You can tell us all then."

"You buying?" Chris asked.

"New guys pick up the tab."

"What?" Jeremy said.

"Text me when and where. Give me a few hours to transfer everything over and set up the new honeypot." Chris closed his computer and put it and Jeremy's computer into his bag.

"Where are you going with that?"

"I'm taking it to my lab."

"I'm going with my computer."

"Fantastic. I'll fill you in on your new laptop. See you later, Don."

Don made reservations for seven at his favorite Thai restaurant and texted Eddleson that they were going out.

Over dinner, they filled Jeremy in on the cyberattacks, the attempted robberies, and assaults.

Then, Don said, "Chris, you have some new information to tell us."

"Okay, I did some digging into who is behind the cyberattacks. I found out that the shell companies behind Stellar Z are mostly funded by some Chinese organizations. The second attack came from one of these companies. Now that we have a second picnic basket, we can verify who the attackers are. What I need are new fake files for them."

"Alright, everyone works on fake documents tonight," Don said.

"I have an idea," Isaac said with a sly smile on his face. "Don, do you have your old test files on me?"

"I have the nonproprietary ones."

"Great! Chris, don't set things up until I get you some files."

Chapter 32 – Mid-November

"Isaac, did you stay up all night?" Sally asked as she came out of the bedroom.

"I modified some of the test data Don collected on me at NASA. Then I enhanced a design for an electromagnetic antigravity device using some of the superconductor materials Monica ordered. It will keep some folks busy for a while trying to figure out how it works. It utilizes multiple spinning electromagnets with some rare-earth metal ceramics. It may actually work to some extent. It would be hilarious to see the Chinese build it."

"Come help me with breakfast. The others will be here in twenty minutes."

"Be there as soon as I copy some files for Chris."

Monica, Don, and Tanya arrived on time. Isaac excitedly went over his fake design with Don, talking about how cool it was while everyone else sat in sleep-deprived silence.

"What do you think, Don?" Isaac had a gleam in his eye.

"I think you've had too much caffeine," Tanya said.

Don and Tanya headed out to hand off the thumb drives containing some actual documents, many fake files, plus Isaac's design. Then, they swung by the antifall office to see how Jeremy was doing.

Monica and Isaac went to make more ceramics for the antifall belts.

The following two weeks went by quickly. Patents were completed and filed. Jeremy changed the name of the antifall belt to *SafeFall Belt* and filed for a trademark. He hired two people to assemble and test the belts. The first hundred were completed, and Jeremy started to market them.

Sally did a random test of some of the belts. Falling into the foam pit brought back memories of her acrobatic act. She asked to install the apparatus she needed to take up ribbon dancing again.

The materials for constructing a lab area arrived on the base, and the work started. The industrial kiln arrived and was installed in the back part of the building. It was large enough to make a five-meter-long rod of thulium ceramic. Monica was eager to get the kiln up and running. In the meantime, she strove to perfect the procedures for making the perfect rods and discs.

Don worked on the design and electronics for a two-meter disc AGD, the maximum size Monica could make with the current kiln.

The focus for Tanya was getting FCC approval on her flight controls for the AGD. They would need that to test negative g AGDs and go beyond the flight limit for drones.

#

Tanya was on one of her morning runs around the civilian section of the airbase when Lt. Meyers caught up with her.

"Good morning, Commander Nash. How do you like our New Mexico mornings?"

"They're great. I'm not used to running at altitude, and I'm really out of shape," she said, huffing and puffing.

"How's the toe? I assume it is better."

"A little pain, but it is healing nicely. Thanks for asking."

"Meet me tomorrow, and I'll show you the exercise course on the other side of the base. There are twenty stations, and the exercises will work on all your muscles. I'll come by at six-thirty."

"Thanks. I'd like that."

"See you then." He sped up and left her to jog.

Tanya watched him, admiring his lean, solid body as a tingle went through hers. She picked up her pace even though she knew she couldn't catch him.

#

On the seventeenth of November, Mr. Brooks called Tanya.

"Tanya, good morning. I got a call from Stellar Z this morning. They want to meet tomorrow to settle the lawsuit." Tanya's heart fluttered with excitement. "Also, my contacts at the patent office have informed me that Stellar Z has filed a dozen patents on an antigravity device. They're sending me copies. I think we need to review what they have before the meeting." Her heart flutter fell to a stomach turn.

"How about right after lunch? Your office." She wondered what patents Stellar Z had filed.

"Great. See you then."

As soon as she hung up, MoonBeam called. "Tanya, how have you and the folks at Adynamia been?"

"We are all great."

"Say, we have finished evaluating the flights and want to test your invention in an unmanned craft. We can have it there early next week."

Tanya's excitement went back up a notch. She worried about how much time the team would have if they met with Stellar Z. "Can you send me the specifics? I'll run the idea by the team. Will the day after tomorrow be good to get back to you?"

"The sooner, the better. Call me with any questions."

"I will." Her phone beeped with a text from Don. "Talk to you later."

She hung up and read. *I got a call from Chris. He demanded we meet for lunch. I suggested the usual pizza place at noon.*

Tanya rushed to enter in a text. *Mr. Brooks wants to meet after lunch. We'll meet at his office to talk about Stellar Z.*

Don texted again. *Eddleson wants to meet this afternoon. I'll tell him we'll be there at four.*

AntiGravity

Tanya sighed and typed. *I'll forward the schedule to everyone else.*

They got their pizza order in, then Chris leaned in and whispered, "Our new picnic basket was picked clean. Stellar Z and the Chinese both fell for the honeypot. Instead of a broadcast of the location, I used an intermittent signal with a delay. It took a few days, but we've got them."

"How sure are you?" Monica asked.

"Totally sure. I hid the honeypot in Isaac's design. The design is on dozens of computers at Stellar Z, including Cooper's."

"Yeah!" Isaac yelled, thrusting his hands up. This startled Emily, who began to cry. "It's okay, sweetie." He tried to reassure his daughter that everything was fine. Then he turned to the rest. "I waited until now to tell everyone. Director Anderson called and wanted to know if I knew why NASA received requests from China and Stellar Z on how to make the superconducting ceramic I put into the design. More proof that they're crooks."

"Keep your voice down," Tanya commanded. "One of the things Mr. Brooks wanted us to look at after lunch are the patents Stellar Z submitted for an antigravity device. If they're Isaac's fake design, they won't be able to deny that they're behind the cyberattacks."

"The meeting with their lawyers tomorrow should be a lot of fun," Monica said.

"One more thing," Isaac said. "I received an email from Carrie Hounchell at AstroLift. They want to meet with us."

Sally looked puzzled. "They were on the contact list. Didn't they respond to you, Tanya?"

"The response to my initial contact stated that they do not work with former Stellar Z employees or contractors."

"So, it looks like they went around you to Isaac."

"At least they are now talking to us. Blue Origin ignores me, or I have the wrong contact." She slid back from the table to let the waiter set the pizzas down.

#

Mr. Brooks slid a thumb drive across the table. "Here are the electronic copies of the patents Stellar Z filed a couple of days ago. They look rushed. They don't look like what you filed, but they may be what you're working on. They said they will have a proposal for us tomorrow that will end our dispute. We'll meet without the mediator, whom I contacted and promised to forward the minutes. Please, let me do all the talking. I don't want any emotional comments." He raised his eyebrows at the team.

"One thing you should know," Chris said. "I've confirmed a second round of cyberattacks by Stellar Z and the Chinese corporation. I'll have the attacks well documented for the meeting."

"That will provide some leverage," Mr. Brooks replied. "Let me know what you find out on those patents."

They went back to the research facility and loaded up the patents on their computers. A minute later, Isaac shouted, "They patented my design!"

"They were too eager to get the patents first," said Don. "I doubt they even evaluated the design to see if it would work."

"It might get the device to be twenty percent lighter, but it will never get off the ground," Isaac said. He stood and skipped around the room.

"And it would take a reactor to power the thing." Don chuckled and closed his laptop.

Tanya breathed a sigh of relief. Sally left with Emily to put her down for an afternoon nap. Monica checked on the progress of the lab construction. Don hovered over his lab bench.

About an hour later, Monica rubbed Don's neck. "Time to meet with Eddleson."

Detective Eddleson was pacing in the conference room when the four arrived. "Take a seat, folks. I have some things to tell you that can't be mentioned outside of this room."

The team glanced at each other while they took a seat.

The detective stood at the head of the table. "Chris has kept me and the cybersecurity center apprised of his antihacking measures. I've been working with the FBI to monitor Adynamia. First, surveillance of your old office revealed that the facility is being watched. We arrested a woman last night who was buying one of your belts from an employee."

"From Jeremey Goble?" Don asked.

"No. One of the persons who does assembly. Mr. Goble has not been informed at this time. All he probably knows is that he was one person short today. The woman is not talking and did not have any identification."

"Another mystery," Isaac said.

"It is critical that you don't talk to anyone outside of this room about the cyberattacks."

"Including Chris?" Isaac asked.

"Chris and I are in contact, and he has orders not to talk to the four of you."

"Did you know that we are meeting with the lawyers from Stellar Z tomorrow?" Tanya said.

"No. I'll be there."

Isaac spoke up. "One thing that might be important, maybe. We have copies of patents filed by Stellar Z. They're a fake design we planted on the computer they hacked."

"The FBI is aware of the planted design and the filed patents."

AntiGravity

"Yes," Isaac said with a fist pump. "The Chinese requested documentation from NASA on how to make the superconductor I put into the designs."

"That I did *not* know. Where did you get that information?"

"From Director Anderson."

"I'll contact him. Anything else?"

"Did you find out anything about the two guys who attacked us?"

"The FBI took them off my hands. I understand that they have made several suicide attempts. The four of you have kept the department and me busy the last few months. I hope the meetings in the next few days put an end to the conflicts you have. Now, don't even talk with each other about what was said in this room. I'll see you tomorrow." The detective left.

#

It was a cold, snowy day, so Don drove everyone to Mr. Brook's office.

When Mr. Cooper followed Roland and the other Stellar Z lawyers into the conference room, Tanya and Monica looked at each other with eyebrows raised.

Everyone exchanged introductions, then Mr. Brooks began. "Welcome everyone. My clients are eager to hear your offer." He gestured toward Mr. Cooper and the Stellar Z lawyers.

One of the lawyers stood and buttoned his coat. "Stellar Z continues to claim that Monica Shultz and Tanya Nash stole trade secrets. In addition, we allege that Monica Shultz did not return all the documents to Stellar Z. We are willing to drop those charges if Isaac Thomas agrees to make a test flight on an *Osprey*. On the flight, we reserve the right to perform any measurement we determine as relevant."

Isaac started to speak, but Mr. Brooks held out his hand. "Before we can agree to Isaac being a test subject, we insist on complete specifications of the craft and the flight ..." He turned to Tanya. "What is the term for directions?"

"The flight plan and trajectory," Tanya said. "And forgive me for adding, we need to be able to monitor Isaac's health in real time throughout the flight and have the right to end his involvement at any time."

"We'll forward the details," Roland said.

Detective Eddleson opened the door. "Sorry I'm late."

Isaac's eyes lit up.

"Detective, please join us," Mr. Brooks said.

The Stellar Z lawyers glanced at each other.

Mr. Brooks picked up a document. "We also have the allegations of cyberattacks to address. I asked Detective Eddleson to join us and provide an update."

"I hope we are not going to bring up that nonsense again," Roland said.

Chris let out a choking cough.

The detective glanced at his phone and looked at Mr. Cooper and his lawyers. "Before I say anything, I need to respond to a message. I'll be right back."

Archie Kregear

Everyone stared at Eddleson as he left the room. Isaac twirled his thumbs under the table. Monica and Tanya's faces showed satisfying smiles. Mr. Brooks began to tap his fingers in sequence on the table.

Mr. Cooper's phone beeped. He pulled it out of his breast pocket and focused on it. Maybe a minute went by before he stood. "Something has come up. Can we reschedule for a later time?" He moved toward the door, but it opened before he got there.

"Mr. Cooper, please sit down." Detective Eddleson remained in the doorway.

"I have something I need to attend to immediately." Mr. Cooper took a step to go around the detective.

A uniformed officer stood in his way.

With his hand in the way and a stern expression, Eddleson said, "I was not expecting you at today's meeting, Mr. Cooper. But now that you're here, you must stay and hear what I have to say."

"May we have a moment to discuss things?" Mr. Cooper stood tall a few inches from the detective.

"I'm afraid not. Please sit."

The other lawyers looked at their boss with a concerned look.

Isaac started chuckling. Tanya slapped him lightly on the arm. They waited with everyone fidgeting in their own way.

Mr. Cooper straightened his suit jacket and took his time to return to his seat.

Roland spoke up. "Detective Eddleson, I don't think you can hold Mr. Cooper against his will."

The detective moved a step into the room, followed by two men in uniform. "At this moment, the FBI is serving a search warrant on Stellar Z for corporate espionage."

A Stellar Z lawyer stood. "Let me say for the record here, there have been no cyberattacks. You better have solid evidence."

Unable to contain his excitement, Isaac interrupted, "Are the patents Stellar Z recently filed on the useless device I designed enough evidence?"

Eddleson gave Isaac a stern glance. "The FBI has sufficient evidence to get a search warrant on Stellar Z."

Embarrassment rolled over Mr. Cooper's face. He opened his mouth to say something, then stopped.

"Can't speak with a tongue stuck in a honeypot," Chris chuckled.

The lawyer adjusted his coat. "We didn't come here to face outrageous accusations." He stood. The other lawyers gathered their things.

Eddleson said, "Just a minute. The allegations involve the Economic Espionage Act of 1996, which governs the stealing of trade secrets from other corporations. Specifically, the acquisition of trade secrets by hacking a computer at an Adynamia facility. Said computer is the property of an employee of Augsburger Manufacturing."

Roland stared at his boss and sat back in his chair.

Eddleson continued, "What I would also like to know, and it would make my life so much easier, is if you know anything about these three individuals." He pulled out three photographs and placed them on the table.

Mr. Cooper took a glance at the photos, and his eyes returned to stare at the floor.

"There have been two attempted robberies of Adynamia. One assailant is at large, and these two are in custody." He pointed at the photos. "The woman was apprehended attempting to illegally purchase a product of Adynamia. I hope for your sake they're not associated with Stellar Z. But if you have any information on them, please let me know."

"Thank you, detective. Enjoy your evening, folks. We'll be in touch," Roland said as he started to walk out of the room.

Mr. Cooper stood, straightened his suit, and fastened a button.

"Not so fast, Mr. Cooper. There's a warrant for your arrest. I must hold you for the FBI."

Tanya and Monica were clasping hands so tight their knuckles turned white.

"Do you have a copy of the warrant?" Roland demanded.

"It's on the way. As I said, I didn't expect Mr. Cooper at this meeting. Since he's here, I have no choice but to take him into custody. Shall we continue this at the station?" He took a set of handcuffs from one of the officers, and Mr. Cooper cooperated by putting his hands out.

As the cuffs clicked, shut, Mr. Cooper looked down the table and said, "The five of you are in a heap of trouble. I'll bury Adynamia."

The Stellar Z lawyers filed out followed by the two policemen escorting Mr. Cooper.

Isaac jumped up, went weightless, and celebrated by throwing his arms and legs into the air. Chris leaned back in his chair and crossed his arms, radiating satisfaction. Tanya and Monica hugged, and Monica burst into tears. Don snuck down the table to look at the photographs. He wanted to put a face on the persons who had nearly killed him.

Detective Eddleson came back into the room. Everyone quieted down. "The FBI is at Stellar Z right now. Be prepared for when they come to talk to you."

"Thank you for everything," Don said.

Mr. Brooks turned to his clients. "Tomorrow, Stellar Z will be front-page news and Adynamia's name will be mentioned in all the articles. The newshounds will be sniffing about. Are you ready?"

"Shit!" Eddleson said.

Chapter 33 – November

"Here, Isaac, take one of these. It will help with the hangover." Tanya placed a pill next to Isaac's plate.

Isaac had his elbows on the table and held his head with both hands. He opened his eyes to look at the pill. "What is it?"

"Midol. It works great for hangovers."

"Are you sure it won't upset his stomach? He was sick half the night," Sally said.

"If the lightweight can eat some of his pancakes, that will help his stomach, pun intended." Don put the last bite of his breakfast in his mouth.

"Whose idea was it to buy champagne last night?" Sally asked.

"Mine." Monica raised her hand and opened her tired, bloodshot eyes.

On his way from the table to the sink with the dishes, Don's phone rang. He set the plates in the sink and answered his phone. He listened, then said to everyone, "Jeremy says there is a cop car and reporters in front of the old place." Then he tells Jeremy, "We made the news this morning. Tell the reporters you have no comment. Call me when you get inside." He listened. "The police are there to protect you, not arrest you. Right. Call me back."

Isaac's phone rang. "Oh, crud. I can't talk to anyone like this." He picked up the phone. "Yeah, this is Isaac," he said into the phone, then listened for a moment. "Carrie from AstroLift wants to confirm our meeting today," he said to everyone.

Tanya's phone rang. "This is Tanya Nash. I'm glad you called this morning, Mr. Augsburger." She said his name loud enough for everyone to hear and walked toward the front door. "We were told to keep everything confidential. Yes, this is something you should have been informed of." She stepped outside.

Don answered his ringing phone. "Jeremy, let me fill you in on what's happening. Oh, Chris. I was expecting a call from Jeremy."

A phone charging on the desk rang. Sally carried Emily over and answered, "Mother. Everything is just fine. Your granddaughter is safe. I'm safe. Isaac is a little hungover."

Monica began to clear the table. Her phone rang. "Hello, Jeremy. Don took another call. Yes, I can fill you in."

Isaac said, "Let me confirm with everyone on the team for eleven. Just a little under the weather this morning. It was a long night. I'll call you back." Isaac hung up, then picked up the Midol tablet and uttered, "You better work" before throwing the pill to the back of his mouth.

Tanya came back in to see everyone ending their calls nearly at the same time. "My call was from Augsburger. He's pissed that he did not know what was going on."

AntiGravity

"Jeremy said the same thing. He's upset and a little scared."

"Chris said that there was an amateurish attempted break-in last night and some novice hacking attempts."

"AstroLift wants to meet at eleven. Is anyone not able to make that?" Isaac said.

Sally added, "My mother is coming. Her flight lands at five."

Isaac's phone rang. "It's Anderson," he said as he swiped to answer it.

"Good morning, Isaac. I hope I didn't catch you at a bad time."

"Honestly, sir, this is a crazy morning but a good time to talk."

"I have a proposition for you and your team."

"Don, Tanya, Monica, and Sally are all here. May I put you on speaker?"

"Yes, please. This concerns everyone."

"Speaker is on."

Everyone offered their greetings. Director Anderson continued, "What I would like to propose is a working relationship between NASA and Adynamia. I think we can offer a lot of expertise and equipment to test what you have."

"What do you think we have?" Don asked.

"The L.A. *Times* reported that Stellar Z stole plans for an antigravity device from you. If you have one, I think you might want to put it to the test. NASA can help with that."

Isaac chuckled. "Those were fake plans we put on a computer."

Tanya leaned toward the phone. "If we did have a device that could do what Isaac does, how would we benefit by partnering with NASA for the tests?"

"The primary things NASA will provide are equipment and funding."

"We have those. What we need is FCC approval to fly what we have."

"NASA has a long track record with the FCC. We don't need their approval to do testing."

"That sounds like a great possibility. Can you send over a written proposal?" Don asked.

"I'll send it by email within the hour."

"Thank you, sir. We look forward to working with you."

The call ended. Everyone sat in silence, attempting to digest the information from the commotion.

Tanya went to the desk and grabbed a pen and a tablet of paper. "Let's figure out an action plan for today."

They reviewed the proposal from NASA. Everyone liked what they saw but agreed to see what AstroLift wanted to talk about before deciding. A call to Mr. Brooks's office secured his conference room.

Tanya got back to MoonBeam regarding next Tuesday's test. The folks were more than eager to come by. Her MoonBeam contact hinted that they were interested in buying a stake in Adynamia if the test went well. Tanya asked them to email their offer.

"Shouldn't we have a press release or something?" Sally asked.

"Good idea," Don said. "Can you write a draft one we can review?"

"Sure, I'll get it together."

It was about ten when Tanya got a call from Mr. Augsburger. She put him on speaker. "This morning, I met with our legal team. They want to file a joint lawsuit with Adynamia against Stellar Z. We'll ask for one hundred million in damages. Are you willing to go in with us?"

Heads around the room nodded approval.

Tanya said, "We think that's a good idea."

"Great. I'll get the lawyers working on it and get you something to review in a couple of days."

"We approve."

"What else is going on over there?"

"We have been in touch with NASA, AstroLift, and MoonBeam this morning. We are getting a press release together as we speak. The SafeFall Belt will be mentioned prominently as our first product." Tanya motioned to Sally, who smiled, nodded, and returned to typing.

"Listen, I supported Adynamia to get my foot in the door on your technology. I hope you'll honor that verbal agreement."

"We have not forgotten, Mr. Augsburger. You'll be in our plans."

"What are those plans?"

"We have a lot to work out. Would a daily update be adequate?"

"Just don't make any deals unless I approve."

The eyes in the room got wide as saucers and focused on Tanya. She said, "We are pleased to be working with you."

"And get over to help Jeremy. The press is holding him hostage, and my sister has called to chew me out for putting him into such a volatile situation."

"We'll drop by and hand out press releases within the hour, Mr. Augsburger."

"Good to know. I won't take up any more time as it sounds like you're fighting to stay on top of the shit pile coming down on you."

The call ended.

"Oh my god," Monica exclaimed and put her palms to her temples. "There is just too much to deal with right now."

Don put his arm around Monica. "We are all in this together, honey."

Sally handed out copies of the press release. "Mark this up, and I'll get the edits in, then we can print."

Tanya started reading. "Good. You have SafeFall in partnership with Augsburger Manufacturing in the first paragraph."

A few minutes later, Isaac, Tanya, Don, and Monica headed to the old office with a handful of press releases.

AntiGravity

Reporters mobbed Don's SUV when they stopped. Isaac said, "I got this." He took the press releases and launched himself over the SUV away from the building. He landed and began to hand out the release, ignoring questions. Don and Monica went into the building. Tanya strolled over to lean against the door watching the mob around Isaac.

Inside, Jeremy rushed to Don and Monica. "I thought you would never get here. I didn't know what to say. The news and social media are blowing up about you."

"Isaac is out there handing out press releases."

"You guys need a website and social media accounts. I was working on accounts for SafeFall but have not made them public."

"If you're ready, make them public and post the release," Don said.

Monica added, "Go out and talk about SafeFall to the reporters. But don't say anything about the hacking or the AGD."

"AGD?"

"You don't know anything about those, so deflect the questions."

"So, I deflect them to you?"

"No, we have to leave."

"What about questions on hacking?"

"The lawyers insist that you not talk about the hacking."

"Okay." Jeremy took a few deep breaths.

"Bring a box." Don grabbed a packaged SafeFall Belt and thrust it at Jeremy.

Monica and Don led Jeremy out. Jeremy stayed by the door while Tanya joined the other two and walked to the SUV. Isaac continued to hold the reporters' attention.

"I have to go," Isaac yelled and pushed his way through the crowd.

He had almost reached the SUV when Jeremy yelled, "Ladies and gentlemen of the press! I'm here to show you the first product of Adynamia, the SafeFall Belt."

\#

The four entered the conference room at Mr. Brooks's office a few minutes after one. Carrie introduced herself and the other two men representing AstroLift.

"The floor is yours." Mr. Brooks gestured to the folks from AstroLift.

One of the men stood. "A few years ago, Isaac Thomas drew the attention of AstroLift." He nodded toward Isaac. "It seems we missed the opportunity to bring you on board. Now that you have ventured out and possibly have some promising technology, we again would like to bring you, and the rest of your team, into the AstroLift family.

"Pending verification of your technology, we are willing to offer a hundred million for Adynamia."

Monica's jaw dropped. The corners of Isaac's mouth stretched towards his ears. Don's eyes narrowed.

Tanya folded her hands on the table and said, "I don't know if that's enough money."

"If our information is correct, the four of you own all of Adynamia. Twenty-five million each and the opportunity to be part of the most advanced corporation in human history is not enough? What figure do you have in mind?"

"I think we need time to consider the generous offer," Don said.

"Things are happening way too fast," Isaac added.

The other man from AstroLift handed a document to Mr. Brooks. "Here is our offer for your review."

Monica said, "Thank you for coming to meet with us. We are trying to assimilate all that's going on at this time, and this gives us an appealing option." She took Don's hand and squeezed.

"We'll let you have the weekend to evaluate our proposal. I'll contact you on Monday."

They left the room.

"Holy shit!" Don exclaimed.

"Before you get into this, I have one more thing to discuss," Mr. Brooks said. "I'm a patents lawyer. You've buried me in other legal issues. I will continue to handle your patent needs, but I'm unable to take on the rest. Here are some recommendations, all of whom are reputable firms here in Albuquerque."

"Sorry to overwhelm you. But we are a little overwhelmed ourselves," Isaac confessed.

"Wait here, and I'll have some copies of the proposal made." Mr. Brooks stood and left the room.

"Today's Thursday. That gives us three days to figure out what to do," Don said with a big sigh.

On the way home, the four grabbed sandwiches and steaks they could grill for dinner. Lt. Meyers opened the gates for them at the base. He commanded the reporters, who had somehow found out where they lived, to let Don's SUV in and told them they would be arrested if they stepped foot on the base.

"We need a person to do public relations," Tanya said. "I'll call Mr. Augsburger after lunch. Maybe he has someone who can help."

Lt. Meyers drove Sally, Emily, and Isaac to the airport to pick up Sally's mother.

At least a dozen people were videoing when Sally met her. She loved the attention. She told everyone on the plane that Isaac was her son-in-law.

That evening, discussing what to do with the offers became a debate, then arguments. Monica wanted to take the money from AstroLift. Don wanted to keep control of the technology. Tanya insisted they couldn't abandon MoonBeam or Mr.

AntiGravity

Augsburger. Isaac insisted on NASA having access to the technology. Sally and her mother wanted to take the offer from AstroLift and move to California.

By Friday evening, only Sally's mother was talking, mainly to Emily.

Isaac spent Saturday in his Jetson car, drifting around the workshop. Tanya burned off her energy by running the base workout course three times. Monica made ceramic for the SafeFall Belts. Don spent most of the day tinkering at his workbench.

Isaac called them to a meeting at his house on Sunday afternoon. "I've been thinking about a way to please everyone. Here's my plan."

Chapter 34 – November

On Monday, Isaac told AstroLift about the test with MoonBeam on Tuesday. They agreed to be there.

Late in the afternoon, Don stood up in his test area and said, "I've checked and tested the AGD-II for tomorrow's flight. I'm ready."

Tanya said, "AstroLift, NASA, and Mr. Augsburger have all confirmed that they will be there. Lt. Meyers agreed to escort us to the test site. I informed Eddleson of our plans."

Sally added, "I sent a draft of a press release I wrote to Megan Jellestad, our new public relations manager. She is coming with Mr. Augsburger. She will be taking over marketing for the SafeFall business and helping Adynamia with the media."

"Are you ready to present the plan?" Monica yelled up at Isaac, who was floating around in his car.

Isaac had added a tray table to his car, allowing him to work on his laptop while cruising around. "I'm as ready as I'll ever be. Let's load up and go get a good night's rest." He landed and began to take his car apart.

Don drove his SUV into the warehouse, and they loaded the AGD-II.

Tanya threw in her flight suit for a potential photo opportunity.

#

There was a little light on the horizon when Tanya, Monica, and Sally climbed in a Humvee driven by Lt. Meyers. Isaac joined Don in his SUV. Detective Eddleson met them at the gate in a squad car to lead the convoy.

The staff from MoonBeam was at the site when they arrived. Don and their technicians began to install the AGD-II into the test craft, a cone about three meters in diameter standing over two meters high. Eight computer-controlled thruster nozzles were spaced around the exterior for maneuverability. An antenna jutted out of the side opposite the door and extended a meter over the capsule. The cabin's interior was two meters in diameter and one meter high at the center, with plenty of space for the AGD-II. Don supervised the engineers as they bolted it to the floor. Even though it had batteries, they hooked it up to the craft's electrical supply as well.

By the time Don and the MoonBeam engineers finished the installation, three small planes had landed. One from NASA, one displayed Augsburger Manufacturing on the side, and the last contained people from AstroLift.

Isaac put his car together and took off to greet the guests as they deplaned.

Megan introduced herself to Monica and Tanya. Together, they set up a canopy and arranged fruit, pastries, coffee, and tea on a table.

The sun had cleared the horizon and everyone assembled, the craft ready to make its maiden flight.

AntiGravity

Don picked up the remote control and walked in front of the assembled crowd. "Thank you for joining us here to give the antigravity device a test. We call it the AGD. This is the second version, and in previous tests, it has been able to reverse gravity. While I will control the lift with the AGD, MoonBeam will maintain a position overhead using the thrusters. There is little wind this morning, so I think we can go nearly straight up and down." He looked at the MoonBeam engineers who were sitting behind a two-person control station. "Is MoonBeam ready?"

"Whenever you are," said the CEO of MoonBeam.

"Then up we go. Starting at a negative twenty percent gravity."

A distant bird chirped. Nothing moved.

Don fiddled with the controls and looked at MoonBeam with concern. "Did you put any radiation shielding on the craft?"

"Yes, full radiation shielding."

"A technical difficulty has come up. I can't communicate to the AGD through the radiation shielding. We need to set up an antenna."

"How long will that take?" Mr. Augsburger asked.

"At least a day to install and test," Don replied glumly.

"Hold my coffee." Tanya thrust her cup at Monica. She rushed to the SUV and put on her flight suit.

Isaac saw what she was going to try, and he jumped into his car and flew it next to Don. "Ladies and gentlemen, we may have a workaround. In the meantime, does anyone want to take a spin in a Jetson car? It too has an AGD, only smaller." Isaac nudged Don and pointed to the SUV where Tanya was changing.

A NASA astronaut stepped forward.

"Wonderful, we have a volunteer with flight experience. I'm sorry, I can't remember your name." Isaac held out his hand.

"Colonel Kristina Thompson. Thank you, I was going to ask you if I could take your car for a spin."

"A brief pause here, ladies and gentlemen. I need to take a moment to teach an astronaut how to drive," Isaac announced, bringing a few chuckles from the crowd.

Isaac made sure the colonel was strapped in and went over the controls. He emphasized that the AGD was governed to go up to a maximum of ten percent negative or positive gravity and that she would be weightless while riding around. He finished with, "Watch the wind currents. This craft is underpowered. Battery level is on the gauge." He closed the canopy and saluted.

The Jetson car lifted off, and Colonel Thompson made a circle around the crowd, then went up and down a few times. She took the car up to about a hundred feet before cruising down in a figure eight to land where she started.

Don argued with Tanya, who squeezed herself into the craft around the AGD-II. "You can't go up in this. There is too little space. You won't be secured."

"I can control the altitude, the rate of descent, and see out the window," she said to Don, then addressed the engineers. "If MoonBeam would be so kind as to not make any sudden moves on the thrusters, then being weightless is no problem. We brought all these folks here to show off. This is our chance." She reached for the control in Don's hand.

"Be safe." He let go of the controls.

The MoonBeam engineers looked at Tanya.

"Close the door. I'll give you a minute before I take this up."

They ran back to their station as Don backed away. He was stepping toward the crowd when the craft lifted off the ground a few feet and rose at a complete negative g. Within a minute, it was a speck in the sky.

"Ten thousand feet," called out an engineer.

Everyone stood in silence.

The engineer called out the altitude every minute for the next four minutes. "Twenty thousand feet. Correcting for air currents. Thirty thousand feet. The ascent has slowed. Now steady at thirty-five thousand feet. Now descending. Coming down at ten meters per second and increasing slowly. Correction is minimal."

The crowd was silent. Most had binoculars fixed to their eyes and their necks fully back.

"Back to ten thousand feet. Craft is steady at nine thousand feet. Maintaining position."

A full minute passed while the craft sat in the sky. Periodically, thrusters fired to maintain the position overhead.

"Rapid ascent! Fifty, eighty, now over a hundred meters per second." The engineer announced. "Ascent slowing. Up to fifty thousand feet. Maintaining overhead. The ascent has stopped. Craft is beginning to descend. Coming down at thirty meters per second. Twenty thousand feet. Descent is slowing rapidly. Descent halted at seven thousand feet."

There was a collective sigh in the crowd. The craft was easily visible.

"Stationary at seven thousand feet."

"Come on down," Don said to himself.

Monica, who had come over to hold his arm, said, "Yes, come down. I can't take any more of this." She shivered. Don noticed her and reached to put his arm around and squeezed.

The craft descended slowly from seven thousand feet and hovered about a hundred feet off the ground. Tanya waved at the crowd from the window. She let the craft come down to ten feet and ever so slowly land lightly from where it had taken off.

Don and Monica hugged in relief. Isaac sped over to the craft in his car, but the sprinting MoonBeam engineers beat him there. The door opened. Tanya climbed out and removed her helmet.

"The AGD is the bomb," said one of the engineers.
"Did I get to thirty thousand?" Tanya asked.
"You topped out at over fifty-four thousand."
"No way! You've got to put an altimeter in there."
The crowd applauded.

Lt. Meyers chased a reporter down who had run toward Tanya and the craft. Detective Eddleson and three uniformed police warned the other reporters, who somehow had gotten word of the test, to stay back.

Isaac arrived, climbed out of his car, and hugged Tanya. "Perfect test, Tanya. You dropped their jaws."

Monica and Don arrived and joined in the embrace.

"I'm so glad you're safe." Monica sobbed, letting her emotion out.

The four cherished the moment for a few seconds until Don said, "Time for the pitch. Let's go talk to our potential partners."

Isaac got in his car and started back. The fan died, so Don pulled the car to the crowd. Isaac let the car down and said, "The fan batteries need recharging."

After a few minutes of shaking hands and being congratulated by their guests, Isaac called them together. "I hope you have enjoyed our test today. It definitely sent my heart racing. We need to address our plans for the future. There are four companies here with which we have discussed options for our company. What I would like to propose is a plan that hopefully will be acceptable to all of you.

"First, Adynamia will remain in control of our technology. Second, to Augsburger Manufacturing, we offer to come to you first for the manufacturing and marketing of land-based products we develop, like the SafeFall Belt." He nodded at Mr. Augsburger and received a return acknowledgment. Isaac felt relief as the first part of his plan was approved.

"Third, we offer NASA, MoonBeam, and AstroLift the AGD-II for space missions. The investment is ninety million each to be paid over three years. You build the craft and manage the missions, and Adynamia provides the lift."

"What about after three years?" a member of the AstroLift team asked.

"We have a few ideas, but there are so many variables as to what can happen that anything we decide now would probably not be relevant in three years. What I will tentatively commit to is to continue to work with each of you into the future."

Director Anderson spoke first. "NASA can agree to those terms. There are a lot of details to work out, but it is a good plan." He smiled and winked at Isaac.

A representative from AstroLift said, "The terms are acceptable as long as we have access to the AGD when we require."

"The initial investment will give us a chance to build and do some R&D," Isaac said.

"How soon can we get an AGD to install and continue our testing?" asked a man from MoonBeam.

"Don and Monica will have to determine the date. Conservatively, a couple of months to get each of you an AGD to test."

"What about the soonest?"

Isaac paused. "If we can keep Don and Monica focused on building them, maybe a couple of weeks. We need to have contracts drawn up and finalized before delivery. Can we do that in two weeks?"

Mr. Augsburger stepped forward. "May I offer a suggestion. Let us all put our legal teams together in a hotel to hammer out the agreement. I think an independent Adynamia is better for all of us, and what Isaac has proposed will allow for cooperative development of antigravity."

"Having one agreement is a lot easier on us than four," Isaac said.

The observers milled about for a while. Most examined the capsule and the AGD inside.

Isaac noticed Detective Eddleson talking to Carrie from AstroLift. He wandered over. "What did you two think about today's test flight?"

"It's everything I was told it would be," Carrie said.

Isaac scratched his head. "Now I'm curious, who set your expectations?"

"I did." Detective Eddleson shifted his feet. "This is my sister."

"There is some resemblance. Who is older?"

"He is." Carrie nudged Eddleson.

Isaac smiled. "I'm glad to have AstroLift on board as a partner. And your brother is trying to keep us out of trouble, but we still manage to make enough to keep him busy."

"He's told me the stories."

"You now have one of your own to tell after seeing the first official public flight of the AGD."

"I only know of the unofficial flights." The detective said.

"It looks like the others are getting on the plane. I'll talk to you later," she said to her brother. "Incredible technology, Isaac." She turned to leave.

"Have a good flight." Isaac waved and walked toward the canopy.

Isaac met Monica, Don, and Tanya at the refreshments. They each drank water to calm their nerves. Megan asked a few questions about what she saw and said, "I need to pass out the press releases and try to answer questions."

Don said, "Thank you for saving the day, Tanya. You were incredible."

"We're a team. I was just doing my part."

"You guys make me a nervous wreck," Monica said, still shaking.

"Carrie is Detective Eddleson's sister." Isaac picked up a pastry and took a big bite.

The four looked around at each other.

"I think I should go help Megan with questions." Don started toward the reporters.

Monica looked at a plane taking off. "I'll stay here."

"Where's Sally?"

"She went to change Emily," Monica said.

Isaac headed off to find his wife.

"I'm going to change too, but out of my suit." Tanya walked to the SUV.

#

A few minutes later, Tanya was buttoning up her shirt when Lt. Meyers startled her.

"Sorry, Ms. Nash, I wanted to speak to you privately for a moment."

"Lieutenant, what do you want to talk to me about?"

"I watched you climb into that little craft and take off out of sight. My reaction is one I didn't expect and haven't felt for a long time. My heart told me that I care for you. You're an amazing person, and I want to get to know you better."

"Well, Lieutenant Meyers. The first thing to do if you want to get to know me better is tell me your first name."

"David. Call me Dave."

"I'm Tanya." She stepped forward onto her tiptoes and kissed him on the cheek. "The feeling is mutual." She smiled at him.

He grinned from ear to ear.

#

Isaac found Sally. "I can build our dream home."

"Did they all agree?"

"They did."

"You did it. You've sold your ability."

Isaac put his arm around his wife. "We did. But I have this feeling that just repelling gravity is not enough." He picked up his daughter, and they went back to the food.

Monica met them. "Great plan, Isaac. We can build the facility we need. The ventilation in the current lab is not sufficient. And we keep control over the AGD. Thank you."

"No, thank you. You're the one who figured this mystery out. None of this would be possible without you."

"None of this would be possible without any of us." Monica sighed and, for the first time in months, felt at peace.

Chapter 35 – December–January

Isaac picked up the packages containing the presents he had ordered online and headed across the base. Any normal person would not have been able to carry the load, but the only problem for Isaac was keeping it balanced. They fell across the porch as he put them down. He wondered if he had gone overboard on gifts but knew he could pay for everything as long as the contracts were finalized and payment received.

After getting the boxes in the house, he checked on the status of the contract negotiations. The final was in his email. He electronically signed the contracts.

Later that evening, Isaac showed Sally the Adynamia bank account. Each partner deposited their first installment. The balance was ninety million and change. He knew the money wasn't all his, but he felt like he had earned it all.

#

Over the next week, planes arrived from the respective companies to take the completed AGD-IIs. To celebrate, Isaac took everyone, including Dave, Jeremy, and Megan, out to dinner at the best restaurant in Albuquerque.

Megan tapped her knife on her glass. "I think it's time we discuss all of the other offers to buy or license the AGD. Per the orders of the four owners of Adynamia, I've held onto all of the other offers."

"What others do you have?" Don asked.

"The European Union, six countries, and a couple of dozen corporations."

"I had no idea so many had made offers," Sally said.

"To me, the question comes down to, do we sell the use of the AGD to whoever asks? Or do we send the business to our three partners?" Don asked.

"I don't want it to be used for military purposes," Monica said.

"The government will have a say in letting other countries have or use the AGD," Tanya said.

Isaac spoke up. "In thinking through our plan, I considered this question. My thoughts are to offer the AGD on a mission-by-mission basis. If anyone wants to use an AGD, we take their proposal and consider how much money they want to offer. Then, we let our partners know the price and let them bid on the mission. If they don't want the business, we can do it directly but only after our partners are out of the picture."

"Sounds like a good plan," Tanya said.

Megan hesitated a moment. "I'll draft up a statement to inform these other companies that we'll get back to them when we are ready. Everyone agree?"

Heads nodded in approval.

#

AntiGravity

After Christmas, Don walked toward Isaac, who was sitting in his car reading. "Hey Isaac, I've been invited to watch the next test by AstroLift. They placed an AGD in one of the old Cargo Demon spacecrafts and will take it up beyond low Earth orbit after the first of the year."

"That's quick. We only gave them the devices last week."

"They started getting ready after the MoonBeam test. Monica says tests make her too nervous, so she's staying here."

"I'll talk it over with Sally. She's busy designing her dream home with her mother."

"So, is the mother-in-law here to stay?"

"Yep. Sally's dad is closing his architecture business and coming out. I'll put him in charge of designing our new facility if we can find some land."

"Keep me informed on the progress."

"Sally and I are trying to keep up. I need to keep Tanya more involved. She's been spending time with Dave."

"No, I've kept her busy with the control interfaces for a lifter I'm designing."

"Something new?"

"Yes. I'll fill you in on the flight next week. Right now, you get back to studying."

"Great, this biology project is a living hell."

"Yep, that's life."

#

On the flight to California, Don said, "Here is my new idea. The test by AstroLift will prove the device can work. When a craft is in space, it will need only a little adjustment to remain at a stationary altitude. Even a small AGD could provide the alterations to gravity necessary for a module to remain in place. We make a device that will remain attached to a payload, keeping it in space. Objects won't need to obtain orbital velocity. They don't need fuel at all. What we make is a lifter—the Cargo Demon weighs about five thousand kilograms. What I want to make is an AGD to lift fifty thousand kilograms. It takes a payload into space, leaves it there, and returns to do it again. The energy cost is nothing compared to booster rockets."

Isaac turned in his seat to face Don. "I like that. And if someone did want to put something into orbit, the lifter takes it up with a rocket that can accelerate the payload to orbital speed. When I was coming up with the amount we charge these companies to access the AGD, I found that it costs about ten thousand dollars to get one kilogram into space. Fifty thousand kilograms at that rate would cost five hundred million dollars. We are saving everyone tons of money."

"Exactly. And we maintain control of the lifters, charging a fraction of what it would take for anyone else to take something into space."

"Wow." Isaac turned his head and looked up out the airplane window.

Don and Isaac arrived late in the afternoon on the day before the test flight of the Cargo Demon. AstroLift treated them like royalty with a reception dinner party with a view of the Pacific Ocean. Isaac was happy that Sally and her mother had taken him shopping for some new polo shirts and chinos.

At one point, three women approached Isaac and introduced themselves. One asked, "Can you show us how you defy gravity?"

"Not again," he said and went weightless, pulling his feet off the floor while remaining stationary in front of them. At first, they did not notice and looked disappointed.

Another of the women said, "I'm sure you're tired of showing off, but I want to get a picture with you flying." She handed her camera to one of her friends.

Someone accidentally bumped Isaac from behind, which sent him awkwardly into the woman, spilling her drink.

Isaac turned a shade of red. "Oh, I'm so sorry. It is impossible to control myself when weightless." He dropped to the floor.

Of course, the incident was caught on video, and lucky for Isaac, the nudge was easy to see.

To make up for spilling the woman's drink, he held her hand, took her weightless, and posed for photos. The line formed; everyone wanted a picture of themselves hanging in the air with Isaac. He became the life of the party.

Don assisted by making sure that whoever Isaac took weightless landed on their feet.

By the time everyone had a photo to cherish, Isaac and Don were exhausted by the social interaction. They returned to their two-bedroom suite in the hotel and went to bed without talking.

#

The test by AstroLift was to take the Cargo Demon to an altitude of 2500 kilometers, just beyond low Earth orbit. This mission would be different from all other space missions, as the craft was to go straight up and down. The issue to solve was the trajectory without horizontal momentum and to avoid all the satellites and space junk. One goal was to minimalize the use of the Demon's thrusters.

The computers aboard the craft controlled the entire flight. It lifted straight into the air. Isaac and Don watched monitors as the spacecraft rose to 2500 kilometers above the earth. It hovered there, maintaining the horizontal speed at takeoff, approximately 1200 km/hour, while the earth rotated below it.

"Now we wait until tomorrow afternoon," an engineer said. "We have to let the earth come around so we can land where we started."

Isaac thought for a moment. "That makes sense. But why couldn't you give it enough momentum to remain over where it took off?"

"We could. But this is what we wanted to test, a flight completely without thrusters."

AntiGravity

"That's incredible," Don said.

"Well, Don, since we have all day, why don't we take a drive along the coast? I haven't seen much of the ocean."

"Good idea."

\#

The following day Don and Isaac arrived at the launch site. The monitors showed a video feed from the Cargo Demon of the earth slowly rotating.

"Descent beginning," an engineer said.

A few minutes later, the Cargo Demon came into view. The horizontal thrusters fired to adjust its position directly over the launch pad. It landed like a feather to the applause of everyone at AstroLift.

Isaac was surprised by all the handshakes, offers of congratulations, and praise. As they walked back to the car, he said, "Game changed."

Don replied, "We've given the world new rules to play by. It scares me with what's next."

\#

Spencer Elliot of MoonBeam invited the team to their test in Utah a week later. Don and Isaac declined, claiming that they were too busy. Isaac didn't want to be a photo opportunity again. Thus, Tanya went alone to represent Adynamia. The craft she had taken up two months previously was going to attempt to replicate what AstroLift had done.

The launch went smoothly. Tanya spent the day meeting with the press and folks from MoonBeam.

The next afternoon, she was at the landing site, watching the monitors from behind the engineers until the craft could be seen with her eyes.

The craft got larger quicker than she thought it should. She said in a low voice, "It's coming in too fast." Her voice got louder. "Slow down. It's off-target. Oh my god!"

The spacecraft crashed on a hill a few hundred meters on the other side of the landing pad.

She held her hands over her mouth, envisioning the handful of people who were moments earlier standing and watching the landing where the craft crashed in a ball of fire. "What happened?"

The MoonBeam engineer said, "I don't know. It could be any number of failures. The craft was slowing, but—it didn't."

Tanya watched the chaos as people and emergency personnel rushed to the crash scene. Her instruction as an astronaut went over accidents and how to handle them. Every mission had a multitude of things that had to go right to succeed. One failure usually meant disaster.

A reporter asked, "Did the antigravity device from Adynamia fail?" before sticking a microphone into her face.

She shook her head a bit to bring herself out of the shock. She looked at the reporter and camera over his shoulder. "I have no idea what might have gone wrong."

"Could a failure of Adynamia's device cause such an accident?" the reporter asked.

Tanya felt cornered by the question. *How should I answer? I should walk away. Anything I say might be used against us.* She took a deep breath. "A couple of months ago, I piloted that very spacecraft over sixteen kilometers above the earth and came back safely. I trusted MoonBeam's craft and Adynamia's technology with my life. To see it crash today is a shock."

"Would you have gone up in that craft for this test?"

Tanya paused. "I'm sorry. I don't want to answer any more questions." She walked away from the reporter, who pursued her to her car. After getting in, she went to the airport to wait for her flight.

AntiGravity

Chapter 36 – February

"Monica, have you heard from Tanya?" Isaac asked as he entered the lab.

"She's on a plane. Meyers will pick her up."

"What do you think happened?"

"The ceramic was perfect. Nothing I did. Don is worried sick."

"I'll go talk to him. I don't think the AGD is responsible. There's nothing you could have done differently."

"I could have not come up with the idea." Her voice cracked.

"It's the greatest thing for the human race since fire."

"And look at how many people got burned by that," she said harshly.

"No, that's not what I meant." Isaac shuffled his feet and rubbed his hands on his shirt.

"I'm not in the mood to talk about the crash. I'm sorry I said that. Go talk to Don or get in your car and fly around."

Isaac's head dropped, and he walked away. "I'm sorry. You and Don are the smartest people I know. I—"

"You want the problem to go away like I do. I can't solve it," Monica said.

"Neither can I." Isaac stepped toward the lab door, but Monica caught up and hugged him. Isaac awkwardly hugged her back.

They held each other for a moment.

"Thanks," she said. "That's what I needed."

He blinked back his tears and sniffled. "Maybe that's what I needed too."

Isaac found Don at his house. "What do you know?"

"Not a damned thing. I've replayed the video, hoping to get a clue. The craft came down too fast and in the wrong place. The National Transportation Safety Board called and wanted the specifications on the AGD."

"What are you going to tell them?"

"I was just writing up the inputs and where to look for breaks."

"They're going to take the AGD apart."

"Probably. For now, all tests of the AGD are on hold."

"What do you think we should do?"

"Cooperate and rethink the design of the AGD. I can't see how this is our fault unless the ceramic broke at the last minute of the flight. What I need is some space to think."

"I'll leave you alone." Isaac walked home and spent the evening with Emily and Sally. His mother-in-law agitated him almost to the point where he was ready to go outside and fly to the moon. Luckily, Emily smiled at him. He gathered his daughter in his arms and walked around the yard.

#

Three agonizing days later, the National Transportation Safety Board got back in touch with Don. "Mr. Greenwell, using the specifications you gave us for operating the antigravity device, we hooked up some controls. When we increased the power, as you documented, the device became lighter. The problem came when we applied the power to make the device go negative."

"What happened?" Don said, thinking that the mechanism to apply horizontal pressure to the ceramic had failed.

"The device rose and pulled the controls away from the operator. We can't get it off the ceiling of the hanger."

The weight of knowing that the AGD worked ideally lifted Don like he had gone weightless. "That sounds like the antigravity device is working perfectly," he said with confidence.

"How do we get it down?"

Don began laughing. "It's mechanical. If you can get ahold of the controls, change the negative g dial to zero and the anti-g dial to ninety-nine. It will lower at an acceleration rate of about one-tenth of a meter per second. Let it hit the floor and move everything to zero."

"I was hoping there was an easier way. Your device is at the ceiling over the rest of the wreckage. Getting up there is the problem, and we can't work under it."

"The lift is mechanical, and it will stay there. If you would like, I'll send Isaac Thomas over to bring it down."

"For safety reasons, we are stopping work in the hanger until the device is neutralized."

"I'll have Isaac catch a flight in the morning. One question. Have you looked at the control software?"

"The software controlling the craft was acquired from AstroLift. After their successful test, we don't think it was the problem."

"I'll have Isaac call you with his travel plans."

The first thing Don did was call AstroLift to get a copy of the control software. Then he called Isaac and got Sally on the line. "Tell Isaac to catch the next flight to Utah. The NTSB needs him."

He called Chris and got voicemail. "Chris, I'm sending you the software that was controlling the MoonBeam spacecraft that crashed. Tell me what you can figure out."

#

Don brought Monica lunch and was laying it out on a desk when Isaac called. "Isaac, did you get the device down?" He put his phone on speaker so Monica could listen in.

"They wouldn't let me use my car, so I had to use my abilities to get the AGD. It's working fine."

"What do you mean they wouldn't let you use your car?" Monica asked.

AntiGravity

"Hey, Monica," Isaac said. "All AGDs are grounded until they figure out what caused the crash. That includes the car. I've been in discussion with them about the SafeFall Belt. They want to halt that as well."

"Any hints on how the investigation is going?" Don asked.

"They're sorting out the parts. The person I talked to thinks it will be a few months before they know why the craft crashed. They were a little pissed when I started looking around."

"Come back home. Nothing else you can do there," Don said.

"I'll head to the airport in a few minutes. See you tonight."

#

Chris called Don late that afternoon. "Don, come over to my office as soon as you can. I have something you might like to see."

Monica messaged Tanya to see if she would like to join them at Chris's office.

Tanya had stayed at Dave's place since she had returned from Utah. She agreed with Monica that she needed to get out. She arrived with Dave, and the four went to see Chris.

Chris ushered them into his back room, which looked like it was also his home. There was a cot in one corner with a sleeping bag, a pile of dirty clothes, and a few T-shirts hanging on a rod near the bed. The rest of the room was filled with computers and computer parts. A large flat-screened TV was on one wall opposite a lounge chair. "Excuse the mess. Pay attention to the screen. First, I'll show you the landing of the AstroLift test." He played it in fast motion. "I sped it up to get to the good part; it lands. Next is the landing and crash of the MoonBeam craft."

Tanya buried her face in Dave's shoulder.

"Now, I'm going to show both overlaid together." The video showed the two craft dropping from space at the same rate until the MoonBeam craft crashed. The AstroLift craft went on to land. "Did you see that? Exactly the same until the crash.

"I got a friend to integrate the control software in his trajectory simulation programs. If I change the landing of the MoonBeam crash to California, it lands perfectly." He let the simulation play out on the screen. "Next, I'll show the AstroLift craft attempting to land in Utah." The Cargo Dragon descended and crashed at the same place as the MoonBeam craft.

"I don't get it," Monica said.

Tanya stepped toward Chris. "This makes total sense. Can this program land either craft right here?" She pointed to the floor.

"Sure. I just change the longitude and latitude of the landing site and rerun the landing."

They watched each craft crash a few hundred yards away from Chris' office.

"Now try ..." Tanya thought about where to land. "Central Park in New York."

Chris entered the coordinates. The simulation landed both craft perfectly.

"What the hell?" Don asked.

"The software does not take into account the altitude of the landing site. AstroLift wrote it to land at their site on the California coast."

Dave said, "This is fucked up, but who is to blame?"

"Definitely not us," Don said.

Monica grabbed Don. "I was so worried that we screwed up somehow."

"I knew we didn't fail, honey. We're all right."

"Six people lost their lives because of some stupid software," Tanya bellowed.

Meyers put his arms around Tanya. "Watching people die is never easy. We'll get through this together."

Chris turned off the TV. "I thought everyone would be excited to see this."

Don said, "This is what we needed. Now we can begin to heal. Thanks, Chris."

"This group always has the most interesting problems. I'll send you my bill."

Don smiled. "You haven't sent the last one."

"I need to hire an accountant to bill my clients but don't have enough money," Chris quipped.

They all chuckled for a moment.

Don asked, "By any chance did you record the simulations you just showed us?"

"No, but I can rerun them."

"Let's do. Tanya, do you want to narrate?"

She wiped a tear from each of her eyes. "Yes, I'd like to."

That evening, Don uploaded the video and sent a message to their partners and the NTSB: *We ran some simulations of the tragic test mission. The linked video is the result.*

#

Director Anderson called Don as he was eating lunch. "After reviewing the video, your explanation fits the information we know. AstroLift has agreed to forward the software."

"Thank you. Let us know what you find out."

A few minutes later, Carrie called Isaac. "Mr. Thomas. Thank you for confirming that the software AstroLift offered to MoonBeam works as designed to land a capsule at sea level. We appreciate your contribution to the investigation. We'll be in touch."

"One more thing Carrie." Isaac paused wondering how to word what he wanted to say. "How much information did your brother tell you about Adynamia?"

"Not much."

"When did he first mention us?"

"He never did mention your company. And I don't remember when he first complained about having to watch over a technology company that was a target of espionage. He did mention that he took the head of Stellar Z into custody. We appreciate the elimination of that competitor."

"You're welcome." Isaac hung up. *I knew Eddleson told his sister things. AstroLift was in the know all along.*

\#

During the weeks after the crash, Isaac had more time to study and be with Sally and Emily. Together they were able to work through the design of the house she wanted. Her initial design added a bedroom and living area for her parents. He was able to get her to agree to build an entire house next to theirs. Sally's mother also wanted their home to be attached, but Isaac was able to convince Victor that owning a separate house would be better. Sally's spirits rose now that she got to plan the home of her dreams and have a place for Emily. Isaac did not want a lot of material things in the house except a few grownup toys, and for the rest he gave in to his wife's design.

\#

The down days allowed Tanya to search for a location where they could build a facility for Adynamia. She located a site east of town and the team put in a bid for the land. It would be a few months before the deal was closed and construction could begin. Working with Victor, she drew out the initial plans for the new research facility and a cul-de-sac for eight half-acre homesites. She drew in one for Don and Monica, one for her and Dave, a place for Sally and Isaac, and a separate house for Victor and Mary. The others could be used by Megan, Jeremy, and others as the team expanded.

\#

Isaac was in his car studying when Megan called. "The NTSB will release their report on the MoonBeam crash Friday."

"That's tomorrow. Super! Record time for them."

"I think NASA and everyone else pushed them to wrap things up."

"One more day to wait instead of months or years is great. I'm worried about what they will say about the SafeFall Belt," Isaac said.

"I'm confident they found out it works. I tested it out myself, it's amazing. I need to call the others." Meghan hung up.

The ability to set a cellphone to be silent until a certain time was one that Megan appreciated, at least until eight on a Saturday morning when her phone startled her. *Three incoming calls and thirteen voicemails.* She blinked and answered a call. Unfortunately, it was a video call.

"Good morning. I'm Paul Osterman of Saturn Ventures. We want to partner with Adynamia. Did I catch you at a bad time?"

"Sorry, I wasn't expecting a video call. May I call you back in an hour?"

"Please."

Megan decided to let the other calls go to voice mail and get ready. Her weekend would be busy.

By five that afternoon, she had talked to four corporate CEOs, representatives from six countries, fifteen reporters, and one of New Mexico's senators. Her stomach growled from the two pots of coffee with nothing to eat. Her message to everyone was the same. Adynamia has partners who can be contacted and will offer to lift payloads into space. There are no plans to sell AGDs directly. Orders for SafeFall Belts can be entered on the web page. We have no need for venture capital. The schedule for testing is currently unknown; contact our partners: NASA, AstroLift, and MoonBeam.

She reviewed the notes typed into her computer. The urgent items included Saturn Ventures, which was adamant about partnering with Adynamia; the Chinese Space Program; and the senator, who had implied that the lack of regulation was a national problem. In a rush she wrote up a summary of whom she had talked to and emailed it to the five principles of Adynamia.

#

On Monday, AstroLift announced their next test flight, past the moon and back. It was a month away, but the excitement of testing returned to the team.

The AGD designed to keep a satellite at a stable orbit was nearly ready. Don reviewed the specifications, explained to Monica what he needed from the ceramic, and emailed Director Anderson at NASA. The test he wanted was to send up a payload and let the new AGD stabilize it for at least a week before bringing it back down.

Tanya and Isaac called Paul Osterman of Saturn Ventures back. He said, "I'm willing to offer double what the partners paid. That's sixty million dollars immediately in your account."

"We need time to evaluate how it would fit into our overall plan," Isaac said. "We did not want to set up a lot of competitors for taking payloads into space."

"With three, they can still set their prices high. You're limiting competition. I don't want to have to force you to make this available through legal action or legislation."

"As Isaac said, our plan is in place, and we are acting on it as fast as we can. Another partner at this point won't necessarily be better for us."

"It's a death sentence for Saturn Ventures," Osterman said as he hung up.

"What a jerk," Tanya said.

"Type-A personality with a capital 'A' and asss whole lot more," Isaac said.

AntiGravity

Chapter 37 – Early March

Isaac returned home from a morning midterm where Lt. Meyers and another soldier sat nearby while he took the test. He didn't feel as prepared as he had hoped and was frustrated. He couldn't fail a class in his last semester.

He gobbled down lunch, then Sally asked, "We're almost out of diapers and rash cream. Can you run to the store?"

"No problem." He put on his coat, grabbed the car keys, and left.

At the gate, a new guard stopped him. "I'm sorry, sir. There are no escorts available."

"I need to get to the store." He pounded the steering wheel.

"I'll call you when an escort is available."

Isaac turned the car around and headed home. He looked at the fence, thought about going over it, and remembered a closed gate at the north end of the compound. He drove to the gate and took the car up and over, landing on the other side, then went to the store to get what his daughter needed.

With a couple of bags, he fumbled for his keys, opened the door, and shoved his packages in the back. He felt a prick on his neck and reached up to swat at whatever was there. He felt a hand and turned to stare at himself in a pair of reflective sunglasses. "Hello?"

"Are you the man who can turn off gravity?"

Hands grabbed his arms. He struggled to get away. He became dizzy; his vision blurred. He thought about going weightless, but everything went blank.

#

Don picked up his phone.

"Have you seen Isaac?" Sally asked, panic filling her voice.

"Not since this morning," he replied. "When was the last time you saw him?"

"Just after lunch. He went to get groceries."

"It's now after five. You're right. He should be home by now. I'll be over in a few minutes." He ended the call and started for the door. "Monica, Isaac is late from a shopping trip. I'm going to keep Sally company!" he yelled across the warehouse.

"I'm coming too." Monica put on her coat and ran to catch up.

Don called Tanya. "Isaac is late, and Sally is worried. We're heading to Isaac's place."

"I'll meet you there," Tanya replied.

As they entered her home, Sally said, "He's not answering his phone. He left four hours ago. Where could he be?"

Tanya took out her phone. "I'm going to call Dave. He always has someone accompany us into town."

Don and Monica played with Emily while Sally paced.

"Crap," Tanya said. "Dave was not aware that Isaac was outside the base. The guard stationed near the gate said he denied Isaac leaving the base. He'd left a message around two when escorts were available. I'll check with Eddleson."

A moment later, Tanya said, "No one has information on Isaac leaving the base."

Don sighed. "You and I should go look for him. Monica, can you stay here?"

"Yes, no problem."

Dave intercepted Don and Tanya at the gate to the airbase. "Get in. I'll drive you around."

Tanya's phone rang. "Yes, detective. You found Isaac's car. But not Isaac. We'll be at the store in a few minutes."

A police car with two uniformed officers stood next to Isaac's car in the grocery store parking lot. Detective Eddleson drove up as they got out of their vehicle.

One of the officers told the detective, "The vehicle is locked. The phone is on the front seat, and groceries are in the back."

Eddleson said, "Search around the vehicle. We'll check the store."

Ten minutes or so later, they regrouped at Isaac's car.

The officer said, "The only thing we found is a cap to a hypodermic needle."

Eddleson put on gloves and retrieved an evidence bag from his car. He took a few photos of the location before bagging the cap and holding it up. "Could be nothing or something."

"He knew he shouldn't be out alone," Tanya exclaimed. "He thinks he's invincible."

"Sometimes he's a little absentminded," Don said.

"Get the vehicle towed to the lab," Eddleson said to an officer. Then he addressed Don and Tanya. "I'll file a missing person report. We'll get everyone looking for him. There is nothing you can do. Go home and stay with his wife. I'll let you know as soon as I hear anything."

Don looked into the back seat. "We should get some diapers and anything else Sally might need before we head back."

The night was a long one. Sally finally fell asleep with Emily. Don dozed on the couch while the others tried to get some sleep.

Victor and Mary drove around town, hoping to spot Isaac.

The following day, they were sipping on their second or third cup of coffee when Tanya's phone rang. "Yes, detective. No sign? Okay. We'll stay put."

Tanya hung up. "The lab got nothing off the cap. They need to run further tests, but they're now calling this an abduction. The lot security camera was too dirty to see anything. Cameras inside showed Isaac buying diapers and the other stuff in his car. Eddleson called in the FBI."

AntiGravity

Sally burst into tears, which upset Emily. Mary took the child while Monica comforted Sally.

Just before noon, Director Anderson called Don. He went outside to take the call. "Don, we have everyone looking over the satellite information. We're tracking every vehicle leaving Albuquerque. We'll find Isaac."

"Thanks for letting us know. We hope he's safe. But how did you find out?"

"The FBI often requests access to satellite data. The team notified me that Isaac was missing. We're all praying for him. I'll let you know if anything turns up."

"Thank you, director." He entered and told everyone about NASA helping to find Isaac.

Tanya got a call and took it outside. A couple of minutes later, she came back in. "Mr. Goble called Mr. Augsburger, who called me to convey his support."

Don had never felt so useless.

Monica tried to comfort Sally, with little result.

Dave dropped by. "I wanted to let you folks know that the air force is on alert. Isaac is not going to get out of the country."

"Out of the country?" Sally yelled.

Monica escorted her into her bedroom.

Tanya ushered the lieutenant out of the house.

Don turned on the news.

Isaac's abduction was the headline. "GRAVITY MAN KIDNAPPED!"

"Shit!" Don said angrily. "I feel so damned helpless."

The next day went by. There were no leads, and nobody had a clue where the abductors might have taken Isaac.

#

Isaac shook his head. His arms and feet were chained to a wall. He went weightless to relieve the stress on his aching arms. A spotlight turned on him. He could see nothing of his surroundings.

"Good, you are awake. If you want to see your wife and child again, you will tell me your secrets."

Isaac looked into the light and saw the shadow of a man below him.

"It's all published. Search for it and read." His words echoed.

"Not all. How does the device lift things into space?"

"By reversing gravity waves."

"You must impart some magic. Tell me how?"

Isaac noticed a microphone attached to his shirt. "You're recording this."

"We're interested in what you tell us. And you will tell us. How does it work?"

"If I tell you, will you let me go?"

"Maybe. This time, my orders do not include keeping you alive. But giving a full explanation of the device is your only chance at staying alive."

"It's mechanical. The device bends a thallium rod to reverse gravity waves."
"The details!"
"I don't know the details."
"Let's find out."

A ladder was placed beside him. A man climbed up, grabbed Isaac's arm, and injected a syringe.

He went negative as hard as he could, and the man flew up and fell on his head with a thud.

Isaac felt the pain in his wrists, and his stomach went nauseous. He returned to normal gravity. Warm blood trickled down his arms where he had pulled the chains. He went weightless and took a firm grasp of the chains with his hands. His head spun, and he passed out.

When Isaac opened his eyes, the light still blazed in his eyes.
"Tell me about gravity," the voice said.

Isaac began a rambling discourse of everything he knew about gravity, the AGD, what it could be used for, his dreams about space travel, and lifting things into orbit.

"I want to know how the device turns gravity off."

He spoke about the device's details, at least those he understood. He had never asked Monica about the thallium and how it was made. Then, he rambled for a long time about his dreams and wild ideas. His mind began to see gravity waves all around him. Not just those bent by the mass of the earth, but those parallel and those at odd angles to what he had bent before. The waves pressed upon him. He felt like he was inside a bullet with waves pressing against him all around.

He focused on all the waves, got a firm grip on the chains, and repelled them all.

"STOP. STOP!" the man before him yelled.

Isaac saw the man on the ground and returned to normal gravity.

"What are you doing? Do you want to bury us all in this mountain?"
"I want out of here."
"Bending thallium can't do that?"
"It doesn't. I do."
"How?"
"I just do it. I can't explain how. I've tried to tell everyone but don't have the words and don't understand it myself."

The man turned and walked away. A moment later, another man started up the ladder and gave Isaac a shot. Isaac closed his eyes, reached out with his hand and seized the ladder, and as the man got to the bottom, he repelled all of the gravity.

AntiGravity

The bottom end of the ladder shot the man to the ceiling, and he crashed to the floor. Boulders fell. One smashed the light, and he saw only darkness.

#

Lt. Meyers brought lunch. It was now three days since Isaac was last seen.

Tanya made sure Dave did not say anything in the house that might upset Sally, who had now gone into a silent depression, taking care of Emily and doing nothing else.

Dave's phone rang, and he stepped outside. A moment later, he opened the door. "Don, Tanya, can I talk to you?" They joined him. "We have a lead. They insist on having someone Isaac is familiar with come along."

"Where are you going?" Tanya asked.

"Colorado. Both of you are invited. Get some warm clothes and hiking shoes."

Don entered the house and said, "They have a lead. Tanya and I are going with Meyers. I'll call you later." He hugged Monica and then Sally.

Dave drove them to a private plane waiting on the runway. He nearly pushed the two of them up the stairs and into seats. The plane began to taxi before Dave was seated.

"How did they locate Isaac?" Tanya asked.

"Something called LIGO figured out where he was at," Dave said.

"The Laser Interferometer Gravitational-Wave Observatory. They detect fluctuations in gravity waves and must have sensed Isaac," Don said.

"All I know is that we have a highly probable location. Local law enforcement is sealing off the area. SWAT from Denver will arrive ahead of us. If Isaac is there, we'll have him before nightfall." Meyers got up and went to the front of the plane for a few minutes. He returned and knelt in front of Don and Tanya. "The plan is to land near Leadville and drive to the site."

A black SUV raced over packed snow toward the plane as it rolled to a stop.

"That must be our ride," Meyers said.

The three hustled down the stairs.

A man in a black suit and blue windbreaker got out of the SUV. "I'm Harrison, FBI."

"Lieutenant Meyers here. This is Don and Tanya. They work with Isaac. Where are we going?" Dave asked.

"Camp Hale. It used to be an army base. Get in." Harrison commanded in a stern voice. The SUV was speeding up a two-lane road through the Rocky Mountains a moment later.

"What's the status?" Meyers asked.

"Law enforcement has been at the site for about six hours. They found two vehicles, both with New Mexico license plates. When they made their way up a valley, they encountered small arms fire and earthquakes. That's when we called you. We're uncertain about Isaac's ability and wanted the experts on him available. The SWAT team from Denver arrived a couple of hours ago. They're carefully moving up the valley."

They drove to a large flat area crossed with roads, evidence of the former Camp Hale. Then they sped through the melting snow across the camp to a group of vehicles, where they stopped.

"Stay in the vehicle," Harrison said as he got out.

"Could Isaac cause an earthquake?" Tanya asked Don.

"I don't know what would happen if he went full negative when underground."

"Underground?"

"How else could he cause an earthquake? In the air, he could fly away."

"Oh shit." Tanya held her head in her hands.

Harrison returned. "SWAT is approaching a bunker about a mile up this valley. Footprints are evident outside. A drone spotted three men up a trail to the north, so we think they're leaving the scene. We are going to hike from here. Lt. Meyers, are you certified for automatic weapons?"

"Yes, sir."

"I'll lend you one of mine." Harrison selected a rifle from the back of the SUV and handed it to Dave, who checked it over.

"Tanya, Don, stay behind us."

A dozen armed FBI agents led them up the road briskly.

Don was soon out of breath and lagged behind.

The ground jolted and shook for a few seconds. Birds flew out of the trees, squawking. Everyone froze in their tracks.

"Isaac's never shown that type of power before!" Don yelled from twenty meters behind the rest.

A few minutes later, the group came on a man dressed in SWAT gear. "Perimeter is established around a bunker about a hundred yards ahead. The doors are closed. Six men have been sent up Cataract Creek in pursuit of the suspects. Choppers are coming in from the other side."

A voice came over the SWAT man's radio. "Doors are open. Moving in."

A minute later, a faint voice was heard on the radio. "Get away!"

The ground shook, and there was a rumble down the valley.

"Target located. Retreating," the voice over the radio announced.

"Coming to your location, with subjects known to the target," Harrison said into his radio, then turned to Don and Tanya. "This is why we invited you two along. We can't have Isaac shaking the mountain down on top of anyone."

Around a curve in the road, Don could see two men in SWAT gear on either side of a cement opening in the mountainside. The metal doors open.

Don was breathing heavily but ran toward the bunker. "Isaac, I'm here. It's me, Don."

Harrison caught him. "Take it slow and easy," he said, holding on to Don and shoving a flashlight in his hand.

Tanya accepted another.

"Catch your breath." Harrison held Don and looked around to get approval from the rest of his men. "Okay, go slow and easy. We'll be right behind you."

"Don, stay with me," Tanya said, taking his arm.

They crept into the bunker. The four-meter-tall half-cylinder cement cave went about twenty meters before opening into a larger area.

Don checked out a person lying at the end of the tunnel. "Not Isaac," he whispered.

"Isaac! This is Tanya! We're here to get you out!"

"Speak to us if you can hear us," Don said.

Meyers remained a step behind.

Tanya's flashlight illuminated another person farther into the bunker. "Blond hair and too big to be Isaac." She panned her light up the wall. Isaac was just above the blond man attached to the rock wall with massive chains.

"Isaac!" Don yelled as he ran to him.

"Get some help to get him down," Tanya said to Meyers.

"Isaac, we got you," Don said, reaching up to touch his bloody leg and the chain attached to the ankle.

Isaac mumbled. In the light of the lantern, his eyes were wide, and dark spots of dirt covered his face.

As Meyers had promised, they had rescued Isaac before sunset. Isaac was taken to a med-evac helicopter at Camp Hale and placed aboard.

Don, Tanya, and Dave rode with Harrison to Colorado Springs, where Isaac had been taken.

It was about seven in the evening when they got phone service, and Don called Monica. "We found Isaac alive. He was taken by helicopter to a hospital. We're on the way there now by car."

"Why did it take you so long to call?" Monica said.

"I'm sorry. We were out of cell phone range. How's Sally?"

"She's been a nervous wreck."

"I'll call you again when we get to Colorado Springs."

Two days later, Don and Tanya returned to Albuquerque with Isaac.

Isaac embraced Sally, and they both cried.

Monica hugged Don. Tanya stood with Dave.

Sally sobbed in a breath. "Tell me everything."

"I can tell you what I remember." Isaac took a seat at the table, and everyone else pulled up a chair. "I had just put the groceries in the car when I felt a sting in the back of my neck. I grabbed at it, thinking it was a bee, and turned to see my reflection in the sunglasses of a man. I said, 'Hello.' He answered back, 'Aren't you the man who can turn off gravity?'

"That's when I looked closer. He wore gloves and a blue coat. I thought that was odd, so I didn't answer. I opened the car door and felt dizzy.

"The next thing I remember was hanging in a cave lit by a lantern. There were five men. One began to ask me questions about gravity. I told them what I knew. My hands and feet were chained to the wall, so I went full negative for a moment. The room shook, and the men stepped back. One stuck a needle in my arm. I focused on shaking the mountain, and I guess I passed out."

"He must have injected you with a tranquilizer," Don said. "Do you have any idea how long you were out?"

"No idea. They had a spotlight on me. When I woke, I felt really funny, like I was high or really drunk."

"The doctors found multiple drugs in your system," Tanya said. "One of them is a common truth serum."

"That makes sense because I answered all of their questions. The funny thing is that I hung there, thinking that they weren't asking the right questions. I told them about gravity, how I altered gravity waves, and about thallium, but they never asked about the ceramic. They asked about the AGD and how it worked. I told them it changed gravity waves and the wild ideas I have about how the AGD could send a man to the moon, Mars, and the other planets. I remember rattling on and on about the potential for space flight."

"We have never talked about those things," Don said.

"Somehow, my mind was just rambling, telling them all kinds of things that my imagination has come up with."

Sally said, "I know your thoughts can be way out there at times."

"They came at me with another syringe. As the man grabbed my arm and stuck in a needle, I went negative. He flew to the ceiling and back down. They said I killed him. After dragging the man to the entrance, they came at me again. One man threatened me, 'If you do that again, I'll kill you.' That's when I began to hallucinate."

Don said, "Traces of LSD, DMT, and stimulants were found in your blood. The doctors said that this combination makes a person talk about everything a mind can come up with."

"I don't remember what I said. I know I shook the mountain a few times. I had the vision of myself hurtling through space inside a giant bullet. I don't remember anything about those men after that, except thinking that the man who spoke to me sounded like Deron. I must have blacked out for a while. It was totally dark. I hung there thinking some archaeologists would find my bones in a thousand years or so.

AntiGravity

"There was some banging, and a little light came; some lights were moving around. I shook the mountain, and they ran. A while later, I heard Don's voice and relaxed."

"The bunker has a ten-meter ceiling. High enough that falling up and then down would be enough to kill a person," Don added.

"How many were found dead?" Isaac asked.

"Five of them," Tanya replied. "Two in the cave and the other three shot themselves during a gunfight."

"Who were they?" Sally asked.

"The FBI thinks they were Russian. They had satellite-based communication devices, so everything Isaac said was transmitted to whoever ordered the abduction. I'll let Harrison know that Isaac thinks one was Deron."

"I still think it's odd," Isaac said. "He didn't ask about the ceramic. We know so much more than they do."

Chapter 38 – Mid-March

The following morning, Tanya and Dave were jogging through new snow on their morning run when a jeep caught up to them. "Lieutenant Meyers, the base commander is ordering you to appear in his office at oh-nine-hundred hours. Ms. Nash, please accompany him."

Meyers noticed the captain stripes, stopped, and saluted. "May I ask what this is about?"

"I received no information on the purpose of the meeting," the captain said, then drove away.

Tanya, with her hands on her hips, took a couple of deep breaths. "Chris said we would be absorbed into the military. The NTSB report detailed what the AGD can do, and now after Isaac's abduction by suspected Russians, the military will envelop us."

"The air force has known about Isaac all along and the AGD since you moved onto the base. What has changed is the technology is now public."

"Have you told the air force anything?" Tanya demanded. Her gander showed some anger.

"I've only said 'yes' or 'no' to their questions."

"Did you have an order to find out what Adynamia does?" She took a step forward and got into his face.

"I was asked to keep an eye on the company to protect it. But ..."

"No buts! Honesty."

"Tanya, you have my heart first. I told them that I wouldn't violate my relationship with you to be a spy," Dave said with a firm tone.

"If I ever find out you were using me to find out about Adynamia's technology, I will feed your balls to a pig." She grinned.

Lt. Meyers stood at attention. "A fitting punishment for a person who commits treason. You do not need to search out a pig farm."

Tanya sprinted away to burn off the energy of her anger. Meyers raced after her.

They showered together at the apartment and dressed formally for their meeting.

"Lieutenant Meyers and Tanya Nash reporting to the base commander as ordered," Dave said to the orderly behind the desk.

The orderly saluted and opened the door. "Meyers and Nash have arrived." He held the door.

A colonel with short hair around his bald head, the base commander, stood behind his desk. "Lieutenant Meyers, Commander Nash, please come in." He introduced five air force generals who stood around the room and continued,

AntiGravity

"Forgive the tight accommodations for this large of a group. General Williams, the floor is yours."

"Four years ago, a young man defied gravity at a conference in Los Angeles. The Pentagon felt it prudent to place Isaac under their watch. I received reports monthly from NASA on the progress of discovering his secret, and over the years, I grew pessimistic that Isaac would lead to a new understanding of gravity. Their conclusion to their efforts last summer drew my interest to a close.

"A few months ago, the company Stellar Z filed patents for a device that would repel gravity. The patents were immediately directed to a team that has in the past researched such technologies. After a day of review, they filed a report concluding unworkable. When the news broke about the crimes of Stellar Z, Adynamia came to my attention. I asked the base commander to keep an eye on what you were doing. To keep this short, I want you to know we worked with the NTSB on testing the antigravity device involved in the crash of the MoonBeam spacecraft."

Tanya shuddered, predicting where the general was going with his speech.

"The technology Adynamia has is impressive. Very impressive indeed. Altering gravity in an aircraft or spacecraft, or even a soldier, changes the nature of warfare." General Williams looked around the room at the other generals. "We are here to informally request that you work with us in developing applications for the antigravity device."

Tanya stood tall. "Thank you, General Williams. I feel I can speak for all the owners of Adynamia. We are committed to applications that will allow humanity to explore space and provide a better life for humanity. The SafeFall Belt is an example of how we can help people. We have no interest in military applications."

"Commander Nash, the Pentagon always prefers to work with private companies to develop military applications on a friendly basis. We envision tremendous potential in working with Adynamia. Some technologies are too disruptive to be available to our nation's enemies when we do not have them. We are aware of the efforts by the Chinese to acquire your technology. The latest abduction of Isaac Thomas by suspected Russians has pushed us to act. You might not be aware of the Chinese and Russian threats to national security. We can't allow them to have the technology and insist that the United States military does."

Tanya stood at attention and spoke directly. "With all due respect, General, Adynamia is committed to our partners at this time. Each is focused on exploration. I believe discovery is a world unifier while the military is a divider. We are well aware that you could, by saying the command, absorb Adynamia into the military and make our technology a national secret. Those of us who know how it works would probably be confined, and the AGD becomes a black-budget project. You might find that we won't be cooperative with revealing our secrets with anyone else."

For a moment, the only sound was a fly zipping between windows frantically looking for a way out.

Tanya listened to the pounding of her heart and thought that everyone in the room could hear it.

"For now, Commander Nash, you may continue. Even though you're not willing to work with the US military, we are obligated to secure Adynamia from all threats. Lieutenant Meyers, you're now at FPCON Delta. Adynamia and their technology are Top Secret."

Meyers stood at attention. "Yes, sir."

"Dismissed, Lieutenant. Thank you for your time, Commander Nash." Gen. Williams glared in their direction.

Dave put his right foot behind him, turned on a dime, and opened the door.

Tanya felt confused and hesitated.

Dave touched her arm and quietly said, "Time to go."

Tanya walked out of the office, followed by Dave. Once outside, she asked, "What does FPCON Delta mean to our lives?"

"The general put Adynamia under the highest level of security possible. Armed soldiers will now accompany everyone at Adynamia, and all AGDs will have personnel assigned to protect them. I have a lot of work to do. Can you stay in the house today?"

AntiGravity

Chapter 39 – April

Isaac took an AGD II up and down in the warehouse just to pass the time.

"Thank God it's Friday," Don said from a few meters away.

"What does it matter, since we never take a day off?" Monica asked, placing three round ceramic pieces down on a workbench.

"We could go camping this weekend, as long as we could find a place large enough for a platoon of soldiers," Isaac said. *Maybe being away from here would help me sleep.*

"The last time I was off the base, I needed to use the restroom. My escorts accompanied me. No thanks to camping," Monica said.

Everyone's phone chirped. Don had his out first. "Tanya is calling a meeting at her place."

"Let's go," said Isaac.

They arrived to find Tanya sitting at her table, working on her computer. "Take a seat. We have a lot of things to cover."

"Oh, great," said Isaac attempting to swing his leg over the back of a chair and ending up off-balance."

"You're too short for the Riker maneuver, Isaac." Don chuckled.

"What's the Riker maneuver?" Tanya asked.

"I'll tell you later," Monica said. "Go on with the news."

"First, I spoke with Mr. Brooks. The government has approved all our patents."

"So fast?" Don asked.

"Our patents are classified Top Secret, as will any further patents we file. They want us to file everything we can come up with. General Williams has assigned a guard to Mr. Brooks's office. Chris is billing us for the security upgrade to our lawyers' computers."

"Did he ever bill us for his time?" Monica asked.

"Yes. I paid him," Tanya said. "Second, AstroLift is scheduled to fly around the moon next week. We never got back to them on whether we would be there for Tuesday's launch."

"Not me," Monica said.

"I think Isaac and I should go. You and Don can keep working."

"I could use some help making materials. The process to make ceramic for the belts is perfected, and I could train someone to do it."

"I'll go if I can bring my car."

"Don't fly in the wind," Don said.

"Isaac and I will leave on Monday and come back on Wednesday. I don't want to be there if anything goes wrong. Meyers and a team of five will escort us on the trip.

"That brings us to number three. Stellar Z is being liquidated. If there is anything we need that they might have, we can get it for next to nothing."

"They have lots of lab equipment I could use," Monica said.

"I would love to see a list of equipment. I'm sure they have some toys I could play with," Don said.

"Can we get the *Osprey*?" Isaac asked.

"In settlement of our lawsuit, we have a substantial credit to spend at the auction of Stellar Z's assets. It seems that the government blocked foreign investors from buying anything. I'll forward a list when I get it."

"Stuff for nothing," Isaac said.

"That brings me to the last thing. Due to the failure of MoonBeam's test flight, they are in financial trouble. Saturn Ventures offered to merge. This means our contract with MoonBeam will be available to Paul Osterman. What does everyone think about that?"

The team exchanged glances. The silence told Isaac that no one wanted to be the first to offer an opinion. *They usually overrule me, so I'll be negative.* "I think that voids the contract as it is nontransferable."

"It is not actually a transfer," Don said. "I think it's okay."

"Fine with me," Monica said. "They will be an equal competitor to AstroLift and NASA."

Tanya added, "I couldn't come up with a reason not to let the contract remain. I'll let the lawyers know the majority of us are in favor of letting the contract continue with the merged company."

Isaac smiled and felt like he had scored another win.

#

The midday launch of the "Over the Moon" jump was uneventful and dull compared to a rocket launch. The Cargo Dragon, which some called a cow for this mission, lifted slightly off the ground, hovered for a few seconds, and rose straight up into the air. There was no billowing thrust or thunderous noise, and no smoke trail to follow the flight. A minute after liftoff, the craft was out of sight.

"The end of exciting liftoffs," Tanya told Isaac.

The after-launch barbeque was a chance for Tanya to get to know the principal players of AstroLift and ask what they thought they wanted to do with the AGD. Most responded with a base on the moon and a mission to Mars. The response that Tanya found most interesting was the idea of replacing the existing satellites now in orbit. Everything could be upgraded at a bargain price.

The selfie crowd pestered Isaac for photos while hanging in the air. Isaac obliged by standing by the pool, taking people ten feet into the air for photos. Two

AntiGravity

middle-aged women each took one of Isaac's hands, and someone, who probably had too much to drink, rushed to get their picture, caught a foot on a chair, and stumbled into the women and Isaac. The woman closest to the pool shrieked and started to fall in. Isaac turned off gravity just in time to keep her from getting wet. A moment later, Isaac was over the pool, holding on to two women with no horizontal momentum. They were stuck.

"Don't let us go!" one yelled, grabbing Isaac around the neck.

The other hugged Isaac tightly around the waist. The crowd stood with their phones aimed at the trio. One of the women lost a shoe.

Isaac yelled, "Without a force to provide some momentum, we are stuck! Do any of you engineers have a way to give us a little horizontal velocity?"

Tanya looked at the scene and got in Isaac's car. She maneuvered it against Isaac and gave the three a little push to where they moved at snail's pace to the opposite side of the pool. Isaac let them down as easily as a feather, landing on the ground to a round of cheering.

Now to really impress them. He took a slow dive into the pool but went weightless, flying just over the surface. Halfway through a flip, he snatched the shoe from the water. After another flip, he landed in the grass on the other side and held up the shoe, which emptied the water it contained on his head.

Tanya landed with a thud close to him. "You big show-off."

Isaac shook his head at Tanya, showering her with a few drops. "This was more exciting than the launch." He ran his fingers through his hair to put his medium-length fringe cut back in shape. Isaac returned the soggy shoe and gladly received praise from everyone. He enjoyed being on the show, mostly because he did not have to engage in small talk with anyone. *A sideshow act has its benefits.*

They boarded a private jet the following day to bring them home. Isaac sat in the back of the plane, playing games on his laptop.

#

The following week, Tanya, Dave, and Isaac went to Florida with the same five escorts for NASA's test launch. The plan was to send up a replica of a space station module and let it hang stationary above the earth for a week. The stabilizer AGD Don designed would be tested to hold the module in place. They would bring everything back to Earth, landing where it lifted off.

They arrived the night before.

The early morning launch went off without a hitch; it was as dull as the AstroLift launch the previous week.

Isaac ran into Susan Millar, who had set up the flight plan to rescue the astronauts from the space station. "Susan, I never got the chance to thank you for figuring out the calculations on the ISS rescue mission."

"Isaac, so good to see you again. You're welcome. I was so pleased that you were able to rescue those astronauts."

"It wasn't all me. Tanya Nash did an incredible job. If I can find her"—he looked around—"I'll introduce you."

"I would like to meet her. There is something I wanted to ask her."

"What is that?"

"I've wondered if I had the incorrect weight of the *Osprey*; it shouldn't have been out of fuel."

"It was too heavy." Isaac proceeded to tell Susan the story of the extra equipment and how that was what led to the inventing of the AGD.

"Fascinating!" exclaimed Susan. "Another example of a man's greed leading to his demise."

"What have you been working on lately?"

"I've worked up some new programs for the AGD flights. I've been working on flights to retrieve the modules and parts of the International Space Station and put it back together. The AGD will make that possible next year. Then, if today's test works, NASA will begin plans for a stationary space station. Then there is the flight to Triton."

"That's one of the moons of Neptune, right?"

"Yes."

"It's the moon with a retrograde orbit and on which Voyager 2 found ice geysers," he said, showing off his knowledge.

"That's the one. Using the AGD, the spacecraft could get there ten times faster than initially planned. I've been working out what would be the best flight path, but it depends where the planets are in their relative orbits."

"Wow. I didn't have any idea that mission was in the works. There are a few ideas that have been floating around in my head."

"What ideas?" A slight smile grew across Susan's face.

"I've been wondering how fast we can get to Mars or the other planets using the AGD. If we take a craft up beyond the moon, let it fall toward the earth to gain momentum and slingshot past while reversing gravity, we would be going incredibly fast."

Susan began talking with her hands like she was referencing a screen. "My initial calculations show that a craft could get to a speed about twenty-five times faster than the space station was orbiting by sling-shotting Earth. At one hundred kilometers per hour, half my theoretical maximum, a craft could reach Mars in eighteen days. This is far faster than the nine months with previous technology. The main problem would be slowing down once the ship reached Mars. The spaceship would need a lot of fuel to brake to supplement the lower reverse gravity and transition into an orbit. Then a lander could easily go to the surface."

"Turn it around and reverse gravity," Isaac said smugly.

Susan paused. Her eyes looked up as if seeing calculations in her head. "Interesting idea. I've had fun with the calculation to drop toward the sun then slingshot to the outer planets or Triton. We're talking months travel time instead of years. Theoretically, we can use reverse gravity to slow. I have work to do."

"I knew the AGD would make the solar system smaller."

"Not just the solar system. One project I hope to complete is to figure out the optimum flight path to another sun. If we can get a craft to ten percent of the speed of light, we could fly to Alpha Centauri in forty years instead of hundreds of years. Maybe we could get close-up photos in our lifetime."

"That would be amazing." Isaac shuddered. The bullet image idea that he had while hallucinating came into his mind. He cleared his throat. "What if we could get to half the speed of light?"

"We could be to Alpha Centauri in about eight years."

Isaac's head tilted back until his gaze met the sky. "Eight years to another solar system. That's what I want to see."

Archie Kregear

Chapter 40 – Late April–May

"Oh, crap!" Monica got up from her computer.

"What's wrong?" Don asked as his heart jumped.

"Jeremy's business report for the first quarter shows orders for over 20,000 belts. On my best day, I made two hundred. I'm three months behind."

"Construction on the new kiln is underway. We can get more small kilns if that would help."

"I need people to do the work."

"We offered jobs to four people you knew from Stellar Z. Haven't they completed their security clearance yet? Who's in charge of hiring anyway?"

"Under rules of FPCON Delta, new hires need to pass the government requirements. These folks worked for a company that was in bed with the Chinese. Do you expect them to get a quick clearance? I can't make ceramic and recruit people at the same time."

"Let's see if we can get Isaac and Tanya to do the legwork on hiring while we focus on making things. Maybe they can find some people who already have a security clearance."

Don poured his second cup of coffee, and the sun wasn't even up. Instead of calling, he wrote an email to Tanya and Isaac. Then he searched for recruitment firms.

That morning at eight o'clock, Director Anderson called him. "Good morning, Don. I hope this isn't too early for you?"

"Not at all. I was about to make a second pot of coffee."

"The demands for AGDs must be keeping you busy, and I hate to put something else on your plate. What I need is a device that can lift something around fifty kilotons. The Europeans have an urgent experiment they want to do in space. Launch windows with rockets are a few years away, but with a larger AGD, we can get it up sooner."

"I understand the need for a heavy lifter and have already designed one, but we need to get the larger kiln built," Don said in an exasperated tone.

"Anything I can do?"

"There might be. We need people. A few to help Monica make ceramic. Do you have anyone with a materials background and a security clearance? An electrical engineer would also be helpful."

"I'll get the word out."

"How are the plans to salvage the International Space Station going?" Don asked, eager to have a mission with the AGD that was not a test.

"The first launch is next week. We need to get up there and grab what modules we can and see what we can reuse. Now that we don't need a booster rocket to get payloads into space, and we can bring spacecraft down without nearly burning up, we can progress a lot faster."

"We're working as fast as we can."

"Progress takes time. I'm amazed at what you have accomplished in the past year. Let me know if there is anything you need. There are lots of resources at my disposal."

"Will do, sir." Don hung up. He had always been a doer, since he could do things faster and better than anyone else. Training people took a lot of time and managing them took a lot more. He could use the help if they were the right people. Don filled his coffee cup and took the pot over to fill Monica's mug. "I just spoke to Anderson; he's going to help us with recruiting."

"I thought you were going to ask Isaac to do that?"

"I sent him an email, but since the director was on the phone, I inquired. Are you ready to head to the lab?"

"I was waiting for you to get off the phone."

They stepped out of their home into a spring rainstorm and ran into Tanya.

Don asked, "How is the building going?"

Tanya pulled the hood of her raincoat up. "The good news is that the framing for the foundation of our new facility is complete. The bad news is that it is too wet to pour cement."

"They're moving along quicker than expected," Don said.

"The incentives we set up for finishing at our desired date is making them work."

"Make sure the inspectors check for quality. I don't want them to cut corners," Don said.

"I set up the contract so that the final payment will be made one year after completion."

"Good plan. I spoke to Director Anderson this morning. The Europeans have something large they want to put up. Keep pressure on the contractors as we need the ten-meter industrial kiln to make the ceramic for a heavy-lifting AGD."

They entered the shop.

"Hey, Don, Monica, Tanya," Isaac said. "I got your email and have already put in a call to a couple of local recruiting agencies. One works nationally. Can I forward the job descriptions you were using, or do they need to be updated?"

Monica said, "Forward those. I don't have time to update them."

"Will do. Hey, did you guys hear that the men the Europeans put into suspended animation for a year woke up and are doing fine?"

"No, I didn't hear that. For a year? Really?" Tanya said.

"The article said they were considering another long test."

"If I connect the dots, the Europeans want to test suspended animation in space," Don said.

"Super cool. Let's get NASA a heavy-lift AGD," Isaac said.
"We can't because it's too wet to pour cement," Monica said.

#

Isaac brought up the video feed of the NASA launch to salvage the wreck of the ISS and sat back in his toy car to watch. He loved floating around the warehouse while he tried to study. Since his abduction, he had requested extensions on all of his schoolwork. He couldn't concentrate and did not sleep well, if he slept at all.

A few minutes later, a metal rod hit the side of his car. "Get out of my work area!"

He looked to see Don pushing him to the other side of the room and returned to the video. The craft went much higher than the orbit of the ISS, where it could use Earth's gravity and rocket engines to achieve orbital velocity. *I wish I knew math well enough to understand how NASA can put a spacecraft next to objects flying at twenty-seven-thousand kilometers an hour.*

Isaac felt a bang on his car.

"Come down," Don said in an angry voice.

Isaac let the car down a couple of meters from Don's workstation and got out.

"I'm sorry, Don. The air currents swirl around the room."

"I know." Don had a line of plastic in his hand and tied one end to a wheel of Isaac's car. He dragged it across the room and tied the other end to an eye hook on the wall opposite from his workstation. "This will keep you in your half of the room." Don blew out a breath and went back to work.

Isaac climbed back in and set a timer to check the video when the craft should arrive at the ISS wreckage. He copied a few minutes of the launch and would piece it together with other significant events of the mission to give to the rest of the team. He proceeded to try to study. Since he was weightless, he didn't mind when his tether caused the car to rotate.

He desperately desired to get a degree in physics and wanted to get a minor in business. The amount of what he called busy work often bored him to tears. Since his abduction, he received permission to take his classes remotely, but he couldn't concentrate. When he did go on campus, the four-person heavily armed security team was an annoyance to teachers, students, and himself. Not that he didn't like Lt. Meyers, but they didn't have anything in common. Dave was a muscular stud and, with Tanya, the life of their dinners together.

#

The last week of April, Detective Eddleson asked for a meeting with the Adynamia team. Mary was happy to watch Emily so that Sally could attend. With Dave and a security team, the five met the detective.

"I asked you all here to provide an update on what we know about Isaac's abductors. The five men are Russian nationals. Russia denies any knowledge of their actions. They claim the men are mercenaries who have been operating in various parts of the world. The current theory is that they came in separately with false passports.

"Russia said their last contact with the five men was in Turkmenistan over a year ago. Their weapons were purchased in the US over ten years ago and reported stolen seven years ago from a militia group in Mississippi. The radio gear is from supplies we sent to Afghanistan.

"The state department put a lot of pressure on the Russians, but they're so interested in getting legitimate access to your technology that they're disavowing any knowledge of Isaac's abductors.

"If LIGO had not located Isaac, the men probably would have gotten away. Forensics on three of the men revealed that two were shot by one man who then shot himself. The FBI confirmed through DNA tests that the man who shot the others and himself was the same person who took the early device and rode it over the golf course. This person's DNA was also found on the boat where Isaac's parents died. The conclusion is that the person known as Deron was behind all three attempts to acquire the antigravity technology. The FBI has no more leads. They're closing the investigation unless some new information turns up. Any questions?"

"I thought the man sounded like Deron." Isaac hung his head low and began to sob.

The rest of the team put their arms around him.

#

Over the next month, Isaac monitored the activity of the three partners: MoonBeam successfully sent up a quickly assembled half-sized model of their new design for a tourist craft, AstroLift launched a satellite into orbit, and four modules of the ISS were collected using Gustavus Net and the vessel that had caused the disaster.

NASA brought the vehicle back to Earth and determined that a ruptured fuel line to the braking thrusters caused the crash. The consensus was that a collision with a small piece of space debris punctured the line. The two deceased astronauts were returned to their respective countries, and the spacecraft, after a thorough inspection by NASA scientists, followed.

The stationary space station was becoming more promising. The fuel required to speed a craft into orbit was unnecessary weight. This resulted in a complete reworking of NASA's program and the type of vessels they needed to lift payloads into space. With this concept, the entire space industry went into a redesign phase. Since a returning craft did not need to burn off the twenty-five to thirty thousand kilometers per hour orbital velocity, it did not need a heat shield and structure to withstand thirty-five-hundred-degree temperatures on reentry.

With each launch into space using the AGD, Isaac felt better about his contribution to the advancement of humanity. He was no longer the sole master of gravity and no longer the center of attention. Yet his nightmares persisted. He would stay up after Sally went to bed, explaining that he wanted to study. What he did was drink until he couldn't stay awake, often never making it to bed and falling asleep on the couch.

Sally became more worried, initially suggesting that he talk to a counselor about his dreams. Isaac refused, instead taking sleeping pills that put him into a deep sleep. As spring progressed, Isaac became more reclusive while claiming to focus on his studies, the space missions, and internet discussions of utilizing the AGD, like flying cars, new airplane designs, potential space missions, and applications for all humanity.

#

At Tanya's invitation, the whole gang went to their new facility. The spring wildflowers were in bloom, making the surrounding hills awash in color, causing Isaac to sneeze. The first thing they noticed was the four-story building that would become their new work area; a two-story building of the same size would be Monica's lab and accommodate a hundred square meter kiln.

Sally wanted to see the site of their new home, so Isaac walked with her to a corner of the hundred-acre property to look at the foundation. The initial plans had plots for eight houses on a cul-de-sac. Because of the increased security requirements, Tanya added homes for Megan, Jeremy, and new employees.

"When can we move in?" Sally asked.

"I don't know." Isaac walked up to the cement foundation with pipes sticking out. "Tanya says she's pushing the construction company as much as she can. We do want quality, so it may take a few months."

"Sally and Isaac, over here," Tanya called out. "I want to show you something."

Isaac and Sally joined the group by some small, manufactured homes. Isaac thought they were for the construction company.

Tanya said, "I've added an area for some temporary housing. We can move in this week and stay here until our homes are built. They aren't much, but they are better than base housing. Later on, they can be used by employees. What does everyone think?"

"I'll be glad to get off the base," Monica said.

"What about security?" Don asked.

"Dave is handling that. The security fence is going up this week; it will replace the construction fencing you see now. Let's take a tour."

#

Isaac enjoyed picking up heavy loads and putting them on the truck effortlessly. He carried their couch out by himself.

Dave yelled out, "Big load for a little guy!"

"I'd like to see you carry a couch all by yourself!"

"Put it down." Dave accepted the challenge. He picked it up, his arm muscles straining to their max, and walked up the ramp onto the truck.

"Show-off," Isaac said.

"Oh, so I'm the show-off?"

"Shall we see who can lift each other the easiest?" Isaac reached for Dave, who grabbed ahold of Isaac.

Dave raised Isaac above his head while Isaac went weightless and lifted Dave off the ground. In a moment, they were above the roofline.

"Now, big Dave. Let's see who has the guts to let go first," Isaac said and held his arms out wide.

Dave began to laugh. "You win. Never again will I let you go or come to any harm."

Isaac felt a lump come to his throat. He and Dave returned to the ground. He choked out the words, "Thanks, Dave." He went to get more of his things and put them on the truck.

None of the team had acquired a lot of possessions; thus, moving had gone smoothly in a couple of days. Dave always maintained a selection of beers and ordered pizzas delivered for everyone. Isaac insisted on paying for the pizza, since Dave was supplying the beer. It now didn't matter to any of their bank accounts.

Isaac set up and made their bed while Sally put Emily down to sleep. They showered and initiated their temporary new home before falling asleep.

There was a loud crash, and Sally let out a panicked scream. "Isaac! Where are you?"

The house shifted, and the glass in the bedroom window shattered. Sally jumped on the bed, lept toward the ceiling, and grabbed Isaac. "Wake up! You're wrecking the house." They fell, the house fell underneath them. The two of them landed on the bed, and the ceiling came at them.

Isaac reacted and caught the ceiling, making it weightless. He held it yelling, "Get Emily and get out!"

Chapter 41 – June

"Hi, Isaac," Don said as Isaac got out of a Humvee driven by Dave. "Would you like a glass of lemonade?"

Monica sat with him at a table outside their home. "Come join us and enjoy the afternoon sunshine."

"Yeah, sure."

"I'll be right back." Don rushed into the house.

"How are you?" Monica asked with concern.

Isaac stared at the house that was now off its foundation and flattened. "Fine. Where are Sally and Emily?"

"Sally is napping with Emily at her mom's right now."

"I'm sorry for waking everyone up last night. I know you were tired."

Don came out with a glass and set it before Isaac. "Do you want to talk about what happened?"

"I just spent five hours talking with a psychiatrist and counselors. They even brought in the hospital chaplain. He implied that I have a demon inside me that needs God's control."

"You don't have a demon, just a wonderful gift. You have never altered gravity in your sleep before. What was different about last night?"

"That's what the shrink tried to figure out. Other than I didn't take any sleeping pills or drink a lot last night, the conclusion is that I have some unresolved trauma from the kidnapping that's giving me nightmares."

"Do you remember the dream?" Monica asked.

"I'm in a bullet, flying like I was shot from a gun. It's the same vision I had in the cave when the kidnappers put those drugs into me. It's what I visualized when I shook the cave."

"So, to get out of the bullet, you go to negative gravity?" Don asked.

"It's more than just going negative. I push in all directions. The psychiatrist kept asking me questions about the bullet and how I was pushing, but he didn't understand my answers. I think I understand what was going on in my dream. So far, we have been pushing away from the gravity of the earth in a plane." Isaac moved his open hand across the table. "We are only altering the gravity waves in two dimensions. A bullet shape, with a thulium ceramic plate on top and then more plates that curve down in a cone, will push aside gravity waves in other dimensions. Then more ceramic on the sides and one on the bottom. My vision is that this shape punches a hole in the sea of gravity waves of all directions."

Don rubbed his chin. His eyes looked up into the sky. Except for his fingers moving on his jaw, he remained motionless. Then his eyes darted onto Isaac. "Yes. A bullet-shaped AGD might push its way through space without a mass to repel or

AntiGravity

attract it. Get out of the bullet, Isaac. Ride it like Slim Pickens did in the movie *Doctor Strangelove*."

Monica said, "How large of a bullet do we need? That's a lot of ceramic to make."

"It's a lot of control devices. Isaac. You're a genius. Like a submarine punching a hole through water, a bullet-like AGD may glide through the fabric of space. But we don't ride in the bullet. We journey on the outside. Right?"

"You must also get out of the bullet, Isaac, let it go," Monica said.

Isaac sighed and looked at Don. "You don't understand, being inside the cave, drugged and chained down, I wanted to blast out of there. To ride, one must be inside the bullet.

Don stood and put his hands on Isaac's shoulders. "I think I understand."

Monica bent over and hugged Isaac. "I can't imagine how terrible that was for you." She stood and wiped tears from her cheeks. "There's more, isn't there, Isaac."

"I'm afraid to go to sleep."

"We thought about that," Don said.

"Monica and I made a plastic tent with a fan for air. We'll put a strap around your ankle while you sleep. If you pull on the strap, it will shock you, hopefully enough to wake you. The stronger you pull, the larger the shock. Plus, it will set off an alarm. I'll come and wake you."

"The two of you are the real geniuses here."

"I'll go see if Sally is up. She'll want to know you're back," Monica said.

Isaac sat back and sipped lemonade. It reminded him of sitting in the Sykeses' yard getting to know Sally.

Chapter 42 – July

Isaac marked another day off on his computer calendar. *Only ten more days without a nightmare, and Sally will let me sleep with her again.* Dave had brought him a canvas military tent to use as a bedroom instead of plastic. He modified Don's shocker to be set off by a switch under the bed's legs. If the bed got lighter after he went to sleep, he got a shock, and an alarm went off on Don's wrist. He committed to quitting drinking and taking sleeping pills. He still had dreams of the bullet AGD, but they were no longer nightmares.

Since wrecking the house, he had become more focused on helping Sally, freeing her to assist Tanya in managing Adynamia and the construction projects. He applied himself to his studies and monitored the partners, providing an interface between them and Don and Monica. His professors had allowed him extensions on his classes, and today was his last final. He grabbed his backpack and headed out to meet Dave, who accompanied him to the university.

He returned home in time for lunch and fed Emily. Then he did the dishes and cleaned the kitchen so that Sally could do her work. He read a story to his daughter before putting her down for a nap. After folding the laundry and doing everything else he could think of doing in the house, he opened his email.

Paul Osterman had a list of what they wanted for the combined MoonBeam-Saturn Ventures company. Their projects included launching satellites, some to be stationary and some in orbit. He spent the next couple of hours working out a priority list with the new requests and the needs of NASA and AstroLift. None of the partners were happy with the rate of production of AGDs. NASA's list had expanded the previous month when Isaac told Russia they needed to work with a partner instead of acquiring AGDs directly. He constantly refused to work with the Chinese and ignored their emails and calls, even though their monetary offers had increased to what he thought were absurdly astronomical—over a billion dollars.

Augsburger sent plans for a flying car. He brought it up and compared it to the design AstroLift had proposed. Both were elegant and would be fun to fly. Before he put either request for flying car AGDs on the priority list, he wanted to see some action from all the government agencies involved in regulations. He didn't want to waste Don's time making AGDs for cars until the regulations were in place.

He spent the next hour putting together his daily partner summary, updating the production schedule based on the new requests, and reviewing Tanya's construction timeline. Monica and her new team continued to focus on making ceramic for the SafeFall belts. Jeremy had recorded a half-million in profit in May. The amount wasn't much compared to the partners' investments, but it was encouraging to everyone that they could help people who needed it.

AntiGravity

After dinner, with the semester over, Isaac began to draw up his design for a bullet AGD. He wanted to make one over the summer. The hard part would be taking time from Monica and Don.

#

Monica set up the lasers she used to find flaws in the ceramic. She studied the latest attempt to make a four-meter circular ceramic. The two engineers she hired to work with her were good, but they had found flaws in the previous three attempts at this size. They thought they had perfected the process by making one-meter, two-meter, and three-meter discs. The problem was not the ceramic but the metal base it rested on while fired in the kiln. The metal expanded in the heat and contracted, resulting in a millimeter or two warping of the finished ceramic. Monica was unwilling to risk any mission to a flaw in her work, especially the first heavy-lift AGD.

By midafternoon, she confidently announced, "This one is perfect."

She sighed and looked over the room. The ten-by-ten-meter kiln sat in the middle of one side of her new twenty-five-meter-square materials lab. A massive heat pump kept the room at twenty degrees Celsius and filtered out dust and chemicals in the air coming into and out of the lab. She felt satisfied and relieved at making a disc large enough to take fifty-thousand-kilogram payloads into space. "Let's call it a day," she said to the two men working with her. Tom, in his early fifties, came from the navy; Rich had worked with NASA and was in his midforties. "Leave anything that can wait until tomorrow."

"My wife won't know what to do with me arriving home this early," Rich said.

"I won't know what to do with myself," Tom said, taking off his lab coat to reveal a white T-shirt with a couple of holes.

"Go buy some new shirts," Rich replied.

Monica laughed. "I guess I've been working you too hard."

"I'm thrilled to be here. This has been the most exciting month of my life," Tom said.

"So, thirty years in the navy and two marriages weren't that exciting?" Rich said.

"Those years were important, the navy, I mean, but here we are pushing the boundaries of technology into a future that I hope will revolutionize humankind."

"See you tomorrow," Monica said. She opened the door into the other half of Adynamia's new facility. It was also twenty-five meters square, but the ceiling was four stories high where the lab was only two. Construction workers were still working on the far end of the building.

Monica approached Don, who sat just outside the lab at his workstation, just a wall apart from Monica's desk. "The four-meter disc is ready. I'm going home to take a long bath."

"That's fantastic!" Don said, jumping up from his chair and hugging her. "I knew you could do it. I'm so proud of you." The relief Monica felt came out in sobs. Don held her tight. "Let's go home and celebrate."

"Give me an hour or two to relax. I want a little time to process all this."

Don checked his watch. "I'll give you until six. Put a bottle of white wine on ice."

She kissed him and made her way through all the equipment to the door. A blast of hot air hit her as she went out into the blinding sunlight. A hundred yards away were the dozen manufactured homes where they lived. She couldn't wait to have a real house. All the employees of Adynamia now lived inside a hundred-acre plot of land surrounded by a three-meter fence topped with barbed wire.

She hurried down the gravel path to get out of the heat but took time to check on the progress of the houses being built on a rise on the north side of the complex. The walls were up on three homes, and one now had a plywood roof. The move-in date was October, just three months away. That was her next goal, get out of the one-bedroom trailer and into a modern, new house. She reminded herself to thank Tanya for managing the construction. She called to have dinner delivered from their favorite Italian restaurant, including a couple of bottles of wine, and climbed into a hot bath to relax for the first time since moving into the new facility.

#

It was late July when NASA announced they had maintained a satellite in a stationary position three-thousand kilometers above the earth, or four times the altitude of low orbits. The AGD designed to maintain a stable altitude worked perfectly. The new model for a space station did not need to have orbital velocity. The advantages included minimal fuel required to get to the station.

The report also included the announcement from AstroLift that they would be landing a craft on the moon within a month. In four missions, they would lift parts of the spacecraft into a medium orbit, where the final module and thrusters would be assembled.

Isaac sent the email and went to read to Emily.

He picked up a book about men on the moon and read, "The astronauts don't walk; they hop. There is less gravity on the moon."

Isaac got up and reduced gravity in himself by seventy-five percent and hopped a few times. Then he picked up his daughter and bounced around the living room like they were on the moon. Emily laughed and enjoyed the ride. He read, "Gravity on Neptune is greater than on Earth. You would be too heavy to walk."

Isaac thought about the experiments with Don. He had tried to increase gravity a few times with little success. But that was three years ago. "Hold on, we'll try to get heavy."

Emily sank into his lap.

He smiled and returned to normal. "Emily, what if we design a belt to make the astronauts on the moon heavy?"

"No walk."

"Right," Isaac said. "I need to make a gravity assist belt."

\#

A few days later, with Don's help, Isaac put on a belt that made him up to twice as heavy. He walked around the lab until his legs were exhausted, all of fifteen minutes. Then he looked for Dave.

After finding him, Isaac said, "I want to repeat our challenge."

"What challenge is that?"

"I bet you can't lift me. I promise not to lift you." He flipped the switch on his belt. With the belt, he might have weighed two hundred and sixty pounds.

Dave placed his hands under Isaac's arms and strained. He got Isaac off the ground.

"You've gained a lot of weight," Dave said with a strained voice. "And so did I."

"I've doubled the gravity in my body. Here, you try." Isaac turned off the belt before taking it off. "It works like a SafeFall Belt only in reverse."

Dave put the belt around his rippled waist.

Isaac set it to thirty percent more gravity. "When you flip the switch, you'll weigh thirty percent more."

Dave gave him a dirty look. "You're not playing a trick on me?"

"Nope, this is serious. If it works, then people on the moon can walk normally."

"Interesting." Dave flipped the switch. "I can feel the extra weight." He jumped up a couple of times. "This is like wearing a backpack." He took a few steps and went into a trot and ran for a few meters.

"Can I increase it?"

"Sure. Turn it off and set it to whatever you want."

Dave turned it up and began to walk back. "This would be a great way to train. It would strengthen the legs. This is a winner for a workout."

A smile spread across Isaac's face.

Dave turned off the belt. "May I have this one?"

"Sorry, Dave. That's the only one, and I need to send it to AstroLift for their moon mission. I'll make you one."

"You're incredible, buddy. You never cease to amaze me." He rubbed Isaac's head.

"Thanks for being willing to test out my inventions." Isaac took the belt, took himself to one-half gravity, and hopped away.

\#

Don finished testing the heavy-lift AGD, running it through the routine for the tenth time. Without getting it outside and attaching tons of weight, there was nothing else he could think of doing. If there were a flaw, he couldn't find it. He messaged Director Anderson that the four-meter AGD was ready. He set a maximum load of 100,000 kilograms. This was massive compared to the Space Shuttle's payload at 27,500 kilograms and almost seven times more than the AGD the partners were working with, which had a limit of 15,000 kilograms. But minuscule to the two-million-kilogram mass of the rockets that launched the space shuttle.

His next project was getting the partners two- and three-meter lifter AGDs with limits of fifty and twenty kilograms, respectively. He didn't know how large of a module the Europeans wanted to take into space, but he figured the four-meter AGD would work, if it worked at all.

He cleaned up his work area and put tools and test equipment away for the first time since he moved into the new facility. Mostly, he was killing time until Monica was ready to head home.

The two men he hired to help him were getting up to speed. He was a lousy teacher, but they knew what they were doing.

Henry was a metalsmith from NASA who claimed that he could make anything out of metal once he had his shop set up. His equipment list was long, and the projection was that it would take him a couple of months to get the items in and operational. Don was happy that he would no longer need to order metal parts from a company in town.

The other new employee, Zeke, a design engineer, came from Boeing. He was getting up to speed on the designs, putting them into a computer that communicated only with his equipment—laser cutters, 3D printers, and such.

With Don's electronic ability, the three believed that they could build anything. All they needed was the idea and time.

Don went into Monica's lab. "Hi, honey. The large lift is ready to go. I'm quitting early. Care to join me for some Italian food?"

"I'd love it." She turned to Rich and Tom. "Can you finish without me? I'm going to take the evening off."

"You deserve a break," Rich said. "We'll finish this batch of belt ceramics and shut things down. See you in the morning."

Don called in an order to the Italian restaurant while he waited, and as usual, added a couple of bottles of wine.

#

NASA took delivery of the four-meter AGD the third week of August. Director Anderson was excited about the option to lift payloads of up to a hundred thousand kilograms with each mission at a fraction of the cost.

Chapter 43 – August and following

Isaac approached Don and Monica as they returned from lunch. "Here's what I think we need to build next."

"What is this?" Monica asked.

"This is a drawing of the Bullet AGD or BAGD."

Monica looked at the drawing. "Okay, explain this to me."

"The exterior is covered with ceramic, each an AGD to repel gravity in all directions. The one on top and the ones in the cone create a negative gravity field in front. The ones along the side maintain the gravity hole. And the AGD at the bottom is also negative gravity. It punches a hole in the waves of space." Isaac stood proudly over his artwork.

Don leaned in to take a close look. "How many individual AGD are there on this?"

"One hundred and twenty-two."

Don stood up straight. "Whoa! That's a lot of ceramic."

Monica sighed and slumped her shoulders. "I don't have molds for most of those shapes at the top."

"The cone at the top does not have round or rectangular ceramic. There are a whole lot of tests needed to determine how they react. After testing, I estimate two weeks to get the electronics together, and I'll have a more exact design." Don turned around to view where Zeke was working and said, "Hey, Zeke. Here's the next design that Isaac has come up with. Can you computerize it?"

Zeke came over and took a few seconds to look over the drawing. "What's the scale?"

Isaac pointed. "I drew it with the top disc at half a meter. And the bottom disc at one meter."

"I can extrapolate from that. I'll get with Henry to go over the internal structure. A couple days work at most. When I get it done depends on priority."

Monica cocked her head at an angle. "What if we used ceramic from my reject pile to make the prototype?"

Don's eyes lit up. "We could put belt ceramic in the cone."

"I have a number of discs with minor flaws that could be used for the top and bottom. We can piece it together, and the side rods are easy," Monica said in a positive tone.

"Get me the dimensions of the discs we can use, and I'll scale the drawing," Zeke said.

Isaac stood with his hands in his pockets, staring at his drawing.

"Are you alright, buddy?" Don asked.

"Yeah, I guess a makeshift prototype will be okay."

"Do you have a test plan?"
"Set it up and see how fast it can go."

#

Two weeks later, they were ready to test the BAGD. They arranged to take it to the abandoned ranch where they had done other tests early on a Sunday morning. Don programmed it to go only ten percent negative gravity, and that for only three seconds. Then it would revert to five percent less than Earth's gravity until it began to descend. It would let itself down to the ground.

Henry had made a metal case with handles to fit over the entire device, with handles to carry it around. They placed it on a pallet with the nose up for launch.

Don handed Isaac the controls. "For this test, all you need to do is turn it on."

Isaac took a deep breath. "This is the good that came from my kidnapping." He flipped the switch.

The BAGD lifted off and rose over twice as fast as Don expected. A few minutes later, it descended as planned and landed a few meters from where it took off.

"It works!" Isaac yelled as he bounded over to the BAGD.

"Amazing," Don said. His mind calculated the possibilities of what he had just seen.

Don and Isaac sat in the back seat as Dave drove them home. Don said, "The BAGD went up faster than expected. We have no maneuverability, and I'm afraid it will get away from us. I think we need to hand it over to NASA to test in space."

Isaac sat still for a while. "You're right. The only way to test how fast it goes is in space. I'll call Anderson tomorrow."

Friday, Dave and Isaac drove the BAGD to the NASA labs at White Sands.

#

By mid-September, NASA had tested the four-meter lifter AGD with loads up to a hundred thousand kilograms to a height of five kilometers. A week later, they took a fifty-thousand-kilogram load to the stationary space station. It included the BAGD.

NASA added communication equipment and eight small thrusters for guidance. Susan added trajectory control software.

The initial tests were to see if the BAGD could rotate and redirect itself. Next was having it move a hundred meters away and return. They sent it further away, making sure it could home back into the stationary space station. Multiple tests over the next weeks followed. In between tests, astronauts would bring it into the station to replace batteries and check it out. By the middle of October, NASA was ready for a full test to see how fast it could accelerate.

Isaac was a nervous wreck waiting for the results. He had demanded that NASA provide him the updates of each test, no matter what time of day.

He was moving a mattress into his family's new home when his phone alerted him of a message. He dropped the mattress in the living room to read the message. *Launch of BAGD is successful. Acceleration rate attained is 20 meters per second. Shut down after two minutes. Maximum velocity attained was 2400 meters per second.*

"We're not sleeping in the living room," Sally said, carrying an armful of bedding.

Isaac jumped up and down on the mattress. "THE BULLET WORKS. THE BULLET WORKS." He fell to his hands and knees. "I'm free." He sobbed.

Sally dropped her load, knelt, and wrapped her arms around him. "I'm so proud of you. You did it. You've given your talent up to humanity."

They held each other and cried.

They lay together until Isaac's phone beeped. He checked the message. *BAGD has returned to base.*

THE END

Epilogue – Years Later

Isaac wrapped an arm around Sally's waist and the two looked out the floor-to-ceiling window of their vacation home. Earth, half lit up in the distance, stole their view. "How do you like this home away from home?" he asked.

"You've fulfilled your promise. The best home in the universe." Sally leaned her head lightly on his shoulder. "The view leaves me speechless. Emily loves it here as long as she can bring a friend.

Isaac was proud of the three-bedroom home he had designed and received permission to attach to the latest stationary space station. At one end of the living area was a video screen; the kitchen was at the other end. The window view of the earth was on one wall, while framed photos of family and spacecraft decorated the wall across from the window. A door by the kitchen led to the rest of the rooms and a docking bay.

Sally said, "Are you sorry you didn't go on one of the missions to the stars?"

"Not in the least bit. I have you and Emily. That's all I need. I don't have the adventurer gene."

"A craft is requesting to dock," the computer voice said.

"Approved," said Isaac. "Show on screen."

"Are you expecting someone?" Sally turned toward the screen.

"No. But I do think it would be rude to refuse docking."

They watched a round craft reconfigure and attach to the docking bay. "That was different." Isaac said under his breath.

A tall man dressed in a golden one-piece suit entered the airlock. "May I speak to Isaac Thomas?"

"Computer, let our guest in and show him to the living room."

A moment later the man stood before them.

"I'm here to issue a summons to Isaac Thomas to testify at the High Council of Sigronway." He held out a golden square device with a black button. "Press the button when you're ready to testify."

"When and where is the court?"

"When you're ready. Preferably during your corporeal existence. The device will take you to the council." He stood still with his arm out.

"What's this about?" Sally asked.

"Questions can be answered by the council. Shall we go now?" His other hand moved over the button.

"No. Not now. How about in fifty years?" Isaac said.

"Ah, yes. You're a trivial being constrained by time. The council is not. Take this. Press when ready. I'm only in your form to lessen the reaction."

Isaac reached out and took the golden box. The man returned to his craft, which disappeared as soon as it disengaged.

"Who do you think that was?" Sally asked.

"Just a messenger of the Council of Sigronway. Whatever that is."

"How will you know when you're ready?"

"I don't know." Isaac stared at the stars over the earth. "Maybe someday we'll be ready to meet some aliens. Maybe someday."

Further reading in the Egress of Humanity series

(Watch for the following stories to be published)

Mission Alpha – Tanya Nash commands humanity's first colonization of the stars.

Mission Beta – AstroLift assembles the best humans they can find and sends them to establish a colony on another planet.

Mission Gamma – The Chinese pay Adynamia a billion dollars for the technology to send a colony to another planet. They leave to conquer the galaxy.

Mission Delta – The colony settles, only to be discovered by space pirates.

Mission Epsilon – The colonists arrive at a lush, beautiful planet without an intelligent species. Or that is what it looked like.

Mission Zeta – The last message from the commander of the ships was that they were approaching a planet with signs of intelligent life. They would do a fly by and continue to another system.

Mission Eta – Colony number four leaves with a hearty crew of volunteers. The aliens are unexpected.

Mission Theta – TBD

Mission Iota – Colonists arrive at a system with two potentially inhabitable planets.

Mission Kappa – TBD

Mission Lambda – TBD

Archie Kregear

Credits:
Book cover: MiblArt — MiblArt.com
Kitsap Writers Critique Group: Search for us on Facebook
Editor: Teresa Grabs — thewordcubby.com
Proofreader: Skye Loyd — edit-guru.com

For more about the author, his books, photography and his wife's art, checkout their web site at — Kregear.com.

Thanks for reading!

Please take a moment to leave a review on Amazon and/or Goodreads.

Should you have questions, thoughts or just want to communicate , find me by email: archiekregear@gmail.com
Twitter: @ArchieKregear
Facebook: Archie Kregear
Instagram: archie_kregear

Printed in Great Britain
by Amazon